CW00821656

THE SILVER-HAIRED SISTERHOOD

JUDY LEIGH

Boldwood

First published in Great Britain in 2024 by Boldwood Books Ltd.

Copyright © Judy Leigh, 2024

Cover Design by JD Design Ltd

Cover Images: Shutterstock

The moral right of Judy Leigh to be identified as the author of this work has been asserted in accordance with the Copyright, Designs and Patents Act 1988.

A CIP catalogue record for this book is available from the British Library.

Paperback ISBN 978-1-78513-241-4

Large Print ISBN 978-1-78513-242-1

Hardback ISBN 978-1-78513-240-7

Ebook ISBN 978-1-78513-243-8

Kindle ISBN 978-1-78513-244-5

Audio CD ISBN 978-1-78513-235-3

MP3 CD ISBN 978-1-78513-236-0

Digital audio download ISBN 978-1-78513-238-4

This book is printed on certified sustainable paper. Boldwood Books is dedicated to putting sustainability at the heart of our business. For more information please visit https://www.boldwoodbooks.com/about-us/sustainability/

Boldwood Books Ltd, 23 Bowerdean Street, London, SW6 3TN

www.boldwoodbooks.com

For Hugh and Ellen. For Skye.

"The best time to plant a tree was twenty years ago. The second best time is now."

— CHINESE PROVERB

GLOSSARY

Cnoc Mor (a Ghrobain) is pronounced Nock Moor and means big hill. Ghrobain is a surname.

Sicín Órga is pronounced shickin orga. It means golden chicken.

* * *

Manchester slang

Belter: a stunner, very good, very powerful
Brassic: a state of having no money
I'm champion: I'm very well, the best
Mingin': smelly
Mint: perfect, great
Mithering: annoying, bothering
Scran: food

* * *

Scottish slang

Bawbag: testicles
Boke: to vomit
Braw: good-looking
Crabbit: bad tempered, grumpy
Mad wae it: under the influence of alcohol
Winch: a kiss

1

Tess Watkins flopped on the bed with an enormous sigh and closed her eyes. She felt like crying. She wasn't sure why, but it was her party and she'd cry if she wanted to.

'Seventy-seven,' she grumbled aloud. It sounded like a lot of years. She tried it again. 'Seventy-seven years old.' She was ancient. Out of the ark. Past it. And in half an hour, her friends would be arriving to celebrate her birthday. Tess didn't feel at all like celebrating being old.

The five women had met at aqua aerobics, and four of them still saw each other there once a week. The fifth, Rose, was in Paris now, but they all remained close. They'd called themselves The Hens since the fabulous hen party four years ago. The hen party that never should have been. The one where Rose found herself and came into her own, becoming cabaret performer Rose-on-Wye and moving to Paris; where Jen decided she didn't want to marry Eddie after all, even though the wedding was booked and he was off celebrating his stag do in Las Vegas with his son Harry. So much had happened in those last four years.

With her eyes closed, Tess was able to run the slide show of their Paris trip, frame by frame. The five Hens were standing beneath the Eiffel Tower, arms linked. Tess was in the middle, laughing; Rose to her left, sophisticated, doing her best impression of Coco Chanel, Della to her right, her face a little wistful, missing her beloved husband back in Exmouth. Jen, the smallest, at one end, smiling for all she was worth like the bride-to-be she never became. She ought to have been in the middle – it was her hen do, after all. And Pam at the other end, tall, willowy, quietly in control. They'd never have managed in Paris without her know-how, her confidence and her spoken French.

Tess wasn't sure if they had ever posed for such a photo beneath the Tour Eiffel, but in her memory, their arms were around each other and they were laughing as if they didn't have a care in the world. She remembered sitting on a bench eating pastries from the Rue Cler with Pam, who had told her she was the life and soul of any party, that she should be so proud of the person she was. That was the problem. She was joyful in company but sad when she was alone. The last few years hadn't helped.

Her husband Alan had held her back for so many years, yet now she was rid of him, she was holding herself back.

Eyes still closed, she thought of Vladimir, the gorgeous Russian she'd met in Paris. Vladimir Borovik-Romanov. The girls had called him Vlad the Impaler and fallen about at the idea of Tess's millionaire conquest. She and Vladimir had dined together in the exclusive Colombe Blanche; she'd stayed on his houseboat on the Seine. It had been like a dream. They had almost become lovers – he'd visited England twice. And after the romantic balloon flight over Bristol with champagne, with Tess's divorce almost finalised, she'd decided she'd take the plunge the next time they met.

They'd arranged a long weekend in Bath. He'd always been

so courteous and respectful, he'd never mentioned them sleeping together but she was sure that they were both ready. She'd imagined her future, living with him in Paris, walking on the banks of the Seine arm-in-arm, happy forever after.

But the weekend in Bath had never happened. Vladimir had moved back to Russia when the war with Ukraine started; she'd received two optimistic emails from Moscow a year ago hoping they'd meet soon, when all the 'sadness' was over, then there was nothing. She'd probably never see him again. What with the end of their special friendship and the bitter divorce from Alan, it had been a tough time. No wonder at seventy-seven she felt soggy in the middle and frayed around the edges.

But tonight was her pot-luck birthday supper – Pam, Jen and Della were coming round with food and wine. They'd be The Hens again for a while, and there would be laughter and lots of reminiscing. Tess would get her mojo back, even if only for a few hours. It was a shame Rose couldn't be there though. She missed her.

She took a deep breath and pulled herself upright, tightening the belt of her dressing gown. After a shower, she'd get dressed. The Hens would be arriving in an hour and then it would be time for feasting and laughter and presents.

Tess felt the barometer of her optimism fall. There was a quiche in a box and a tub of coleslaw in the fridge, both bought from a supermarket, alongside two bottles of champagne. She hadn't cooked from scratch. Pam would bring a fabulous vegetarian dish. Della would have made fried plantain, salt fish, akee. Jen would have baked a birthday cake.

She felt useless again. The fridge wasn't even hers, nor was the house. It was all Rose's. Tess had lived there since she came back from Paris, since she found Alan in bed with... Tess closed her eyes. She'd laughed at the time, taken a photo on her phone of them cavorting, walked away with her nose in the air and her dignity intact. But to this day she couldn't stand the scent of Chanel. And Alan's words were still with her. He'd been 'keeping Celia warm after she'd developed hypothermia on the golf course while walking Pam's spaniel Elvis'. Who was he kidding?

The divorce had been unpleasant. Alan hadn't loved poor Celia – they weren't even together now. But he'd been bitter about Tess leaving, as if it were her fault that she'd found him in her bed with a woman he didn't care for. At least Tess was spared his lies now.

Her phone was ringing – a WhatsApp video call. She snatched it up and her spirits lifted as she saw a woman dressed as Marie Antoinette, her white wig high and swirly as an ice-cream cone.

'Rose.'

'Bonne anniversaire, ma poule,' Rose Grant cooed. 'Daz and I are about to go on stage. I just thought I'd give you a quick call to say happy birthday before the show.'

'You remembered.'

'November girl – Scorpio. That's passion and impetuosity, isn't it?'

Tess forced a grin. 'I'm seventy-seven, far too old to be impetuous.'

'I'm seventy-nine and as impetuous as I've ever been – more so.' Rose laughed. 'I keep telling Daz I'll retire at eighty. He's forever complaining he's getting a helicopter landing pad at thirty-six. I say to him, darling, it won't show beneath that blonde wig.'

It took Tess a few seconds to understand. 'Oh – you mean his hair.'

'How's my house?' Rose asked.

'I haven't burned it down, if that's what you mean,' Tess retorted with a grin.

'You haven't found anywhere else yet?' Rose asked. 'I often think about how much I hated living there. I much prefer the pretty renter Daz and I have that looks out onto the river.'

'Oh, I can buy somewhere whenever I want now, after the divorce.' Tess paused. She wouldn't mention Alan tonight. It was her birthday. 'So – what are you singing?'

'Usual set – we're kicking off with "Gimme! Gimme! Gimme!" and "Money, Money, Money", then ending up with "Dancing Queen" and "Thank You for the Music".' Rose laughed. 'I tell Daz he looks more like Agnetha every day – he's perfected her tragic expression in "The Winner Takes It All". It brings the house down, it's so funny.'

Tess forced a smile. Rose's life seemed so different from her own, so much glamour and fun. She said, 'So – will Rose-on-Wye and Greta Manchester be playing at Monty's for the fore-seeable future?'

'Who knows?' Rose shrugged and her tall wig wobbled. 'What else would I do? Give it all up, move back to Exmouth and live in the same four walls...'

'...that I do?' Tess said.

'Come and visit me,' Rose offered. 'Come to Paris. Live. Have fun. The invitation is always open.'

'I might.' Tess wished she could. She had no excuse. It was just lethargy that held her back. She changed the subject. 'The Hens are coming round soon. I've no idea what to wear.'

'Wear the dress,' Rose said without taking a breath.

'What dress?'

'*The* Paris dress. The One you bought for the date with Vladimir.'

'Vladimir.' Tess sighed.

'You remember, the black and gold cocktail dress – it cost three hundred euros after Della won all that money at the casino.' Rose gushed. 'Oh, you looked so glamorous.'

'Mutton dressed as lamb.' Tess tried to brush off the feeling of inadequacy.

'Lamb's overrated,' Rose said firmly. Those had been Tess's words once.

'I haven't worn that dress since Paris.' Tess pulled a sad face.

'Then you need to bring more Paris into your life,' Rose replied emphatically.

'You're right – I do,' Tess said. Rose had a point. 'Yes, I'll wear the dress. It might liven the tub of coleslaw up a bit.'

Rose frowned. She clearly had no idea what Tess meant. She suddenly stood up, the screen showing her long pink rococo dress covered with frills, feathers and ribbons. 'Sorry, Tess – that was Daz calling. Elton Joan has finished her set. We're on next. Happy birthday, darling. Have a lovely evening. Give my best to The Hens and don't forget, don't let the buggers grind you down.'

'Which buggers?' Tess began, but Rose had gone. Tess smiled. Four years ago, Rose had been dowdy and lacking in confidence. Now she was blooming, in full flower. And Tess was the shrinking violet – she'd taken Rose's place.

Tess thought about the silk cocktail dress. 'It's my time to shine,' she said determinedly and set off at a lick towards the wardrobe to find it. She hoped the moths hadn't got at it.

She shook it out and light glinted and danced on the gold sequins. Just as she'd sparkled in it four years ago. She held it up and looked in the mirror. A trip to the hairdresser's was overdue – silver roots showed beneath the blonde; she needed a cut. The dress had a plunging neckline and Tess stared at her neck. No amount of jewellery would cover up the lines she had accumulated over the years. She shook her head.

'Seventy-seven.'

Tess knew she was being silly. She'd feel better later, when she was surrounded by friends, talking about old times. But that was the past. Where was the future? Tess wished she knew.

She put the dress back in the wardrobe, wondering if she should pass it on to a charity shop. A younger person would look better in it.

She tugged on jeans, a shirt, and felt more comfortable. She'd forgotten all about the shower she'd intended to have. The words 'age appropriate' buzzed in her ears. It felt like an insult. Pam was the same age – she'd be in jeans, but looking great. Della looked sexy whatever she wore and Jen was so small and neat she made Tess feel chubby.

Tess applied some lipstick, brushed her hair and took a breath.

'Come on, Tess – it's your birthday. Pull yourself together.'

Her mother had said that to her so often. Alan too. *Pull yourself together* implied that she was coming apart at the seams.

'I'll open a bottle. That'll cheer me up,' she said to herself.

Immediately, Alan's voice in her head said, 'You're drunk, Tess. It's not very appealing to sleep next to someone with their mouth open.'

Tess let out a wild laugh. 'Well, you'll never sleep next to me again, Alan. So good riddance.'

She hurried to the kitchen, found a bottle of Moët in the fridge and popped the cork, pouring herself a fizzy glass.

She gulped a mouthful, wondering if anyone would ever sleep next to her again.

The doorbell rang.

Glass in hand, her feet bare, Tess scampered to the door and threw it open, whooping wildly as Pam Marshall and Jen Hooper fell into her arms. Pam was in faded jeans, Jen looking like a doll in her pretty dress. Tess glanced over their shoulders; Della Donovan was walking along the road, hand in hand with Sylvester, dapper in his pork pie hat. She looked fabulous in a patterned maxi dress.

Seconds later, they were all standing in the lounge, hugging each other, talking nineteen to the dozen, holding out bottles of wine and dishes of food.

Della said, 'Here we all are, back together again... oh, this is so nice.'

'Rose sends her best. We've just chatted on WhatsApp.' Tess's voice was muffled as Pam kissed her cheek.

'Happy birthday, Tess.' Pam gave her a huge box tied with ribbon.

'Me next.' Jen handed over a soft package.

'Della's brought so much food... she's been cooking since this morning,' Sylvester said. 'You're looking mighty fine, Tess.'

'As ever,' Della added, thrusting a small box towards Tess. 'Oh, I've been looking forward to this all day.'

'All week,' Jen added.

'All month,' Pam said, trumping them all.

'And I'm an honorary Hen for the night.' Sylvester laughed, waving his elbows, clucking.

'Let's sit down,' Tess said, arms full of gifts. 'Oh, it's so good to see you all. You've no idea how much I need this...'

2

By ten-thirty, Tess was tipsy. She was wearing the silver bracelet Della had bought her that must have cost more than she could afford. The silk scarf from Jen was round her neck, and the three novels Pam had wrapped in tissue paper were on the table. She poured more champagne into their glasses and sliced more cake.

'Seventy-seven though...'

Della laughed. 'Isn't seventy the new fifty?'

Tess shook her head. 'Being seventy was OK. I still felt young-ish. I didn't feel past it. But seventy-seven is nearly eighty and then it's, like, will I get to ninety or will everything that lurks in sniper's alley get me?'

'Sniper's what?' Pam asked.

'Sniper's alley...' Jen shuddered.

'Disease, loneliness, immobility, death...' Tess said quietly.

Della groaned. 'I suddenly feel old.'

Sylvester placed a hand over his wife's. 'You are like a fine wine, better with age.' He pursed his lips for a kiss and Della brushed them with hers.

'This man thinks he's still twenty.' Her voice was full of affection. 'But I wouldn't have him any other way.'

'You still put fire in my belly, woman.' Sylvester's laughter suddenly became a paroxysm of coughing. 'The damn sea fog has got on my chest.'

Della handed him a drink of water, her expression troubled. 'I told you to wrap up, Sylvester. You didn't wear your scarf...'

'She never stops fussing.' He laughed, waving a hand, still coughing.

Jen leaned forward for her champagne. 'You have a point though, Tess. I went to the doctor's for a check-up yesterday. The young nurse – she couldn't have been more than twenty-five – said I wasn't doing badly for my age but she said I was far too thin and I could do with putting a bit of weight on. She said my bones were becoming less dense, in such a cold way. I went home and burst into tears.'

'That's disrespectful,' Pam said, irritated. 'Society doesn't allow older people enough dignity.'

'That's true,' Della agreed. 'I get the bus into Exeter sometimes and the young kids take all the seats and leave me standing. It's as if I'm invisible. And the language they use – I don't like to hear all the swearing.'

'I was reading an article...' Pam helped herself to cake. 'It was supposed to be about young people getting financial help from grandparents. The words they used were appalling.' Pam waved a hand. '"Grannies, codgers, wrinklies, past their prime". I could have throttled the writer. It was as if we're just has-beens.'

Sylvester agreed. 'I used to work in a snack bar on the seafront—'

'I made him give it up,' Della interrupted.

'But half the young people I served would want to bump fists with me and say "Yah, mon" in this foolish voice, which I found most vexing.' Sylvester wrinkled his nose. 'And others would call me grandad or boomer – one young scally even called me a coffin dodger.' He glared: it was still fresh in his mind.

'There are no advantages to being old,' Jen said sadly. 'People see the external and assume that inside we're past it too. But we're no different. It's a form of prejudice that no one notices.'

'Exactly,' Pam said. 'I don't jog as much as I used to, but yoga keeps me fit, and swimming and aqua aerobics.'

'Oh, thank goodness for our aqua aerobics.' Della sighed. 'It's the only thing that sorts out my sciatica.'

Pam was on a roll. 'People judge by numerical age and that's ridiculous. And it's so short-sighted – everybody gets older.' She pushed a hand through her spiky cut. 'I let my hair go silver – to hell with it. If people want to judge me, it makes them some kind of ass and I'm better without them.'

'But it's OK to be old.' Tess thumped the table with her fist, making the champagne in her glass leap. 'Life isn't over. People do all sorts of things. They take qualifications, run marathons, they travel – look at Rose. She's amazing.'

'She is.' Della sipped orange juice thoughtfully and patted her frosted hair. 'Older people are still attractive, sexy, talented. We never stop moving forward.'

'Until we drop.' Sylvester's laughter rumbled. 'And that's a long, long way off.'

'To think I nearly got married four years ago,' Jen muttered thoughtfully. 'You know, I actually saw Eddie the other day.'

'Oh?' Pam asked. 'How is he?'

'He's been married for over a year now, to a woman called Diana. I met them on the beach. He introduced her, and she was so meek and timid, the way she clung to him... I wonder if I'd have ended up like that.'

'No way,' Pam said. 'You're far too strong. That's why you

changed your mind.' She turned to Tess. 'You too – you've turned everything around.'

'Have I?' Tess was astonished. 'How?'

'You got rid of Alan, who was a foolish, cheating man...' Della's voice trailed off.

Pam was impressed. 'I think you're amazing, Tess.'

'But I get a bit lonely sometimes,' Tess said in a small voice.

'Maybe you should get a dog – like Elvis,' Jen suggested.

'Elvis is more than a pet – he's a companion.' Pam beamed. 'We're off travelling in a few days.'

'Aren't you going to an ashram in North India?' Tess asked.

'I changed my mind. We're going to Greece. Elvis has a passport.' Pam dug into the cake. 'I'm doing yoga while I'm there and jogging on the beach. Elvis is ten now but he's remarkably chipper... he loves a dip in the sea.'

'It sounds idyllic.' Tess thought she needed a holiday too.

'I'm off on Friday too.' Jen smiled dreamily.

'The land of Fire and Ice...' Tess hoped she didn't sound too jealous.

'You could have come with me,' Jen reminded her. 'I asked you. Two weeks on a cruise around Iceland.'

Tess shook her head. 'I can't spend the settlement money yet – I'll need to buy a house when Rose kicks me out.' She had a moment of anxiety. 'What if I'm on my own for Christmas?'

'I'll be here.' Della wrapped an arm around Tess. 'We'll go Christmas shopping together. We can hit the night market in Exeter, get mince pies and hot spice wine.'

'And we'll be back for Christmas,' Jen added.

Tess tried a smile. 'That'll be good.'

'I love Christmas,' Sylvester said dreamily. 'Aston and Linval come home, the grandchildren, and we'll drink rum, chew the fat, eat so much food till our bellies bust.'

'Gemma's not coming this year,' Tess said slowly. 'And Lisa's too busy doing her own thing...'

'Christmas Day will be a hoot,' Pam said kindly. 'Come round to mine.'

Jen reached out and took Tess's hand. 'We'll get together for Christmas dinner.'

'That would be nice. I'll call on each of you in turn. Like Santa.' Tess forced a grin and reached for the bottle. 'More champagne?'

'It's gone a little flat.' Jen watched the liquid splash in her glass.

'I'll open another,' Tess said determinedly. 'When one bottle's empty, there's always another full one.'

She wandered to the fridge wishing that were true. But she couldn't help thinking that life was passing her by. Jen was off cruising, Pam was taking Elvis to Greece, Della and Sylvester were still totally in love. And Rose, the oldest of them all, was living the dream, playing piano in a nightclub in Paris.

Tess told herself she needed to cheer up. She tugged a cold bottle of Moët from the fridge and held it to her warm cheeks. The cool glass felt good.

She plastered a smile on her face and went back to the dining table. She was strong. She'd turn her life around. She heard the sound of her own voice, high with optimism.

'Bubbly, anyone?'

* * *

Jen turned the key to the door of her house in Barley Mow Avenue. She'd left lights blazing. That was how she lived now, in fear of intruders, burglars. She locked the door firmly, bolted it, and glanced at the wall clock. It was almost half past eleven. The stroll back from Tess's had taken only ten minutes, but she was always nervous about walking alone at night. Exmouth was a safe enough place, but stories about women being mugged were often in the news, and the thought preyed on her mind. She was glad to be in her own home though – not marrying Eddie had been a wise move: he'd have dominated the space, made the decisions. She'd have hated it after a month.

She glanced at her laptop, open on the table. The itinerary for Silver Singles Cruises was visible, with a beautiful photo of the Northern Lights, a green and yellow mist hovering in velvet black skies. The words 'Land of Fire and Ice' were illuminated in blue and red, alongside photos of leaping geysers and white ice caps floating in an indigo sea. She couldn't wait to leave, sailing from Southampton at the end of the week.

Jen went into the kitchen for a glass of water, drinking slowly, pushing a hand through her neat chestnut hair. She liked going on singles cruises – everyone was in the same boat. Literally. The phrase made her grin. She'd encountered interesting people over a few years. On the last cruise, to Egypt, she'd met a man called Henry who'd been a pleasant companion. He'd asked to keep in touch, but Jen felt there was no future in it. He lived in Macclesfield – that was miles away. Besides which, there was something liberating about being on her own, deciding where to go, how long to stay. She'd probably never have another relationship. Colin had been her husband since she was twenty-three. He'd died eight years ago and it seemed like an eternity.

No, Jen thought as she made her way upstairs to bed. Theirs had been a comfortable marriage, about companionship, friendship but definitely not excitement. Excitement, Jen decided sadly, was probably not for her.

* * *

As Pam stepped into the tiny living room, Elvis hurled himself at her, tail wagging, long ears flopping all over the place. Pam whisked the little black spaniel into her arms and kissed the soft fur between his eyes. 'Have you missed me?'

Elvis turned adoring eyes on her, his paws sticking up, completely trusting the safety of the hug. Pam placed him back on all fours and collapsed in front of the TV. Immediately, he bounded up on her knee as she flicked the remote.

'There's a documentary I recorded about Ruth Bader Ginsburg, Elvis...'

Elvis placed a wet nose against her hand, his eyes inquisitive. Pam continued, 'She was the Supreme Court associate justice known for her ground-breaking work on women's rights. She died in 2020. It'll be really informative.'

Elvis understood. His eyes stayed on Pam. 'OK, I'll get myself a cup of herbal tea first, and you can have a veggie dog chew.'

Elvis woofed in agreement. Pam eased herself from her chair and moved towards the kitchen, the spaniel at her heels. As she filled the kettle, she muttered, 'This holiday can't come quick enough. We need a break from the cold weather. Imagine the Greek sunshine on your back, Elvis – and the crystal blue sea. I don't know about you, but my poor aching joints definitely need some vitamin D.'

* * *

Della tucked her knees beneath her sky-blue nightie and snuggled up in bed, wrapping an arm around Sylvester. In the glow from the street lamp outside, the smooth dome of his head shone and her heart expanded with the familiar leap of love. In her embrace, he felt smaller nowadays. The job at the snack van on the seafront had taken it out of him. He'd had pneumonia four years ago, and it had left him with a rasping cough. She hugged him tighter and heard him chortle. 'I'm not going anywhere, woman.'

Della nuzzled the back of his neck. 'You know I love you.'

'And I love you back. A day doesn't go by when I don't count my blessings...' Sylvester mumbled into the pillow, his voice sleepy. 'Fifty-three years, two fine sons, and you to wake up to each morning in my bed. I am a lucky man.'

Della sighed. 'I think poor Tess is feeling a bit down, being on her own.'

'It's better for her than living with that Alan. He was a no-good piece of mischief.' Sylvester was almost asleep.

'She deserves someone lovely, just like she is,' Della agreed. There was silence for a moment, then she murmured, 'Jen's going on a cruise, Pam's off to Greece...'

She heard Sylvester breathe out deeply; he was almost dozing off.

Della continued, 'We never got to Paris, did we? I had such a great time with The Hens there, and I wanted to share it with you.'

'The honeymoon we never had...' Sylvester grunted.

'It would have been nice.'

'Right, my little wife, we'll have to change that. Who cares if the whole trip mashes up my wallet? Let's go.' Sylvester turned round to face Della, his face shining.

'Go?'

'To Paris.'

'When?'

'Before Christmas. We can take four days and get back by Christmas Eve. It will get us in the festive spirit.' Sylvester beamed with delight.

'Sylvester,' Della shook her head, 'We don't have much money.'

'Who cares a damn thing about that?' Sylvester retorted. 'We can't take it with us. The electricity man can wait. Let's do it, me and you – a romantic long weekend.'

Della was almost convinced. 'We could...'

'We'll book it at the weekend,' Sylvester said determinedly.

Della found herself smiling. 'Oh, it would be so nice. You and me at the top of the Eiffel Tower, walking along the Champs-Élysées, visiting the Louvre and we could go to the *Cimetière* at Montparnasse.'

'What's that?'

'A graveyard. There are so many famous people buried there.'

'Damn fool places, graveyards – it'll be a long time until anyone gets me in one of those.' Sylvester kissed her lips. 'We'll have the time of our lives, Della. We'll go on a boat on that long river that runs through Paris and climb all the way to the top of the Eiffel Tower. I don't care how many steps there are.'

'They have lifts.' Della laughed.

'And we'll celebrate in the city of romance.' Sylvester closed his eyes. 'I can hardly wait.'

'Me too,' Della said. A huge sigh shuddered through her. 'Oh, I want to show you all the sights. We can have breakfast in one of those cute little cafés by the river that sell coffee and pastries, and we can walk to the Arc de Triomphe, watch the sunset from Montmartre. Oh, will you just listen to me?' she whispered. 'I sound the real expert, don't I? But imagine Paris, Sylvester. After waiting for so long. It would be a dream come true.'

'Mmm.'

Della kissed his forehead. 'Just imagine, you and me in the city of love...'

She heard a soft sound rattling through his nose. He was fast asleep.

3

On Thursday afternoons, the pool was reserved for aqua aerobics. Tess, Della, Jen, Pam and twenty-five other swimsuited women raised one arm above their head, then the other, copying the movements of their new teacher, Chris, who was male, thirty and undeniably muscular. Kathy, the previous teacher, had left a year ago. Numbers in the class had been dwindling, but since Chris in his red Speedos had taken over, there had been an astonishing increase in interest. Right now, he was leaping up and down at the side of the pool, gleaming pecs and six-pack rippling, with twenty-nine pairs of eyes riveted upon him.

At the end of the session, Chris stood at the poolside in his clingy swimwear talking to three women who reached out every few seconds to pat his biceps. The Hens huddled together by the changing rooms, water dripping from their swimsuits.

'Shall we go for coffee and cake?' Tess asked.

'I can't.' Pam pulled a 'sorry' face. 'I have to get home to Elvis and pack. We're off first thing tomorrow.'

'Nor can I.' Jen shook her head. 'I'm driving to the ship in

Southampton at the crack of dawn on Friday morning. And I have to visit Anna in the care home this evening.'

'How is your sister?' Della asked with concern.

'Not good. Sometimes she doesn't recognise me at all,' Jen said sadly. 'She won't get any better. And she's only seventy-nine.'

'Dementia is such a cruel illness,' Pam said kindly. 'It must be tough.'

'For us both,' Jen agreed. 'The cruise is the break I need. Anna's well cared for though. I picked a good nursing home in Plymouth.'

Della sighed. 'She went downhill fast after her husband died.'

'That was three years ago,' Jen said. 'Pete's funeral was in the October. How time flies.'

'It does.' Tess's voice was full of emotion.

The Hens were quiet for a moment, then Pam said, 'We have to grab life, all of us. So, when Jen and I are back, let's do something really nice.'

'Such as?' Della hoped it wouldn't be expensive – she was going to Paris, and then there was Christmas to pay for, dinner, gifts for Linval and Aston, his wife and children. Linval's children too, although she didn't see them as often as she'd have liked. His ex could be difficult.

'A celebration – just for us.'

'We could go to see Rose,' Tess enthused, not noticing Della's anxious expression.

'Or we could have a wild weekend in London?' Jen suggested.

'Or a party at my house? I'll cook,' Della offered.

'Let's think about it,' Pam said. 'We'll bring in the new year.

We could invite Rose – she should be there too. Her big birth-day's on New Year's Eve. We'll have a party for her.'

'Good plan.' Jen shivered. 'I'm getting cold.'

'Let's get changed.' Pam hugged her towel.

'I'll come for coffee and cake with you,' Della said to Tess.

'On me.' Tess knew Della and Sylvester were feeling the pinch now he had stopped work. 'I'll race you all to the showers.'

'Race?' Della laughed. There was a squeal from the poolside where Chris the instructor was surrounded by excitable fans. 'It's all I can do to crawl home after that session with Aquaman over there.' She rubbed the familiar ache in her back. 'I watch him stretch and lunge, and I realise I'm not getting any younger...'

* * *

On the way to Lime Tree Coffee House, Tess could smell the wafting aroma of frying fish from the nearby chippy. She almost dragged Della in the other direction for a battered cod and fries, but her self-control won that battle temporarily. Minutes later, as she sat in front of a large latte and a gingerbread cinnamon cupcake, calories were the last thing on her mind. She listened, fascinated, to Della, whose eyes shone with happiness.

'So Sylvester and I are going to the travel agents on Saturday afternoon, and we're going to book it. Just imagine! Paris!' She sighed. 'I can hardly believe it. I'll talk to Rose on Sunday and we'll meet up when we get there. I can just imagine Sylvester's face when he goes into Monty's club and sees Wheezy Anna and Filmah Boots on stage...'

'You could book the holiday online,' Tess suggested.

'Online? Sylvester?' Della's laughter pealed. 'He has to sit down with Tammy in Worldwide Travel and actually see a printout on paper.' Her face was soft with love. 'Sylvester is such a technophobe. "Della," he says to me, "technology will ruin the world. You know every mickle meks a muckle." And then he laughs fit to bust.'

'What does that mean?' Tess asked.

'That small things combined can have a big effect. He thinks we'll all be buying our groceries from robots before we shuffle off.'

'Small things combined have a big effect? Like empty calories...' Tess grinned as she took a bite of cinnamon cupcake. 'Ah, you only live once.' She was thoughtful. 'Della, do you think I've put on weight since I left Alan?'

'If you have, then I have too. It's what happens. The body migrates south. We're not all built the same.' Della clearly didn't care less. 'I go by the rule of seven anyway, so it doesn't bother me.'

'The rule of seven? What's that?' Tess slurped creamy latte.

'Every seven years your body changes big time to get ready for the next stage of life. So at seven, you're a child. At fourteen, a growing woman. By twenty-one, a full woman. Twenty-eight, then thirty-five, right up until...'

'Now? Seventy-seven?' Tess gasped. 'Is that the age when a woman is...' she shuddered '...old?'

'Some might say so.' Della shrugged. 'Some would say old is forty-nine. Some would say you're as old as you feel. Sylvester says he's as old as the woman he feels. I tell him that those are the words of an old man who got used to living in a different age but – Tess, I love that man so much. Each year that passes...' her eyes shone with tears, '...I love him more and more.'

'You're so lucky.'

'You never loved Alan? Not ever?' Della asked. She picked up her cupcake and nibbled the edge.

Tess pulled a face. 'I thought I did. When we were in the foolish bloom of youth. Then when we had the girls, we were too busy to think of love. Then he retired and became selfish; he just played golf and I stayed home and watched TV and there was nothing left. Besides, I can't trust a man who cheated on me.'

'That affair with the wife of his golf buddy,' Della remembered.

'He didn't even care for her. And years before, he had a fling with Jeff's wife. Jeff and I worked in the same estate agent's. He and his wife split up but Alan and I tried to make a go of it.' Tess shook her head. 'That was a mistake.'

'And what about that lovely man you met in Paris?' Della asked.

'Vladimir. We lost touch. I dare say he's stuck in Moscow now... his apartment in Paris and his houseboat might be empty.' Tess groaned. 'It was a dream, for a while. Maybe when the political situation is different, we'll meet again...' She pulled herself together visibly. 'But you and Sylvester are going to Paris. At last.'

Della flapped a hand in front of her face. 'Oh, Tess – I'm so excited. I'm going to treat myself to a new nightdress.' She laughed, a hand over her mouth. 'Fifty-three years of marriage to that gorgeous man and I never had a honeymoon before.'

* * *

Tess was sitting at the window staring at the sky. It was blank, the parchment colour of sky when it was crammed with snow. Of course it wouldn't snow – it was far too early, but Tess wished for that light silent falling of feathery flakes that felt magical. She needed some magic in her life. It would be snowing in

Iceland when Jen was there. Tess wished she'd agreed to go with her. She'd decided against it in favour of not spending money from the divorce settlement: she'd need it in the future.

She imagined swimming in the steaming Blue Lagoon, the water bubbling as snowflakes stuck to her eyelashes, a glass of chilled beer in her hand. She'd have felt like a pop star. It would have given her more happiness than money in the bank.

Rose was living it up every night at Monty's. Jen and Pam were setting off on glorious winter breaks – Della was going to Paris. Tess wondered what was keeping her in Exmouth. Beyond the window, the wind buffeted pale clouds and she thought again of snow. A skiing holiday might be nice, Tess on the slopes in epaulettes and movie-star sunglasses, flirting with an instructor called Axel, sipping après-ski drinks through chapsticked lips. The only problem was that she couldn't ski. She imagined falling head first onto Axel, spilling her drink, knocking him into a snowdrift. But it would be nice to be with Jen on a cruise ship bound for Reykjavik with the prospect of seeing the aurora borealis.

Tess imagined being in a jeep in snowy mountains, sipping iced Brennivín liquor to keep out the cold, swathed in fur, staring into the skies. The driver, an impossibly tall, blonde Viking called Ólafur, was pointing out the stars in a gravelly voice. Above, the technicolour canopy of blues and greens took her breath away. Then Ólafur took her breath away by wrapping his arms around her, declaring undying love and kissing her as she'd never been kissed before.

Tess shook herself and laughed.

As if...

In her dreams.

She'd make a cup of tea.

As she passed the open laptop, she paused and sat down. On

impulse, fingers tapping on the keyboard, she typed 'aurora borealis' and pressed enter. There it was, a sky full of swirling brightness that made her catch her breath. She'd love to see the Northern Lights. It was something everyone should do once, a 'bucket list' moment. Then she saw the words 'Experience the Northern Lights on Skye'. She moved the mouse and clicked.

The photo that met her eyes was a beautiful Victorian hotel on the edge of the sea. Above, the sky was overcrowded with colour that seemed to come straight from an impressionist artist's palette. The name of the hotel was Sicín Órga. She leaned forward, moved the mouse and brought up the website. The pictures made her gasp.

The hotel was in Sleat on the Isle of Skye, which Tess knew was in Scotland, north of Glasgow. She supposed it wasn't too far from the Orkneys and John O'Groats. She'd never been further north than Edinburgh.

Sleat, though. The word sounded like soft snow, piled high.

The reviews were all nine out of ten: exceptional. Mr A Spencer had written a year ago: 'A wonderful place, the high-light of our trip to Scotland, so welcoming. Four-poster bed – an incredible view of the sea. Thoroughly recommended.'

Tess thought the hotel looked lovely: the outside was diamond white with bay windows; the spacious bedrooms had open fireplaces. She wiggled the mouse. The owners were Roddy and Isla Fraser. How romantic did that sound? Roddy and Isla. He'd be a tall handsome Scot with a beard and a kilt. She'd be warm and welcoming, cooking gorgeous dishes in her old-fashioned kitchen. They offered Land Rover tours of the mountains to see deer, the aurora borealis, to sample whisky in the snow. The Monad Crag distillery was five minutes from the hotel. She could go for a tasting and stagger back. There was a beach nearby, hiking and biking, laundry service, breakfast. And there would be snow. What else did she need?

Tess felt a surge of excitement.

'Damn it,' Tess said aloud. She stared at the picture of the Northern Lights. They were magical. 'Damn it. I'm going.'

She brought up the Sicín Órga website, checked availability, and found a double room. She entered her credit-card details and booked until the 14th. She'd be back for Christmas, in time for Jen's and Pam's and Della's return. And by then, she'd be feeling bloody marvellous.

One click. It was done. She was going on holiday to Skye in December.

A holiday on Skye!

She sat back in her seat and an unstoppable grin filled her face. She wanted to dance with excitement.

Then it occurred to her that she had no idea how to get there.

4

———

Tess was doing her best to vacuum the living room, pushing the nozzle beneath Rose's beautiful piano to suck up the skeins of dust gathered like tumbleweeds. Tess was always nervous around Rose's piano. It insisted that it was Rose's home, not hers. Rose had kept her beloved piano pristine. Tess ought to polish it.

But she was still thinking about how to get to Skye in December. The train journey was long and expensive, and there was no railway service on the island. It wasn't as pricey by air but she'd need to hire a car from Inverness and drive via Loch Ness. That would work. She needed to make her mind up and arrange something.

A text buzzed in from Pam, who was about to board for Crete, promising to send photos. Jen was already on her way to her cruise ship. Tess thought with a smile that she'd have felt dreadful about the prospect of two weeks by herself, but now she'd booked in at the Sicín Órga, it felt like an adventure. She hadn't even told anyone yet.

She'd tell Della tomorrow, after she and Sylvester had booked their trip to Paris. Della had invited her round for dinner that evening – Tess imagined the squeals of joy over booking a sweet bijoux hotel on the Seine, Tess countering with news of the grand Victorian place on the beach on Skye. It felt good to have something to look forward to.

Tess was so pleased with herself that she decided to make herself something nice. It was almost eleven. On a whim, she'd bought a tin of Himalayan Salt and Caramel Drinking Chocolate Flakes. She hadn't opened it yet, but in her mind she'd already made it with hot milk, whipped cream and shavings of chocolate. A sprinkle of mini marshmallows. And a chocolate brownie.

She grinned. 'Tess, you know how to live.'

Fifteen minutes later, she was sitting at the kitchen table sipping sweet salty chocolate and nibbling a fudgy brownie. There was cream on her nose, a ring of chocolate around her top lip. Glorious. She put her feet up on a chair, leaned back and closed her eyes. For a moment, she was standing on the beach outside the Sicín Órga hotel, the sea breeze in her hair, inhaling the salty seas of Skye. Overhead, the clouds were fluffy-tailed lambs. Then Isla Fraser, the cheerful red-haired owner, came to join her to discuss dinner. It would be served in front of a roaring log fire in an inglenook. She'd be sitting on a tartan chair, a dish of rumbledethumps on her knee. Tess had no idea what rumbledethumps was – a Scottish casserole topped with potato? – but she was snuggled in the tartan chair, forking it into her mouth and it was piping hot. There was music playing – traditional bagpipes, a haunting melody resonating from the high walls where a stag's head overlooked the whole room. Drums were pounding – rat-tat-tata-tat, rat-tat-tat-tat...

Tess opened her eyes.

Someone was knocking on the front door. She frowned: the postman had already called with junk mail addressed to Mrs

Rosemary Grant. Nothing for her again. Feeling safely anony-
mous, Tess took another gulp of hot chocolate and hurried
towards the impatient knocking.

She tugged the door wide and caught her breath. It was
Alan, wearing a stiff suit, clutching a bunch of drooping
chrysanthemums in a cellophane wrapper. Tess stared, taking in
the paunch, the thinning hair, the practised smile, and said,
'Hello, Alan.'

He was staring back. 'You've got a brown smear on your lip.'

Tess wiped the chocolate off with the back of her hand.
There was cream from her nose. She wiped that too. 'What do
you want?'

He brandished the flowers. 'Can I come in?'

Tess wasn't sure. She'd seen him four times in the past three
years. They had met twice to discuss the divorce. Once she'd
been round to the old house to collect the last of her belongings
and they'd argued over who owned a saucepan. The final time
was by accident, a year ago, they'd collided near the laundry
liquid in a supermarket and sprung apart, as if scalded.

She eyed the chrysanths suspiciously. 'What was it you
wanted?'

'I thought we could have a chat.'

'I'm busy.'

'Drinking hot chocolate?' His smile broadened. 'The same
old Tess.' She thought there was affection in his voice, but it
might have been sarcasm. She relented – she'd always relented
where Alan was concerned, except the once, when she'd found
him with Celia in their bed.

'Come in.'

As he walked in, Alan looked around at Rose's shiny piano,
at the vacuum cleaner hose curled like a snake on the carpet. He
followed her into the kitchen and noticed the half-eaten

brownie. He said quietly, 'Rose's place looks nice. When's she coming back?'

'I have no idea.' Tess faced him. 'So – let's get down to the nitty-gritty. What do you really want?'

He put on his smooth voice. 'You could offer me a cup of whatever you're drinking.'

Tess was sharply aware of the old charm offensive. She didn't find him charming now. She sniffed the air. 'What's that smell? Chanel?'

She watched him cringe. Celia had reeked of it as she'd frolicked in their bed. Alan composed himself as best he could and mumbled, 'Bleu de Chanel.'

Tess did her 'as if I care' face. The truth was, she didn't care, not now. She lifted the kettle. 'Instant coffee?'

Alan eyed the hot chocolate, the brownie on a plate. 'Tess, we have things to talk about...'

Tess was about to retort 'no, we don't,' but she held back. She was learning – it was best not to give him an opening for a debate he'd feel compelled to win. She turned her back and filled the kettle, placing a heaped spoonful of coffee in a mug. Two spoonfuls. It would be bitter. Just as she was feeling, to be honest. Alan sat down.

'How long have you been living here?'

'You know how long.'

'Don't you miss the old house?'

Tess ignored him again. The house wasn't important now. And she'd miss a bad cold more than she'd miss living with Alan. He waited for her answer and when none came, he said, 'I miss everything.'

'What do you miss?'

'Us...' He allowed his single word to tick in the air like a time bomb. Tess felt it tick a bit longer, then explode around her. She banged the mug of coffee on the table, feeling a surge of temper.

'You're all alone, then? No one to fill the cold bit in the bed?'

'It's not that.' Alan sighed, as if he was suffering badly. 'I just think that – we made a mistake.'

'We?' Tess lifted an eyebrow. '*We* didn't sleep with our golfing friend's wife.'

Alan flinched, then he placed the flowers on the table. 'These are for you.' He lifted the cup to his lips. 'Have you ever thought – what if we were too hasty, Tess?'

'What if I should have left years ago?'

'We had happy times – we were a family. It was good when Lisa and Gemma were little.'

Tess couldn't deny it, the best times had been when the girls were growing up. But they were grown now and had busy lives. She glanced at her mug. She couldn't drink. Her mouth felt full of straw: there was a nasty taste and she didn't know what to say. Alan's presence made her uncomfortable.

'I don't play golf now,' Alan said, as if it meant something else.

Tess felt anger surge; she was about to ask him if he'd shagged every single golfer's wife and there was no one left in the club to shag. No, she wouldn't lower herself.

She said, 'Right.'

'I sit at home and watch TV. I think about you.'

'You could join a group.' Tess bit her tongue. She was about to suggest the Exmouth WI – there would be plenty of women there...

'The thing is,' Alan did his best impression of Bambi, big eyes, vulnerable, '...I want you back.'

Tess asked herself how she felt and the answer came immediately. Emotionally numb. Her brain ached. She hadn't expected Alan to visit and she hadn't expected him to ask her to come back to him. Cynicism followed, then disbelief. He needed a housekeeper, a skivvy. At best, a placid companion. Or he owed money.

Tess drew herself to her full height and asked the obvious question. 'Why?'

Alan appeared to be thinking of what to say for a few moments. Then he said, 'I love you.'

Tess's laughter pealed. She couldn't help it – it ripped from her.

Alan looked hurt. 'Please don't laugh, Tess. I mean it.'

'And what brought on this sudden realisation?' Tess folded her arms.

'Waking up without you. Being alone. Missing your warmth, the sound of your voice.'

Tess was incredulous. 'When did you decide this?'

'I've always known.' Alan stood up. He took a step towards her, then knelt by the chair, grasping her hand. 'We're good together. We always have been.'

Tess waited for a reaction – for her pulse to race, for her heart to thud. She waited to be flooded with feelings of affection for the man she'd known since her twenties. Instead, she felt pity.

'Alan...'

'Please, Tess.' He gulped audibly, playing the final card up his sleeve. 'I was so wrong to let you go. I've been regretting it every day for the last four years. I've been a fool. I didn't know how happy I was until I lost everything. Until I lost you.'

Tess didn't know whether to laugh again. She wasn't sure if he was performing for her benefit or if he was truly apologetic. That was the problem with Alan – you never knew if he meant what he said or if he was saying it to get his way.

She said gently, 'I think you should get up.'

'I'm on my knees for you.' Alan didn't move. 'Come with me, Tess. Back to our home. Let's start again. I'm begging.'

Tess shook her head weakly. She felt sorry for him now – he had the ability to wear her down and tug at her heartstrings. She did her best to summon the image of Celia and Alan in their bed. That would bring back some perspective.

She took a breath. 'Please – get up.'

Alan eased himself back in the chair, grasping her hand, tugging it to his lips. 'Tell me you'll think about it. I'm a broken man.'

Tess looked at the suit, the paunch; she inhaled Bleu de Chanel. He didn't look like a broken man. It occurred to her that she needed him to go away as soon as possible. Once he was on the other side of the front door, she could think straight.

Tess swallowed. 'Have you finished your coffee?' She could see he hadn't. He'd hardly touched it. He hadn't come round to drink coffee. He turned his most desperate gaze on her.

'I need you.'

Tess stood up. 'I'll give it some thought.'

'Oh, Tess, you won't regret it.' Alan leaped up like a spaniel, as if he'd been offered a biscuit: Tess had seen Elvis make exactly the same bounding movement with Pam. Alan was behaving as if she'd said yes. He'd always done that. It was how he got his way.

Tess folded her arms. 'Now, if you don't mind – I'm busy.'

'Of course.' Alan stood up too. 'I value your space, your free time. I'd never take you for granted. We'd be equals – we'd respect each other. We'd love each other. We'd be...'

Tess started to walk towards the front door. Alan followed her, talking, gesticulating.

'We'd be inseparable. Just like we used to be. We'd do everything together – gardening – cooking – holidays. We'd go on holiday...'

Tess opened the door. 'Bye, Alan.'

'You'll think about it? We'd be young lovers again. I'd bring you breakfast in bed...'

'In bed?' The image was there again, Celia and Alan, Percy Sledge crooning from the speaker downstairs, 'When a Man Loves a Woman'.

Tess shook her head.

'We'd go on a honeymoon – Paris – you like Paris – we'd have a wonderful time – we'd go to shows – drink champagne.'

Tess closed the door with a dull clunk. Alan was still outside wittering about Paris: Tess heard the words 'Eiffel Tower' and 'night boat on the Seine'. She walked away and left him to it, plodding sadly back to the kitchen. Now she was on her own, she knew the truth for sure. She might feel sorry for him, but she'd never go back to him. She'd tell him straight. Next time. If there was one.

She plonked herself down at the table and sighed. She wasn't sure if she wanted to cry.

The holiday on Skye couldn't come soon enough. She longed to feel revitalised, as though the wind had blown her troubles away.

Tess needed someone to talk to. She didn't want to trouble Della – she'd be with Sylvester. They did their supermarket shop on a Friday. Jen was on her way to Southampton. Pam was airborne. She'd ring Rose in Paris.

Tess pressed the buttons on her mobile and Rose's image came up. She was wearing a turban fastened with a glittery brooch, a faux fur coat, sitting outside at a bistro drinking coffee. Behind her, Tess could see a waiter moving between tables. A sign on the wall read Café Clémentine.

Rose's mouth moved, crimson lipstick in motion. 'Tess. How lovely. You caught me having breakfast.'

'It's almost lunch time.' Tess felt a slight surge of envy – her hot chocolate was cold now, the brownie no longer wanted. Rose was living the life.

Tess forced her best bold grin. 'Paris looks wonderful.'

'You must come over. What about popping across for Christmas?'

'I could.' Tess was warming to the idea.

'I'm looking for a new flat, as it happens,' Rose said. 'Daz and I have been talking. I'm eighty next birthday. He's the perfect flatmate – he's young, single, we work together, most evenings, so we thought we'd pool our resources and buy something on the Rive Gauche.'

'Oh?' Tess wondered about the wisdom of Rose buying a place with Daz. He was young. What if he met someone? What if he decided to move on? She tried not to look unenthusiastic. 'What does your son think about it?'

'Paul? He thinks I've lost my wits.' Rose trilled a laugh. 'He won't visit me. He's far too busy with his job and his wife and his children. He's just like Bernard was – sweet in his own way, but he thinks he knows everything. No, Tess,' Rose made a cheeky face into the screen, 'I'm a widow now and I'm going to spend all Paul's inheritance unwisely.'

'That sounds like fun.' Tess was not sure what Rose meant.

'Oh, it will be,' Rose purred. 'So I need some funds to finance my lifestyle. By day I'm Rose Grant, wild extravagant English lady residing in Paris, and by night I'm Rose-on-Wye, dressed as Marie Antoinette, playing the piano for Greta Manchester who sings Abba songs in Monty's glorious nightclub.' She winked. 'It's the perfect life.'

'It must be...' Tess took a breath and wondered how to tell her about Alan, but Rose was still speaking excitedly.

'And that's why I'm glad you rang, Tess. I was just about to ring you. The thing is – I wanted you to know something...'

'Know what?' For a moment, Tess wondered if Rose was going to announce her engagement. Instead, Rose offered a troubled expression.

'What I'm trying to say is, Tess, I've been talking on the phone to Wiley and Nagel.'

'Who?'

'The estate agents in town. I'm really sorry to tell you, but I'm sure you'll find somewhere soon. A better place. There will be plenty of time to sort it out. You see, someone will be coming round to do a valuation later.'

'Round where?'

'To the house, Tess, to value it. I've made up my mind and I wasn't sure how to tell you. I said to Daz, I feel so bad about it but I'd better just spit it out.'

'Spit what out, Rose?'

'I feel completely terrible, really mean. It's your home but...' Rose munched a croissant, her face sad. 'I'm putting my house on the market today. I've decided. The place is for sale.'

5

Della leaned across the bed and kissed Sylvester's nose.

'It's Saturday, sweetheart. Rise and shine.'

She slid from the duvet and moved to the window, glancing across the road at the rows of houses. 'It's a bright morning. No rain. We could pop into town, book the trip to Paris and then get coffee at the place where Tess and I went after aqua aerobics... Then a walk on the beach, a bit of exercise.'

'Mmm.' Sylvester made a sound of contentment. 'Whatever you want, Della. But – I might just roll over for a few minutes...'

'I'll make your breakfast.' Della was wide awake. 'How about a boiled egg? Some toast.'

'Lots of salt, just on the yolk, how I like it...' Sylvester mumbled into the pillow.

Della scurried back to the bed and kissed his forehead. 'You won't be long?'

'Five minutes.' Sylvester smiled. 'Maybe ten.'

'Just long enough for me to make you a sweet coffee and a perfect egg.'

'You're perfect,' Sylvester muttered, then he was asleep again.

Della rushed downstairs. It was past nine – they had both slept in this morning. She busied herself in the kitchen, lifting pans, filling one with water, spooning coffee into the pot, placing it on the stove. She was humming lightly to herself, thinking about Paris. They planned to stay for three nights, four days, maybe from the 3rd to the 5th of December. It might be cheaper midweek. She'd researched online and spotted a budget hotel in the Latin Quarter 900 metres from Notre Dame cathedral; another 600 metres from Trocadero, the River Seine and the Eiffel Tower. She would be happy with either of them.

And Sylvester would love it. She could already picture him saying, 'What's this damn fool little pastry thing you're asking me to eat? It'll blow away on the wind. Don't they have boiled eggs and toast?' And she'd hug him and laugh.

She placed his boiled egg in the cup and cut the toast into squares just as he came into the kitchen. He plonked himself at the table and she poured coffee into the One Love Jamaica mug that Linval had bought him last Christmas. He turned bleary eyes on her. 'I don't need waiting on, Della. I should be making your breakfast.'

'I don't mind.' Della smiled.

'I'm struggling to keep up with myself this morning.' He scratched his ear. 'I didn't sleep well. And I had a bit of a dizzy turn at the top of the stairs. I must be hungrier than I thought.'

'Then I'm glad I got up first. If you're a bit peaky, maybe you can have a nap when we get back from town,' Della said.

'You can come upstairs and lie down with me...' Sylvester laughed, doing his best to make light of his complaints. 'We can get in the mood for Paris.' He knocked the top off his egg. 'Maybe I'll chase you round the bedroom.'

Della was about to retort as she often did, 'But will you remember what to do when you catch me?' Something stopped her. Instead, she asked, 'Are you feeling all right?' She reached out to touch his hand.

Sylvester snorted. 'Ah, no need to fuss, woman. I just haven't woken up yet.' He dipped toast in runny egg. 'Lovely. Just how I like it. And the coffee, steamy and sweet, just like my wife.'

Della frowned. Something about Sylvester was bothering her. She observed him carefully. His shirt was open at the neck, exposing the top of his chest, a stray grey hair or two. She said, 'Don't get cold. You should do up the top button.'

Sylvester moved a finger to his neck, touched the button and went back to his breakfast. 'I don't like those damn buttons done up too tight. I feel all trussed up.'

'I'm just thinking of your chest.' Della remembered when she'd arrived back from Paris after the hen party to an empty house, discovering him in hospital with pneumonia. 'You know how I worry.'

Sylvester slurped coffee. 'Ah, don't fret, Della. I have the constitution of a billy goat. Talking of which...' He wiped toast in yolk and pushed it into his mouth. 'What are you cooking tonight for Tess? She's coming round for dinner, isn't she?'

'She is. What do you fancy?' Sylvester offered her a roguish look and Della laughed. 'For dinner.'

'We haven't had curried goat in a long time.'

'Goat?' Della was unimpressed. 'Tess won't eat goat. What about brown stew chicken?'

'The food of the gods. I remember my mother...' Sylvester's eyes shone. 'She used to make my father his favourite dish. Mannish water.'

Della groaned in mock horror. 'Oh, not the mannish water again.'

'It's an aphrodisiac.' Sylvester pursed his lips in a kiss. 'A cooked goat head, with green bananas, garlic, dumplings,

Scotch bonnet peppers, all served with roasted yam.' He leaned on his palm dreamily. 'Real fire. I wish I was a young man again.'

'You'll feel like a young man when we get to Paris,' Della said encouragingly. 'I've seen this lovely hotel, Les Chênes. You can see the Seine from the rooms.' She stood up, clearing empty plates from the table.

'We'll book whatever you like.' Sylvester levered himself from the table, his egg unfinished.

'I can't wait.' Della closed her eyes as he kissed her. 'We'll have so much fun.'

'And afterwards we'll leave the bedroom and see the sights,' Sylvester said, deliberately misunderstanding her. He looked suddenly tired. 'Della, I think I'll sit in my chair, just for a few minutes. I have a bit of indigestion come on.'

'Oh, I hope I cooked the egg enough,' Della said.

'It was delicious. Just like my lovely wife.' Sylvester fondled her shoulder. 'I'll just sit a little minute.'

'Of course.' Della turned back to the dishes. 'Shall I bring you another coffee?'

'That would be nice. Hot and sweet,' Sylvester said, but his voice was tired. He moved to the door, supporting himself against the chair. 'Don't be surprised if I fall asleep.'

'You get your beauty sleep,' Della called after him as she turned on the tap, watching hot water splash in the bowl, adding washing-up liquid, frothing bubbles. She pulled on a pair of yellow rubber gloves and began to wash the dishes, humming as she worked. Theirs was a little kitchen, but she was proud of it. She was already organising the day ahead – she'd start on supper once the holiday was booked. Tess would enjoy a chicken dish, maybe a classic sweet potato pudding for dessert, with golden raisins soaked in dark rum. Tess had a sweet tooth –

she'd have second helpings. Della was looking forward to the evening.

She tugged off the yellow gloves and poured Sylvester a second coffee from the pot on the stove, adding two spoonfuls of brown sugar. Still humming, she hurried into the living room.

Sylvester was sitting on his favourite chair, a comfy wingback with soft cushions. He was leaning slightly forward, a hand pressed against his chest, wheezing. Della hurried over to him.

'Sylvester? Have you been coughing again?'

His brow was damp; he was panting. He glanced up, his eyes glassy. 'I can't breathe...'

She placed a hand on his shoulder. 'What's happening?'

'Can't breathe,' Sylvester gasped again. He was panicking. 'I have a pain here, here...' He pressed his chest. 'Crazy thing. Up my arms, up in my jaw.'

Della was suddenly springing to action. 'Stay there – right there.'

Sylvester groaned as Della picked up her phone and dialled emergency services. Her voice shook. 'Ambulance, please. I think my husband might be having a heart attack – yes, he's breathing. Yes, please hurry.'

Della tried her best to sound calm while she gave her address and answered simple questions, her eyes on Sylvester all the time, who was increasingly breathless, an open palm against his heart. She put down the phone. 'The ambulance is on its way. You just sit tight, breathe slowly. They told me to tell you to rest while we wait, and to give you an aspirin. You have to chew it slowly – it will help.'

'I... I'll try.' Sylvester gasped.

'Let's get you in the ambulance.' Della fretted. 'It will be here in a moment. Now hang on there – I'll run up to the bathroom and get the aspirin and then the ambulance will be here... oh.'

She wrapped her arms around him. 'Sylvester, why didn't I know? I should have noticed. Just sit, relax best as you can and – let's get you well again.'

He offered a hopeless expression, his chest heaving. Della fled upstairs to the bathroom, her heart thumping, her hands jittering as she searched in the medicine cupboard for an aspirin. She found one at the back of a shelf with trembling fingers, muttering, 'If anything should happen to that man... What would I do?'

She hurried down the stairs to where Sylvester was slumped and she heard a siren approaching. The ambulance was seconds away.

* * *

Tess sat in the bath, surrounded by sweet-ginger-and-cinnamon-scented bubbles. She felt calm now; thoughts of Alan were miles from her mind. She'd booked a plane ticket that afternoon from Bristol to Inverness – it was a short flight – and she'd hired a little car, a Fiat 500, something manageable. It would give her independence when she was on Skye.

She'd been looking online at the places she'd like to visit; it would be cold in December – she doubted she'd have the confidence to swim in the Fairy Pools in Glen Brittle. But she'd drive to Dunvegan Castle, the ancestral home to the Clan MacLeod. Coral Beach was a stone's throw away too – she'd see the Hebrides looming in the distance. She'd take a boat trip from Elgol to Loch Coruisk, a freshwater loch surrounded by the Cuillin mountains. She might go otter spotting, drive to Portree and try archery, clay pigeon shooting, air rifle shooting and axe throwing. The idea of hurling an axe made her smile, being instructed by a six-and-a-half-foot-tall red-bearded man called

Murray, handsome, in a kilt. And, of course, there were the Northern Lights—

Tess sank deeper into the suds and thought it might be nice if she had a companion to travel to Skye. Alan's face came back to her, the suit, the paunch, the scent of Bleu de Chanel. No, not Alan. Definitely not. But it would be good to have someone to talk to over dinner, someone to share walks and whisky with. For a moment, her courage almost failed as she saw herself wandering alone, an old lady in a heavy coat and wellingtons, the wind blowing her hair. She took a deep breath, dunked herself beneath the spicy scented water and up again, her hair dripping.

Being alone meant that she'd have the chance to meet new people, like-minded travellers. She just had to be brave and make the first move, ask questions. It would be good for her. It would make her stronger.

She wondered what the time was. It couldn't be six yet. She had plenty of time. She hoped Della had made a sweet dessert laced with rum. And there would be wine. Tess had bought two bottles this afternoon. Yes, she'd have a great time this evening. It would cheer her up.

The For Sale sign that had just been put up in the garden had temporarily shaken her, but the young man who'd come round to value the house had said it would probably take months to sell. She wouldn't need to look for somewhere else until after Christmas, and he mentioned a pretty cottage had just come onto the market, perfect for a single lady. Tess was secretly a little worried it might cost more than she had in the bank. But she wouldn't think about it until she got back from Skye.

She paused, listening. Someone was hammering on the door downstairs. Tess spoke her first thought aloud. 'Oh, no. Not Alan again.'

The banging continued so Tess reached for a towel, then a fluffy bath robe. She'd leave the water: it surely wouldn't take long to deal with whoever was knocking. She'd send them on their way and come back to a hot tub.

Hugging the bath robe, tying the belt, Tess thumped downstairs and tugged the door open. She was surprised to see Della standing in the doorway, looking cold, shivering. Tess offered her best grin.

'Hi, Della. I thought I was coming to you tonight.' Her smile widened. 'I have bought plenty of wine, so we'll get properly smashed. I'm looking forward to it.'

'Can I come in?' Della muttered and Tess realised immediately that something was wrong.

'Of course.' Tess stepped back, hauling the door wide. 'What's happened? Where's Sylvester?'

'He had a turn at home, in his chair.' Della took a breath, her teeth chattering. 'I phoned an ambulance. We were on our way to the hospital then...'

'How is he?' Tess asked, then she saw the tears in Della's eyes. 'Della?'

'I had to come, Tess. I'm sorry.'

Tess opened her arms. 'Where is he now?'

'I have to tell someone. I haven't even called the boys. I came straight here. I couldn't phone anyone...' Della rushed into the hug and burst into tears. 'Tess, Sylvester had another big heart attack in the ambulance. A massive one, while I sat next to him and held his hand. And that was it. There was nothing they could do – he closed his eyes, breathed out one time and smiled at me as if he was trying to say something then – it was the last thing he did. In one second, it was all over. Over.'

'Della?'

'He's gone, Tess – Sylvester's gone.'

6

─────────

It felt more like a celebration than a wake, Tess thought as she poured rum punch into a tall glass. She swirled the drink, all ice cubes, pineapple chunks, delicious sweetness. She felt sad. The table in Della's little kitchen was packed with sandwiches, quiches, salads, jerk chicken, rice dishes, as well as salt fish, akee, callaloo, plantains, spiced cake. Reggae music bubbled from the smart speaker. There were flowers in vases everywhere – Jen and Pam had sent bunches, Rose too, with their love and apologies for not being there. Tess had brought a potted plant. She closed her eyes a moment, remembering how brave Della had been, how dignified. The funeral had been dignified too, the little chapel packed with people wearing bright colours, Della holding her head high in a yellow dress and a soft brimmed hat. Tess had not stopped crying.

A quiet voice beside her said, 'Can I get you some food, Tess? Or top up your drink?'

Tess looked at Linval Donovan and for a moment she thought it was a young Sylvester. Slim, dapper and smooth-headed in a white suit, he was the image of his father. Tess had drunk two rum punches already. Any more alcohol would make her even more weepy. She muttered, 'No, thanks, Linval. This is delicious though. Did you make it?'

'Of course. It was Dad's recipe, and his dad's too. I can make rum punch with my eyes closed. Lots of rum, pineapple juice, orange, lemon, lime and grenadine.'

'Where's your mum?' Tess asked quietly. The kitchen was empty, apart from a woman in a floral frock filling her plate.

'In the living room, talking to guests,' Linval said. 'She'll be with Aston and the kids. What a huge turnout. Dad would have enjoyed it so much. He'd have thought it was a great party...' His bottom lip quivered. Tess took his hand.

'Della was amazing in the chapel, how she held it together.' Tess took a breath. 'That poem she read was wonderful. I was blubbing right from the first line.'

Linval nodded. 'It was Momma's choice, "Island Man" by Grace Nichols. It said everything perfectly about Daddy, how he lived in a place of tarmac and traffic and dreamed of blue skies and the ocean.' He sighed. 'Daddy came to England from St Ann's Bay when he was sixteen – he met Momma in Stepney over fifty years ago. But I don't think he ever got used to the cold weather.'

Tess smiled. 'And I loved the poem you read. It set me off crying again.'

'"Reggae fi Dada" by Linton Kwesi Johnson.' Linval had tears in his eyes. 'I didn't read all of it – it's long – but it's exactly how I feel.' He sighed. 'It was tough when we were kids, there wasn't much money in the house, but Daddy worked hard, Momma too, and we always had love and laughter and food on the table.'

Tess drained her drink. 'So what will Della do now?'

Linval shrugged. 'I asked her to come back with me to

London. Aston said she could move in with him. But Momma's tough. She wants to stay in Exmouth.'

'Because her memories are here?'

'She said all her friends are here,' Linval said simply and Tess felt a lump in her throat.

'I'm due to go on holiday in a couple of days...' Tess murmured. 'I was going to Skye. But Pam's away, Jen's cruising in Iceland, Rose is in Paris. So I'm going to cancel it and spend time with Della.'

'I'm very grateful.' Linval nodded. 'My mother will tell everyone she can manage. But this house is full of Daddy – his belongings, his memories. I know Momma's strong and capable, but it will be hard being here.'

'It will,' Tess agreed. 'I'd already decided to cancel. I'll call the hotel later and say I can't come. I'd rather stay with Della. I don't want her to be alone.'

'Thanks, Tess,' Linval said gratefully. 'That's kind of you to give up your holiday.'

'You'll do nothing of the sort.' A hushed voice came from the doorway. Della sashayed in, her yellow dress swishing.

'Della.' Tess forced a smile. 'Linval and I were just saying—'

'I heard the end of it.' Della clamped her lips together. 'You're going to Skye in a couple of days, I know.'

'I've decided not to go,' Tess said.

Della placed her hands on her hips. 'And why not?'

'You know why not, Momma,' Linval said helplessly.

'Because I'm a weak widow who just buried my husband?' Della frowned.

Tess's eyes filled with tears. 'Because you're my friend and friends stick together.'

'They do. And?'

'I can't leave you here by yourself, Della.'

'You think I'll fade away?'

'No,' Tess said kindly. 'But it will be hard on your own, what with...'

'Sylvester gone?' Della breathed in deeply, steadying herself. 'I loved that man with all my heart – I still do. And I intend to keep his memory alive. He was the best of men, the kindest, the sassiest, the sweetest...' She paused, wiping her eyes. 'I owe him big time...'

Tess felt a tear slide down her cheek. 'You were such a close couple.'

'And that's why I promised myself.' Della took a breath. 'Sylvester and I were going to book a honeymoon break in Paris. If he could speak to me now, he'd say, "My fool heart gave up on me, Della, but that doesn't mean you can't have some fun for the both of us." And that's what I intend to do.' She squeezed her eyes closed as more tears came.

'You're off to Paris?' Tess said, full of awe as she wiped wet cheeks.

'Not exactly.' Della looked from Tess to Linval, back to Tess. 'You're right about me not wanting to be by myself at the moment. Sylvester is still here, in the walls, in the air around me. I'm grieving and it will take forever and a day to get over that man but...' She took a deep breath. 'I know what he'd want me to do, Tess, and I'm going to do it. That's if you agree.'

'Of course I agree.' Tess was baffled. 'But what am I agreeing to?'

'I'm coming to Scotland with you. Both of us are going, just as Sylvester would have liked.' Della turned to Linval. 'Now, son, I want you to get out that little laptop thing you're always on and book me a plane ticket to Inverness. I'll lock up the house with all its memories and give myself time to breathe again. In a couple of days, Tess and I are going to Skye.'

* * *

Tess walked back to Rose's house slowly, thinking about the funeral, allowing the fact that Sylvester had gone to sink into her skin. She'd been one of the last to leave Della's – it was past five, and Della was sitting in Sylvester's wingback chair drinking tea, talking to Linval. He had bought her a return plane ticket to Inverness and Tess had tried to ring the hotel on Skye to book another room, but no one was answering the phone – Tess assumed it was a busy time – so Linval booked the room online. Della had forced a smile, reached for Tess's hand and said, 'It's done. We're going.'

There were two cars parked outside Rose's house, next to the green placard with Wiley and Nagel: For Sale. Tess frowned as she approached her home: she didn't recognise the black Audi or the white Renault Zoe. Her first thought was that Alan might have bought a new car, and she glanced around the small front garden to see if he was loitering.

She turned her key in the lock and stepped into the hall, pausing to listen. A man was talking in a light persuasive tone: '...very keenly priced to sell as the vendor wants to move quickly. And it's virtually vacant possession.'

A woman replied, 'I thought there was a tenant?'

'Oh, I believe she can leave at short notice,' the man replied smoothly.

Tess strode into the living room. 'That would be me.' She smiled at a tall balding man in glasses, who was talking to a woman in a green anorak. The woman took a step back, a little surprised. The man was immediately professional.

'I'm pleased to meet you. I thought you were out. I don't have a contact number for you, or I'd have phoned ahead. Mrs Grant sent me a key.'

'I've been to a funeral,' Tess said quickly. Her eyes fell on the man's clipboard and a key he'd deposited on her newly polished piano. 'Rose is very particular about her piano. In fact, she's particular about everything.'

The estate agent picked up the key and clipboard, looking a little awkward. The woman in the anorak turned to Tess.

'It's a lovely house. I think I'd like a second viewing so I can bring my husband and my daughter. It would be perfect for us – the primary school's just a short walk away.'

'It's nice,' Tess agreed, turning her back to the estate agent. 'It has a warm atmosphere. Rose was happy here.'

'But she lives in Paris now – is that right?' the woman asked Tess.

'She's a concert pianist,' the estate agent butted in.

'Rose is nearly eighty. I'm so proud of her.' Tess ignored him. 'She and her partner are cabaret performers in a drag club.'

The woman clapped her hands. 'How wonderful. But what about you? I mean – isn't this your home?'

'Temporarily. But I'm off to Skye the day after tomorrow for a break.' Tess waved a hand to show the house was unimportant. 'If you really wanted to buy, I can move out quickly.' She was stunned by her own words. She had no idea where she'd go. But she didn't want Rose to miss a sale.

'Oh.' The woman seemed delighted. 'Imagine – the new year in a new home. Seeing snow fall from this window.'

'The Christmas tree could go where the old piano is,' the estate agent chimed in, not wanting to miss an opportunity.

'*Old* piano?' Tess threw him a look. 'That piano is worth thousands – Rose bought it from Liberace in the seventies.' She pressed her lips together to prevent a laugh escaping. 'They played together on this very piano in Ronnie Scott's in London.' She searched for something else to say. 'With Elton John.'

The woman in the anorak was clearly impressed. 'Oh, she must be very talented.'

'Rose is the best.' Tess ignored the dagger eyes the estate agent was making. She pretended to have just noticed him. 'What did you say your name was?'

'Nagel, Andrew Nagel.'

'I'm Tess Watkins,' Tess said benevolently. She strode into the centre of the room. 'Well, Andrew, I'll let you finish your tour. Just take care of that valuable piano.' She addressed the woman in the anorak. 'It was so nice meeting you.'

Tess whirled away, up the stairs and into her bedroom, flopping onto the bed. She felt suddenly exhausted. The prospect of being homeless made her feel tired, although she suspected no sale would be completed until well into the new year.

Sylvester's funeral had taken its toll on her – it was hard to imagine him not being with Della any more, laughing, chasing her around the table. But Tess intended to make sure Della had the best chance to rest, to relax and to heal.

It was up to her to make sure they both had a good time on Skye.

7

On Sunday afternoon, Tess and Della sat on the plane, their shoulders touching, feeling the engines vibrate beneath them. Tess looked anxious. 'Are you all right with this?'

'You mean flying?' Della asked tentatively.

'I mean everything.'

'You mean Sylvester.' Della shook her head. 'Oh, Tess. The house is empty. The bed is empty.' She took a breath. 'My life is empty. Other than that I'm fine.' She met Tess's eyes. 'I cried myself to sleep last night. It feels wrong without him.'

'I bet.' Tess nodded: in truth, she had no idea.

'So – we need ground rules for this holiday,' Della said firmly.

'Do we?'

'We do. I'm bound to get upset from time to time and you can just let me get on with it.' Della took Tess's hand, her face earnest. 'I don't want you pussyfooting round things. I might cry and that's how it's going to be. Don't think you can't mention his name, even if I do sob my heart out – I lived with that man for fifty-three years and I don't want to be afraid to talk about him.'

Della's face crumpled. She tugged out a hanky and blew her nose.

'Just tell me what to do for the best.'

Della forced a smile. 'You're doing it. You're letting me come away with you. And I'm determined to have a wonderful time, and I won't be a killjoy and a sourpuss, but I'm grateful for your company and I don't want you compensating by being too nice or thinking you have to distract me. And in turn, I'll try not to be a wet blanket.'

'Wet blanket, sourpuss and killjoy you are definitely not.' Tess squeezed Della's hand. 'You be who you are. That's who I want to be on holiday with. We'll be fine.'

'Everything will remind me of Sylvester, wherever I go.' Della sniffed. 'I've never been to Skye before though. I'll take him with me in my heart, but this break is about you and me, Tess, making new memories.' Della sniffed again, as if it was the final one she'd allow herself. 'Now let's get this party started. Where's cabin crew? I need a drink.'

Tess said, 'Do you remember when the five of us flew to Paris?'

'The hens in flight...' Della smiled.

'We sat on the plane and I was wearing that embarrassing beret and striped Breton shirt – whatever was I thinking?'

'And the string of garlic necklace?'

'I just wanted Jen to be in the hen-party mood. Then I found myself sitting next to a disapproving Frenchman and I felt so awkward.'

'I spent every airborne minute worrying how Sylvester would manage without me and what did that man do? He stayed out in the rain and got pneumonia. Oh, Tess – do you think that's what made his heart weak? Should I have taken better care of him?' Della's lip trembled.

'Of course not,' Tess said kindly. 'You took the best care of that man.'

'But he was stubborn and adorable. I still have the image of him in the ambulance, and a woman with a defibrillator, and nothing was happening, just Sylvester, his eyes open, not seeing me.' Della's eyes filled again. 'Oh, look – cabin crew.' She took a breath, reaching out a hand as a young man in a white shirt and a red waistcoat hurried past. His name badge said Sam, so Della called out, 'Sam?'

The young man turned back. 'What can I get you?'

'I'll have a rum,' Della said firmly. 'Jamaican, if you have it. And if not, whatever you have. And my friend will have...'

'A lemonade, please,' Tess muttered. 'Remember I'm picking up our hire car at Inverness.'

'Oh, I forgot. Right, a rum and Coke and a lemonade, please,' Della said cheerily.

'Of course, madam,' Sam replied efficiently.

'I didn't know you drank rum,' Tess whispered.

'I never used to but – do you know, Sylvester loved it. And it will remind me of his sweet rum kisses...' Della took a breath. 'So, we'll pick up our hire car and drive to Skye. I'm guessing it will be quite dark and the roads will be narrow.'

'And filled with badgers and deer and wild boar.' Tess was suddenly nervous. 'And lochs to fall into. And ice on the road.'

'Then I'll just have the one drink.' Della smiled. 'Since I'm going to be co-pilot.'

'I have directions on my phone.'

'When we arrive at our hotel, we'll treat ourselves to a drink and an early night, then we'll be ready for a hearty breakfast of porridge and pancakes tomorrow.'

'How do you know they do pancakes?' Tess asked.

'Linval told me.' Della smiled at Sam as he placed a miniature of rum in front of her, a can of cola, and a lemonade for Tess. Della paid with her card. 'He showed me the website. He said it all looked a bit outdated. But apparently, the woman who owns the place, Isla Fraser, is an incredible chef. So the food will be wonderful.'

'That's good to know.'

Della poured the miniature and raised her glass. 'To great holidays.'

'Great holidays.'

'And great breakfasts.'

'Great breakfasts.'

'And the isle of Skye.'

'Skye.'

'And of course,' Della said with a flourish, 'to Sylvester...'

'To Sylvester,' Tess agreed. The friends clinked their glasses and took a swig. Della closed her eyes, smacked her lips and said, 'I wish I'd ordered a double.' She had almost finished her drink.

It was going to be an interesting holiday.

* * *

The wind outside Inverness airport was so strong Tess was almost blown over. She tugged up her jacket hood firmly and it was immediately whisked off again. Her hair lashed her face in blonde strands. Della gasped as a huge gust drove her back towards the revolving doors.

'This place is seriously blowy!'

'Let's find the hire-car.' Tess waved her ticket. 'We're looking for a Fiat 500. We'll get in, turn the heater up to meltdown and drive to Skye.'

Twenty minutes later they were hunched in a little mint-coloured car, trying to find the exit. Tess ignored the directions on her phone as they drove around Inverness because she was busy staring at the beautiful old castle and took a wrong turn, following the A9 to Perth. Della yelled, 'This is the wrong way,' and Tess had to retrace the road. She whizzed round a round-about twice, and eventually negotiated three more roundabouts, feeling small between large lorries, before following the A82 to Loch Ness.

'Why are we going this way?' Della asked. 'Your phone said...'

'Oh, that thing's just for advice,' Tess said. 'I want to take the scenic route past the loch.'

'Loch Ness?' Della frowned. 'Won't it be dark by the time we get there?'

'It might be dusky, but we'll be able to stop and take photos.' Tess was excited. 'It will be inky by the time we get to Skye though. I looked at a map before we left Exmouth. If we follow the loch road, we get to see a couple of castles and some moun-tains, then we go over a bridge and that takes us to Skye. It looked incredible in the pictures.'

'Even though it's going to be too dark to see anything?' Della asked again dubiously.

Tess wondered if Della was feeling low and offered her widest smile. 'But we'll get the atmosphere.'

As they continued down the road, Della tried to avoid the sinking feeling that Tess wasn't the best driver in the world. She was veering very close to the hedges and paying far too much attention to the scenery: every few minutes she'd shriek, 'Aww, look at that.' Della had no idea what she was pointing to.

'What am I supposed to look at now?'

'A lovely little squirrel scampering up a tree,' Tess cooed.

'You might want to look at the lovely road,' Della muttered.

Tess was oblivious. 'We're just coming up to Loch Ness. It's very twisty and turny here...'

'Let's try to stay out of the water, shall we?' Della said under her breath but Tess was shrieking again.

'Ohh, but ohhh – just look, Della. Ohhh.'

She slammed on the brakes and the car came to a jerking halt in a lay-by. Behind them, a car blared a warning honk. Tess didn't seem to hear.

'Just look.'

'Have you seen the monster?'

'The mists, Della – just look at the low-hanging mists. So atmospheric, just like a scene in a film – and the sun is going down behind the loch. I have to take a photo...'

Tess leaped from the car clutching her phone. The wind almost blew it from her hand and she squealed with laughter. 'Oh, but – Della – this is Scotland. Look at it, in all its glory.'

She peered through her phone, taking snap after snap of the inky loch. Swirling scarves of hazy mist sat just above the water like coils of low cloud. She was a little disappointed that the photos looked blurred rather than mysteriously misty. She'd hoped to send a few to Rose, Pam and Jen. She turned to see Della huddled round-shouldered in the Fiat, staring at her. Tess supposed that Della wasn't in the mood to take photos, and that was completely understandable She crept back to the car.

'Well, thanks for letting me take some pics, Della. The loch is so beautiful.'

Della said nothing and Tess started the car. She hadn't driven a mile, when she noticed a castle by the side of the road and braked heavily.

'Oh – ooooh, look, Della. Oh my, oh my, oh my.'

Della sounded tired. 'What is it now?'

'A castle – an old ruined Scottish castle.' Tess pulled into another lay-by and leaped out. 'I need tons of pictures... tons.' She pointed the camera, the wind blowing her hair across the lens, tugging at her coat, then she was back inside the car. 'It's so cold outside.'

'The castle's called Urquhart.' Della forced a smile. 'It's one of the largest ruins in the Highlands. I looked it up online before we left home.' She stifled a yawn. 'It might be nice to visit it on the way back, when we're not so tired and it's light and you can see it properly.'

Tess realised at once that Della hadn't been sleeping well. 'Oh, I'm sorry – you must be worn out, and here's me taking photos and jabbering about views and mist.' She started the car. 'Let's get a move on – I think the journey should take a couple of hours.'

'Two and a half, according to your phone.' Della closed her eyes. 'I have to admit, I'm looking forward to a good night's sleep.'

'The four-poster beds will be heavenly,' Tess said. 'I can't wait to curl up with a good book. I love having all the space to myself – one of the perks of having kicked Alan out.' She stopped speaking, realising what she'd said. 'Oh, Della, I'm so sorry...'

'Not at all.' Della struggled to keep her voice strong. 'Alan deserved everything he got.' She was thoughtful for a moment. 'I miss Sylvester though, especially at night, when the bed's cold and empty. I even miss that rattling snore I used to complain about...' She sighed. 'Oh, look at the mountains, Tess.' She pointed into the distance. 'Even though it's almost dark now, you can see the snow gleaming on the top. It's so uplifting.'

Tess looked at black velvet mountains iced with shining snow, a low bronze moon in the fading sky. Her voice was a whisper. 'It's beautiful.'

She drove steadily through undulating roads flanked by high mountains, dropping down to the Kyle of Lochalsh and across the high bridge, almost hypnotised by the twinkling lights in the distance. Della had fallen asleep, her body twisted beneath the seat belt. She was breathing deeply. Tess glanced towards the edge of the bridge. There was the island of Skye, rising mountains in dark humps, a few scattered houses with small lights behind windows. Tess glanced anxiously at the satnav. She'd need it now to guide her to Sleat, to the Sicín Órga hotel. It was forty-five minutes away.

A warm welcome and a hot cup of tea couldn't come soon enough.

8

Tess drove along the bumpy road to the hotel car park in total darkness except for the wavering headlights of the Fiat. Della was fast asleep, her head on one side. It was almost nine o'clock. The hotel was almost in blackout, the lamp over the door shedding soft light. There were no other cars parked apart from a tatty-looking Land Rover. Tess eased Della's head up gently. 'Wakey wakey – we're here.'

They looked at the grand white building in front of them. It appeared desolate and – Tess didn't like the words that came into her head – hauntingly empty. Della opened her eyes.

'Sorry. I wasn't much help as a navigator. I didn't intend to doze off.'

'Don't worry. Let's get inside,' Tess said quietly. She pushed the car door open and immediately felt the blast of the wind biting her ankles. Della was wide awake now.

'It's icy out there.'

'There's a steaming hot cup of tea with my name on it in that hotel,' Tess said. 'Let's grab our luggage.'

'Oh.' Della opened her eyes wide. 'I can hear the sea.'

Tess listened: the low rush of the ocean whispered. She couldn't help smiling. 'We're here, Della – we're on Skye.' She was out of the car, dancing, despite the case in her hand, whirling round. 'We're here!'

Della clambered out of the passenger side and stifled a smile. 'Well, I don't know where the other guests are, Tess – the lights are all off.'

Tess hugged herself to feel warmer and hurried to the door, pressing the bell. It made a low clanking sound inside. Della struggled next to her, placing two bags on the floor, moving closer for warmth. 'That wind has ice in it.'

'Come on, come on...' Tess rubbed her hands together impatiently. 'What are the owners called?'

'Mr and Mrs Fraser,' Della remembered. 'Isla and Roddy.'

'Lovely names.' Tess was beaming. 'And this is the sick... what's the name of the hotel?'

'Sicín Órga,' Della reminded her.

'Sicking orca?' Tess was still smiling as she rang the bell again. 'Come on, Isla – I'm freezing to death.'

'I'd kill for a hot drink,' Della said. 'A nice local whisky will do.'

'Oh, a whisky in front of a roaring fire – one of those lovely inglenooks.'

'Holding a toasting fork...' Della's teeth chattered. 'Hot crumpets.'

'Dripping melted butter. And browning marshmallows.' Tess rolled her eyes. 'A mug of hot chocolate with fresh cream on top.'

'And grated chocolate...' Della began. The door opened and a man was standing in the gap, looking unhappy, grumpy even. He frowned. 'Yes?'

'I'm Tess Watkins and this is Della Donovan.' Tess smiled.

The man's face didn't change. He was tall, lean, with dark hair that curled over his collar and a craggy chin.

'Aye?'

'We've booked to stay here tonight.'

'I've no bookings,' the man said, his accent a less-than-friendly Scottish drawl.

'Oh, don't worry.' Della took over. 'We booked online.'

'I don't do online bookings.' The man made to close the door.

'Wait.' Tess took a deep breath. 'We've booked rooms here. We need to sleep.'

The man wasn't interested. 'Not my problem, lassie. You can't stay here. I'm not taking bookings, not now. Probably not ever.'

'Excuse me.' Tess wondered whether it would help to be assertive. 'We're tired out. We've come from England, for goodness' sake.'

'There might be somewhere in Portree, a bed and breakfast.' He took a step back. 'You could drive there and ask.'

Della put on her most soothing voice. 'Are you Mr Fraser?'

'I am.'

'Roddy, it's so nice to meet you,' Della purred. 'Look, you have rooms, and we need one. Might we stay, just for tonight?'

'I'm not doing bed and breakfast any more. I'm not doing anything.' Roddy Fraser's face was uninterested. 'The hotel is closed for the foreseeable—'

'One night, please?' Della coaxed. 'Then tomorrow we could make other arrangements.'

'Yes, perhaps we could speak to Isla, your wife.'

'There's no wife here.' Roddy was about to close the door again. 'No wife, no hotel, no bed and breakfast.'

'I'm sorry,' Della said gently. 'But please, just for one night... we're exhausted. Please.'

'Well, I'm not sure... maybe I could...' Roddy was relenting. 'I have two singles in one room I can let you have. The beds haven't been slept in. The room's not aired, but I suppose you can stay there.'

'Singles? What about the four-poster?' Tess asked.

'Singles are fine. Thank you – you've no idea how good that sounds,' Della insisted. Roddy left the door open and disappeared inside. Della grabbed her bags and followed him before he changed his mind, Tess on her heels.

He flicked on lights and the hall was illuminated by a chandelier with several bulbs missing. The space had been grand once, but it was run-down now. The beautiful mahogany staircase and the red tartan carpet were dusty and worn; the black and white floor tiles were grubby and the wallpaper was peeling. An ornate grandfather clock stood tall in the corner, the time five minutes to three; it no longer worked. Roddy Fraser shrugged as if he no longer worked either. In the light he looked really tired. He muttered, 'Follow me.'

Tess and Della followed him up creaking stairs, past a huge window with velvet drapes to the left, an oil painting of a regal-looking man in a kilt, his hands on his hips, on the wall.

Tess asked, 'Is that Robert the Bruce?'

'It's my great-grandfather, Dougal Fraser. He owned this hotel years ago.' Roddy's voice was as flat and dull as his footfall. He crossed a landing where a long corridor led to several bedrooms.

'What a beautiful place,' Della remarked kindly.

'It was,' Roddy said. 'Once. I had plans to bring it back to its original state. I was going to have every room decorated.'

'Restore it to its former glory?' Tess encouraged.

'That would be fabulous,' Della agreed.

'Not any more,' Roddy mumbled, pushing a key into a door, heaving it open and flicking a switch. 'Your room. It is what it is.'

Tess and Della stepped inside, letting their cases drop simultaneously. The vertical-striped wallpaper was peeling and grubby; the red velvet drapes faded. Two single beds stood side by side. An open door led to a bathroom; inside, Tess glimpsed a white standalone bath with dull gold taps. She offered Roddy a smile.

'En suite. That's lovely.'

'It's the best I can do.' His face didn't change. 'Goodnight.'

'I don't suppose you have any food?' Della asked hesitantly. 'We didn't have time to eat.'

'Doesn't the hotel do meals? I'd love a glass of wine,' Tess said hopefully. 'On the website, it said...'

'We used to do a lot of things.' Roddy turned to go.

'Not even a cup of tea?' Tess asked sweetly, placing her palms together as if praying.

Roddy didn't speak. His shoulders hunched, he moved to the door and was gone. Tess and Della stared around the room.

'It'll do,' Tess said grimly.

'It'll have to.' Della sounded relieved. 'I thought we'd have to spend the night in the car.'

'So did I. And it's so cold out there.' Tess pulled an unimpressed face. 'Roddy Fraser didn't look happy.'

'I felt sorry for him,' Della said. 'It wasn't the warm Scottish welcome I'd been expecting, the roaring fire...'

'This place is chilly,' Tess agreed. 'Is the heating even on?' She moved to a radiator and shook her head. 'Stone cold.'

'He didn't even know about our booking. There are no other guests.'

'That's awful. I'll be starving by breakfast.' Tess said. 'We'll have to find somewhere else. There must be somewhere on the island. Did he say to try Portree?'

'We'll look tomorrow.' Della stretched her arms and yawned. 'I'm just so tired now.'

'I wonder if the bath works.' Tess wandered into the en suite and turned on the taps. Hot water splashed into the bath. 'Oh, Della – it's steaming. Lovely. I'm going to have a long soak. I wonder if there's lashings of water?'

'Sylvester used to get into our bath after I'd bathed – he'd say, I want to wash in the water you wash in, Della, and I'll come out smelling of roses.' Della closed her eyes, remembering. Tess hugged her.

'You have the bath tonight, Della, and I'll have one tomorrow morning.'

There was a sharp knock at the door. The friends turned at the same time. Della called, 'Come in.'

The door creaked open and a lean, dark figure stood in the gap, holding something. For a moment, Tess wasn't sure if she was looking at the hotel's resident ghost. Then Roddy Fraser said flatly, 'You told me you were hungry.'

He stepped into the room carrying a tray. Tess looked at a bottle of red wine, two glasses and a family-sized bag of tortilla chips. She whooped, hurried across the room and grabbed the tray as if it were the Last Supper.

'Thank you, Mr Fraser – thank you so much.'

'It's all I could find,' he said modestly although the expression on Tess's face was one of pure gratitude, akin to love.

'It's wonderful. Look, Della, wine – and crisps.'

Roddy seemed even more embarrassed. 'I could probably make you a bit of toast for breakfast... I can do coffee or tea.'

Della nodded, understanding. 'You've no idea how grateful we are. I'm guessing you're a bit short-staffed – maybe because it's winter and Skye is a small island – but we're really grateful.' She watched Tess, who was unscrewing the lid of the wine bottle, pouring red liquid into glasses as though her life depended on it. 'Thank you.'

'My pleasure.' Roddy shifted awkwardly back through the door and was gone.

Tess held out a glass of wine as she shovelled tortilla chips into her mouth. 'Nothing has ever tasted this good. I was so hungry my stomach was eating itself.'

Della couldn't help a small smile. 'This is the life, Tess. The perfect dinner.' She gave a single laugh. 'I bet Jen's enjoying fine dining on the cruise ship.'

'And Pam will be on a pleasure boat with Elvis, eating dolmades and baklava...' Tess waved a tortilla chip. 'But this is heaven. Della – oh, do you think we should have asked Roddy to join us?'

Della shook her head. 'He looked worn out, poor man. He's probably having whisky-laced tea as we speak.'

'Oh no... he said the hotel was closed.' Tess put on her most horrified face. 'We're the only ones here.'

'What do you mean?' Della looked worried.

'Do you think Roddy's like that man in the Bates Motel in *Psycho*? He might kill the residents in the shower?'

Della shook her head. 'I think he's very sweet, bringing us a bottle of wine.'

'But why isn't the hotel open if it's being advertised online? The website looked quite old.'

'Perhaps his wife's unwell.' Della was thinking of Sylvester. 'Things aren't always as they seem.'

'He said they were going to do the place up – it certainly needs a lick of paint.'

'But then he said he wasn't going to.' Della frowned. 'I

wonder what's happened.' She listened. 'We've left the bath running.'

'Take your wine and have a long soak, put some bubble bath in. There's some in my travel bag,' Tess said.

'I'd love that. My back's killing me. Don't you want a bath?'

'You enjoy it. I'll finish the wine,' Tess offered generously. 'And the crisps.'

'Then we'll get a good night's sleep.' Della looked at the two single beds and immediately doubted her own words. 'Tomorrow morning, we'll find ourselves some better accommodation.'

9

After sleeping like logs, Tess and Della crept down the huge staircase at half past eight. The banister was dusty, the mahogany scraped, and the huge window was grimy. Outside, the sky was full of fluffy clouds. Beyond the garden, a vast sandy beach stretched towards a rolling ocean.

'Monday morning and the place is deserted,' Della said. 'It's a shame we can't stay here. There's something gloriously down-at-heel about this hotel, a sort of faded beauty.'

'Definitely. But wouldn't somewhere modern be nicer?' Tess took a deep breath. 'Can you smell breakfast? I can't. Imagine, Della...' She closed her eyes, ecstatic for a moment. 'A pretty bijou hotel, a Scottish breakfast with haggis; hot strong coffee served by a hot strong...'

'OK, Tess.' Della smiled. 'I get the picture.' She hurried down the stairs. 'Right now I'd settle for tea and toast.'

Tess agreed. 'I was hungry last night – the tortilla chips were a lifesaver.'

'It was kind of Roddy.' They had reached the bottom. Della

pointed to an open door. 'Do you think the breakfast room is this way?'

'Let's find out.' Tess hurried forward with new urgency into a large room that might once have been a ballroom. There were seven or eight tables covered in white cloths, the same vertical striped wallpaper on all walls, a low chandelier, large windows, a thick tartan carpet and the requisite stag's head on the wall. Tess pulled a face. 'This place would be beautiful if it was decorated. Oh, look!' She pointed to the far corner. 'Rose would love that.'

A grand piano stood, covered in a layer of dust, a candelabrum perched on top.

Della agreed. 'I can just see Rose-on-Wye playing that, dressed in her tall wig and a flouncy dress.'

Tess indicated the door at the far end of the room, left slightly ajar. 'Do you think it leads to the kitchen?'

'Let's go and see,' Della suggested. 'There might even be breakfast.'

'Coffee,' Tess said, licking her lips. 'Porridge.'

They paused just outside the door. There were voices coming from inside, a man's and a woman's. The man sounded flat, defeated – it was Roddy.

'Couldn't you just stay and make breakfast? I have two guests in room two.'

'You know how the coffee machine works, and the toaster, Roddy. That's not why I came.'

The woman sounded irritated. Tess met Della's eyes and placed a finger over her lips, listening.

Roddy muttered, 'I don't want to sell, but there's no way I can manage by myself.'

'No one wants to work here. Sleat's too remote. And I certainly don't want anything to do with it.'

'The hotel used to be so good, Isla. *We* used to be so good.'

'In your dreams.' The woman's voice dripped with sarcasm. 'I've put up with second best for too long. I know what I want now.'

Roddy sounded crushed. 'You want Alasdair Barclay.'

'He and I are good. I've had enough of Sleat, of Skye.'

'And of me, I know. I wish I hadn't asked Barclay to come here and quote for the decorating. You were happy with me before he changed your mind.'

'He didn't change my mind.'

'We'd have made this place wonderful.'

'It's crumbling. Like we were crumbling.'

Della and Tess exchanged glances. So that was what had happened. Poor Roddy.

'So you think I should sell, Isla?'

'As quickly as possible. Alasdair and I plan to move to Inverness, set up there...'

'But the hotel was my father's, and my great-grandfather Dougal Fraser built it. He told me how Sicín Órga was the grandest hotel on Skye.'

'Sicín Órga,' Isla sneered. 'Now it's just a dead duck.'

Tess met Della's eyes and mouthed, 'dead duck?'

There was silence, as if Roddy might be crying. When his voice came, it was cracked. 'Won't you reconsider, Isla?'

'I'm doing you a favour. You can't run the hotel by yourself. You know you have visitors coming today?'

'The two women upstairs?'

'Two more are booked in room nine. The Wilsons – it's on the screen, right in front of your nose.'

'Oh?' Roddy didn't have a clue.

'They'll be here this afternoon. They booked online. They're expecting dinner.'

'I forgot.'

'Two more guests to disappoint. I kept this place going single-handedly, Roddy. You'll just run it into the ground – you're hopeless.'

'I didn't used to be, Isla. I was the heart and soul. It was a warm, happy place. It's just that since you've left me, I'm a...'

'Broken man? You keep saying that.' Isla actually laughed and Della opened wide eyes, shocked at Isla's callousness.

'Please – think again,' Roddy wheedled.

'I've found my way out of a bad marriage. Now just sell the hotel. I'm entitled to half.'

'It's not right.'

'Oh, I think you'll find it is,' Isla snapped. 'You can get a job somewhere. Or you could retire. You're fifty-two.'

Roddy sighed loudly. 'Is that why you left me? For a younger man?'

'Younger, fitter, better looking – take your pick,' Isla said. 'Right. I'll be in touch to make sure you've put it on the market. Meanwhile – what you do with yourself is up to you. I don't care. I wash my hands of this place and you and...' She sauntered through the door, stopping in front of Tess and Della. She looked them up and down. 'Roddy, I think your guests are here for breakfast.' She gave a cold grunt. She spoke directly to Della. 'There's a hotel in Portree, The Grand Highland. It's more upmarket than this dive – and I hear they do wonderful food.' She glanced at Tess. 'Just a bit of free advice. This hotel is finished. Get out while you can.'

She swept towards the door and was gone. Roddy stood haplessly as Della walked in, followed by Tess. He slumped against the counter, his head in his hands, in the centre of a gleaming stainless-steel kitchen, equipped to professional standards.

Tess couldn't help herself. 'If that was your wife, she's not very nice.'

'She wasn't always so cold. We were all right once.' Roddy didn't move. His hands were over his face. 'This is what happens when a marriage breaks down.'

Tess's voice was breezy. 'Tell me about it. I won Olympic gold medal in the failed marriages marathon.'

'Oh?' Roddy looked up, surprised.

'I came back from a hen party in Paris and found my husband in bed with a woman who reeked of Chanel. He was playing Percy Sledge as a soundtrack to seduction.'

'What happened?' Roddy asked, his face a mask of sadness.

Tess shrugged. 'I dumped him. Last week he knocked at my door and begged me to take him back. He's lonely, apparently – or he thinks I'd help with the bills and the cooking.'

'I didn't know that,' Della said.

'I won't go near him again.' Tess snorted. 'It hurts like mad at first when someone cheats on you, but have courage, Roddy. You'll find a way forward.'

'I don't think so.' Roddy eased himself upright. 'I'm sorry – I promised you toast and tea,' he groaned. 'I'm not a good host.'

'Not at all.' Tess felt a surge of empathy – Roddy was a kindred spirit. 'You're doing so well – the wine and crisps last night were spot-on. It's a huge hotel to run by yourself.'

'And I'm failing,' Roddy groaned. 'I'll sell it and move on, like Isla told me to...'

Della's hands were on her hips, ever practical. 'Have you had breakfast, Roddy?'

He shook his head. 'I don't think I've had anything since yesterday morning...'

Della opened the stainless-steel fridge. 'Well, this is a good sign – we have eggs, milk, cheese.'

'Isla was the cook here,' Roddy said hopelessly. 'I used to manage the bookings but recently I can't seem to concentrate.' He looked sad. 'I wouldn't know what to make from eggs and milk.'

Della was already filling a coffee pot, heating a frying pan on the range. 'Tess, take Roddy to one of the tables and set it for three people, please. How does a plate of pancakes sound?'

'It sounds perfect.' Tess took Roddy by the arm. 'Come on – you show me where everything is, and I'll pop back and help Della. I was a Saturday waitress when I was a teenager. I'm very good with customers, you know, even if there are only three of us...'

* * *

Roddy stared at the table in awe. As if from nowhere, a pile of pillowy pancakes sat on a plate, perfectly browned, the edges crispy, all smothered in honey. He gaped as if it were a miracle. Tess poured hot coffee from a pretty pot, handing him a cup. He sipped and closed his eyes, as if the ecstasy was too much to bear.

'Thank you.'

Tess helped herself to a pancake. 'Yes, thank you, Della.'

'It's a pleasure. It's a lovely kitchen, Roddy.'

'The best room in the hotel. Made to Isla's specifications...' Roddy's words faded away.

Tess leaned forward with interest. 'So, when did she leave?'

'Three weeks ago.' Roddy exhaled sharply, as if the memory was painful. 'We'd decided to get the hotel upgraded. A decorator came in to give us a quote, from Portree, Alasdair Barclay – the rest is history. I could see it from the beginning – she was making eyes and he was strutting about like a cockerel. I knew what was coming.'

Della was amazed. 'How long had you been married?'

'Almost twenty years. She's a wee bit younger than me. But she always had an eye for the guests – Isla liked to flirt. It was her way.'

'Flirting's one thing – going off with the decorator is another,' Tess said.

'Our marriage had been flat for a long time but I loved her,' Roddy admitted. 'It was nice at the beginning. The hotel was doing well. We'd have the fire going in the lounge, and I'd run trips to different places on the island.'

'The Northern Lights.' Tess sighed.

'And we'd do days out, whisky tasting in the evening, banquets – people used to come here from Inverness, Dingwall, Perth...' Roddy shook his head, dismayed.

Della's gaze was level. 'And the hotel was a success?'

'It was.'

'Then why can't it be like that again?' she asked.

Roddy looked defeated. 'My marriage is over. What's the point?'

Tess elbowed him gently, prompting him to take another pancake. 'Life goes on.'

Della shuddered a sigh. 'It does. I lost my husband recently. He was the love of my life.'

Roddy shuffled in his seat. 'I'm sorry... I didn't realise.'

'That's the reason I'm here.' Della pressed long fingers against her temples. 'To try to escape the heartbreak of being at home and seeing him in every corner.'

'Ah.' Roddy was momentarily embarrassed. 'And I gave you the most awful welcome last night. I'm sorry.'

'You did well,' Tess said, full of enthusiasm. 'The midnight feast hit the spot.'

'And I enjoyed cooking breakfast in your kitchen.' Della smiled in an effort to cheer him up.

'I suppose we could all crumble and fall apart, but we're here, the three of us,' Tess said philosophically as she helped herself to another pancake. 'That thought should be enough to keep us going.'

'But I can't run the hotel alone.' Roddy slumped forward. 'And then there's the problem of Murdo.'

'Who's Murdo?' Tess asked. 'Your dog?'

'Your son?' Della wanted to know.

'Uncle Murdo's my father's brother. He lives in a cottage in the village. He works for me.' Roddy rubbed his face. 'Working keeps him out of trouble.'

'Is he a criminal?' Tess asked, interested.

'Murdo's just Murdo,' Roddy said enigmatically. 'He does island tours, boat trips, takes guests out. I pay him over the odds. The guests seem to like him although he's an old reprobate.'

'Why?' Tess asked.

'He's all right.' Roddy smiled affectionately. 'Isla used to say he's more trouble than he's worth. But he has a heart of gold… And when I sell up, he'll have nothing to do, and a bored Murdo is bad news.'

Tess imagined the night skies, rumpled and colourful, and sighed. 'Maybe he can take us for a trip to see the Northern Lights?'

'There's the matter of where we are going to stay tonight,' Della said, ever practical.

'I won't charge you anything for last night. How can I?' Roddy said. 'And you've made breakfast.'

'So what will you do about the Wilsons?' Tess asked.

'What Wilsons?' Roddy couldn't remember.

'The ones your wife said were coming this evening, expecting dinner.' Tess folded her arms. 'The ones who booked online. How many other bookings do you have?'

'I don't know.' Roddy shrugged helplessly. 'I'll turn them away.'

'Or...' Tess's eyes gleamed. 'We could help you.'

'Tess?' Della frowned. 'How can we?'

'I'm just thinking...' A smile spread across Tess's face. 'If we help out for a few days while Roddy gets back on his feet, make breakfasts, sort out the bookings – maybe we could stay here at a lower rate. And...' she was pleased with herself '...perhaps Uncle Murdo would take us on a few trips, the Northern Lights, maybe a whisky tasting?'

'Oh, you don't want to go whisky tasting with Murdo.' Roddy shuddered. 'And as for the rest...'

Della wasn't sure. 'Won't that take up all our holiday time?'

'We could make breakfast early, check the online bookings,' Tess said excitedly. 'Then we'd go out. Roddy, you'd have to make sure the rooms were clean and the beds changed. Della and I are on holiday after all.' Her grin broadened. 'But it would be a way of helping. It would give you time.'

'Time to see if I can get this place up and working again?' Roddy seemed to respond to Tess's enthusiasm and energy. 'Would you do that?' He glanced at Della. 'Your breakfast this morning was exceptional.'

'A busman's holiday?' Della said thoughtfully. 'It might work. As long as we get some free time.'

'Oh, I can promise you guided tours, the best advice about Skye...' Roddy put a hand to his head. 'It would certainly show Isla that I'm not sinking beneath all the heartache she's caused.

And it would give me great pleasure for Alasdair Barclay not to see me fail. But why would you do that?'

'Because it's good to help. Because you seem like a man who needs a bit of luck,' Della suggested.

'And it would pay Alan back,' Tess said smugly. 'All the Alans and Islas of this world who think it's all right to cheat and lie and take our livelihoods, then come skulking back years later with tails between their legs.' She took a breath. 'That's why I'm doing it. To stick it to all the Islas and all the Alans. To show them they can't get to us.'

Tess turned to Roddy and saw that he was smiling. He suddenly looked ten years younger.

'Yes, let's stick it to all the Islas and all the Alans,' he said determinedly. 'Thanks, Della. Thanks, Tess. You're right. We can do this.'

10

Tess sat in the little office just off the hall peering at the laptop over her reading glasses, checking the day's bookings, Della and Roddy behind her. The desk was littered with papers, bills, unopened letters. She'd mention to Roddy later that they needed sorting out – she'd deal with today's problem first.

'So, Tom and Kate Wilson from Edinburgh are coming this afternoon. They've booked a double room, Roddy, and they're expecting dinner.'

'Dinner?' Roddy was suddenly anxious. 'I can get a room ready, but I can't do dinner. Perhaps they'll find a takeaway somewhere?'

'Do you have a freezer?' Della asked.

'Yes, there's one in the outbuilding.'

'If it's well stocked, dinner won't be hard. I can get a couple of chops or steaks out and make some chips.'

'They're vegetarian, according to their booking,' Tess explained.

'That's easy. We'll offer a veggie lasagne and salad, brownies and ice cream, and more pancakes for tomorrow's breakfast,' Della suggested.

'Can you do that?' Roddy asked, mouth open.

'Quite quickly, from scratch. I'll make double portions and freeze them,' Della said. 'It's not a lot of work if you wait on tables for me, Tess.'

'Easy peasy.' Tess pointed at the screen. 'Tomorrow there are more visitors booked. Jon Parsons and Stephen Walsh from Stafford, and Mr and Mrs Beckworth from Aberdeen. No special dietary requirements. We can put them in rooms one and three.'

'I'll cook jerk chicken and rice and peas, if that sounds acceptable,' Della said. 'And a full Scottish breakfast. You'll need to ask them about breakfast orders the night before, Roddy, and check the menu is OK for them as soon as they arrive. Then we'll be organised. And make sure you have wine and soft drinks in stock.'

'I can do that.'

'Right.' Tess glanced at the wall clock. 'So – is there anything else?'

'Can I have a quick look around the kitchen to get my bearings, and maybe give you a shopping list?' Della asked Roddy.

'It would give me something to do today instead of licking my wounds.'

'Don't forget that the rooms need preparing. And the laundry,' Tess said.

'I suppose I can do that...' Roddy sighed.

Tess could see he was flagging. She picked up a piece of paper and wrote in large print: 'STICK IT TO ALL THE ISLAS AND ALANS'. She placed it in front of the computer screen.

'Right. I'm on it.' Roddy smiled, getting her point immediately like a shot in the arm.

'And after we've fed the Wilsons tonight, we'll have dinner together,' Tess said.

'Like a business dinner?' Della asked. 'So we can organise tomorrow.'

'That's a good idea.' Tess thought about the unopened bills on the table. If she could help Roddy to be at least a little prepared, by the time she and Della left, it would put him on the front foot. Perhaps he'd really make a go of the hotel.

'A team dinner,' she repeated.

'With wine,' Roddy added. 'We'll deserve it.'

'And we ought to open up the living room,' Tess said. 'Set the big fire in the inglenook. Offer the guests whisky there as a nightcap. They'll be keen to come back.'

'Hot chocolate? Crumpets?' Della added. 'Not everyone wants whisky.'

Roddy was beginning to get the idea. 'I'll add crumpets and hot chocolate to my shopping list.'

'Meanwhile,' Tess said cheerfully, 'Della, you and I will go out for a little walk and stretch our legs. Let's investigate Sleat, and do a bit of sightseeing.'

'You will come back, won't you?' Roddy was suddenly nervous. 'I mean – I don't know what I'd do if you left me in the lurch.'

'Don't worry,' Tess soothed. 'We're here for twelve days. By the end of a week, we'll make the hotel so well organised, it'll run itself.'

* * *

It felt good to be out in the fresh air. Della wanted to stroll on the beach first, to 'blow the cobwebs away', and Tess agreed whole-heartedly. Arm in arm, they ambled across rocks and pebbles, down to where the fine white sand stretched to the ocean. There was no one around. The wind arranged their hair, making their faces and ears tingle. They could smell the salt of the sea, taste the tang of it on their tongues. The whisper of the waves was soothing as Tess looked up at the turquoise swirl of sky. In the distance, mountains clung to the clouds like crouching giants. She caught her breath.

'Isn't this incredible, Della?'

Della swallowed a lump of sadness in her throat. 'It's just what I need, Tess.'

Tess pulled her close, their arms threaded. 'Tell me how you're feeling.'

'I'm so glad we're helping Roddy. To tell you the truth, it's good for me to have someone to focus on. That's what I do best, I care for others. That's what I've always done. It stops me feeling sorry for myself.'

'Aren't we both the same?' Tess said. 'So, what's going on inside your heart during the quiet times?'

'I feel fragile...' Della took a deep breath. 'Like I'm only just holding it all together and I can't predict whether in the next moment I'll be weak or strong. The smallest thing might set me off, such as...' A sob caught in her throat and her eyes glistened. 'It's so beautiful here. And I'll never get to share it with Sylvester. We spent all our lives struggling to make ends meet and we never had much of this stuff – holidays. The fun was just him and me, at home, making each other laugh, making memories...' Della's face was covered in tears.

Tess hugged her. 'You're bound to feel like that. But you're right – it's not fair.'

'We had something rare and special, Sylvester and me, something not everyone gets to share. That makes it hurt all the more to lose it.' Della wiped her eyes. 'The rest of my life will be just me, without him...' More tears streamed. 'I can't seem to make myself accept it.'

'It hurts,' Tess said gently. 'I lost my mum when the girls were tiny. She never got to know them. I carried on, looking after them and Alan, as if I deserved no help from anyone. I kept the feeling of missing her locked away. But it was hard. And lonely.'

'So lonely.' Della's eyes were red from crying and the force of the buffeting wind. 'Thank goodness for friends, Tess, for you and the others who are so sweet to support me. And I have Aston and Linval, grandchildren. But losing Sylvester is like losing a part of me, an arm – worse than that – my heart. It's gone...' She took another shaky breath. 'He'd have loved this beach so much.'

'He would have.' Tess watched the surf spattering against the sand, the waves that tumbled and rolled. 'We must enjoy moments like this for ourselves now, I suppose. Sylvester is in your heart.'

'I'll make the best of things. That's all I can do. Thanks for letting me come to Skye with you.'

'Thank you for coming. It's a privilege,' Tess said.

Her words were lost in the low rumbling of a revving engine. She turned to see a man on a quad bike not far away, driving in circles on the sand. She grasped Della's arm and they watched the man together. He was wearing a cap pulled low; his salt-and-pepper grey hair stuck out. He had a thick beard, a tartan shirt, the sleeves rolled up. Tess thought that he needed a coat as the wind tugged at his clothes. She wondered what he was doing, revving the engine, accelerating, driving round and round in tight circles.

The quad bike tipped over and the man went sprawling on the sand. The bike was on its side, two wheels spinning in the air; the man was on his side too, not moving. Tess pulled Della's arm. 'Do you think he's all right?'

Della's eyebrows came together. 'I think he's unconscious – you don't think he's had a heart attack?'

Both women raced towards the man and found him curled up like a baby, his knees drawn up, his thumb close to his mouth. Tess crouched down and examined his face. 'Are you all right? Can you speak? Have you hurt yourself?'

The man glanced up. He was laughing. The heap of his body shook as he lay there; he clearly found falling off a quad bike hilarious.

'Are you hurt?' Della asked. 'Do you need help?'

Tess could smell whisky. 'Or are you a bit tipsy?'

The man eased himself to a sitting position and started to laugh again. 'Are ye sea nymphs come from the ocean to rescue me? Beautiful mermaids whose singing voices will enchant me forever?'

'Pardon?' Della placed her hands on her hips. 'Do you need a lift up with the bike?'

'Or are ye nosy old biddies who've come to take the pish?' The man found his comment even funnier. 'Just because I fell off my bike and landed flat on my arse?'

Tess folded her arms. 'You're drunk in charge of a motor vehicle.'

The man dragged himself to his feet, a bundle of tall rags, and addressed Tess directly. 'I'm sorry, madam – are you a hofficer of the law come to arrest me? It's a long time since a lassie handcuffed me to the bed, pulled up my kilt and spanked my bottom.'

Tess was a little offended. 'You're inebriated.'

'Aye, I might be that, but I'll be sober soon and ye'll still be a mingin' old woman.' The man dusted sand from his clothes and heaved the quad bike upright, clambering over it.

He turned to Della, a wide grin curving his lips. 'I don't know where ye come from, lassie, but I suggest ye go back quickly before the wind changes direction and ye have to keep that miserable face for ever. And as you're leaving, don't forget to take your pet pig with you.' He winked at Tess, made a low oinking noise, revved the engine and roared away.

'Pet pig?' Tess watched him disappear into the distance. She shivered and felt tension set into her shoulders like concrete. 'What a horrible man. And he reeked.'

'We offered to help.' Della looked down at the grooves the tyres had made in the sand. 'He was just a silly man. Pay him no mind, Tess. We won't see him again.' She hooked an arm through Tess's. 'How about we take a walk into Sleat and find a coffee shop? We could treat ourselves to a cuppa. We deserve it.'

'We do.' Tess shivered, following Della on careful feet as they walked towards the ricks. But she didn't feel like talking now. She couldn't get the image of the rude man out of her mind, his tattered clothes and the stench of his breath.

She sighed. It didn't matter where you went, how beautiful the place was, there was always someone who wanted to spoil it. And she'd had enough of being called names by a ridiculous man to last her the rest of her life.

She especially didn't like being called a pig. It upset her more than she cared to say. The word reminded her of an insult Alan always used when they'd argued. They'd quarrelled over Alan's spending all the time: he'd buy expensive clothes, the best golf clubs. He knew that he was being selfish, but instead of admitting Tess was right when she pointed out that he wasn't being fair, he'd give her a disdainful look and say, 'When you wrestle with a pig, you both get muddy and the pig likes it.'

It was a two-handed slap, implying that Tess liked arguments and she looked like a pig. She felt tears fill her eyes. She was fed up with being upset, with fielding insults from men who thought they were entitled to hurt her feelings. She wouldn't let it get to her, again, not ever. Alan was in the past – his abuse, the sound of his voice, the smell of Bleu de Chanel – everything. Gone.

She caught up with Della and grinned widely, determined to look optimistic.

'Yes, let's grab a coffee, Della. And why don't we have a muffin each? On me...'

11

By four o'clock, Della was in the kitchen clanking pots and pans, busily organising the evening meal. Tess met the Wilsons from Edinburgh at the front door, welcoming them into the hall, warmer now Roddy had turned the central heating on. Tom Wilson was a redhead with gentle green eyes; Kate was dark-haired, short, with a pleather jacket and gold-framed glasses. Tess shook their hands in turn.

'Pleased to meet you – I'm Tess, the housekeeper. We've put you in room one, which has a four-poster bed. I hope that's all right?'

'It sounds marvellous,' Kate said. 'We're going to the Orkneys tomorrow. Tom has friends there.'

'It's my friend Richie who I've known since uni – it's his thirtieth birthday,' Tom said.

Tess pointed towards the staircase. The banister gleamed and the carpet was freshly vacuumed. Roddy had followed her instructions to the letter. 'I'll take you up. Oh, there is one thing. I notice you ordered dinner tonight and you're both vegetarian...'

'Is that a problem?' Kate frowned.

'Far from it,' Tess said. 'Chef thought about preparing a vegetarian lasagne with butternut squash, parsnips, mushrooms and fresh salad leaves with basil and tomatoes.'

'That sounds wonderful,' Tom said.

'I'll have to pick out the mushrooms.' Kate made a face. 'I hate them.'

'And I love them,' Tom said. 'It's the only thing we disagree on.'

'That's no problem.' Tess smiled professionally. 'Chef can put mushrooms at one end of the dish and none at the other. That way you'll both be happy when we serve up.'

'That's so kind,' Kate said.

'Chocolate brownie for dessert?'

'Yes, please.' Tom rubbed his hands together.

'And for breakfast tomorrow – pancakes, full Scottish veggie or porridge?'

'Pancakes,' they said in unison.

'Of course, wholemeal toast too.' Tess was halfway upstairs. 'If you like whisky, we can offer you a complimentary glass of Monad Crag in front of the fire after dinner.'

'That sounds romantic,' Kate said.

'Yes please to that.' Tom was delighted. 'It's been a long drive.'

Tess had reached room one. She pushed open the door. 'Here we are.'

She stood back to survey the space: Roddy had made a good job of it. The curtains were drawn and the spacious room dimly lit, a dreamy glow of lamps. The four-poster was hung with white curtains. Beyond the open door to the en suite bathroom, the Victorian-style bath gleamed. The room smelled of freshly laundered linen from the plug-in air freshener Della had put on Roddy's shopping list.

'It's lovely.' Tom's eyes gleamed.

'Well, I'll leave you to settle in.' Tess smiled in welcome. 'Enjoy your stay at the...' She'd almost forgotten the name of the hotel. 'The Sicín Órga.'

'Oh, we will.' Tom put down his case. 'Thank you.'

'My pleasure.' Tess walked back to the stairs. Being a house-keeper gave her a small glow of warmth and accomplishment. She was enjoying it.

She arrived in the kitchen to hear Della singing softly. The fudgy chocolate brownies were cooling on a rack, the vegetables were steaming, and she seemed more contented than Tess had seen her in a while. Roddy was sitting on a stool drinking coffee, looking exhausted.

'The Wilsons are installed,' Tess said cheerily. 'Della, can you do the lasagne with mushrooms in just one half?'

'No problem,' Della said. 'There's coffee on the stove, Tess. Help yourself.'

'You made a good job of cleaning up,' Tess told Roddy.

'I did my best.' He groaned, pushing a hand through his hair. 'It was hard work. I don't know what I'd do without you. I feel a bit bad – this is your holiday.'

'It's our *cut-price* holiday,' Della said. 'Roddy's idea – we're not to pay a penny for the accommodation while we're helping out here.'

'We have two sets of guests coming tomorrow.' Roddy looked worried. 'That's twice the work.'

'We'll sort everything out later,' Della said. 'I'm making enough lasagne for all of us. And the brownies are going to be a hit.'

'It's my fault this place is falling apart – Isla used to do everything. Now she's gone, I don't know what I'll do…' Roddy shook his head. 'Especially after you leave.'

'We'll get you back on your feet,' Tess said briskly. 'You need to employ a chef and a cleaner, to start as soon as possible. You'll have to organise everything else – bookings, food, housekeeping, welcoming the guests when they arrive.'

Roddy pushed a hand over his forehead. 'I'll need a system.'

'We can help you with that too,' Tess offered.

'Roddy was just saying…' Della inspected the steaming vegetables '…there's someone who can take us to see the Northern Lights one evening and tomorrow we could visit a deserted castle.'

'Armadale Castle was a stately mansion house that was largely destroyed by fire in the mid-nineteenth century,' Roddy explained. 'But it's worth a visit. Dunscaith Castle is very nice too. Of course, you have a car – you can explore the whole island. Dunvegan Castle is beautiful – or you might go to Kilmore Church, not far from here, where St Columba landed and preached around 585 AD.'

'You sound like a tour guide,' Della said kindly. 'The visitors will love all of those places. I can't wait to see them all.'

'We could do the rest of Sleat tomorrow and then on Thursday and Friday we could go farther afield, the north of Skye, or the west coast,' Tess suggested.

'As long as you're back in time to help with dinner,' Roddy fretted. 'I might ask my uncle to give you an island tour one day. It would be good for him to get out of Sleat. He has a Land Rover he uses to take tourists to the Northern Lights. Of course, we can't always see them here.'

'The Northern Lights…' Tess said. 'That would be the high-light of my holiday.'

'That reminds me, I had a text from Jen earlier,' Della said.

'She sent love. And Pam texted first thing, sending her best – she and Elvis are enjoying Crete.'

'Oh, I had a text from Rose – I want to give her a call.' Tess pulled her phone from her pocket. 'I'll do it now before she and Daz go on stage.'

She pressed a button and the phone rang. Rose's face popped onto the screen. She was wearing glasses and something loose and white. Behind her, there was a huge window. Tess frowned. 'Hi Rose. Where are you?'

'Oh, never mind that.' Rose spoke quickly, as if she was in a hurry. Her mouth moved strangely – Tess wondered if she was chewing gum. The picture wasn't clear. But something about Rose wasn't right – Tess felt it instinctively.

'Is everything OK?'

'I need to tell you.' Rose shook her head. 'The house is sold. I accepted an offer.'

'Oh?' Tess thought Rose was being a bit abrupt.

'They want to move quickly. Sorry, Tess. Can you be out at the beginning of the new year?'

'Yes – of course, I can stay with Della or Pam or Jen until I find somewhere to buy.' Tess felt suddenly adrift. She hadn't expected the house to sell so quickly – or for Rose to be so blunt. She was surprised to feel tears prickle her eyes.

'That's good. I wanted to check you were all right. I promised you could stay as long as you needed but if you have somewhere else, that's good,' Rose muttered in a strange voice. 'That's one more thing crossed off my list.'

'Have you found anywhere to move to?' Tess thought she'd ask politely.

'Who knows?' Rose wasn't giving anything away. 'I don't know what to do yet.'

'Oh?'

'I'm sorry – I should have asked first. How's your holiday, Tess?'

'On Skye? It's lovely. We...' Tess was about to gush about the hotel, how she and Della were in charge of running everything, how it was quite good fun, but something about Rose's frowning face stopped her. She said, 'It's very nice.'

'And what's the hotel called?'

'The Sicín Órga.'

'And where is it?'

'Skye.'

'But where on Skye?'

'Sleat. In the south.'

'Right.' Rose suddenly looked even more cross. 'Well, I've told you about the house. Daz will be here in a moment. Now I have to go because I have a lot to do. Sorry to rush but we'll catch up soon, Tess. It's been a bit – fraught. I'm busy tonight.'

'Aren't you at Monty's? I thought you'd be getting changed to go on stage...'

'No, no, I have different plans,' Rose said quickly in her unusual voice. 'I'd better go. I've got things to do.'

'Are you sure you're all right?' Tess was becoming even more concerned – Rose wasn't behaving like herself at all.

'I will be fine, once I've sorted myself out,' Rose said impatiently. 'I can't talk now, Tess. I just wanted you to know about the house and to make sure you'd have time to organise a new place. Well, I can't be sitting around here all day. Sitting around – that's a joke. Right – I'll ring soon...'

Rose's face disappeared from the screen, leaving Tess blinking and confused.

'Well, that was very odd.'

'What was odd?' Della asked.

'Rose was strange – she might have been drinking,' Tess mumbled.

'Well she is in Paris, and a performer. She's allowed. Are you worried about her? Shall I ring?'

'I'm not sure what to do, Della – she just seemed weird. And she told me the house is sold. I'll have to find somewhere.'

'Stay with me.' Della didn't miss a beat. 'As long as you need to.'

'Thanks. Pam said the same,' Tess said. She was feeling a little calmer. 'I'll leave Rose for a couple of days and get in touch later. Perhaps I just caught her at a bad moment.'

Roddy was on his feet. 'Right, what can I do? I've sat about feeling sorry for myself, watching my two guests organise my life for long enough.'

'I like the call to action, Roddy. What brought this on?' Della said.

'You've both been so kind. Twenty-four hours ago I was thinking about putting the hotel on the market but now...' Roddy stood tall. 'Now I'm thinking, what if I can make the business work? The Sicín Órga's the Fraser family home, the ancestral seat, and I'm not letting Isla take it away from me without a fight. This is the new Roddy Fraser you're looking at, ladies. I'll make everything a success. I can do it.'

Della clapped her hands. 'Bravo. It's a lovely hotel, Roddy. When we've gone, you just need to take on staff and advertise the rooms.'

'It's the winter season though.' Roddy seemed easily deflated. 'I'd need to fill them all regularly to make a profit.'

'Then fill your website full of pictures of snow,' Tess suggested.

'And lots of Christmas pictures,' Della added.

'Can you do websites?' Roddy asked tentatively. 'It's not my area of expertise and the one we have is so out of date.'

'Not me, but,' Della said with a smile, 'my son Aston does it for a living. I'll email him and ask him if he has time.'

'Would you?' Roddy exhaled in relief. 'Oh, my goodness, you're lifesavers.'

'Guardian angels.' Tess beamed. 'Which reminds me, we'll need to be setting the table for dinner. Roddy, can you get plates organised, and napkins? And wine, in case the Wilsons want it? And get an extra bottle breathing too – we'll need one with our dinner afterwards.'

* * *

Tess and Della were ready for dinner by nine o'clock. The Wilsons were sipping whisky contentedly by the roaring fire in the lounge, having mentioned three times how much they'd enjoyed Della's food. Roddy, Della and Tess sat in the large refectory, eating supper, drinking wine, feeling pleased with themselves. Roddy had drunk more than his fair share and his eyes shone with happiness and relief.

'The Wilsons' meal went so well. Della, you're a much better cook than Isla was.'

Della smiled at the compliment. 'Years of practice. Busy family. Making something from nothing. Hungry husband...' Her eyes were misty. 'No, I'm enjoying it, Roddy. Tess and I needed a break, but this is perfect for me – seeing the sights, exploring Skye, but having something to take my mind off... off what I've lost. It's the perfect combination. Thank you...' She turned to Tess and laid a hand over hers. 'And thanks, Tess – without you I'd be at home sobbing into my pillow.'

'You're allowed to sob into your pillow,' Tess said kindly. 'I agree, though – it's fun working here short-term with you both. Otherwise I'd be out by myself walking on... what are the local hills called?'

'Red Cuillin.' Roddy smiled.

'And fretting that I have to move out of Rose's house and Alan might call round and invite me back to live with him again...' Tess put a hand to her mouth. 'What if I'd given in, in a moment of weakness, because I was frightened of being homeless, and went back to him? I would give him five minutes before the charm offensive stopped and he started to call me a pig again.'

'He called you a pig?' Roddy's brow furrowed. 'I've no time for a man who can't speak properly to a woman. Isla was unkind to me – I mean, she was a cheating cow – but I'd never call her a pig.'

'I think pigs are lovely creatures.' Della put her hand to her lips to hide the smile. 'You know you can stay with me, Tess.' She glanced at the clock. 'It's nine-thirty. I'd better get our brownies.'

'Oh, yes, please.' Tess looked around the room. 'The refectory is so beautiful, Roddy. It must have been magnificent in its day. You even have a grand piano.'

'This was used as a ballroom when my great-grandfather built it.' Roddy closed his eyes. 'As a child, I remember it being full of important people, dignified men in kilts, laughing ladies in their finery, bagpipes and the best food, music, dancing – it all happened here.'

'You should open it up again, bring it back to how it used to be,' Tess said.

'I could take some photos and ask Aston to use them on the website.' Della stood up. 'Right, chocolate brownies and cream and some coffee all round.'

'I'll help.' Tess pushed back her chair. 'Then we'll get

tomorrow organised and we'll pack up and be ready for an early start.' She offered Roddy a wide grin. 'I'm really enjoying being here.'

'And I'm grateful that you're here.' Roddy finished his glass of wine. 'I was a broken man.'

'And now you're on the mend,' Tess said.

'But what about when Isla comes back?' Roddy was momentarily anxious. 'What about when she demands to know why the hotel isn't on the market?'

'You can get solicitors to deal with all that. I know – I've been through it.' Tess pushed the memory away. 'Where were we?'

'Dessert,' Della said.

She turned just as a tall, bearded man came rushing into the room, almost cannoning into her, shouting, 'I'm late for dinner, Roddy. I hope you saved me some of that lasagne you—' He paused, looking from Tess to Della and back to Tess, his expression frozen with horror. 'Well, if it isn't the two women from the beach.'

'And you're the drunken man who fell off your bike.' Tess put her hands on her hips.

'Ah,' the man said, lost for words. He took off his cap, scratched unruly grey curls and put it back on again. 'Aye, that was me.'

Roddy stood up tentatively. 'Tess, Della – meet my uncle. This is Murdoch Fraser.'

Murdo looked sheepish, putting his hands in his pockets, taking them out again. 'Ah...'

'Ah, indeed,' Tess said. 'I suppose you're looking for food now to wash down all the alcohol you drank earlier?'

'I was,' Murdo muttered. 'The dinner smells good though. And my belly's rumbling.'

'Well, I have to say,' Della huffed, 'I cook soul food, everything prepared with love and kindness. So, a man who insults my friend needs to think very carefully about his manners if he wants to sit down at my table and break bread with me.' She sniffed loudly. 'But you're lucky I'm the kind soul that I am.' She took in Murdo's crestfallen expression and she smiled kindly. 'There's plenty of food to go round. I'll get an extra portion for the rude boy here to soak up all that whisky.'

'Of course you can eat with us, but I think you need to apologise first.' Tess folded her arms across her chest like a schoolteacher. 'No man will be rude to my friend, call me a pet pig and get away with it...'

12

'No, I'll not stay.' Murdo held up his hands. 'I've hurt these ladies' feelings – I'm sorry for it, truly...'

'Uncle—' Roddy began.

'I'll go home. I'm embarrassed by what I did.' Murdo turned to Della. 'You're right – I shouldn't have said those things. You caught me at a bad moment. I was rude. I'll take myself off back to my cold cottage. I apologise for bothering you – I hope you enjoy the delicious food that I can smell even as we speak.' He held up a hand like a dog's sore paw. 'I'll bid you good night.'

'Oh, no – don't go...' Della said kindly. 'There's plenty to go round.'

Tess muttered, 'Of course. We're just saying – perhaps you should talk to people politely.'

'Uncle Murdo,' Roddy pleaded.

'No, no, I won't stay where I've offended your guests. I'll go back to my cottage... into the dim and darkness.' Murdo drew himself to his full height and swayed away, as if attempting to retain the smallest amount of dignity.

'Uncle?' Roddy called again, but Murdo had crashed out of the refectory, the door slamming behind him.

'Don't go hungry,' Della shouted.

'Was he joking?' Tess looked sad. 'I felt sorry for him.'

'So did I.' Della sighed. 'I don't like to see anyone starve.'

'I hate the idea of him being in a cold house,' Tess said.

'Did I upset him?' Della asked Roddy. She wished the poor man had stayed, at least for a brownie.

'Uncle Murdo forgets how to be around new people, especially women. He used to come here for his food before...' Roddy sighed. 'I invited him here tonight, because he offered to take you out in the Land Rover. I'd no idea you'd met already – and clearly nor had he.'

'He wasn't very endearing this afternoon,' Della said honestly.

'He was drunk,' Tess added.

'He's had his share of problems,' Roddy murmured sadly. 'Mine pale into insignificance.' He sniffed loudly. 'Maybe he'll lick his wounds and come back tomorrow.'

'I hope so.' Tess wanted to ask what had happened to Murdo, but Della spoke for her.

'I'll put him some lasagne by and a couple of brownies. He can have them tomorrow.' She exhaled. 'Poor man.'

'Thanks, Della. Uncle Murdo isn't bad. He gets things wrong sometimes,' Roddy said thoughtfully, then he remembered. 'But we promised ourselves brownies. And what about the coffee?'

'I'll get it,' Tess offered. 'Della, you rest – you did all the cooking. And, Roddy, you need to be up early tomorrow. We have breakfast for the Wilsons to prepare, four new guests to organise and a new website to plan.'

* * *

The next morning, Tess, Della and Roddy watched as the Wilsons waved goodbye, promising to leave a good review on Tripadvisor and to recommend the Sicín Órga to their friends. Roddy scurried off to clean the bedrooms, Della texted Aston to ask if he might work on the hotel website, then she and Tess tugged on warm clothes and boots. They were off to see the sights of southern Skye.

When they stepped through the door, they were surprised to see a metallic red Land Rover Defender, the engine idling.

Tess looked to Della for guidance. 'Do you think it's one of the guests who's arrived early?'

Della recognised the driver, the hat pulled down low, the wiry curls, the bushy beard. Murdo hung out of the window, waving a bouquet of flowers so hard that some of the tops fell off. 'My profuse apologies, ladies. Your taxi awaits – if you'll allow a sober and very penitent Scotsman to take you on a tour of the island for the day.'

'Oh?' Tess tried not to smile.

'I proffer copious apologies for my bad behaviour yesterday. Consider me remorseful.' Murdo guffawed. 'I put cushions in the back and sprayed one of those floral air fresheners about to make it smell nice. It stank of my old boots. And I bought snacks for lunch – do you like pop and crisps?' He beamed at Tess, then Della. 'I'd be honoured if you'd let me be your tour guide – by way of apology.'

Tess wrinkled her nose. 'I didn't like being called a pig.'

'Or being told I'm miserable,' Della said. 'Even though I have every right to be.'

'Roddy explained to me in no uncertain terms that I'd over-stepped the mark. I can assure you it won't happen again.' Murdo took off his cap, scratched his head, and replaced it firmly over his hair. 'And I'm an experienced tour guide. I'll show you around, give you all the historical facts and figures.'

Tess was almost convinced. 'It might be nice.'

'Thank you,' Della said. 'We'll come along.'

'It's the least I can do to compensate for my inappropriate introduction.' Murdo stretched out an arm and flung the passenger door open. 'Climb in – there's room for three in the front.'

Tess and Della clambered in. Murdo thrust the flowers at Tess, who was squashed in the middle, moving her legs out of the way of the gear lever as he took off at what he probably thought was a gentle pace, crunching over gravel and accelerating away.

'Where are we going?' Della was nervous.

'Oh, you can trust me – I'm a dab hand.' Murdo took a deep breath. 'First, ladies, we are going to Isleornsay, a picturesque little harbour village on the Sleat Peninsula, a beautiful spot to sit and de-stress. It was formerly a thriving herring fishing port and home to the Isle of Skye's first public toilet.'

'You've done this before,' Tess said.

Murdo nodded energetically. 'I did lots of tours, before Isla became a heartless sow and tried to take Roddy's livelihood away so she could have it off with a no good slimeball.'

'Tell it like it is,' Tess said.

'You have a thing about women and pigs,' Della commented.

'I can only apologise again.' Murdo looked chastised. 'Roddy was my elder brother Bruce's boy. He's worked hard on the hotel since he took it over. Boy and man, he learned the trade from his father. Isla was never much of a wife. She spent his money on clothes and playing golf.'

'Never a good sign,' Tess muttered.

'And she had a roving eye. I could see it when guests came, as if she was looking for a better offer. I'm no misogynist, mind.'

'Clearly not,' Tess said.

'I keep an eye out for Roddy, always have done. He was one of those milksop kids who wailed when he grazed his knee... not roughty toughty like his father.'

'And you?' Della asked.

Murdo appeared not to notice her sarcasm. 'Roddy's too kind-hearted, if you know what I mean.'

Tess shook her head. 'He said Isla was a good cook – she gave you all your meals.'

Murdo made a low sound of disgust. 'Ping meals.'

'What does that mean?' Della said.

'Microwaved – irradiated.' Murdo shrugged. 'Not that I grumbled. Roddy says your food is much better.'

Della said nothing; Murdo complained too much and didn't like women. He braked suddenly and the Land Rover came to a jolting halt.

'Here we are – first stop on the Murdo trail...' He pointed at a silver stretch of water and a pretty harbour. Bobbing boats and snow-capped mountains rose in the distance. 'I thought we'd take a little stroll around Isleornsay and then have lunch.'

'Pop and crisps?' Della remembered, trying not to wrinkle her nose.

Murdo smiled. 'Murdo's gourmet style.'

Two hours later, after a stroll around the village at a break-neck pace, Murdo talking non-stop about the island's first public toilet, they paused for lunch, drinking tonic water and eating cheese, oatcakes and haggis-flavoured crisps. Then they were on their way again, Murdo making the Land Rover bump across the tarmac. Tess and Della were glad when he braked outside an old crumbling church.

'Kilmore Church,' he said, his voice full of awe.

Tess peered through the window. It seemed dilapidated and very old. 'Is it called Kilmore because more people were killed here?' she asked mischievously.

Murdo didn't smile. 'The original church was burnt to the ground after a battle between the MacIntyres and the MacLeods. The MacIntyres fled to take sanctuary and the evil MacLeods barricaded them in before setting fire to the building, killing everyone inside.'

'That's awful,' Della shuddered.

'My mother was descended from MacIntyres,' Murdo muttered. 'I'll just stay here. Off you go.'

'Go where?' Tess asked.

'For a nose around the churchyard. Isn't that what old bidd— English visitors like to do?' Murdo sniffed. 'I'll have forty winks.'

Tess and Della were pleased to leave him behind. Tess pushed her arm through Della's and they clambered across damp grass, around gravestones that jutted out like broken teeth, towards the grey shell of the church.

'This is a grim place.' Della was thinking of Sylvester. 'It wouldn't have been my first choice.'

'Are you all right?' Tess asked gently.

'It's a beautiful old building that's full of history. Let's look around. I'll say a prayer in my heart for him.'

Tess knew Della wasn't referring to Murdo. She murmured, 'He's a strange man, though, Murdo – all he wants to talk about is public toilets.'

'Mmm.' Della made a sound of sympathy. 'He strikes me as someone who doesn't spend much time around people, who's forgotten how to be nice. Do you know what I mean?'

'I do,' Tess said. 'The pop and cheese and crisps were a sweet gesture, the flowers too.' They approached the old church through a crumbling stone arch. 'Do you think he had his heart broken?'

'He certainly gives off a sense of gloom. A bit like this place.' Della walked beneath the broken stone doorway into a roofless building, grass and rubble beneath her feet, and caught her breath. 'What a creepy atmosphere.'

Tess shuddered. 'You can sense the bloody murder of the MacIntyres.' She turned to Della. 'Why would he bring us here? It's hardly uplifting.'

Della shook her head. 'Shall we go back?'

'And try to cheer him up?' Tess smiled. 'I've had enough of this eerie place. Yes, maybe that's the answer. We'll turn Murdo into Mr Happy.'

'I bet you can't,' Della said.

'I bet I can.' Tess's eyes twinkled. She was ready for a challenge.

Della said, 'Oh no – what time is it?' She pulled out her phone. 'Tess, it's quarter to four. We should be back at the hotel sorting out dinner.'

They both ran back to the Land Rover dodging grave-stones and rubble. When they arrived, the door was locked and Murdo was fast asleep, mouth open, his head resting against the window, his cap over his eyes. Tess knocked hard.

'Wake up, Murdo. We need to be back at the hotel.'

Murdo sat up with a shock and muttered something that sounded like 'Crivvens!' His eyes were wide and he looked alarmed and angry. His muffled voice came through the glass. 'Ye nearly scared me witless ye auld bat...' Then he was fully awake and he opened the door. 'Sorry – I was fast asleep there. I was dreaming.'

Tess met his eyes. 'We're late, Murdo.'

Della said, 'I promised Roddy we'd be back in time to start cooking.'

'Ah, no problem. Leap in.' Murdo gave them both a reassuring smile. 'I'll drive extra fast.'

Tess and Della clambered in, clicking their seat belts. 'Make sure we get back safely, please...' Della said.

'And we aren't sick on the way,' Tess added.

'Oh, I'm the safest fast driver on the island nowadays.' They took off at a bounce and cannoned down the bumpy road. 'Hold tight, ladies – I'll give ye the ride of your lives. And when we're back to the hotel, I'll even give you a hand in the kitchen.'

He pressed his foot harder on the accelerator and they lurched and sped forward. 'This old banger can do a hundred miles an hour if I put my foot down. The locals don't call me Mad Dog Murdo for nothing.'

13

The following morning, Roddy sat in the tiny office, Della and Tess peeping over his shoulders at the laptop screen. He was perplexed. 'We have no guests today. It doesn't look so bad for Friday and Saturday – we have some bookings. But you're the only people staying here tonight.'

'Then let's use the time wisely,' Della suggested. 'Let's have a meeting over dinner and sort out December, get Christmas organised, and the new year...'

'Even though you won't be here after the 14th?' Roddy's eyebrows met in the middle. 'Why are you both so supportive? I'm not used to people being kind. I mean, you're giving up your holiday. It's not – what I'm used to.'

'Well, it's great fun,' Tess said.

'We're from a generation where we don't let the world get on top of us – we're fighters.' Della was thinking of her childhood, the early days with Sylvester, trying to make ends meet. 'You're a nice man and your wife doesn't think that you can make the business work – let's prove her wrong.'

'Plus we get to stay here cheaply, which means we can spend

our holiday money on Skye,' Tess exclaimed. 'Things are going so well – the guests loved your jerk chicken and rice last night, Della.'

'And the full Scottish breakfast with black pudding and tattie scones,' Roddy said, his eyes shining. 'I don't know how you do it, Della – Isla used to do porridge in the microwave.'

Della remembered Murdo had said something similar. 'It gives me satisfaction, cooking for guests who appreciate it. And it gives me focus.' She sighed. 'I'm not sleeping well...'

'Of course,' Tess said sympathetically. 'It's to be expected.'

'The boys message me every day. Which reminds me...' Della waved a hand, remembering, 'Aston's put a few ideas together for your website, Roddy. I've sent him some photos, the bedrooms, the hall, the refectory and a few of the places we visited.'

'Not the burned-out church.' Tess shivered.

'No – we don't want the MacLeods and the MacIntyres scaring the guests away,' Roddy muttered. 'I hear Uncle Murdo told you the gory tale.'

'He did. We'll make today a cheery day,' Tess said emphatically. 'What shall we do, Della?'

'Let's take the car and go west. Go to the mountains and have a nice gentle walk,' Della suggested.

'I think Uncle Murdo has other plans,' Roddy said. 'He texted me that he's waiting outside right now.'

'Oh no.' Tess felt her stomach sink. She hadn't quite got over the bumpy ride yesterday. 'Do we have to go with Murdo?'

'He enjoyed being your chauffeur.' Roddy smiled. 'I'm sure he'll take you wherever you like. It's good for him, getting out and meeting people.' He tried harder. 'He likes you.'

'He called me a pet pig.' Tess still couldn't let it go. 'How does he behave to people he doesn't like?'

'Well, if he's happy to drive, Tess, maybe we could treat him to a pub lunch somewhere?' Della suggested.

'Oh, don't let Murdo anywhere near alcohol,' Roddy said quickly. 'The two can't mix – ever.'

'I think we noticed that on the beach,' Tess recalled.

'Does he have drink problems?' Della asked tactfully.

'Murdo just has problems,' Roddy said. 'He drinks to forget sometimes.'

'To forget what?' Tess couldn't help herself.

'Oh, I better get cracking.' Roddy slid his chair back, clambering out of the seat. 'I have to strip the bedrooms and do the laundry.' He offered a smile. 'I'll see you later.'

'I was thinking of making something special for dinner – do you have any mullet in the freezer, Roddy?' Della asked.

'I can pick up some fresh pollack.'

'Fish and rice, then,' Della said.

'And a bottle of wine,' Tess added. 'After all, we are on holiday...'

They watched Roddy disappear from the office and Tess raised an eyebrow. She kept her voice low. 'So Murdo and booze shouldn't mix? I wonder what his secret is.'

'I've no idea but we won't let him drink and drive,' Della said. 'We'd better see what he has in store for us. No morbid churches, I hope...'

Murdo was waiting in the garden wearing a dark donkey jacket, faded jeans and the familiar cap. There was no sign of the Land Rover. He had a large pair of boots on and a tartan scarf.

'I booked for three of us,' he said with a sheepish grin.

'Booked where?' Tess was intrigued.

'Aren't we driving there?' Della asked.

'Shanks's pony is all we need for this journey. We won't want to drive,' Murdo said.

'Why?' Tess noticed his boots. 'Are we hiking?' She looked down at her own footwear, a pair of sturdy trainers. 'Will I be all right in these?'

'You'll be tickety-boo,' Murdo said. 'Come on – we shouldn't be late. It's starting at eleven.'

'What's starting?' Della panted, running to keep up with Murdo. Tess was at her shoulder. 'Are we going to a show?'

'It'll be a show all right,' Murdo said. 'You'll enjoy it, I promise you.'

'And is it just for me and Della or will you come?'

'Will I be there? That's funny.' Murdo laughed too loud. 'Dinnae teach yer granny tae suck eggs!'

Tess had no idea what he was talking about, but she followed him and Della down the road, Murdo leading the way at a pace, Della panting to keep up and Tess straggling behind. Wherever they were going, Murdo was keen to get there.

They hurried down the road, turned the corner and Della's heart sank. She knew why Murdo had been in a rush. There it was, a huge sign in blue and white: The Monad Crag distillery, open for whisky tasting.

'Here we go,' Murdo said with a grin. 'The tour takes an hour.'

'Have you done it before?' Tess asked unwisely.

'Have I...?' Murdo started to laugh. 'Kenny runs the place – he's one of my best friends.' He laughed harder. 'Especially when I'm drinking his whisky.'

At the entrance there was a reception window; behind it, a small dark woman with winged glasses was selling tickets. She purred, 'Hello to you, Murdo. Just go on in. And these are your guests? Welcome – and enjoy the tasting.'

'We'll try,' Tess said nervously.

'Thanks, Lorna,' Murdo said with a wink. 'Is Kenny ready for us?'

'Yes, he's brought extra stock.' She gave a light laugh. 'Make sure there's some left for everyone else, eh, laddie?'

Della and Tess exchanged glances: this didn't bode well.

'Don't stand on ceremony, ladies – we're already late for Christmas.' Murdo was on his way into the large room of barrels and bottles among signs for varieties of Monad Crag whisky: smoky and peated, blended. Della had no idea what the difference was – she thought whisky was just whisky. Tess approached a man in a red and yellow tartan kilt. 'Are you the owner?'

'Kenny Hague.' He thrust out a huge paw, shaking Tess's hand vigorously. She looked into his twinkling eyes, taking in the tawny curls, the friendly smile.

'Murdo has brought us for a tasting,' she announced.

'And a tasting you shall have – although if I know Murdo, the drink will be down his throat before he tastes it.'

'Oh?' Della was by Tess's side.

'Aye – whisky is whisky to Murdo.' Kenny nodded politely. 'But you two lassies are here, so we'll start now, shall we?' He handed them a card with a variety of words printed.

Tess frowned as she read. '"Appearance, Nose, Taste, Finish, Complexity"? What does this all mean?'

'And what's the difference between peaty, woody and spicy?' Della asked, reading over her shoulder.

'Come with me and we'll taste a few whiskies. You'll soon get the hang of it,' Kenny said.

'Are you tasting with us, Murdo?' Tess looked over her shoulder. Murdo was already unscrewing a bottle of dark liquid he'd lifted from a shelf, filling a tumbler. He muttered, 'You get on with the tasting. I'll be mad wae it by the time you've finished...'

'Mad with what?' Tess wondered, but Kenny Hague was

already pouring a tiny drop in two tumblers and placing them on barrels.

'So, first we examine the colour the wood has given the whisky. Hold it up and give it a swirl. What colour is it?'

'Brown?' Tess ventured.

'Amber?' Della tried.

They glanced over their shoulders. Murdo was refilling his glass already, grunting. 'Gone.'

'The whisky is neat, undiluted, served at room temperature with no ice,' Kenny continued. 'Now look for the streaks of liquid which run down the inside.'

Tess watched Murdo drinking as if his life depended on it. She remembered what Roddy had said, took her glass over to him and tugged his sleeve. 'Won't you join us? We could use your expertise.' She eyed him nervously; he had no intention of slowing down.

'I'm doing my own tasting.' Murdo took another gulp. 'I've heard the talk before. It's all a bit slow for me.'

Tess took the bottle from his hand, determined to stop him drinking. 'Well, just humour us...' She walked back to Della with Murdo's whisky and he slunk behind her, following.

He nodded at Kenny. 'Which one do we have here?'

'The smoky island Monad Crag,' Kenny said. 'One of your favourites, Murdo.' He poured a huge tumbler full and handed it over, then gave Della his full attention. 'Take a good sip. Taste comes from the tongue while flavour comes from your nose, so breathe to aid your orthonasal perception. Take in the texture and swallow.'

'What's orthonasal perception?' Tess was curious.

'It means sniffing,' Murdo said, his nose in the glass. He gulped and smacked his lips. 'Och, I cut out the middleman. I just swig it...'

Tess watched in despair as he downed several samples. She glanced at the clock. The tour took an hour and they'd been there for only twenty minutes.

'Let's move to the single malt,' Kenny said smoothly.

'Yes, let's.' Murdo drained his glass and held it out. Kenny refilled it.

Tess met Kenny's eyes. 'Shouldn't Murdo be having the same as we are?'

'Murdo's need is greater,' Kenny said with a shrug. 'He has a high tolerance. Now, the single malt...'

Della sniffed her glass nervously, glancing at Kenny. Tess had already finished hers. She smacked her lips. 'Well, I like this one. Which one was it?'

'The single – it has a unique fruity taste that is soft on the palate and a dry finish. However, the double malt offers a mix of flavours, is sharper in taste and has a more lingering finish...'

'This one isn't lingering for long.' Murdo drained his glass again and turned to Tess. 'Another of my favourites.'

'It's nice,' Tess said, accepting another glass from Kenny. She glanced at the clock again. She'd tried only a few samples but the whisky was strong, making her feel a little wobbly on her feet, and the tour was nowhere near finished. Besides, Murdo was a lost cause – there was nothing she could do to stop him drinking.

She sighed. 'I've probably had enough whisky.'

'I think I'll go back to the hotel,' Della said. 'I'd like to read my book. I'll need to be sharp to help with supper.'

Tess stood where she was, blinking, her vision clouding. 'We should go.' She took a deep breath to steady herself. 'I can hardly stand up.'

'I'm just getting started,' Murdo said, swaying from side to side. 'Kenny, it's time for the double malt.'

Kenny lifted a new bottle. 'Now, this definitely is your personal favourite.'

'They're all my favourites.' Murdo held out his glass. 'Make it a triple, pal...'

'Now it's definitely time to go home,' Della said firmly. 'I think we've all had enough.'

'Not me.' Murdo chuckled. 'I'm not steaming yet.' He waved his arm in the air and lost his footing, cannoning into a shelf. The bottles of whisky rattled precariously. He gave a low laugh. 'Careful, Murdo – ye don't want to spill any.'

'We need you to walk us back to the hotel,' Tess said loudly.

'*He* needs walking back to the hotel,' Della said honestly. 'Come on.'

'I'll buy a bottle of the single malt... we can take it back,' Tess said quickly, hoping Murdo would follow her if she had a full bottle. He could sleep it off in one of Roddy's rooms.

'Now you're talking,' Murdo guffawed. 'Kenny – get the lassie a bottle.'

'Of course – that will be fifty-six pounds,' Kenny said happily, reaching up for a glossy labelled bottle and placing it inside a tube.

'How much?' Tess flourished her card and whispered to Della, 'Well, we have a free holiday – and if it gets Murdo out of here in one piece...'

'Exactly.' Della rolled her eyes in sympathy.

Murdo allowed himself to be led into the fresh air, Della clinging to one side and Tess on the other. He was grinning, swaying, his breath reeking. He almost stood on Tess's foot. She was puzzled. 'Why did you try to get drunk again?'

'I was well on the way...' He indicated the bottle in her hand. 'But if you let me get stuck into that one, I'll do my best to get properly pished...'

Della gave him a disapproving look. 'Murdo, we went for a nice whisky tasting and you just drank and drank.'

Murdo caught his breath in a hiccup. 'It's best not to remember.'

Now Tess was in the open air, the cold blast from the sea was making her feel suddenly very tipsy. 'I need to lie down now.'

'I'll come and join you,' Murdo suggested.

'You'll do nothing of the sort,' Della said firmly. 'You can sleep it off by yourself in one of the rooms, Murdo.'

'Och, but when I'm alone, the memories come.' Murdo sighed.

'What memories?' Tess asked.

Murdo started to laugh. 'As they say, if I told you, I'd have to kill you. But then...' His laughter became tears that streamed down his cheeks. He laughed some more. 'There's been enough killing. That's the problem. That's why I need a drink.' He shook his head to clear his memory and plodded along, staring into the distance. 'The whole thing is killing me.'

Tess and Della exchanged glances, wondering what on earth he was talking about. Murdo staggered ahead on bendy legs, muttering to himself about how miserable he was. Tess could hear him mumbling as he hurried towards the hotel. He sounded close to tears. Something or someone had clearly broken his heart.

Tess suddenly felt truly sorry for him.

14

That evening, Della made an extra plate of fish and rice for Murdo to eat later – he'd taken himself upstairs hours ago to sleep in one of the rooms. After their meal, Della, Tess and Roddy sat with coffee and a notepad, making plans for December. Tess put a hand to her head. 'I'm still feeling the effects of the whisky tasting.'

'I brewed the coffee good and strong,' Della said, taking a slurp. 'Tasting each different type was interesting. I enjoyed the whisky – but not as much as Murdo did.'

Tess met Roddy's eyes. 'What's the story with Murdo?'

'Not my story to tell. He's a good man, but his past comes back to haunt him from time to time.'

Tess was persistent. 'Did he do something bad?'

Roddy shook his head. 'Something Murdo feels guilty about.'

'You're being very mysterious.' Tess couldn't hide her interest.

'So – about this spanking-new website?' Roddy changed the subject.

'Aston's sent me some ideas.' Della reached for her tablet. 'Here, I'll show you. He's got some great headings and pictures, and he's started on the layout. Take a look.'

Roddy examined the pictures, holding the tablet too close to his face. 'This is incredible. Did you take the photos?'

'I did,' Della said proudly. 'Just simple ones on my camera.'

'You have an eye – and your son is really talented.'

'He is.' Della felt suddenly sad. 'Aston gets it from his father. Sylvester was always the creative one. He never really made the most of his skills. He could draw, that man. He drew a sketch of me once.' Tears glistened on her cheeks. 'It was too beautiful, but it was how he saw me.'

'I saw it framed – it looked exactly like you.' Tess wrapped an arm around her friend.

Della wiped her face with her hand. 'I'd like more coffee.'

'You won't sleep,' Tess soothed.

'I won't anyway.'

'I'll just run this plate of fish and rice up to Murdo then we'll take a glass of something in the lounge, shall we?' Tess said kindly. She grabbed Murdo's plate. 'It's still warm. Which room is he in, Roddy?'

'He'll be in the one that reeks of whisky.' Roddy made a face. 'I'll get the coffee and we'll sit by the fire. It's lit and roaring.'

'Lovely. I'll go on ahead,' Della agreed, her eyes still full of tears. 'A few minutes by myself might be good.'

Tess understood. With the plate in her hand, she hurried towards the stairs.

Della walked aimlessly to the warm living room, which was spacious, dimly lit, with red drapes and a tall grandfather clock that ticked like a low whisper. From the high walls, an imperious stag looked down. She was drawn to the fire. She sat on a rug close to the hearth, tugging her phone from her pocket, bringing up a photo of Sylvester and herself. Sylvester was dapper, in a blue pinstriped suit and pork pie hat, smiling in that mischievous way that he had, his arm through hers. It was their last wedding anniversary. Della caught a sob as it rose in her throat.

Her thumb flicked through photos although her head warned her that it was unwise, too soon. There he was, smiling again, flanked by Aston and Linval in the garden; again, at the door to their home, Della kissing his cheek while he goggled into the lens. Gorgeous photos. Wonderful times. Della couldn't believe that they had come to an abrupt end, that there would be no more. She stifled another sob, then the tears came. She couldn't stop them – a gulp, a sniff, then she was weeping and wiping her cheeks.

A cool voice from behind her said, 'It didn't take you long to get your feet under the table.'

Della looked up sharply at a slim woman in a fur-collared coat and knee boots, standing with her hands on her hips. Her dark hair was piled high and Della was struck by the cold glint in her eyes. She'd only seen her once before, but she recognised Isla Fraser immediately.

Isla hadn't finished. 'I wouldn't have thought you were his type, but I expect you're a gold-digger. Did he find you online or did you find him? Lonely hearts, was it?'

Tugged from her moment of grief, Della was stunned. 'Pardon?'

'You saw an opening.' Isla knitted her brows. 'That's it, isn't it? I leave the hotel and suddenly you're here, trying to persuade my husband to let you take my place.'

'What?' Della couldn't find any more words.

'I hear you've installed yourself here as a cook. I suppose you've installed yourself in his bed too.'

Della blinked once and suddenly she felt the swell of injustice lift her to her feet. 'Now listen to me—'

Isla continued in a beat. 'I heard you're cooking special meals from – wherever it is you come from, sleeping with Roddy, making a friend of Murdo.'

'That's rubbish.' Della folded her arms. 'I'm here on holiday.'

'That's a new word for it. A holiday to find a new husband?'

'Wait – I've just buried my beloved—'

'Roddy told me you were a widow a moment ago when I was in the kitchen. I wanted to find out what's going on. And it's clear you're desperate to replace the old one.' Isla smirked.

'You're a bad-minded woman,' Della said. 'How dare you?'

'How dare *you*? You think you can persuade my husband not to sell when half the money's mine – you think you can both make a go of it here? Well, you have me to reckon with, and I promise you, you don't want to make an enemy of me. My bark is bad but my bite is so much worse, lady.'

'Your anger issues are not my problem,' Della said.

Isla took a step forward, holding up a wagging finger. Her voice rose higher. 'I'll make them your problem. You won't take my place. I won't let you transform my husband's business. I want this place sold. You're just trying to push my buttons—'

'I'm *not* trying to push your buttons – if I was, I'd be looking for mute,' Della said quietly. 'You listen to me. I've heard enough of your nonsense. Just kibba yuh mout' and take your muss ugly face away before I'm tempted to slap it.'

Isla took a breath. 'You haven't heard the last of this.' She swivelled on a boot heel and marched out.

Della squeezed her eyes closed, held the phone to her heart and muttered, 'Thank you, Sylvester, my love. I'm sure you helped me... those good old Jamaican phrases came back to me like you'd whispered them in my ear.'

* * *

Tess pushed open the door and tiptoed into room one, holding out the plate of fish and rice. 'Murdo?'

There was no one there. The four-poster bed was empty, the drapes fresh, the room dim. Tess tried the door to room three, opposite. It was locked.

The next room along was room two, her room. The door was open and Tess could hear the rattling sound of snoring inside. Murdo had chosen her room to crash out in. She was not pleased.

She saw him curled up on her bed. His cap was off and he'd rolled into the foetal position, a big man-baby with loose curls, his hands clasped in front of him as if in prayer. Tess approached the sleeping hulk quietly and was tempted to smooth his hair from his eyes. She extended a hand, pushing a loose lock back, and Murdo sighed, a deep sound of satisfaction, as if he was releasing his troubles. Tess thought about kissing his cheek as she might a slumbering child, then she smelled the reek of stale whisky as he blew out air. She placed the supper dish down and said gently, 'Murdo, I brought you some fish...'

He snorted and made a muffled sound that might have been 'I'm a bit peely-wally,' then he hunkered back onto the pillow and began to snore again.

Tess didn't understand – she wasn't impressed that he was dribbling onto her pillow. She took his hand. 'Murdo, you should probably wake up.'

He continued to snore. Tess moved her face closer to his, despite the whisky stench, and whispered in his ear. 'Murdo. Wakey wakey. I have some rice and fish for you.'

Murdo opened his eyes wide and yelled, jerking back. 'Agh, I was half scared to death – I thought you'd come to give me a winch.'

'A winch?'

'A kiss.'

Tess was offended. 'As if I'd give you a kiss, Murdo. There's no need to react like that. Plenty of men would be flattered. But I wouldn't kiss you – you stink like a drain.'

Murdo sat bolt upright, pulling the duvet around him. 'Sorry, Tess – I was half asleep.' He picked up the plate. 'It's kind of you to bring me the scran.' He pulled a face. 'I'm sure it's tasty but I'm not hungry. On top of the whisky I feel a bit out of sorts. I wasn't trying to call you a munter or anything – I mean, you're pretty. It's just that I opened my eyes and saw you and I thought I might boke – I mean be sick – I mean…'

Tess smiled. 'You're not helping.'

'I'm not,' he agreed.

'So – why don't you eat supper, then you can come down and sit by the fire with me, Roddy and Della?'

'I might…'

'And that's my bed you're sleeping in.'

'It smells sweet.' Murdo met her gaze awkwardly. 'Nice perfume.'

'Poison – my favourite,' Tess said. Murdo shook his head, confused. She used her most coaxing tone. 'Now eat up – I brought it specially. Della made it with coconut cream and lime juice.'

'It smells good, but my stomach…' Murdo pulled a face. He was clearly not feeling well.

'Try a spoonful.' Tess sat next to him on the bed, patting his knee.

'The truth is – I'm not really up to it,' Murdo said.

'You drank quite a lot.'

'I did.'

'And you were drunk when we first met and you were rude to me on the beach.'

'Ah, I'm sorry.' Murdo stared at the plate. 'It's been a heavy week. I'm not usually so bad.'

'I don't want to pry.' Tess was curious, she wanted to know why Murdo was so sad, but she didn't want to hurt his feelings. 'Something is bothering you. Have you asked for help?'

'Help?' Murdo laughed. 'From whom?'

Tess shrugged. 'Friends, doctors. What about your wife?'

Murdo stared down at his plate. 'She was called Mairi.'

'That's a lovely name.'

'She was lovely...'

'And do you have children?'

Murdo shook his head. 'I have no one in the world other than Roddy.' He almost smiled, a wide gape, the same expression as a baby with wind. 'Just her. We were Murdo and Mairi, Mairi and Murdo. I used to say we had two bodies, one mind, one soul. She was special.'

'Was?' Tess prompted. She didn't want to ask if Murdo didn't want to tell.

'Gone.' Murdo's eyes were round and shining with tears. 'Five years ago. It was December, just like now. I remember the cold weather, the bite of snow.' He patted Tess's arm. 'I'm thirsty all of a sudden. Do you have anything to drink?'

'I can make you a cup of tea.'

'Anything stronger?'

'No,' Tess said gently. 'It's best you don't.'

Murdo nodded then he shook his head. 'I don't think I can eat the rice. Thank you – and thank Della – you've been kind, but I'll give it a miss.'

Tess shook her head. 'You don't look so good.' Murdo's skin had taken on a greenish pallor. 'Do you want to lie down again?'

'I don't know what I want.' Murdo didn't move. 'I drink, then it hits me in the face just like a punch from a prize-fighter. I can't get past it.'

Tess was filled with sadness for him. 'Life can be tough. Della has just lost her husband. I hear her at night, crying into the pillow...'

'Poor Della.' Murdo sniffed. 'But I bet it wasn't her fault, what happened.'

'It was heartbreaking, just the same,' Tess said. 'And I'm on my own.'

'Widowed?' Murdo asked.

'No. I found my ex, Alan, in bed with the wife of someone he played golf with. He told me she had hypothermia and he was keeping her warm.'

'What a bampot, cheating on someone like you,' Murdo said quietly. 'He didn't know when he was well off.'

'He didn't,' Tess agreed, her voice hushed. 'And I'm about to be made homeless and I don't know what to do next. That's why I came on holiday, to cheer myself up.'

'And here's me dragging you down.'

'Not at all.' Tess took the plate of fish from him, filled a fork. 'I don't mind cheering you up. You've had a hard time. And I'm sure after a bit of Della's home cooking you'll feel better.' She shovelled rice in his mouth. White grains stuck to his lips. She beamed encouragingly and pushed in a second forkful, flakes of fish poking out.

'Well done, Murdo,' Tess said encouragingly.

'I'm not...' Murdo's skin had turned a deeper shade of green. For a moment he couldn't move. His body was in a state of shock and revulsion. Suddenly, his eyes bulged and he made a low retching sound, clutching his stomach, then he leaned forward over Tess's bed and was violently sick.

15

Thursday was a bright new day, the sun shining. Tess and Della were determined to drive somewhere special. They sat at breakfast with Roddy, discussing where to go.

Tess said, 'It'd be nice to be up in the snowy mountains, breathing the sharp air, watching a clear spring gurgle down gleaming rocks.'

'I'm sorry about what happened yesterday.' Roddy was full of apologies. 'Uncle Murdo didn't cover himself in glory.'

'No, he didn't, poor man. He covered my bedding with something entirely different,' Tess said. 'I changed the duvet but the room still smells of sweat and whisky.'

'It does,' Della agreed. 'I opened the windows wide to let some fresh air in this morning.'

'And Isla's foul temper didn't help,' Roddy said awkwardly. 'She tore into me when I was in the kitchen and I just stood there and took it, then she went off in search of you.'

'I know,' Della said simply. 'I met her in the living room.'

'I saw her afterwards – she was furious.' Roddy held himself stiffly about the shoulders, as if he were still being reprimanded. 'She told me you'd exchanged words.'

'You could call it that.' Della didn't like arguing but when it came to it, she wouldn't back down. 'I wasn't having her badmouthing me. She left with a flea in her ear. And she'll get more of the same if she comes back.'

'Well done, Della.' Tess was full of admiration. 'So, let's have a day out. We'll eat our porridge and drive to – Dunvegan. Is that right?'

'It's a perfect place, on the other side of the island,' Roddy said. 'I'd come with you but I'm getting supplies – Murdo's spending the day at his cottage licking his wounds.'

'I'm not sure he'd be fit to drive,' Tess said.

'I've bedding to wash and cleaning and the shopping to do, and I want to have a look at the new website, after all the good work your son has done, Della.' Roddy offered a smile. 'We have guests tonight. They've asked for dinner.'

'Oh? How long are they staying?' Tess asked.

'Five nights, maybe more,' Roddy said. 'A Mr Chadwick has booked the family room. So I'll need to get that ready.'

'Right. We'll be back at four to give you a hand.'

'Are you sure?' Roddy asked. 'You're on holiday, after all. I could manage.'

'We're happy to help.' Tess beamed.

'It's a good distraction,' Della agreed. 'Besides, after my little run-in with your wife yesterday, I'm damn determined this hotel isn't going to go under. By the time Tess and I leave, it will have a new website, a new menu and guests booked from Christmas right through to the end of January.'

Roddy let out a low whistle. 'Oh, that would be good.'

'I'll show that woman, you see if I don't,' Della muttered.

Tess met Roddy's eyes and winked. 'Isla made a mistake crossing our Della...'

'Sylvester used to say it was a damn fool blunder to get on the wrong side of me,' Della said with a smile and her eyes filled with tears.

An hour later, Tess was driving the little Fiat 500 along the winding A863 and Della was still talking about Isla Fraser in a roundabout way.

'I think Roddy's a nice man but he's been henpecked. A woman should empower her partner and respect him and he should do the same for her. A partnership is a strong bond.' Della swallowed, thinking. 'She's emasculated that man and left him like a capon.'

'Capon?' Tess was focusing on the road.

'She's taken away his manhood and he's let her do it.' Della frowned. 'I wonder if that's why the hotel is called the Sicín Órga?'

'Sicking Orca? You mean Murdo?' Tess laughed at her own joke.

'Golden Chicken, that's what it means. It's on the new website. Roddy has a heart of gold, but he's afraid of Isla.'

'We'll do our best to help,' Tess said. 'But I want us to have a great time too. Dunvegan today, maybe we can hike on the Old Man of Storr tomorrow and visit the Fairy Pools.'

'No more whisky tasting,' Della added.

'Poor Murdo,' Tess muttered. 'He told me he had a wife, Mairi. I wonder what happened to her.'

'Didn't he say?'

'He started to.' Tess pointed to her left. 'Look...'

'That's the Loch of Harport,' Della glanced at the tourist book in her hands, then back at the deep blue water, flanked by snow-capped mountains and fat, fleecy clouds.

'It's beautiful,' Tess said. 'Oh, this island is heaven. I was just thinking this morning – Rose is in Paris, Pam in Crete, Jen in Iceland – but I'm so glad we came here.'

'Me too.' Della watched the scenery as it flashed by outside. She took in the gigantic mountains, their white meringue peaks holding up hovering skies, and the enormity of it all made her want to cry. Sylvester would have enjoyed sitting next to her, taking in the beauty of it all, and she knew exactly what he would have said. The wide expanse of sky seemed to overhang the mountains; Della wondered if heaven was beyond, if Sylvester was there, if he knew where she was and how she felt. She swallowed hard.

Tess sensed her thoughts. 'It makes you feel very close to nature – like we're a small part of the big picture.'

Della nodded. 'I feel very small nowadays...'

'We're all small,' Tess said. 'But we can do big things. Like helping Roddy. That's a huge thing. He's very fragile, I think.'

Della was about to say that she felt fragile too, but she said, 'How far are we from Dunvegan?'

'Twenty minutes?' Tess glanced at the satnav. 'Shall we visit the castle first?'

'Dunvegan Castle, stronghold of the Chiefs of MacLeod for nearly 800 years...' Della flicked through the guidebook. 'Closed between 16 October and the end of March...'

'Oh no.' Tess was disappointed. 'We should have checked.'

'But we can go to Claigan Coral Beach.' Della began to read excitedly. '"With its white sand and turquoise sea it has an almost ethereal quality. The beach is not in fact sand and neither is it coral. It's formed by the deposit of small pieces of 'coralline' hard seaweed called *maerl* that is crushed by wave action, dried and sun bleached on the shore." Let's go there.'

'It sounds glorious,' Tess agreed, turning the car into Dunvegan, passing through an avenue of low overhanging trees. 'I can't wait.'

They parked the car, pulled on wellingtons and warm jackets and hurried through a wide gate and over a stony path, through squelching mud. Tess was a little unsure. 'Does this seem like the way to a beach?'

'I saw a signpost.' Della tugged up the hood to her jacket. 'The cold wind is making my ears freeze.'

Tess was thinking the same thing – the blast was strong. 'My face is so cold, my lips are numb and I can hardly speak,' she muttered. 'Do you think we'll be all right walking all this way? After all we're...'

'Two women in our seventies?' Della grasped Tess's arm for comfort. 'Tess, there are women in their seventies and women in their seventies. Some are happy to be defined by the number of years they've been on the planet, by their wrinkles and other people's views of their exteriors, whereas we...'

'We're women in our prime.' Tess laughed. 'Or just past it. Who cares? We are who we are and we're happy being us. Whatever – I'm determined to have the best time. Being seventy-seven is cool.'

'And we're alive. The alternative isn't so great,' Della said wistfully and Tess hugged her closer.

Two figures were running towards them over croft land; they were handsome, rugged young men jogging in woollen hats, layers of clothes, tracksuits, padded jackets. As they passed, Tess noticed their icy breath and their determined expressions. She called out, 'You can stop running after your dreams – we're right here,' and burst out laughing.

One of the men muttered something: 'Right y'are, darlin'.'

'Tess – what are you like?' Della was shocked but she couldn't help smiling.

'I was inspired by what you said. About not being judged by my age...' She took in Della's surprised expression. 'What? I can still turn heads.'

'Of course you can,' Della said, hugging her arm. 'So do you think you still might... one day...?'

'Might what?' Tess asked.

'You know...' Della said again. 'If a good man came along...'

'Oh, definitely – I'd grab him with both hands,' Tess said. 'Alan was never really the one for me. I spent a whole marriage trying to persuade myself that we were all right. We were, for a while – when the girls were little, we were a family, and that brought out the best in us, I suppose, but there was no real passion, no romantic love. Not like you and Sylvester – you were soulmates. That's what I've missed. Alan was a cold fish. It's taken me a lifetime to realise that I need a man with a big heart, and big strong arms and great big – oh, will you look at that?' She caught her breath and pointed. 'There's the beach. Come on. I want to get right down there and stand in the sea breeze.'

'Just look.' Della stopped dead. Beyond the grassy slope, the beach was a half-moon curve of white sand, rolling turquoise waves stretching towards the mountains and sky. In the distance, the Outer Hebrides loomed, misty shadows. She caught her breath. 'It's stunning.'

'It is.' Tess took out her phone, taking photos, then she was on the move, loping over the grass. 'I'll beat you down to the beach... if my ankles hold out.'

'And my sciatica... and my plantar fasciitis,' Della screamed into the wind.

Tess's voice carried back, 'Plant a what?' and the yelp of her laughter.

They tumbled downhill, standing on the beach, the cold

wind in their faces, breathing in the icy blast. Della sighed. 'This is good for the soul. The air is so pure.'

'Like whisky on the breath.' Tess sighed.

'Not Murdo's, poor man,' Della said, and Tess wondered if he was alone in his cottage, feeling sorry for himself. Perhaps she should have invited him along.

But Della was right: standing in the stiff sea breeze, Tess felt uplifted, happy, surrounded by beauty. She pointed to the right. 'There's a flat-topped hill up there…'

'That's Cnoc Mor a Ghrobain,' Della said in her best phonetic pronunciation. 'If I remember the guidebook right. From the top you can see Dunvegan Head.'

'What are we waiting for?' Tess yelled, grabbing Della's arm.

'I'm feeling every year of my seventy-seven.' Della held back. 'Tess, it's not a good place to be if your heart fails… we'd be isolated.'

'Our hearts are good for a few years.' Tess wasn't sure what else to say, but she knew what fears loomed large in Della's imagination. 'Let's give it our best shot.'

They slogged to the top, against the charging wind, hoods blown back from their jackets, hair flattened against their scalps. They stood in the force of a blustering wind, looking out at the shining sea, the rising mountains and the shoreline shrouded in mist. Tess took Della's hand and held out her phone in the other. 'Let's do it.'

'Do what?'

'Lean into the wind and see if it can support us.'

'Why would we do that?'

Tess beamed. 'I read in a magazine that if you lean into the wind you get a real sense of being hugged – you feel locked in the arms of the present moment, allowing life to shape you as it is meant to.'

'I could do with some of that.' Della reached for Tess's other hand as she held out the camera for a selfie. Both women tentatively leaned forward. The wind blew their clothes, their hair, and suddenly they felt the equilibrium, supported in the wind's embrace.

Tess yelled, 'This is incredible. Like being hugged by Mother Nature.'

Della closed her eyes and imagined. If only Sylvester were somehow there in the wind, in the swirling of nature; if only his arms were around her now. She imagined his voice, filled with love and anxiety, 'You'll get cold in this bluster... and watch out for the damn fool rain...'

For a moment it felt real, and she laughed out loud.

Tess stood upright. 'What time is it?'

'Time for a cup of tea in a nice café,' Della said. She felt filled with happiness.

'Then we better get back to the hotel.' Tess knitted her brow. 'And start cooking something for the guests.'

'Look.' Della pointed towards the ocean, where the mist of the Outer Hebrides had become even hazier, and a dark cloud was hurtling towards them at speed. 'Look at the cloud...'

'It's a rain cloud – it's coming this way,' Tess yelled. 'And it's going to burst.'

'We better run.' Della grasped Tess's hand and they scampered downhill.

By the time they were halfway down, the skies had darkened to an ominous grey and water spilled from on high. Tess yelled, 'Let's get back to the car. We'll get soaked.'

Della put her head down, pushing forward into the driving rain, listening to the squelch of her boots in mud. 'I was sure Sylvester warned me this would happen back there,' she murmured.

Tess hadn't heard. 'The rain's getting heavy.' She tugged her hood over damp hair and the wind blew it back again. 'We'll get back to the hotel before the new guests arrive and have a hot bath.' They had reached the path and were splashing towards the gate. 'I hope Roddy remembers to close the windows.'

They drove back to the hotel in the hurtling rain, the windscreen wipers swishing. Della was almost asleep by the time they stopped in the car park and Tess wished that she had time for a short nap before the new visitors arrived. But just as they clambered out, ready to rush inside, a taxi appeared, slowing down. The driver hunched his shoulders against the rain and busied himself with luggage. The door opened and a young man clambered out wearing a dark jacket and skinny jeans.

Tess recognised him instantly. The taxi driver and the young man assembled a wheelchair, then they helped the elderly occupant out, the younger man holding an umbrella over her head. She was swathed in a woollen coat, giving orders, waving a finger: 'Take care. It's absolutely bucketing down. What kind of damp, dark place have we come to? My best shoes are already soaking wet...'

Tess and Della would have recognised the bossy tone of her voice anywhere. They turned to the taxi at the same time and called out in surprise.

'Rose?'

16

Daz pushed the wheelchair into the hall, Rose talking nineteen to the dozen as Della and Tess exchanged glances.

'So, as soon as I was discharged from hospital, I thought, let's come here. We got on the train from Paris... it took ages, and I had to stop overnight at Manchester on the way just to rest,' Rose said irritably. 'But I wanted to see you both and tell you everything.' She met Tess's glance. 'I know I was a bit abrupt the other day when we spoke on WhatsApp. Face to face is much better...'

Tess stood in the hall, her hand on the wheelchair. 'So, what happened, Rose?'

'I've been really lucky – and it's all thanks to Daz.'

Della placed a hand on Daz's as he pushed the chair. 'Why?'

'Well...' Rose took a deep breath, 'We'd been on stage, as usual, playing all the songs to a packed house. I said to Daz, I'd been feeling a bit funny. Then I woke in the middle of the night with pins and needles shooting through my body, and my face. I was terrified.'

Daz took over. 'I was just about to turn in. I heard Rose cry out and I rushed in. There she was, sliding in between the bed and the bedside table, all confused. So I got her straight to hospital.'

'And I'm so glad he did. I'd had a stroke...'

'Oh, my goodness,' Della said. She squatted down next to Rose. 'How are you now?'

'Thanks to Daz, I'm going to be fine. I'm already much better than I was. My speech is better – the only really annoying thing is that I can't play the piano like I used to.'

'Oh no.' Tess grabbed Rose's hand and held it in hers. 'Will the skill come back?'

'I'll be darned if it won't,' Rose said through gritted teeth. 'That's why we're here.'

'It's good to see you. How can we help?' Della asked.

'I thought you'd need *my* help, what with Sylvester – passing.' Rose met her eyes. 'And I need a break to recuperate. Monty's left my job at the club open – she's been wonderful.'

'Too right – she told us to come back when we're ready.' Daz smiled at Rose fondly. 'And that's what I'm going to do – help Rose get her strength back. She'll do a bit of walking – she's got sticks to help – and she'll get good rest in the fresh air, away from Paris. The doctor gave me a list to help recovery. Sleep is important, good food, steady exercise.'

'And being with the people I love.' Rose's eyes shone. 'My son's far too busy to support me, and I wanted to be with you two. And Daz.' She threw him a look of affection. 'He's been marvellous.'

'We're a team, Rose and me. And not just on stage. We just get on,' Daz said, pushing a hand through neatly groomed hair. 'The French people are so switched-on – they don't bat an eyelid about me being Rose's carer. I know if we were back in England, someone would think it was odd, a man in his thirties enjoying being in the company of a woman...'

'Who's a little bit older.' Rose winked. 'I have Daz to thank that things aren't as bad as they could be. The doctor thinks I can make a full recovery. And I just *have* to play the piano again...'

'We'll get there, with care and patience, the doctor said so. It's no sweat to take care of you, Rose,' Daz said. 'I'm not in a relationship. I live for my job, being on stage, singing all the songs in the spotlight, the costumes.'

'Did you find another flat in Paris to buy?'

'All that's on hold.' Rose shook her head. 'Until I'm well again. Even though the house in Exmouth has been sold.' Her face lit up. 'I'm starving. What's the food like here?'

Tess glanced at Della. 'Oh, it's the best. You wouldn't believe how good it is.'

'I notice there's no lift upstairs.' Rose made a dissatisfied sound.

'I'll carry you up.' Daz puffed out his chest nobly.

'I'll get up on my sticks,' Rose said. 'I'm convalescing but I'm not incapable.'

'And we'll help you,' Tess added. 'You know we will.'

'It's so good to see you,' Della said and suddenly the three women were in each other's arms, hugging, tears shining.

'So if you need owt, Rose, just ask us. This is Team Rose now.' Daz flung himself into the hug, the four of them huddled over the wheelchair. 'Let's get you and your stuff up to the room and get settled in. Then we can have some scran and a small glass of wine, and put the world to rights.'

Rose smiled, looking up at three happy faces, a sigh of relief shuddering from her small frame. 'It feels so good to be together again. Now I can concentrate on getting better.' She looked around, a frown creasing her brow. 'Is there anyone working here? I was expecting at least a receptionist or a housekeeper to meet me at the door.'

'Well, the thing is, what we haven't told you yet is...' Tess smiled.

'...the staff here are pretty special,' Della added.

'Second to none, in fact,' Tess said. She saw Rose's puzzled expression, then she and Della burst out laughing.

* * *

That evening, Rose eased herself from the wheelchair into the soft-backed chair at the dining table, and lifted a forkful of risotto into her mouth while Daz smiled like a fond parent. Tess and Della held their breath as one, having no idea if she could manage cutlery. Rose gave a triumphant smile. 'See? I can feed myself, no problem. And my speech is almost back to normal.'

'The doctor said Rose was a fighter,' Daz said proudly. 'And she's come on in leaps and bounds in just a few days.'

'It was just a tiny stroke.' Rose turned wide eyes on Tess. 'I said to Dr Fauret, will I have another one? Will it be worse next time? And she said all strokes and patients are different, but a positive attitude does wonders.'

Daz patted her shoulder. 'The doc said she was doing well and told Rose that the recovery is in her hands.'

'That's the problem.' Rose held up her right hand. 'This poor little paw is my life – it's the one I use to play the melody – and it's just not back to normal. It's so frustrating. Daz said I should rest it completely, maybe just do a few finger-stretching exercises every day, but the thought of not playing again is unbearable.'

'And she mustn't stress. Hypertension is bad. The hand has

been really mithering her,' Daz explained. 'It's best to let it rest a bit.'

'Or...' Rose glanced hopefully towards the corner. 'I notice there's a piano over there. Perhaps I can just do some basic practice on the keyboard each morning?'

'I'm sure you could.' Tess reached for a bottle of wine, filling up the glasses.

'How's the food?' Della asked.

'Oh, it's just so good.' Rose smiled. 'I can't believe you let yourself be talked into working here though.'

'We weren't talked into it,' Tess said.

'We offered. If you'd met Roddy's wife...' Della made a face '...you'd see why. Poor Roddy.'

'But we're here on holiday until the 9th,' Daz said.

'At least,' Rose added.

'So what can we all do during the day?' Daz asked. 'Rose needs to have some fun, and I'd love to find out about Skye. I'm from Salford – I've never been north of Blackpool.'

Della pressed his hand. 'So, first thing, I'll make scrambled eggs – then we can go out. I was thinking about the Fairy Pools. Or somewhere else.' She turned to see Roddy rushing towards them, carrying a huge tray. 'Oh, lovely – you brought the sticky toffee pudding.'

Roddy puffed beneath the weight of the tray and five bowls of cake covered in a thick caramel sauce. He plonked it down and took a seat, gulping the wine Tess had poured already. Della was piling empty plates onto the tray, moving it to an adjacent table. Rose proffered a hand, her fingers decked with rings. 'I'm Rose.'

'Roddy,' Roddy said breathlessly.

'So...' Rose's expression was haughty. 'What's this about you making my friends work all hours in your hotel?'

Roddy looked alarmed for a moment, then Daz said, 'She's just kidding.'

Rose said, 'Delicious pudding, Della – you can cook every night, the food is so gorgeous. But you must take plenty of time off.' She was suddenly concerned. 'You're recovering too.'

Roddy was still awkward. 'I don't know what I'd have done without Tess and Della.'

'It's a good job the hotel isn't packed,' Rose said.

'Well,' Roddy held up his spoon. 'The thing is... I have two more guests booked in for tomorrow night – they are staying for a few days. And I'm going to put the new website up and we'll see what increased trade that brings in for Christmas and Hogmanay.'

'Have you advertised for a chef and a housekeeper yet?' Tess asked.

'I have. The ads have gone in – I'm just waiting to see what the take-up is like,' Roddy said nervously. 'So, tomorrow afternoon, Robin Craig and his son Jamie will arrive. They have no special dietary requests. They've booked a room each, so I'll put them in the far ones, rooms seven and six. And they want dinner.'

Tess was unfazed. 'No problem. I'll offer a set menu. It's easier if Della knows what she's cooking in advance and we all have the same thing.'

'Saturday night – maybe I'll make a beef bourguignon. I can leave it slow cooking all day – maybe we'll have some buttery couscous on the side,' Della suggested.

'Sounds divine,' Daz said.

'But you need to have fun as well,' Rose insisted, lifting a finger. 'We need a nice day out. It's your holiday.'

'What do you suggest?' Tess turned to Roddy.

'Well, as it happens, Murdo has offered to take you all out.'

'Murdo?' Rose asked.

'Not whisky tasting?' Tess groaned.

'Murdo's very keen to stay away from the whisky, as it happens.' Roddy looked around uncomfortably. 'He wants to take you all to Loch Coruisk, on a boat trip. He says the weather should be good tomorrow and he'll call round at half nine.'

'Sounds good,' Tess said. 'What's Loch Coruisk?'

'It's a beautiful lake, surrounded by the Cuillin mountains. When I first met Isla, we went there together...' Roddy's eyes were misty. 'It's perfect for a cruise on a boat, and Murdo will look after you.'

'Who's Murdo?' Rose arched an eyebrow.

'Roddy's uncle and the hotel tour guide,' Della said simply.

'Will Rose be all right, stuck in a boat all day with a cold wind blowing in from the mountains?' Daz asked protectively.

'Rose?' Roddy was momentarily perplexed. 'Oh, you mean your mother?'

'My best friend,' Daz said. 'I can't have her doing anything too strenuous or getting cold.'

'Murdo will make sure you're comfortable.' Roddy offered Rose his most reassuring smile. 'And I hope the family room is comfortable. Room four is opposite Tess and Della.'

'I'll let you know how comfortable it is tomorrow,' Rose said enigmatically. 'My doctor has put me on so many tablets and they're supposed to help me sleep, but they don't.' She pushed her glass towards Tess. 'A little bit more of this lovely red wine might help. I'm allowed a small amount. My doctor is French.'

'Right.' Tess refilled Rose's glass halfway. 'Let's finish up here and then have an early night. Della and I will be up early to make scrambled eggs, then we'll let Murdo show us the delights of the Loch.'

'I'm looking forward to it,' Rose said, attempting to slide

her chair back. Daz was quickly next to her, offering her a hand, guiding her towards the wheelchair. Tess and Della watched from their seats as he eased her into the chair and wheeled her away. They exchanged glances; so far, they weren't sure whether Rose was making a good recovery or whether she was putting a brave face on it. Something felt wrong.

At midnight, Rose lay on her back with her eyes wide open. She could hear Daz snoring in the adjoining room, a light snuffle, but she couldn't sleep yet. There were too many thoughts whirling in her mind. She was almost eighty years old; she expected there to be a few aches and pains, stiffness in her joints, occasional senior moments of memory loss. But she hadn't expected to have a stroke. She should have seen it coming. And although she'd got off lightly – those were the exact words she'd used to Daz – the doctor had been honest on the day she'd discharged her about the possibility of a second stroke, and the thought wouldn't leave her alone. The doctor's voice echoed in her mind, the light French accent, the careless way she dropped each word as if it were routine because she wasn't used to the subtle niceties of English.

'The chances of a second stroke are high, Rose. The next few days, weeks, months are crucial. You must keep yourself calm, and take things easy. Do not rush back to work. Do not hurry back to your piano and worry about playing it again. You need to walk away from it.'

Rose had frowned. 'Walk away, Doctor? From playing the piano? From being on stage? But it's my life.'

'It's your life you're risking each time you go on to the stage,' the doctor had said simply. 'You're an old lady. Just go away and concentrate on being what you are.'

Rose had been furious. Daz had picked her up from the hospital, calmed her down by taking her for lunch at their favourite bistro, and they'd made the plan to go to Skye. He'd told her being able to relax among friends on a remote island with nothing to do all day would do her the world of good. Then she'd be well enough to return to work at Monty's.

Daz had been incredible. He'd promised Rose that he was committed to support her recovery. He'd pledged to look after her food, her mobility, her convalescence and Rose had cried tears. She couldn't do it without him.

But Rose couldn't relax. The very idea of it – doing nothing – would kill her. Besides which, there was a piano in the dining room, just waiting to be played. And the room was glorious, high ceilings, decorative arches, looked as though it had once been grand. There was certainly enough space for an audience.

Rose moved her fingers up and down on the duvet, just for the exercise, as if she were playing a tune. It was the intro to Abba's 'Mamma Mia'. She knew each note like the back of her hand. Literally. Then she played 'Does Your Mamma Know' and 'Money, Money, Money'. She felt her heartbeat quicken, as it always did on stage, the thrum of the music in her ears, the gasping delight of the audience, the smell of stale perfume and spilled wine and the dust of costumes.

Entertaining was everything to her. She wouldn't give it up – she couldn't – not without a fight.

17

Della hadn't slept. How could she, in a cold, empty bed? The silence was dreadful, no incessant purr from Sylvester, no warm body next to her. The minutes and hours stretched.

Just a few feet away Tess had been dreaming. In the middle of the night she'd shouted something out – 'Murder!' or 'Murdo!' The sadness of being alone now, a widow, had made Della cry. She felt foolish and selfish and mawkish – all of those things: poor Tess hadn't known real love in her whole life, not from that dry, selfish Alan. Della had been the luckiest of all her friends. But then the pendulum had swung the other way – losing the most wonderful man in the world brought a pain no one could know unless they'd been as truly blessed and happy as she'd been. It was unfair, and Della had sobbed silently into the pillow, her face contorted in pain, until she thought her heart would break. Mercifully, as the moon shed a long beam of silver light through the window, she finally fell asleep.

It was half past seven when she woke, slithered from her bed and pulled on clean clothes. She intended to go downstairs herself, creep into the kitchen and start breakfast alone, but as her fingers folded around the door handle, Tess croaked from beneath the heaped duvet, 'Not without me, you don't.'

Della's voice was a whisper. 'I'll just go down and put the kettle on.'

'Hang on – I'm here.' Tess knew instinctively, surrounded by darkness, that her friend had not slept well. She wriggled into clothes; Della could hear her grunting as she zipped up her jeans. Tess's voice was as cheery as she could make it. 'Another day, another breakfast.'

Once they were on the landing, opposite room four, Della muttered, 'I wonder how Rose slept.'

'I hope she's recovering,' Tess whispered. 'She looked well though, considering, didn't she?' The question hung in the air.

'Strokes can be devastating,' Della said.

'And they can be just a blip,' Tess said, although she hadn't a clue what she was talking about. 'We'll make Rose happy; she'll enjoy being on Skye and she'll get better.'

Della sighed. 'There's been enough sadness...'

Tess took her hand. 'There has.'

There was a light on in the dining hall and beyond, in the kitchen. Della made her voice jolly, trying to change the subject. 'Oh, Roddy's up already.'

'Roddy,' Tess called out, joking. 'I'll have an egg and bacon roll, if you've got the pan on.'

They opened the kitchen door to find Daz standing by the fridge, wearing a white vest and pyjama bottoms, drinking water from a jug. 'It's only me. I was gagging for a pint of water. That radiator upstairs sucks all the moisture from the air.'

Tess offered him a grin. 'I'll make us a drink. Tea or coffee?'

Daz flourished a teabag. 'Rose and I'll have green tea – I brought some.' He folded his arms. 'I'm determined she's going to get better.'

'We'll do what we can,' Della agreed.

'It's all in here.' Daz tapped his temple with his finger. 'Psychological.'

'How do you mean?' Tess asked.

'If she thinks she'll get worse, then she will.' Daz frowned, thinking. 'She has to believe she can get back to normal again.'

'And do you think she will?' Tess asked anxiously.

'I'm doing all the right stuff – checking her pills, keeping positive, encouraging healthy eating, although she's a monkey for a cream bun. And she gets tired really easily. But you two will cheer her up.'

'I hope so,' Della said.

Daz's face was sombre. 'I was sorry to hear your husband passed, Della...'

Della took a deep breath. 'That's why I'm here, keeping busy in the kitchen.'

'Right. So, I can cook a good fried breakfast,' Daz said. 'I'm a Salford boy through and through. I can do you all sausage, bacon, egg and beans.'

'Is that what Rose has?' Tess asked, amazed.

'No-o-o-o.' Daz put up both hands in protest. 'Not on your life. She's having her go-to, get-Rose-well-again breakfast... scrambled eggs, muesli, an apple, a plain yogurt and grapes.'

'We've got all that,' Della offered smugly.

'I know – I just took a gander in the fridge,' Daz said. 'Right, let's set to. Breakfast for just the five of us, is it? And then two more tomorrow.'

'You remembered.' Tess was impressed.

'Oh, I did a number of jobs before I landed the dream job of my life as Greta Manchester.' Daz winked. 'I worked in catering several times. Well, I've washed up.'

'Then get the kettle on,' Della said. 'Breakfast for five coming up. I expect Roddy's about somewhere.'

Daz was clanking cups. 'I passed him on the stairs coming down. He was going to get milk from the village.'

'Right, well, breakfast is easy. Let me deal with it,' Tess said, suddenly in charge. 'You get the beef bourguignon in the slow cooker, Della, and then we can go out all day with Murdo.'

Della couldn't help smiling as she recalled what Tess had called out in her sleep. 'Did you dream about him last night?'

'I did, as a matter of fact – it was a nightmare.' Tess's face took on a shocked expression. 'I dreamed we went to the loch with him and he was driving the Land Rover. Then suddenly, his eyes went fiery red and he developed tentacles and began to chase me and I fell into the loch and he was swimming after me, like the shark in *Jaws*, and I was drowning...'

'No wonder you called out his name in your sleep,' Della said, open-mouthed. She was frying chunks of meat in a pan.

'Did I?' Tess was equally baffled.

'Well, they say it's all psychological, dreams,' Daz explained. 'People who are more prone to nightmares are creative thinkers – that's a good thing, right? Nightmares represent our inner fears and anxiety. In fact they can reveal a lot about our personality, and give a deeper interpretation of our subconscious mind, thoughts and feelings.'

'Can they?' Tess was astonished.

'I just think it's normal to have bad dreams sometimes,' Della said matter-of-factly.

'No, nightmares are symbolic of our inability to control a particular situation in our life,' Daz explained as he prepared Rose's muesli, his expression serious. 'Your nightmare represents a lack of freedom and power, Tess. In other words, there's something you're really frightened of in real life, and the nightmare is telling you to prepare for it.'

'Homelessness, old age, loneliness. Take your pick.' Tess shuddered. 'Alan...'

Della wrapped an arm around her. 'We'll look after each other.'

'Of course we will.' Tess hugged Della back, wondering if she'd been a bit selfish. 'So – scrambled eggs, Della? Toast? Coming up.'

'And Rose's breakfast is on the tray. I'll just go upstairs and get her ready,' Daz said cheerily. 'I won't be more than ten minutes. The eggs will be done just right.'

'You're so good to Rose,' Tess said from her heart.

'She's my best mate and she needs me – and I made a promise,' Daz said simply.

'Thanks, Daz,' Della called as she watched him head through the door. 'He's such a nice young man.'

'And he and Rose are devoted to each other. He's like a son,' Tess said. 'If only my girls were half as attentive... or Rose's Paul.'

'Our children have their own lives,' Della said philosophically as she dropped seasoned meat into the slow cooker. 'We have to give them space.'

'We do, you're right,' Tess said as she whisked eggs in a bowl. She wished she could be as nice as Della. She decided today she'd try extra hard to be nice to everyone.

Then a yell came from outside the kitchen. 'Something smells good... is there enough for another one?' Murdo appeared, in a jacket and walking boots, a wide smile on his face. Tess thought he looked well – his eyes sparkled. 'I can't tell you how hungry I am. And we'll need a face full of food if we're going to explore Loch Coruisk.'

Half an hour later, everyone was seated around the table,

chatter bubbling. Rose proclaimed that she felt starving for the first time in ages; Tess's scrambled eggs were the best she'd had. Murdo piled brown sauce on his and Roddy asked for second helpings, explaining that he had bedrooms to clean later and would need the extra energy. Rose definitely had an appetite; she finished every scrap of breakfast and all the fruit. 'Being on Skye agrees with me,' she declared.

They scurried round, preparing for the trip. Tess, Della and Murdo waited at the door in warm coats, hats and gloves while Daz helped Rose upstairs to the loo. She came down fifteen minutes later swathed in a huge coat, an oversized fur hat and a red-lipstick smile.

Tess said, 'You look a million dollars, Rose.'

'When in Paris,' Rose murmured. 'The coat and hat are fake fur, so you needn't worry.' She negotiated the bottom step precariously, hanging onto Daz's hand. 'Well, Mr Murdo – I don't think we've been properly introduced. We were both too busy feeding our faces over breakfast. I am Rose Grant.'

Murdo kissed her gloved hand. 'Murdoch Fraser at your service,' he said gallantly. His eyes moved to Tess and Della. 'So, Roddy told me about Rose, about her love of music, so I have a little surprise for you all today.' He shook hands with Daz. 'And you must be Daz. It's all ready for you.'

'What is?' Tess was suddenly anxious. She wasn't sure if Murdo's hare-brained schemes could be trusted.

'I have a friend and he's lent me a boat on a loch.' Murdo was pleased with himself.

'Oh, that sounds wonderful,' Rose enthused.

'Mint,' Daz agreed.

'Well, we're all wrapped up and warm, and I promised Roddy I'd drive the Land Rover so steadily as if I had a custard tart on the seat next to me.' He eyed Tess nervously. 'Not that I'm calling you a custard tart.'

'It makes a change from a pig,' Tess said between her teeth.

'Can we be back by four, Murdo?' Della asked. 'We have two extra guests for tea, so it's beef bourguignon for eight of us, that's if you'll join us.' She offered him a charming smile.

'I'd love to.' Murdo gave a little bow. 'The chariot awaits. It's about an hour and a quarter to Loch Coruisk. But it will be worth it once you arrive. And you wait until you see the boat I have borrowed for us.'

* * *

Tess stared at the boat and couldn't believe her eyes. Apparently, it belonged to one of Murdo's friends, an ex-sailor now a self-made millionaire whom Murdo called Aul Crabbit Harris, who was reputed to have more money than sense. There was no sign of him today. But he and Murdo went back a long way: they were like brothers, according to Murdo, who was currently indicating with a proud smile the boat they would cruise in for the next three and a half hours.

Apparently Aul Crabbit didn't care what anyone thought of him and Tess could see why. She stared at the boat in dismay. It was bright red, spacious, with built-in seats, cushions and a heater, and there was plenty of room for Rose to sit sheltered from the wind that skirted around the loch. The painted figurines on the outside were naked mermaids with ecstatic expressions, cavorting in a turquoise sea around a very proud sailor – she couldn't bring herself to say why. But the whole design was in terrible taste.

She clambered aboard tentatively. Murdo offered a hand,

asking, 'What do you think of Aul Crabbit's dayboat, Tess?' and she shook her head in disbelief.

'I've never seen anything quite like it. Are we really cruising around the loch in this?'

'It's full of fuel. And it's free.' Murdo was pleased with himself. 'And no one will fail to notice us.'

'They certainly won't,' Tess said.

'Oh, I just love it!' Rose thought it was hilarious. 'A boat called *The Nauti Buoy*? With a design on the side of a sailor in a cap and a striped shirt, with an oversized pink banana for a...'

'Willy.' Daz finished the sentence. 'And all those cheering mermaids. I think it would go down a storm in Monty's. I can just imagine Latrine Kleen and Jenna Cide perched on top of the masts, singing "Come All You Sailors" at the top of their voices.'

Rose was thrilled. 'Murdo – this is absolutely wonderful.'

Tess wasn't so sure, but she bit her tongue: Rose seemed very happy and Della was doing her best to pretend that she hadn't noticed the ridiculous well-endowed seaman. Once everyone was on board and the engine was rumbling, Murdo pressed a button and suddenly Abba began to sing 'Waterloo' through huge speakers. He beamed with delight.

'I made you a soundtrack.' Murdo took Rose's hand. 'And Roddy has given me a hamper for lunch – alcohol free, might I add.' Murdo glanced at Tess. 'Today is about having fun.'

'Oh, it's already fun.' Rose adjusted her fur hat. 'Whizzing round the loch in *The Nauti Buoy*. Daz, we'll have to take lots of photos for the girls back in Paris – they'll love it.'

Tess and Della exchanged looks and Tess rolled her eyes.

Murdo yelled, 'Anchors aweigh,' Rose clapped her hands and they were off, cruising through the inky water of the loch.

* * *

It had been a perfect day. They had eaten pork pies, cucumber sandwiches, walnut cake, and drunk sparkling elderflower to the most joyous music. Murdo had worn a captain's hat at the beginning of the journey but by the end Rose had had it on and he'd been sporting her fur bucket hat over his wiry curls. Daz had clambered up onto the deck to conduct an invisible orchestra while he'd sung 'You Make Me Feel (Mighty Real)'. His voice had been lost in the echo of the jagged snow-capped mountains, dark as shadows, and Murdo had told everyone to stare into the murky loch. He'd explained that it was reputed to be the home of a kelpie or water horse and if they looked hard enough, they might see a sprite swimming in the cloudy depths.

As Murdo drove the Land Rover back to Sleat, the sky was already darkening. Daz was sitting in the front, he and Murdo discussing something, but Tess, Della and Rose were too busy in the back seat singing, their arms around each other. They had done 'Sloop John B' three times, Rod Stewart's 'Sailing' twice and were currently on their fourth rendition of 'What Shall We Do with the Drunken Sailor?'

Rose was in the middle, Della's and Tess's arms around her, Murdo's captain's hat tilted as she sang her heart out. With her eyes closed, wrapped in a warm hug, she had no fear; here with her friends, nothing else mattered but the moment and the fun. Murdo drove carefully along dim lanes, swinging the Land Rover into the car park. The sky was indigo now, a mass of peep-hole stars. Three silhouettes of cars were in the car park as Murdo braked. Tess glanced towards the hotel door where two men were waiting, shuffling their feet.

She yelled, 'It's the new guests – Robin and Jamie Craig. They're early.'

From a distance, the men were just dark shadows. Tess left Della and Daz to help Rose from the car and rushed forwards.

The two men were hesitating awkwardly in front of the door, one of them around her age, tall, white-bearded, the younger one probably in his thirties, smooth-faced, wearing an anorak and carrying a case. Both of them looked perplexed.

Tess looked from one face to the other and gushed, 'Mr Craig – and Mr Craig – I'm sorry you've been kept waiting. I expected you to be a bit later... but never mind. I'll show you to your rooms – you can get settled in and...'

Something made her stop. She followed their gaze and her eyes came to rest on the white wall, next to the door. Several words had been painted there – the large letters were still wet and dripping. She caught her breath as Della joined her, then Murdo and lastly Daz helping Rose. Together they stared at the sign and their hearts sank.

It read:

WORST HOTEL EVER. JUST TURN AROUND AND LEAVE.

18

———

Tess laughed – it was her best attempt to dismiss the nonsense of the graffiti.

'Mr Craig.' She addressed both men together. 'I'm so sorry you had to witness this awful mess. You wouldn't believe it in a glorious place like Skye but we've... we've... got a bit of a problem with one or two local children. They like to practise their art skills.' Tess whooped again, as if it were hilarious.

'There's one kid in particular – he thinks he's Banksy,' Daz said.

'He or she – we don't know,' Rose added.

'There's similar graffiti in other places,' Della said, her face too honest to lie. 'I mean, not just our hotel...'

'I'll cover it all up,' Murdo announced to everyone. 'Straight after dinner.'

'Dinner – oh yes, dinner is slow-cooked beef bourguignon and couscous,' Della said proudly.

'I forgot to say when we booked – I'm vegetarian,' the older man said.

'Not a problem – I can do spicy roasted vegetables with the couscous,' Della said.

The man looked at her. 'Are you the chef?'

'I am.' Della didn't sound too certain.

'And I'm the housekeeper.' Tess was rummaging in her bag for a key. She had left it behind. 'I'll just ring the bell so that we can get in... it's chilly out here.' She looked up at the star-crammed sky.

'It seems a peculiar thing to paint on someone's hotel wall with the words "worst hotel ever". It's like some sort of warning.' The younger man, Jamie Craig frowned.

Robin Craig tried a friendly smile. 'I suppose it's all a local joke, kids...'

'It is. We all find it so funny,' Murdo said. 'Ha, ha, ha.'

'Skye is a unique island,' Tess tried. 'We like to provide a blank canvas for all the children – laptops, easels, hotel walls...' She rang the bell again, her face desperate.

'Look, I'm a guest here. My partner and I have a suite of rooms.' Rose's voice boomed as she indicated Daz, who wrapped an arm around her. 'And I can assure you it's a lovely place. Why, when we arrived last night, we had the most gorgeous dinner, a glass of whisky before bed.' She attempted a step forward and stumbled, Daz catching her in his arms as her captain's hat slipped forward over her eyes. 'Whisky,' she said for emphasis.

Robin Craig didn't seem impressed. 'We've booked here for five nights.'

'It might be all right, Dad,' Jamie said tentatively.

The door opened with a bang and Roddy stood in the light, his arms folded. 'Thank God you're here, Tess – my bloody wife has been round again shouting the odds, threatening to run this place into the ground and— Oh.' He noticed the father and son, their faces equally unimpressed. 'Hello – welcome.'

Murdo's voice rumbled. 'There's been a bit of graffiti on the wall, Roddy. I'll paint over it after dinner.'

Roddy's face fell as he read each word. 'That bloody woman – I'll swing for her.'

'Let's go inside, Mr Craig,' Tess said, taking over. She led the Craigs into the bright warmth of the hall.

Daz swept Rose into his arms. 'You must be tired out, our Rose. And I don't want you getting cold. I'll take you upstairs to our room and run a bath.'

'Oh, that would be heaven, darling. Then I'll dress for dinner,' Rose said happily as Daz whisked her up the staircase.

The Craigs exchanged glances, Jamie shaking his head as he muttered, 'Not a honeymoon couple, surely?'

'Daz and Rose are friends,' Tess said firmly. 'Now, you're in rooms seven and six. I'll take you there to settle in. You'll be very comfortable.' She met Roddy's eyes over Jamie Craig's shoulders; he was nodding furiously, letting her know both rooms were ready.

'Dinner will be at seven in the dining room,' Della said smoothly.

'And complimentary whisky will be served afterwards by the fire in the lounge,' Roddy said hopefully.

'So if you'll follow me, your rooms await.' Tess's voice was completely professional. 'Welcome to the Sicking Orca.'

* * *

The fire crackled and flames leaped, making the amber whisky glow in each glass. Della smiled, feeling proud. 'So was dinner all right for everyone?'

'It was better than all right.' Jamie stretched out his legs, enjoying the heat. 'I'm used to Dad's vegetarian cooking when

I'm home, or I make something simple in my flat in Aberdeen. Your food's special, Della.'

'It is.' Robin's eyes gleamed in the firelight. 'The roasted vegetables – what spice did you use?'

'Harissa – that's red chillies, garlic, cumin, coriander and caraway seeds,' Della said.

'It was on the list of things she made me buy,' Roddy admitted. 'Della's transforming things around here. I'll be sad when she and Tess leave.'

'Are you leaving?' Robin sounded a little disappointed.

'I'm a guest,' Della said. 'I'm helping out while Roddy finds a proper chef.'

'The thing is – we told a little lie,' Tess admitted. 'We're all guests – apart from Murdo here.' She shot a glance in his direction; he'd hardly touched his glass of whisky. She gave him an encouraging smile. 'Roddy's wife probably did the graffiti.'

'Or her new man.' Roddy pulled a sour face. 'Alasdair Barclay, the decorator from Portree.'

'We haven't met him,' Tess said. 'What's he like?'

'A weasel,' Roddy murmured.

'A bampot. Ugly as sin. Not half as nice as Roddy,' Murdo said loyally.

'So why is she with him?' Daz was seated at Rose's feet, sipping whisky.

'Maybe he has some attribute that's not immediately apparent,' Rose suggested. 'Good conversation?'

'I have good conversation,' Roddy insisted. 'She left me because she's a flirt and he's a dirtbag and they suit each other. However, I'm not bitter...' Roddy took a breath. 'I just want to make a go of the hotel and pay her off.'

'And we're glad to help,' Della said kindly.

'So – you're staying for five nights.' Tess turned brightly to

Robin. 'And we're here until the 14th. So we'll make sure you have a lovely time.'

'I'm here for both work and pleasure,' Robin said excitedly. 'I'll be out most days, but an evening meal here would be wonderful.'

'Maybe I could play that piano during dinner,' Rose offered.

Daz shook his head. 'You need to take your time,' he murmured quietly. He turned to Jamie. 'What do you have planned while you're on Skye?'

'While Dad's out researching, I'll be working in my room,' Jamie said. 'I have a deadline to meet on Monday, then I'll help Dad with his research for a couple of days.'

'What's your line of work?' Daz asked, his face bright with interest.

'Music blogging.' Jamie sighed. 'I did an interview with a jazz musician I admire. I need to write it up – do her justice.'

'Anyone we know?' Rose asked, leaning forward.

'Georgia Lord, the singer – I don't think many people know her work, but she's one of my favourites. I Zoom-called her in Chicago for the interview.'

'Not Georgia Lord who sang "Time for Hire"?' Daz was astonished.

'The same.' Jamie was surprised that he'd heard of her.

Daz started to sing, his voice low.

> *'Each day that goes by*
> *I'm on fire*
> *Waiting for you*
> *And time for hire...'*

Jamie couldn't help the smile on his face. 'That's amazing – you have a really good voice.'

'He does.' Rose patted Daz's hair proudly. 'He's man of many talents.'

'And what do you do, Robin?' Tess asked, a little flirtatiously.

'I'm here to research hunter-gatherers,' Robin explained. 'I'm writing a book about them. There's so much useful history on this island.'

'I heard something about an excavation at An Corran, by Staffin Bay,' Murdo said. He still hadn't drunk more than a mouthful.

'They found hazelnuts.' Robin stared into the fire. 'From the hunter-gatherer period, from more than eight thousand years ago.'

'On Skye? Fascinating,' Roddy said.

'It is.' Robin rubbed his hands together, holding them towards the flame. 'The hazelnuts were found in soil samples. Radiocarbon dating shows they're from the Mesolithic period, seventh millennium BC. There were samples of charred shells from 6600 BC.'

'Wow,' Tess said. She leaned towards Della with a grin. 'And I thought I was old.'

Della smiled, her eyes sad. 'I'm feeling my age too. I have to go and load the dishes into the dishwasher before I go to bed.'

'No need,' Daz said. 'I already did it. There's nothing more mingin' than dirty dishes, so I shoved them in and pressed go. They'll be dry by now.'

'Oh, that's wonderful. So – what would everyone like for breakfast tomorrow? Robin, Jamie...' Della looked from father to son. 'What can I get you? Full Scottish? Bacon roll? Avo on toast?'

Jamie licked his lips. 'Can you do pancakes? The fluffy ones with honey drizzled all over?'

'I certainly can.'

'Oh, yes, please,' Robin said.

'Perfect. Coffee, tea and toast, all ready for eight o'clock. Will that do?' Della grinned.

'I can't think of anything better.' Robin stretched his arms languorously.

Della yawned. 'Well, I'm ready for my bed. All the mountain air from Loch Coruisk has made me sleepy.' She closed her eyes and hoped for a better night than last night.

'Me too.' Tess stood up. 'Well, that's me. Goodnight, everyone. Pleased to meet you, Jamie and Robin.'

'Likewise,' Robin said. 'I'm so glad we weren't put off by that awful graffiti outside – it's been a lovely evening.'

'That reminds me.' Murdo was suddenly wide awake. 'I'll paint over it before I go home.'

'It's cold out,' Tess said, troubled by the idea of him working so late.

Murdo swallowed his whisky in one gulp. 'Medicinal. To keep the chill out.' He winked at Tess and was on his way.

Daz turned to Rose. 'We need our beauty sleep.'

Rose shook her head. 'Can you give me five minutes by myself before we go up, Daz?'

He lowered his voice. 'What do you need, lovey?'

'I just want to sit in the dining room for a few minutes.'

'Of course. Come on then, our kid.' Daz helped Rose to her feet, holding her arm while she took one step after another.

Tess watched them go, admiring Daz's loyalty, feeling concerned for Rose. She could move slowly, determinedly, but each step was harder than the one before. The stroke had hit her badly, despite Rose's protests that it was just a small one. Tess wasn't sure how well she'd recover. She peered into her empty glass and promised herself she'd do everything she could. Della would help too. They were friends through thick and thin. Tess would make sure Rose got her mojo back.

* * *

Daz was in the kitchen, emptying the dishwasher, clanking about organising plates for the following day. Rose sat at the piano and stared at her fingers as they hovered over the keys. She realised she was frowning as she took a breath and her left hand descended, fingers lightly pressing the notes. She'd start with something she knew well. Abba's 'Gimme! Gimme! Gimme! (A Man After Midnight)'.

She belted out a thumping bass, a simple sequence of notes. Rose's left hand moved fluidly; it was second nature. She concentrated hard, staring at the ringed fingers. So far so good. She took a breath and swept the five fingers of her right hand over the keys. She knew the riff well – a simple flick of the wrist, notes pressed quickly from index finger to smallest finger and back again, a trill. But her hand wouldn't move properly. She hit the wrong keys, a crashing discord. Rose inhaled deeply and tried again. The left-hand accompaniment worked well, then in she came with that sweep from the right hand and, again, the fingers were stiff and heavy, and the notes were wrong. She slammed both hands down on the keys and muttered, 'Shit!'

Daz was by her side. 'Baby steps, our Rose. You know what the doctor said...'

Rose stared up at him through hot tears. 'I can't play, Daz. My fingers won't work.'

'You can't play *yet*,' Daz said. 'But you will.'

'I can't.'

'But you will. I know you will. You're Rose-on-Wye,' Daz said. 'What would Greta Manchester do without you?'

'What if I'm finished – what if this is as good as it gets?'

'Look.' Daz squatted beside her, taking her right hand in his. 'You'll get the movement back with practice. Even if I have to sit next to you and move your fingers one by one, we'll get it back. Seriously, Rose, it may seem difficult right now, but we'll practise just a bit every day, to keep your hand in.' He laughed lightly at his own joke, then his eyes were serious. 'I promise you.'

'I'm scared.'

'Of course you are,' Daz agreed. 'It will take guts, bravery, a lot of bloody-mindedness. But that's my Rose and if anyone can do it, you can. Positive mental attitude.'

'You're right.' A tear slithered down her cheek. 'I've had tough times before and come through them. I'll make this hand work like magic, you watch me.'

'Like I said, baby steps.' Daz smiled kindly. He pushed a hand beneath her arm. 'And talking of small steps – come on, it's your bedtime.'

Rose met his eyes. 'You're just so kind. Whatever would I do without—?'

'You'll never have to find out. Now come on, Rose, it's time we tucked you up. You'll feel more positive in the morning. Let's get upstairs. I'm fair tuckered out myself.'

Daz took her arm and the pair of them moved slowly towards the door. Rose glanced back into the dining room, taking one last fond look at the piano, then Daz switched the light off and the room was shrouded in darkness.

19

Della opened her eyes the next morning to a silence that felt strange. She lay on her back and listened to nothing at all. Tess was sound asleep. It was almost seven. And of course, there was no one next to her on the pillow, no one muttering that she was a damn fine woman.

She'd never get used to the emptiness. She'd never manage to accept that, for the split second when she woke, it was as if nothing had changed, Sylvester were still alive. Then realisation dawned, the avalanche of remembering that he'd gone, that the future would always be without him. She missed Sylvester so much her bones ached; even her spine was stiff with the shock of it. Nothing would change that.

The silence stayed. It was an eerie silence – no birdsong outside, no movement, not even the distant rush of the sea. She clambered from her bed in pyjamas and wandered to the window.

She opened the curtain and was immediately dazzled by the white glare. Snow had fallen overnight and there were drifts of it piled in the garden, in the car park beyond, on the beach further away. The sky was blank as paper; rumples of snow lay in the road; each car had a frosty topping. Della frowned; she needed to get moving. In an hour everyone would be wanting breakfast. She reached for a warm jumper, clean clothes, and lurched for the door, trying her best not to disturb Tess.

In the kitchen, Daz had already set the coffee pot on the ring and was organising Rose's breakfast. Roddy was shivering, sipping from a mug, wearing an anorak, rolled-up jeans and damp socks. He explained, 'I've just been out to check. It seems we're fairly snowed in. Murdo's outside, putting a second coat of paint on the graffiti. He'll be freezing when he comes in.'

'There's enough here for him too.' Della was already whisking pancake mix, heating a compote of apples, pears, apricots and figs, spooning yogurt into dishes.

Roddy scratched his head. 'The roads will be blocked. We'll be able to walk into Sleat but I can't see Robin being able to travel very far to look around the island.'

'We have food for tonight though,' Della reminded herself. 'I must go out the back and take a look at your freezer. You've got it well stocked.'

'There's half a deer in there,' Roddy said glibly.

Della met his eyes. 'I hope I'm not expected to cook that.'

'No – that's our Christmas venison,' Roddy said.

'I'll take something out to defrost for tomorrow – but it won't be the deer,' Della smiled.

'The new chef will roast that on Christmas Day.'

'Have you got someone lined up?'

'Only one applicant – it's a small island. But he'll be very useful.' Roddy sounded hopeful. 'He's called Sandy Lowe. He's coming for an interview first thing on Monday.'

'That's good.'

'I was hoping you'd meet him, Della. I mean – I don't have a clue about chefs and I hoped you'd – well – interview him with me.'

'Oh?' Della frowned. 'I suppose I could.'

'He said in his email that he was very experienced – he's worked across the Highlands. And he lives in Armadale, so it's not too far for him to travel.'

'As long as the weather's OK,' Della said.

'I was going to take Rose for a walk today, just a little amble around the hotel, maybe towards the beach, but it'll have to wait,' Daz mumbled. 'It's too cold for her out there.'

'She'll be able to rest here – and get better,' Della said anxiously.

'Early days. But she's a fighter, that one,' Daz replied. 'I'll pop upstairs and get her.'

Della heard him mutter a greeting to someone as he left, then Murdo was in the kitchen, his jacket and hat damp. He rubbed large hands together. 'That's the painting done. But it's cold enough to freeze your bawbag out there.' He met Della's eyes and smiled to cover his sudden awkwardness. 'Any chance of a brew?'

'Hot tea coming up.' Della flicked the switch on the kettle. 'Sugar? Honey?'

'A tot of whisky?' Murdo asked hopefully.

Della shook her head. 'Breakfast's in a few minutes, Murdo. I'm doing pancakes, but there's toast too, and I can do scrambled eggs if you'd prefer that instead of pancakes.'

'All three, please,' Murdo said. 'You and Tess have transformed this place.'

'They have.' Roddy looked momentarily sad. 'We won't know what to do when you're gone. By the way, Della – do you think you might have another look at my website after breakfast?'

'And I don't suppose you or Tess are any good at sewing?'

Murdo asked. 'Only I've this big gaping hole in my work breeches...'

'No. I'm no seamstress.' Della pulled a face. 'And I can't see our Tess ever sewing any man's trousers, not in a million years.'

The morning passed slowly. After breakfast, Della spent several hours with Roddy, talking about the website. She even emailed Aston to ask for his thoughts, but the new Sicín Órga site was almost complete, with a beautiful photograph of the hotel front and the words 'A Little Bit of Heaven on Skye'. Then after making soup for everyone for lunch, Della went for a lie-down and Roddy busied himself with cleaning and washing. Rose sat in the conservatory staring out at the beach. Robin Craig was in his room reading and Jamie had found a quiet corner to talk to Daz about jazz music. Tess passed them, listening to their excited babble.

Daz said, 'For me it's Charlie Parker – the sound of that sax! And for vocals, it's Billie Holiday – that voice is mint.'

Jamie answered, 'Miles Davis every time – his haunting, bittersweet lyricism. And Nina Simone.'

Tess smiled and was on her way. She pushed the door open to the lounge and stepped inside. Murdo was there, his hands outstretched towards the fire. He shrugged. 'It's freezing outside. I cleared a path. The roads aren't too bad now.'

'Do you think it will snow again?' Tess asked, sitting next to him.

'I'm sure of it – the skies are full.' Murdo reached for a glass of black liquid and took a swig.

Tess pulled a face. 'What's that? Rum and Coke?'

'Vimto,' Murdo said. 'I'm doing my best to stay off the hard stuff. Especially after what happened. I was mortified about being sick on your bed.'

'It wasn't your best moment,' Tess said kindly. 'I did feel sorry for you though. You were really pickled. I don't think I've ever seen anyone drink so much.'

'I can put it away when I'm in a dark mood,' Murdo agreed. 'But I won't get that blootered again. It's bad for my health and my head and...' he patted his curls in jest '...it does nothing for my bonnie face.'

Tess stared into the fire. 'Maybe the time for us to worry about our looks is over.'

'What makes you say that?' Murdo asked. He reached out a paw and patted her hand. 'I think your husband must have been a bampot.'

'How do you mean?' Tess couldn't remember what she'd told him about Alan.

'It would take a stupid man to lose a woman like you.'

'That's a bit rich – you said I looked like a pig...' Tess met his eyes. 'You were drunk in charge of a quad bike.'

'I was steaming. And I'm sorry for what I said. You're a braw woman, Tess.'

'Braw?'

'Bonnie. You and Della both.'

'Oh.' Tess felt a bit disappointed. She thought he'd been paying her a compliment. It wasn't the same if Della was complimented at the same time.

Murdo swigged from his glass. 'You told me you found your husband in bed with another woman.'

'Did I?' The image still haunted her and she shuddered.

'I was lying on your bed half drunk and I couldn't believe how nice you were being to me. You told me he was called Alan and that he was unfaithful.'

'He was.'

'Did it break your heart?' Murdo asked, his gaze level.

'Not at all.' Tess lifted her chin in defiance. 'He was a good-for-nothing toe rag and seeing him with a poor woman from the golf club was really the tip of the iceberg – or the last straw, I'm not sure which.' Tess gave a shrug. 'But I am well rid.'

'So – what now?'

'Now I'm here on Skye, having the best time I can,' Tess said.

'And after that? What then?' Murdo asked.

'How do you mean, what then? It will be Christmas and I'll be...' Tess paused, remembering. It took her a few seconds to compose her thoughts. 'I'll go to Della's or Pam's or Jen's – my other friends – for Christmas and we'll have a whale of a time and then I'll worry about where I'm going to live afterwards.'

Murdo was impressed. 'That's just incredible.'

'What is?'

'You're inspirational, Tess. You're full of joy and positivity. You take one day at a time and you enjoy life to the max.'

Tess laughed. 'You should see me on a bad day.'

'I think it's amazing, how you're so kind to everyone – I heard Della's just become a widow, and Rose has had a stroke, and you may have nowhere to live, but you're so cheery. I envy that.'

'You do all right – you keep yourself busy, Murdo. You've been painting and clearing the path – and you're a wonderful tour guide. We all had a fabulous time on *The Nauti Buoy*...'

'Och, you should meet Aul Crabbit Harris some time, Tess. He'd make you laugh. Why, he can sink a glass of whisky in four seconds flat.'

'He sounds like a bad influence.'

'I'm my own bad influence,' Murdo said, edging close to the fire where he'd hung his damp socks. Tess noticed the steam rising. 'I hardly drank when Mairi was alive. But after she died, well, it helps me deal with things.'

Tess wriggled closer. 'What things?'

Murdo murmured, 'The manner of her death.'

'Why? What happened?'

'It was all down to me...' Murdo whispered. Tess was sure she saw a single tear glisten in his eye. She waited for him to speak – it was the kindest thing to do. But no words came.

'Murdo?' she coaxed.

She watched him take a deep shuddering breath. 'Mairi would be alive if it hadn't been for me. I blame myself, to this day.'

'Why?' Tess edged closer, touching his huge wrist. 'What did you do?'

'Nothing.' Murdo raised his head, his eyes gleaming. He was about to speak. Then there was someone shouting from the hall, a loud shriek, followed by a torrent of angry expletives, a woman's voice. Murdo jerked upright and said, 'That's Isla. I wonder what she wants now.'

He was on his feet, hurrying into the hall, Tess just behind him. Roddy was standing by the stairs, his body shrinking backwards. Tess had heard the unpleasant expression of a face looking like a smacked bum – it fitted Roddy exactly. His cheeks were tingling red with embarrassment and crumpled with sadness. Isla was in full flow.

'I'm not asking now – I'm telling you straight. I'm losing patience. Ali says we should have got a solicitor already.'

'But I can make a go of the hotel,' Roddy said weakly.

'Like you made a go of our marriage?' Isla snickered. 'Roddy, you're a loser. This hotel is a shithole. I made that clear with my little painted sign. If you don't put it up for sale, I'll ruin you.'

Murdo spoke up. 'Now that's not fair, Isla.'

'Isn't it?' Isla turned on him, teeth bared. She was wearing a black and white coat with a fur collar; there was snow on her boots. 'No one asked you to open your mouth, Murdo. This has nothing to do with you.'

'It's my home, this hotel,' Roddy said, taking courage from his uncle's arrival. 'I can make it work. I have a new website, a chef coming...'

'Don't make me laugh.' Isla's voice dripped acid. 'You have a granny who can cook a bit and you think you're the bloody Ritz.' She gave a nasty cackle. 'You listen to me. I want this place sold. I want half the money by the new year or there'll be hell.'

Roddy looked genuinely scared. 'What will you do?'

'What will I do?' Isla's laugh was colder than ever. 'Ali and I have our own plans. And if the money's not in our hands by January, he'll come round here with some of his friends and make you pay.'

'That weaselly little git?' Murdo's hands were balled on his hips. 'I'd like to see him try. I'd punch his lights out.'

'Empty threats – that's all you're capable of, Murdo,' Isla scoffed. She turned back to Roddy, who was visibly quaking by the banister. 'You've been warned. Half the money belongs to me by rights. I'll make you pay up – you see if I don't.'

'You'll get your half, I promise,' Roddy said. 'I know you're entitled to it. But just let me get the hotel back on its feet. Then I'll go to the bank. I'll raise the money somehow. I just need time.'

Isla sneered. 'You've made a mess of the whole business.'

'That's in the past,' Murdo chimed in. 'But he'll make a go of it now, and we're going to help.'

'You?' Isla laughed.

'I will, I'll have your money by the new year.' Roddy looked sorry for himself.

'You'll fail, Roddy. Just as you failed as a husband.' Isla narrowed her eyes. 'And I won't wait for you to make another excuse. I want this place on the market.'

'Why don't you just go?' Tess suggested.

'I'm not leaving until Roddy promises.' Isla frowned. 'He knows what I'm capable of...'

'You've outstayed your welcome,' Tess said quietly. 'I hope the rest of your day is as pleasant as you are.'

'Who the hell are you? Roddy's new squeeze? Or Murdo's?' Isla whirled round in Tess's direction, snarling. She paused. Della had arrived, hands on hips. She coughed, a signal for Isla to stop. Jamie, Daz and Rose stood behind her. Rose spoke up, her voice bored.

'I heard a horrible screeching noise coming from the hall. I thought we had bats. Roddy, please can you tell this howling harpy to sling her hook. I'm trying to get some rest.'

Isla's mouth opened. Roddy murmured, 'You should go.'

Isla took in each face, then she drew herself up tall. 'You mark my words, I'll be back. Half this hotel is mine.' She turned to Roddy. 'Think on what I said.' She strode forward, slamming the door behind her.

An icy blast circulated around the hall and Daz grinned. 'Was that the ice queen or what?'

Tess moved to Roddy. 'Are you all right?'

Roddy shook his head. 'She's really angry.'

Rose laughed. 'I've met that type. All hot air.'

'All mouth and no action,' Daz said.

'No...' Roddy's voice was hushed. 'If you get on the wrong side of Isla, she has to get even. She meant every word she said.' He looked around nervously. 'It was Isla who painted the graffiti on the wall. You all heard her – she said she'll ruin me.' He took a breath. 'And what Isla says, she does.'

20

More snow fell stealthily overnight and the following morning it was still snowing, thick flakes twirling fast. In the dining room, eight people clustered round the table over a piping-hot breakfast, wondering what to do with themselves. Roddy was still reeling from Isla's visit and he had hardly eaten. Murdo clapped him on the back.

'Don't worry yourself – there's no danger of the woman coming back today. It's like K2 out there.'

Roddy pushed his fork into the scrambled eggs. 'I sat up half the night working out my finances to see if I could sell something or borrow money to buy her out. Or maybe I could renovate the old attic and turn it into more bedrooms. But I need money up front.'

Murdo sighed. 'I wouldn't get enough for my cottage to help you out, or I'd sell it.'

Roddy gave him a grateful look, then sank his head into his hands.

'I know she's your wife, Roddy, but...' Rose felt sorry for him as she looked over the rim of her cup of tea '...this is your home, your parents' home, your grandparents'. Surely that's worth something in the eyes of the law?'

Robin Craig shook his head. 'I don't think so – when a couple split up, isn't everything shared equally?'

'But this hotel is his livelihood,' Della protested. 'She could have half the takings… if she's patient, this place will be a great earner.'

'A solicitor would have to witness an agreement,' Jamie said.

'And Isla wants to take her half and go.' Roddy sighed.

'Why did you take up with her?' Della asked. 'She's a piece of work.'

'She was nice, really nice, at the beginning. I couldn't believe such a lovely woman had eyes for me.' Roddy looked sad. 'The first year was OK, then we had nineteen years of arguing unless I did what she wanted. I sensed she was always looking round for something better.'

'Someone she could fleece,' Murdo said between his teeth.

'People like that…' Daz lifted his fork in emphasis '…they don't go away without a fight. My uncle Nobby married a woman – Millicent, she was called – she bled him dry and went off with his mate. He was brassic by the time she'd finished with him. And broken-hearted.'

'I know the feeling,' Roddy muttered beneath his breath.

'Most women aren't like that.' Rose felt it necessary to restore equilibrium.

'She won't get away with it.' Della banged her fist on the table. 'You need to see a solicitor and say that you want to keep the hotel.'

'Perhaps when the takings come flying in for Christmas and Hogmanay, Isla will change her mind,' Rose said.

'Christmas…' Tess woke up from a daydream, her eyes shining. 'That's what we need.'

'I'd like to sit in front of that roaring fire and read all day,' Robin said. 'I won't get much research done outside in this snow.'

'And I have my article to finish,' Jamie added.

'Yes but...' Tess waved a knife '...Roddy needs cheering up. So I suggest...' All eyes were on her. Tess's face shone with excitement. 'Let's cook a feast – a huge Christmas dinner. All the trimmings. All together. Roasties and veg... gravy, a turkey or something. Then while it's cooking, let's go out in the snow and have fun.'

Daz was immediately excited. 'Tobogganing, snowball fights.'

'I took a turkey out of the freezer yesterday – it will be perfectly defrosted,' Della said.

'We could go down to the beach and paddle in the water in our wellies,' Roddy added. 'And there's food in the freezer.'

Della patted Robin's arm. 'I'll make a nut roast for you.'

'That sounds wonderful,' Robin said. 'Imagine how the hunter-gatherers existed on Skye when so much snow fell.'

'So it's fun in the snow first, then Christmas scran.' Daz smiled. 'I'm buzzing...' He turned to Rose. 'We'll wrap you up warm, scarf and gloves and that furry hat, and maybe you can chuck a few snowballs at me?'

'I'll do my best,' Rose said grimly. 'I can prop myself up in the kitchen and whizz up Yorkshire puddings. In the old days, Bernard – bless him – and Paul used to swear by my Yorkshires.'

'It's decided,' Tess said. 'Today we're practising for your big Christmas.' She winked at Roddy. 'Then when we're not here, you'll be able to do it perfectly.'

Roddy wasn't sure.

'We'll do the prep, split the work.' Della rubbed her hands together. 'We'll have soup ready for lunch then we'll—'

'Hit the slopes,' Daz exclaimed.

'That sounds really good.' Robin's face shone.

'Perfect.' Roddy was smiling now. 'Della, we have plenty of seasonal veggies.'

'I'll get a good fire stoked up,' Murdo said. 'There's plenty of wood in the shed.'

'And while you're all busy, I might sit at the old piano for half an hour and tinkle – just to see if I can get these fingers to work...' She met Daz's eyes hopefully. 'If you'd give me a helping hand. I'm determined to master that Abba frill better than Benny Andersson by the time we go out for our snowball fight...'

* * *

After lunch, the snow was still falling like fat feathers. Dinner had been prepared; the meat was already in the oven and the veggies were sitting in roasting tins. Della had even made a batch of mince pies, using some dried fruit, candied peel, brandy and pastry that she made from scratch. Now the garden was a hive of activity as everyone screamed and shouted.

Rose watched from her chair, wrapped in blankets and coats, while the others had fun. She smiled at their antics. Murdo was taking Tess on a sledge ride down a slope in the garden, sitting behind her like a huge bear, in a checked jacket and a cap. Tess whooped and shrieked while he clutched her protectively, both tumbling in one ball into the snow at the bottom. Della was making a huge snowman outside the house with Roddy, helped by Jamie and his father, who had snow in his beard. Daz stood behind Rose's chair, handing her a mug of warm tea from a flask.

'Are you all right, our kid?' he asked affectionately.

'I'm champion,' Rose replied, mimicking his accent. She sipped the tea, the mug clutched in gloved hands.

'I was impressed with your piano playing this morning,' Daz said. 'It's coming back.'

'Oh, I don't think so.' Rose had been disappointed; she hadn't made much progress.

'I disagree – you're improving in leaps and bounds. Small steps though, Rose...' Daz said quietly.

'I suppose so.' She sighed. 'I wish I could take small steps to the top of that hill, Daz. Just look at Tess and Murdo. They are having such fun.' She caught her breath. 'I don't suppose I'll be able to do that again...'

They stared at the top of the mound, where Tess sat on the sledge, Murdo behind her, cannoning down, Tess screaming as they tumbled for the tenth time into a drift of snow. Tess stood up, brushing snow from her clothes and laughing.

Murdo roared, 'Your turn, Della.'

Della looked up from placing a carrot nose on the snowman and shook her head. 'Not for me.'

'Oh, come on,' Murdo yelled. 'You'll be safe.'

'Yes, come and join us, Della,' Tess called. Della gave an exaggerated shrug and hurried towards them.

Roddy shoved a shrivelled orange on the snowman's face as a mouth, and called to Rose, 'Does this remind you of anyone?'

'It's Irritating Isla to a tee.' Rose didn't pause for breath and Roddy immediately burst out laughing. Rose noticed how bright his cheeks were – he looked so much better for being outdoors. She turned to Daz. 'You go and have fun with the others. Have a go on Murdo's rickety wooden sledge.'

'Oh, you're all right.' Daz rubbed her shoulders beneath the thick coat. 'I'm enjoying being with you.'

Rose watched Della and Murdo hurtling down the slope on the sledge while Tess was taking photos on her phone. She waved it in the air and shouted, 'Jen and Pam will love these. I'll send them over dinner with tons more.'

Murdo extended a hand, tugging Della from the snow where she had fallen. Rose thought she still seemed sad behind her smile, but she seemed better than a few days ago, when she probably hadn't been sleeping at all. Rose's heart went out to her. Della would find it difficult to go home to Exmouth; memories of Sylvester would be everywhere but the house would be empty.

A soft scattering of snow fell on her shoulder and Rose turned to where Daz was laughing, a white powdery clump stuck on the front of his jacket. Jamie had just thrown a fat snowball. Daz bent down, packed a tight ball and hurled one back, catching Jamie's woolly hat. Jamie shrieked with laughter and threw another. His shot was wide, and it landed with a plop in Rose's lap.

Jamie froze, not sure how to react, then he gave a lopsided grin. 'Sorry, Rose.'

'Right...' Rose eased herself from the wheelchair until she stood upright. She brushed herself down deliberately, bending over, cupping a handful of snow into a ball, sending it catapulting. It hit Jamie full in the chest. 'Don't you underestimate me, young man.' She laughed.

She collected more snow, throwing again and again. Two more snowballs landed on Jamie's coat. A third caught him full in the face, Daz grinning and chucking packed snow at him for all he was worth. He threw one playfully at Roddy, who turned in alarm.

Another snowball soared, two, three; Robin joined in, and Daz was making ammunition for Rose to fling at them all. Rose laughed. 'I was a dab hand as a kid.' She threw another snowball and it thudded against the snowman, hitting the carrot. The nose shot off and fell into the snow.

Roddy shouted, 'Oh, I wish I could do that to the real Isla,' and started to laugh.

In a single movement, the snowball fighters turned their attention on the snowman – or snowwoman – propelling missiles for all they were worth. Roddy threw his hardest, laughing hysterically each time the snow connected, yelling, 'Take that, Isla.' Rose wasn't sure that his anger towards his wife was altogether healthy, but it was clearly making him feel better. She glanced around for the others; Tess and Della were on their way towards her, waving, but Murdo had gone. Rose assumed he'd taken himself off for a quick dram. She returned her attention to brushing snow from her coat. She was snuggly warm inside; only her nose and cheeks were cold.

Daz asked, 'Are you tired?'

'I'm fine – is it time to go in yet?'

'It's only three. It doesn't get dark for a bit – although it does get dark here early,' Daz said.

'Jen's in Iceland,' Tess called as she approached, arm in arm with Della. 'It's dark all day there apart from a couple of hours over lunch... imagine that!'

'She seems to spend all her time drinking on board the ship and flirting with the other guests,' Della said.

They paused; a throaty sound of an engine was coming from the road, a spluttering rattle, then Murdo appeared on his quad bike. Jamie waved an arm. 'Oh, look. I bet it's really fun to ride that across the island.'

Murdo brought it to a halt outside the hotel. He rushed across to Rose and held out a hand. 'Your chariot, madam.'

'What?' Rose's brow furrowed. 'You want me to get on that?'

'I do,' Murdo said. 'The others have been on the sledge and

you deserve a ride. If you sit up behind me and hold tight, I'll go ever so steadily.'

'Right. You're on.' Rose didn't hesitate. Daz helped her towards the quad bike, giving her a hand up, tucking her coat around her as she clung on. Then Murdo was off, on his way towards the beach, Rose behind him, the snow falling all around. She could be heard singing 'Mamma Mia' as the quad bike chugged noisily away.

Tess met Daz's eyes. 'She's doing so well.'

'She's trying her best,' Daz murmured. 'She'll get better or bust in the attempt.'

'We'll help,' Della said.

'Oh, you've no idea how much good being here has done her,' Daz said. 'A few days ago, it was like her life was over. She thought she wouldn't play the piano again.'

'And will she?' Tess asked anxiously.

'Like I said.' Daz shrugged. 'She's determined.'

'That's our Rose,' Tess said.

Jamie and Robin had joined them. Jamie was still watching Murdo and Rose on the bike. 'Do you think he'd let me have a go?'

'Jamie's been on quad bikes since he was a kid,' Robin said.

'Let's ask. I'll ride with you.' Daz's eyes gleamed.

'You're on,' Jamie said. He raised his voice. 'Murdo – any chance?'

'Of course.' Murdo steered the quad bike over, braked gently and came to a halt. 'Don't overdo the throttle or you'll be tipped off.'

'I've had enough of being a speed queen.' Rose allowed herself to be helped down. She patted Robin's arm. 'And you can keep me company.'

'It would be my pleasure,' Robin offered gallantly.

Roddy muttered, 'We should check the roast.' He turned to Della, hoping she'd help him.

Della sensed his lack of confidence. 'All right. It's time to put the potatoes in – and the nut roast.'

'I'll come with you,' Tess offered. 'I might make some hot toddy with the whisky I bought. I'll make it weak, so Murdo can have a bit, but it'll warm us all up.'

'Sounds lovely,' Della said.

They had reached the hotel door and Roddy pushed it open. The hotel was in semi-darkness. 'That's funny. I was sure I left the lights on...'

Roddy reached for the switch. Nothing happened. He flicked it again. 'No lights.'

'That's strange.' Tess frowned. 'Do you think a bulb has gone?'

They walked through the half-light towards the kitchen and Della said, 'Can you smell anything?'

'No.' Roddy sounded nervous.

'Nor can I,' Tess said. 'That's odd.'

'Odd? How?' Roddy asked.

'We should be able to smell turkey roasting.' Della shook her head in disbelief. They had reached the kitchen. It was dim, almost in darkness.

'I don't understand.' Roddy was confused.

'There's no electricity,' Tess explained.

'It's not working – any of it.' Della said. She rushed to the oven and opened the door. 'The food hasn't even started to cook. There'll be no feast tonight – no roast, no Christmas dinner, nothing... It's all stone cold.'

21

Della, Tess and Roddy stood in the shadowy dining room, staring out of the window as snow spiralled like magic dust. There was noise and activity outside, Murdo pushing Rose in her chair around the cleared path as she chattered happily to Robin; Daz and Jamie shouting with joy, roaring up the hill on the quad bike. Della said, 'They'll all be starving when they come in.'

Tess shook her head. 'Do you think a fuse has blown?'

'It could be a power failure because of the snow,' Roddy said. 'Maybe half the island is in blackout.'

'We could light candles,' Tess said hopefully.

'Oh, I have plenty in stock,' Roddy replied. 'But what will we do for food?'

'Can we toast crumpets in front of the fire?' Tess suggested.

'That's hardly a Christmas roast.' Roddy was disappointed.

'I remember when Sylvester and I were first married, and the boys were babies,' Della said. 'We rented this old place in Stepney, and the electric meter was always running out. We didn't always have coins – Sylvester brought home an old camping stove. I don't suppose you have anything like that, Roddy?'

'I don't think so,' Roddy said. 'But there's the old Aga out the back.'

'Aga?' Della's eyes lit up.

'It's a big old oil thing in the outbuilding next to the water pump and the freezer. My grandma used to cook on it.'

'So – have you got oil?' Della asked.

'We keep some in stock.'

'Where?' Tess looked around.

'In the outbuilding,' Roddy said and Della seized his sleeve.

'What are we waiting for? Does the Aga work?'

'It can be made to.'

'Then let's cook a roast,' Della said. 'Christmas dinner's back on.'

Tess picked up a tray of potatoes. 'We have wine, port, whisky – let's rock and roll.'

Half an hour later, the Aga was hot enough, and the outbuilding glowed with the soft light of a dozen candles. Della was busy cramming the oven with meat and vegetables. 'We can roast everything – potatoes, swedes, carrots, Brussels sprouts. And the gravy will come from the meat juices – I'll make a different one for the nut roast.' Her eyes sparkled.

Tess flourished a bottle. 'I found this in the dining room cupboard.'

'Sherry.' Roddy had brought glasses. 'We deserve a tipple.'

'So – this outbuilding...' Tess inspected the brick walls, the old iron Aga, the dusty shelves, two huge freezers, low-hanging cobwebs in the corner. 'It's a useful space.'

'It was the kitchen years ago.' Roddy's eyes shone. 'I had such plans – it's big enough to turn into a gîte. The dining room was a ballroom back in the day. It's been boarded up – there was a stage behind it. People used to dance and listen to orchestras play. My father always talked about opening up the attic, adding more rooms to make this the grandest place on the island. I'd love to have brought the Sicín Órga back to its former glory.'

'You still could,' Tess soothed.

Roddy shook his head. 'I know when I'm beaten. Isla always gets her way.'

'No,' Della said firmly. 'Once bookings come in for Christmas and Hogmanay...'

'And you employ a new chef,' Tess added.

Roddy's face was glum, defeated. 'That might keep me going for a while but...'

'Burns Night – January,' Tess suggested.

'Valentine's Day – then it's springtime,' Della said.

'And then it's summer – the island will be packed with holidaymakers.' Tess folded her arms. 'You'll make it work.'

Roddy's expression didn't change. 'I should cut my losses and give Isla what she wants.'

'No,' Della and Tess said at the same time.

'Sicín Órga is your heritage,' Della told him. 'Yes, Isla is entitled to something, but not at the expense of your happiness.'

'Why is it called that?' Tess asked.

'Sicín Órga means golden chicken. My grandfather said that there was an old tale – his grandfather brought a golden chicken to the island from Edinburgh many years ago and it laid golden eggs, the likes of which had never been seen on the island. He sold them, made a fortune and bought a hotel. The rest is history.'

'See – this hotel is your family history.' Tess took a swig of sherry.

'Of course, it's a myth,' Roddy said sadly.

Della shook her head. 'This hotel is full of memories and

we're making new ones – food cooked on the Aga, new friends and old, family, celebrations...'

'Eating by candlelight,' Tess said. 'I'm off to lay the table. Roddy, give me a hand – you know where everything is.'

'And I'll check on dinner.' Della opened the oven door and was greeted with a waft of steam and the scent of roasting. It reminded her of last Christmas and tears filled her eyes.

An hour later, the dining hall echoed with chatter and the sound of munching. Daz groaned with delight as he shovelled Yorkshire pudding into his mouth. 'You know, we eat lovely food in Paris but I'd forgotten how good proper home-cooked scran is.' He closed his eyes, taking a mouthful of wine. 'Happy non-Christmas, everybody.'

Robin was enjoying his nut loaf. 'When we booked, I thought the hotel was perfectly placed to do research. But it's so much more.' He offered Della a smile, then Tess. 'The food is second to none, and so's the welcome. I'm enjoying being here.'

'I'll second that.' Murdo sipped wine. 'Normally I'd be at home, feeling sorry for myself with a ping meal on my knee. It's funny – I haven't thought about a glass of whisky all afternoon. I was having too much fun in the snow.' He glanced at Rose. 'Did you enjoy yourself?'

'I did – and it was good exercise.' Rose smiled. 'I'd love to get a quad bike. It would be so empowering.'

'Small steps,' Daz reminded her.

'I know what you mean though,' Jamie said. 'I finished my work this morning and being out in the snow was fun. I loved the quad bike. Thanks, Murdo.'

'My pleasure.' Murdo's eyes shone in the candlelight. 'And thanks, Della and Tess, for the wonderful meal.'

They all raised their glasses. 'Della and Tess.'

Tess had cleared her plate. 'Well, that was delicious. All the more so for cooking it in the old Aga and eating it by candlelight.'

Roddy frowned. 'I wonder when the power will be back on.'

'Oh, not too soon, I hope,' Rose muttered. 'I like the candles. It's all shadows and calm.'

'Why don't we take the mince pies and brandy into the living room?' Della suggested.

'The fire's roaring in there,' Roddy said. 'It would be just like my great-grandfather's era, sitting together, talking, no television or laptops.'

'Like hunter-gatherers – after a shared meal, conversation around a fire, storytelling,' Robin murmured.

'Let's do it.' Tess was on her feet.

Daz helped Rose up steadily. 'Are you up for it?'

'I certainly am.' Rose was already standing.

'Right.' Murdo stood up with a grin. 'You get yourself comfortable in the living room. There's something I need to check on…'

'Oh?' Tess watched him go, wondering if he was going to find a bottle or two.

* * *

It was very cosy in the lounge, light glimmering from flickering candles in jars. Della brought in mince pies and cream as Roddy poured brandy. Rose was helped into an armchair, Jamie and Robin sat on the burgundy sofa, and Della and Tess crouched in front of the fire, feeling the heat on their faces. Tess held up her glass, watching the flames flicker as she swirled the dark liquid. She said, 'It was so romantic, eating dinner in the dark.'

Robin nodded. 'Candlelight's very atmospheric.'

Della made a muffled, contented sound. 'That was always my

idea of romance, Sylvester and I eating food, eyes meeting, and I know what he's thinking, and he knows exactly what I'm about to say...'

'I tried my best at romance,' Roddy muttered. 'I remember once on Isla's birthday I took her breakfast in bed and I put a ruby ring in her croissant, hoping she'd discover it and be thrilled.'

'Oh, how gorgeous.' Tess closed her eyes, imagining. 'A man who cares enough to hide a piece of jewellery.'

'Not at all,' Roddy groaned. 'She almost chipped a tooth. I suppose it was a crazy idea – she might have swallowed it and choked.'

'It would have saved you all this trouble,' Rose said grimly.

'Steady, our Rose.' Daz laughed.

'I loved Bernard, but he never really understood me,' Rose persisted. 'He'd never buy me a card or a present. He said it was a waste of money – he said it was just another day. But every year I wished he'd do something to make me feel special.'

Tess forced a laugh. 'Alan would give me something he'd think I'd like – perfume, jewellery, chocolate. Then he'd either tell me how much it cost or, if it was chocolate, he'd eat most of it and say he was helping me out or I'd get fat.'

'I'd get Susan a surprise, something she'd never have thought of for herself. She said she liked surprises,' Robin said wistfully.

'That's really sweet,' Tess said.

'The surprise she gave me wasn't sweet, Tess.' Robin heaved his shoulders. 'She left me five years ago. She hadn't loved me since Jamie was a boy. My beard scratched when I kissed her, I walked like a T-Rex and I snuffled in my sleep – that's what she said.'

Della closed her eyes. 'There's nothing wrong with snoring. It reminds us we're still alive.'

Tess took her hand. 'Romance is important though, to men as well as women.'

'It is,' Robin agreed. 'Susan wasn't the romantic sort.'

Daz frowned. 'I was with Simon for years in Paris – he was my partner on stage and at home. We were Greta Manchester and Ashley de la Zouch, before Rose came along. I waited all those years but he never told me he loved me, not once.' Daz forced a laugh. 'He did say I made the best cup of coffee though.'

'That must have hurt,' Jamie said quietly.

'It did, a bit.' Daz made a face, trying to look as if he didn't care. 'He said my feet were cold in bed.' He sighed. 'Onwards and upwards, I say. There are plenty more fish...' He caught Della's eye and was suddenly quiet.

'Friends count for a lot,' Rose said. 'They're the family you choose, the ones who hold us together when we come apart.'

'I can see that.' Robin's eyes glimmered. 'It's good not to be alone.'

Tess lifted her glass. 'To friends.'

'Friends,' came the chorus.

Daz began to sing softly:

> *'Each day that goes by*
> *I'm on fire*
> *Waiting for you*
> *And time for hire...'*

'Gloria Lord's song,' Jamie said thoughtfully. 'I finished my article...'

Suddenly the room was illuminated with bright light. Della

blinked the tears from her eyes; Daz's song had made her feel weepy.

'The power's back on.' Roddy beamed. 'Oh, that's great.'

The door opened wide and Murdo came in. He looked pleased with himself. 'And then there was light.'

'Did you fix something?' Tess asked.

'In a manner of speaking.' Murdo gave a laugh. 'I flicked on the main switch and – hallelujah!'

Della frowned. 'So the electric had been switched off?'

'At the mains. One switch,' Murdo said.

'How?' Rose asked.

'That's what I'd like to know,' Murdo muttered quietly. 'The main box is in the outbuilding.'

'I should have checked,' Roddy groaned.

'That's not the point,' Murdo replied.

'What do you mean?' Robin asked.

'I mean that someone went in there while we were messing around in the snow and deliberately switched the electricity off,' Murdo said grimly. 'I had a look around the back of the house and I found some tyre tracks. I bet they came from a Land Rover. So...'

'So?' Rose asked.

'Who might have come down from Portree in the snow in their new boyfriend's Land Rover to turn off the power? No-one ever parks round the back – unless they know it's a good place to avoid being seen.' Murdo's eyes gleamed. 'I can only think of one person.'

Roddy shuddered. 'Isla.'

'It makes sense,' Tess said. 'She admitted to the graffiti on the hotel wall.'

'She's got her knickers in a twist. I wouldn't put anything past her...' Murdo said. 'The question is – now she's thrown all her toys out of the pram, she's got nothing to lose. First, the graffiti. Then the electricity. What's she going to do next?'

22

Rose woke on Monday morning and wriggled her toes. They moved freely, no pins and needles. She felt newly positive, and she hadn't even taken her meds yet. Carefully, she eased herself out of bed and pressed her feet on the rug. The sensation of the furry fabric was delicious. It was the right time. She'd try to walk by herself.

She stood up. Her weak arm hurt a little but at least she was vertical. This would be her first step without sticks. She took a single pace.

So far, so good.

Rose breathed out slowly. A second pace, wobbly, but still upright. She looked ahead to the window. If she could make it to the curtains unaided, it would be such an achievement. At an estimate, it was six more paces. She gritted her teeth.

One.

Rose concentrated on her balance. Her legs felt weak, but she was still standing. She started to sing the Elton John song of the same name to help her focus.

Two.

The right foot felt a little numb. She put the left down firmly, her arms out like Rose from the *Titanic* movie. They shared the same name and the same giddiness right now.

Three.

Four.

Her legs felt weak as sponge. Rose paused, refocused, stared ahead to the drawn curtains.

Five.

She was almost there.

She remembered something that happened in her youth – she'd been nine years old, trying to complete her first width of the swimming pool. She'd failed four times – she recalled her fifth grim attempt, her father watching from the poolside. She'd pushed off, reached the halfway mark and felt herself beginning to slow down, to sink. She'd fixed her eyes on the edge of the pool, using her last moments of strength to push forwards. She felt just the same now, wobbly, her energy draining but she wouldn't fail.

Six.

She wasn't there yet. She needed one more pace. Rose hurled herself forward, grasping the window ledge with shaking arms.

Seven.

She'd made it.

She tugged open the curtains and saw blinding snow, drifts of it, and caught her breath: four deer were standing in the garden, looking around on delicate legs. She watched them carefully to see what they'd do. One of them glanced up with round eyes and Rose decided it was the deer's way of saying congratulations.

Rose replied, 'I'll take that, Bambi.'

'Take what?' Daz's voice came from behind her. She turned round. He was standing in his silk dressing gown and boxers.

'I just walked. It was only seven steps but...'

Daz was at her side, holding her up. 'Well done you. I said all those sitting and standing exercises would pay off. That's incredible.'

'I'm on a roll,' Rose said determinedly. 'Now I'm going to dress myself and go downstairs with a stick. Will you help me? I mean – don't help unless I really need it. Just be there.' She met his eyes, her own fierce. 'I'm going to do this, Daz. Then I'm going to practise on that piano.'

'Not till you've had brekkie and a brew,' Daz said. 'Come on, champ. You've done very well. The small steps are getting bigger now.'

'I'm on the mend,' Rose said. 'It's done me good being here. So – we're definitely going home the day after tomorrow.'

'Same as Jamie and his dad,' Daz muttered.

'It's been wonderful.' Rose's eyes shone. 'The snow, the beautiful outdoors, the company – Della and Tess...'

'We need to head back to Paris though. Monty needs me to perform on Saturday night.'

'I won't have my right hand back by then.' Rose sighed. 'It will take me a while, but I'm determined to be good as ever by Christmas. Perhaps she'll let me play then?'

'We'll give it our best shot.' Daz hugged her. 'Come on, missus – I'm starving. Let's get breakfast.'

'I'm hungry too,' Rose said. 'And you can forget about that healthy cereal today. There's a Scottish fry-up down there with my name on it.'

Breakfast was a lively affair. Della had never cooked so many eggs or made so many pieces of French toast. By the time she plonked herself at the table, everyone else had finished. Murdo, who turned up for all his meals now, had eaten two portions of everything and was still gulping coffee. Robin indicated his watch and nudged Jamie gently.

'We're off around the island now the snow's eased,' Robin said. 'You know, the first people came here around 14000 BC. They walked along Doggerland, which is the North Sea, following the elk and deer. There's still some evidence of hunting camps.'

'So that's what Dad's looking for,' Jamie added. 'I promised I'd help him, now my interview with Gloria Lord's out there.'

'Rose and I are going to practise our act,' Daz said.

'And I want to try a walk around the garden.' Rose smiled. 'I've seen deer.'

'Oh, they're a nuisance,' Roddy grumbled. 'They eat everything. Isla used to grow strawberries in the summer and the deer ate them all...' He stopped and put a hand to his face. 'I'm sorry – I'm just having a moment.'

Della patted his hand. 'It's allowed.'

'I'm taking the Land Rover up to the Old Man of Storr,' Murdo jumped in, to lighten the mood. 'The snow won't last, and the view will be magnificent.' He turned to Della. 'We have seven hours of light today. Let's make the most of it.'

'Oh – aren't we interviewing the new chef?' Della asked.

'I can do that by myself,' Roddy said, but he didn't look confident.

'I'm happy to help.' Della watched the relief spread on his face.

Murdo turned to Tess. 'So it's just you and me, then?'

'I'll treat you to lunch,' Tess offered. 'Then we'll come back and help.'

'I know a lovely little inn, a blazing log fire, good food.' Murdo licked his lips. 'Of course, I'm driving, so it's lemonade shandy for me.'

'Are you sure you can't come, Della?' Tess asked as Della shook her head. 'Rose? Daz?'

'You go, Tess,' Rose said. 'We'll be busy. We have a Zoom call with Monty later to organise the weekend show.'

'When are you leaving?' Jamie asked.

'The day after tomorrow... the same as you.' Daz met his eyes. 'All good things come to an end.'

'I need to catch up with you, Tess, Della,' Roddy remembered. 'We have more guests booked in. The website's doing the trick. So I wondered if you'd help me plan up to the 14th – I can't believe you've only got six days left. I'd better get a wriggle on and tidy up. The prospective new chef will be here soon...' He leaped up. 'Sandy Lowe. I wonder what he's like.'

* * *

Della wasn't sure what she expected, but when Sandy arrived ten minutes early carrying a huge plastic box under his arm, she saw a short man in his late twenties with long red hair in a ponytail, a wide grin and sparkling light blue eyes. He was wearing shorts, despite the snow, clumpy hiking boots and a purple anorak, which he stripped off to reveal a yellow T-shirt sporting the words 'Never Mind the Bollocks – Here's the Sex Pistols'. His arms were plastered with tattoos – a colourful dragon, a bright rose, several inky italicised words: Mum, Family, Shona, Maisie. He stood in the kitchen, staring at the shining stainless-steel equipment, and muttered, 'I'd love it here.' He plonked the plastic box down with a grin. 'But I don't have the job – not yet.'

Roddy had put on a shirt, tie and jacket for the occasion. He gave a nervous cough. 'Hello, Sandy – I'm Roddy Fraser, the owner. So, right, we're looking for an all-round chef to build business towards Christmas and Hogmanay. I need a reliable self-motivated cook who can organise meals. We have eight rooms, so if they were all filled that would be fourteen guests plus the family room. Of course, it's all a bit ad hoc at the moment – we're never fully booked, but I'm hoping that will change and if it does, we'll get more staff. We're going through a bit of a slump though... there are only a couple of rooms booked and...' He paused. He wasn't selling the job. His eyes flickered towards Della, imploring, and she took over.

'I'm doing the cooking temporarily.'

'You must be Mrs Fraser.' Sandy stuck out a hand.

Della shook it. 'No, I'm...' She considered how to explain. 'I'm helping out. But I'm only here for a few more days.'

'I can start immediately – right now, this minute...' Sandy said for emphasis.

'Right.' Roddy looked unconvinced. 'So, er, I have to ask – um – your application was a bit sketchy. You've worked as a chef before?'

'Och yes, I've worked in all sorts of places,' Sandy said. 'I'm very keen.'

'You didn't offer any references,' Roddy tried again. 'Why was that?'

'I'm from Perth,' Sandy said, as if that were an explanation. He winked at Della. 'That's Scotland, not Australia.'

'So where did you work in Perth, Scotland?' Della asked.

'Och, all over.' Sandy shrugged. 'The Leather Bottle, The Brazen Head, The Caravel, The Fountain.' He tried again. 'The Brass Button.'

'As a chef?' Della asked.

'Chef, bottle boy, barman – whatever was needed.' Sandy threw out his arms to show he was eager. 'I'll do anything.'

'Have you worked in a hotel?' Roddy asked.

'I started my training a few years ago – at the... The Queen's.' Sandy didn't seem too sure.

'Where's that?' Della was confused.

'The Queen's... Hotel in... Riddrie, in the north-east of Glasgow – that's in Scotland too.'

Roddy shook his head. 'It rings a bell.'

'Och, it was a great place to train,' Sandy enthused. 'Great teachers there. I did everything – bread, pastry, dinners.' He added as an afterthought, 'Puddings – all the puddings.' He took a breath. 'Stew.'

'So how long did you train for?' Della asked.

'Two and a half years – but they let me off with good behaviour.' Sandy laughed. He looked around for approval at two mystified faces, so he assumed a serious expression.

'So when did you qualify?' Roddy asked.

'Three months ago,' Sandy admitted.

'And where did you work for the last three months?' Roddy tried again.

'I came to Skye, found a place for my family. I live in Armadale. It's not far from here. I could come in on my bike.'

'Motorbike?' Roddy asked.

'Yamaha V-Star 250.' Sandy gave his most pleading look. 'I really would love to work here, honestly.'

'Why?' Della asked.

'Who wouldn't?' Sandy's eyes were wide. 'Beautiful place, the old-fashioned feel to it, and the chance of working in this gorgeous kitchen.'

'So...' Roddy unfolded a piece of paper from his pocket. It had questions scribbled down in biro. 'So, let's say, hypothetically, a man and his son arrive for their first night here, and it's December, like it is now. What would you feed them for dinner?'

'Well, I'd look in the cupboards and see what there was in stock.'
Sandy examined Roddy's face for approval and tried again. 'Maybe
they'd like a jacket potato – have you got a microwave?' He shook his
head. 'Maybe the son would like chips – all kids like chips.'

'They're adults,' Roddy said.

'Och, I know, I'd make them oysters. That's posh, isn't it?
They'd enjoy that. Or...' Sandy was clearly just saying the first
thing that came into his head. He frowned at Roddy's expres-
sionless face. 'Mackerel, herring – that's cheap to buy on the
island. It would save you money. And for pudding, I'd... I'd make
jam sponge and custard... or... ice cream... maybe something
else...' His voice trailed off. 'What do you think I should make?'

'Maybe you should ask them what they like,' Della
suggested. 'What if they were vegetarian? Vegan?'

'I'd tell them to change. I'd offer them a big juicy steak each.
They'd probably love it,' Sandy joked. His face fell: no one else
was smiling. 'Look – I'm messing this up. I always talk nonsense
and try to make people laugh when I'm nervous. It's because I
really want his job. But I can cook – and bake.' He turned his
attention to the plastic box. 'I made these for you.' He tugged off
the lid and displayed the contents.

Roddy gaped at a selection of perfect cakes and pastries.
'What do we have here?'

Sandy pointed at each one. 'Scottish Fruited Gingerbread,
Melting Moments biscuits, little Dundee cakes, Clootie
Dumplings, Scottish Scones.' He offered his most persuasive
smile. 'I was always making them at the... Queen's. Try one. You
won't be disappointed.'

Della selected a fruity bun. 'What's this, did you say?'

'Clootie Dumplings. Clootie means cloth. It's dried fruit,
spices, oatmeal or breadcrumbs, flour, and beef suet. It's boiled
or steamed.'

Della licked her lips. 'Delicious. A bit like a Christmas pudding. I can imagine this with cream or ice cream as a dessert.'

Roddy tried one.

'Lovely texture. Perfect.'

Sandy was pleased with himself. 'You could have it here on Burns Night with a wee dram and custard or ice cream.'

Della picked up a cherry-topped biscuit and took a bite. 'This is so crumbly – it's divine.'

'Melting moments.' Sandy was delighted. 'Like kisses from the sugar fairy.'

'And you made these?' Roddy asked, helping himself to gingerbread.

'For my interview. I thought I'd let the baking do the talking.'

'And is all your cooking this good?' Della asked.

'Better.' Sandy paused. There was no sound but for the munching – Roddy had started on a scone. 'Oh, please – give us the job,' Sandy begged. 'I have a partner to support and a four-year-old lassie. I'd work my arse off for you – I mean...' He grinned to cover his embarrassment. 'I'd be really good, I promise.'

'Well – we'll let you know...' Roddy said. Sandy's face fell.

Della tugged Roddy to one side and whispered in his ear. 'Why don't we set him a test and how he gets on?'

'How would we do that?'

'Get him to make a meal for everyone.'

Roddy nodded. 'OK. Whatever you think. Can you organise that?'

'I can.' Della walked back to Sandy, who had started to stroll around the kitchen, opening the oven doors, touching the work-tops. 'Sandy – how would a trial suit you?'

'A trial? Why – what have I done?' Sandy laughed. 'Och, you mean a trial at the job, here? I'd love that.'

'Right. So here's your first big event. Tomorrow night I'd like you to prepare a meal for eight guests – one's a vegetarian. I want a starter, something we can all share, so a veggie starter for eight. Then a fish course for the seven of us and a tasty veggie option for one, and then a delicious dessert...' She pointed towards the plastic box. 'I know you have loads of potential. But Roddy's offering you a chance here – the meal needs to be ready for seven-thirty. And I'll be your sous chef, plate up, wait on the table. How's that?'

'I reckon I can cook something and serve it up myself.' Sandy scratched his head. 'And if I do well and pass the test, do I get to stay in the job?'

'We'll see how you go – but, yes,' Roddy said.

'Och, thanks, thank you...' Sandy shook Roddy's hand, then Della's, his grin wider than ever. 'You won't regret taking me on. I'll be in at noon tomorrow and get set up. I couldn't be happier. And I'll be in Shona's good books – you wait until I tell her...'

'Is that your wife?' Roddy asked.

'Partner, yes. She'll be over the moon.' Sandy clicked the lid on the plastic box, tugged on the anorak. 'Right, I'll be seeing you tomorrow. I'll take the rest of the cakes home – my little one loves my baking.' He winked. 'Nice to meet you both.' And with that he hurried out of the kitchen.

'Well,' Roddy said tentatively. 'It seems that we have a chef.'

'Perhaps.' Della was not sure. 'We'll just have to wait until tomorrow and see if he's any good...'

23

Tuesday was one of those bright days where the sky was a wide canopy of blue, crammed with clouds, a perfect day for an outing. The snow had dissolved into slushy puddles, the roads were open and the air was sharp and pure. Murdo suggested at breakfast that, given the success of his trip with Tess to the Old Man of Storr, complete with the best Cullen Skink on the island in a local pub, he'd take everyone out for the day. He wanted to devise a trip for everyone: Robin could take lots more photos of glorious archaeological sites, Rose would be treated to wonderful views without having to walk far, and everyone would experience the delights of Skye. He offered to lead the way in the Land Rover with Tess, Della, Rose and Daz, and Robin could follow with Jamie in their car.

Roddy, of course, had to stay behind in the hotel. He was, after all, owner-manager and there was work to be done. He looked nervous, muttering more than once that he hoped Isla wouldn't turn up and even more that she wouldn't bring Alasdair Barclay. He was still anxious about her threats.

'Hang on in there until lunchtime,' Tess soothed. 'The new chef will be here and, by all accounts, he'll be able to take care of you if Isla shows up.'

'Oh, I hope it works out with him,' Della said. 'We only have a few days left. It would be great if you had proper staff in place by then.'

'Just imagine if the business took off. Isla and I never had more than three rooms filled, four at Hogmanay, and in the summer, either we were rushed off our feet or it was deadly quiet. But we've got more bookings for December,' Roddy murmured.

'Don't worry – I'll have everyone back before dark, and we'll take a look at bookings. I'm thrilled you've offered the "See Skye with Murdo" trips on the website,' Murdo said.

'Della's idea.' Tess linked an arm through her friend's.

'There have been lots of enquiries about it,' Roddy said happily. 'Especially the Northern Lights.'

'That's the reason I came here – I can't wait to see them,' Tess agreed.

'I'd love to see them too,' Robin murmured. 'How incredible to see the skies lit up, as they've been for millions of years.'

'I'll keep an eye on the aurora forecast,' Murdo promised.

'I'd come back just for that,' Rose said.

'Let's get on. Later, we'll make an evening of it.' Tess led the way to the door, with a wave to Roddy. 'And don't get in any trouble. And if Isla comes here, just find one of your grandad's chamber pots and throw it over her head.'

'Exactly.' Rose was wrapped in her warmest coat and the furry hat. She offered Daz her arm, leaning on it heavily. 'I'm looking forward to seeing the sights and sounds of Skye. I have to say, I'm a bit sad. Daz and I will be back in Paris by the weekend...'

'Paris though.' Jamie glanced towards Daz. Daz held his eyes for a moment and exhaled deeply.

'Right, let's hit the road... gently,' Murdo said with a smile. 'I promise you – this will be the best tour you'll get on Skye.'

* * *

True to his word, Murdo packed lots into the day. They visited the High Pasture Cave first, which everyone loved – a huge mound in grassland, the mountains looming behind. Robin had been excited beyond belief: he'd rushed round in a frenzy, muttering, 'The Mesolithic... remains... evidence of humans... Iron Age... rituals... deities.'

Tess admired his passion and she had to agree that, another time, delving into the cave itself would be fascinating.

Rose loved the Fairy Pools, clear water at the foot of the Black Cuillin mountains. Everyone had walked around while she and Della, who tried not to complain that the sciatica in her back was playing her up after all the cooking, took photos to send to Pam and Jen. Rose was so proud of the pictures of the fountains, the black mountains behind swathed in chiffon mist, that she sent some to Monty in Paris.

Jen and Pam immediately replied with lots of their own. Jen sent a photo of herself smiling enigmatically in an evening dress, posing on deck with a man in a tuxedo. She was holding a cocktail of some sort, a white drink filled with ice. Behind her there were equally white mountains covered in more ice. Pam sent photos of Elvis posing in front of the turquoise sea in Crete, another of her swimming with the little spaniel – Rose wondered who had taken it. She was pleased that both women had managed to make friends on their holidays. Looking at Jen, perhaps she had made more than a friend of the handsome man in the tux.

Murdo took everyone to a small café for hot drinks before driving them to Dunscaith Castle. Robin forged ahead, camera in his hand, then Daz and Jamie followed behind, talking, their heads close. Rose was able to manage only a short walk between Della and Tess because the ground was stony, but she was delighted with her progress. She paused to take photos while the others went on ahead. The ruins were dramatic, and the view from the top down to the swirling sea was spectacular. Murdo hurried down the hill and lifted Rose on his back, bleating into the wind about how the castle was a prehistoric fort, but the ruins were built by the MacDonald Clan of Sleat in the thirteenth or fourteenth century. Rose told him she didn't want to be carried around like a toddler and hit him playfully with her small fists until he relented and took her back to the Land Rover.

The skies were darkening as they drove home, Rose almost asleep on Daz's shoulder, Robin and Jamie in the car behind. Della was talking excitedly about the evening meal, wondering what the new chef would cook. He'd be there now, organising dinner, if he'd turned up.

Tess's eyes were on Murdo as he drove along the road, negotiating the last of the melting drifts of snow. She muttered, 'You're a great driver, Murdo. So sensible.'

He didn't reply for a moment, then he said, 'Old age, Tess – that's what's calmed me down, and the experience of life's lessons. I haven't always been steady. I was a boy racer in my time.' He laughed, a single bark. 'You saw me on the beach when you and Della first came, drunk in charge of a quad bike.' He shook his head. 'I'm trying my best.'

'You are,' Tess said quietly. Della was listening now. 'You haven't... overdone it since the whisky tasting.'

'Oh, I had a bellyful that day. It was a mistake.' Murdo gave a shuddering sigh. 'I was ashamed of myself, being sick.'

Tess patted his shoulder. 'You're a changed man.'

'Och, I'm not going on a bender now if I can help it. If I overstep the line, I lose all sense.'

'You're impressive, Murdo,' Della said.

'It's thanks to you and Tess.' Murdo glanced at Della. 'You've both been amazing.'

'Have we?' Tess was mystified. She didn't think she'd done anything.

'I lost my wife in an accident and I've been beating myself up over it ever since. If I'd done something different, maybe Mairi would be alive. But since you two came here...' Murdo said. 'I don't know what it is. I suppose you've given me a purpose, got me to help Roddy more, to keep myself busy. You're a good influence.'

'So, when we go back to England, will you be able to stay sober?' Della asked kindly.

'I think the whisky tasting was the last straw. It brought me up sharp. I realised how stupid I looked. That and...' Murdo caught Tess's eye. 'I offended you on the beach – with what I said. I was mortified that the drink could make me so rude.'

'You didn't cover yourself with glory.' Tess laughed.

'It's been an honour meeting you both,' Murdo said quietly. 'I'll miss you when you go.'

'Oh, I'm sure we'll come back before too long,' Tess said cheerily. 'Won't we, Della?'

Della nodded. 'All my memories are at home though. They're waiting for me... as soon as I walk through that door, they'll be there.'

'Are you worried about it?' Tess pressed her hand. 'Has it been bothering you?'

'I'm not sure. Coming here has helped me see the world in perspective.' Della sniffed. 'But I don't know how I'll feel when I walk into that house and all Sylvester's things are there. I suppose I have to face it but – I'm not sure if I'm ready for how much it's going to hurt...'

Tess squeezed her hand. At that moment, a ringtone came from the back of the car and Daz could be heard talking into his mobile in fast French. They were not far from the hotel now. Tess had to admit, she was feeling strangely troubled. Whether it was what Della had just said about going home to the house that held so many memories, or Murdo's conversation about his wife's death, or that Rose was leaving for Paris tomorrow, or simply that when she left Skye, she'd have to face up to the fact that the house she lived in had been sold and she'd need to pack up and move. She felt ungrounded and ill at ease.

* * *

Eight people sat around the table, dressed for dinner apart from Murdo, who was in a checked shirt, jeans and his cap. Tess and Della wore pretty dresses; Roddy, Robin and Jamie wore crisp shirts and Daz was in a burgundy velvet suit. Rose had on a long red dress with a huge flower corsage and a little fascinator with a net veil. They were drinking wine except Murdo, who had a small glass of beer. The conversation buzzed about the places they'd visited, but everyone was aware of the amazing savoury aromas that were drifting from the kitchen.

Tess asked, 'I wonder what he's cooking?'

'He's been in there since midday with the door shut.' Roddy shook his head. 'He came here on a clapped-out motorbike, in those shorts and that anorak, and he had a bag on his back

crammed with stuff. He told me to stay away – he wanted to surprise us.'

'Maybe he's heating up a takeaway,' Murdo said.

Jamie sniffed the air. 'It smells like heaven.'

'I can smell cumin,' Rose said.

'No, you can't.' Daz laughed. 'How can anyone recognise cumin?'

'I have a delicate nose,' Rose retorted. 'I can sniff out a spice.'

'It's definitely spice,' Della agreed.

The kitchen door opened and Sandy emerged with a tray. He was wearing a white chef's uniform over his shorts; the top seemed to have been stained with red as if he'd committed murder. He placed the food in front of eight surprised faces.

'So, to start—' Sandy smiled '—here's freshly made hummus, flatbread, falafels and Fattoush. That's a salad with beans and bits of bread in. I have a bit of a Middle Eastern theme going on here tonight. So – eat up. Or if you like – *astamtie bitaeamik!*'

'My goodness me.' Rose gasped. 'Did you make all this today?'

Sandy beamed. 'I did. I had to work fast, mind. And when it came to the pudding, I made a bit of it at home this morning. But I wanted you to be impressed.'

'I am.' Roddy's eyes were wide.

Tess was already digging in. 'Mmm...'

'Sublime,' Robin said.

'This is gorgeous,' Della added.

'What a feast.' Daz was pouring wine.

Sandy strutted away like a little rooster, pleased with himself. By the time the starter was finished, he was back to take away the bowls, returning with more food. He piled it on the table with a flourish.

'So – here we have baked fish with cumin, za'atar and sumac butter, a huge roasted vegetable tagine to share, buttery couscous and a little tabbouleh...'

The guests stared at the food, colourful as jewels. Sandy was unsure about their reaction. 'It was hard to get pomegranate for the tabbouleh but I managed to persuade a mate to bring me one from Inverness.'

'You've gone to so much trouble,' Roddy said.

'Och, I have most of the spices at home – I like to use them,' Sandy murmured.

Rose said, 'We eat Moroccan in Paris a lot, but this is incredible.'

'Where did you learn to cook like this?' Daz asked, amazed.

'The Queen's cooking school,' Sandy said. 'Enjoy your meal.'

'We certainly will.' Robin licked his lips. 'I'm booking another visit here if the food's like this. I have a lot more work to do on Skye on hunter-gatherers... and everything's just so nice.'

'I'd definitely come back,' Jamie said.

'So would I,' Rose agreed. 'People would travel miles for this food.'

Sandy sashayed back to the kitchen whistling, and Rose leaned towards Roddy. 'Where did you find him?'

'He's local – I can hardly believe my luck.' Roddy turned to Della. 'What do you think?'

'Sign him up as quickly as you can,' Della whispered.

'He's amazing,' Rose said. 'And I love his tattoos. Do you remember when we were in Paris with Pam and Jen and we got a tattoo each?'

'We did,' Della said. 'The word "Paris" and a heart.'

Tess flashed a smile. 'Mine will probably never be seen by the human eye again, not even my own, but I know where it is.'

Murdo's expression was pure admiration. He raised his glass. 'To some of the most incredible people I ever met.'

'Cheers to that,' Robin said.

They ate and drank for a while, talking softly, making low sounds of contentment, then Sandy returned to take the plates. Della said, 'That was gorgeous – I can't wait for dessert.'

'You know your job hangs on it?' Daz joked.

'It doesn't at all – the job's his,' Roddy said quickly.

Sandy was back soon with a tray of honeyed baklava and a silky, creamy dessert in glasses with jewelled rose petals on top.

'Whatever is this?' Rose asked.

'Oh, they are easier to make than you'd think. I whipped them up – they are *muhallebi*,' Sandy said. 'Almonds, pistachios, cardamom, cinnamon. And each portion is less than 150 calories.'

'Where did you get rose petals on Skye?' Roddy asked, amazed.

'Och, I have this friend in Inverness,' Sandy said enigmatically.

'Well, this is brilliant.' Murdo raised his beer glass. 'How about a toast to the hotel's new chef?'

'Indeed.' Roddy lifted his glass with a flourish. 'To Sandy.'

'To Sandy,' everyone chorused.

'I don't think I ever ate such food,' Robin said. 'I live off lentil stew.'

'Well,' Rose said as she dug her spoon into the creamy dessert. 'I wonder what we'll be eating tomorrow night. I expect we'll be stuck on a train somewhere with a sandwich.'

'No – not exactly.' Daz pulled a face. 'There's something I need to tell you, Rose. I suppose now's as good a time as any.'

'Oh?' Rose looked worried. 'What's happened?'

Tess leaned forwards. 'Is something the matter, Daz?'

'I had a phone call from Monty this afternoon, on the way back,' Daz began, picking up a hunk of baklava. He shoved it into his mouth. 'Monty's is closed.'

'Closed?' Rose was incredulous.

'For the foreseeable. Food poisoning. So – Roddy...' Daz said encouragingly. 'I don't suppose Rose and I can hang onto the family room a little longer?'

24

The following morning, as Tess and Della came downstairs, they could smell sizzling eggs and roasting coffee. Rose, Daz, Robin and Jamie were already at the table filling their faces. Roddy was pouring drinks into guests' cups.

'Our new chef turned up bright and early. He's even got porridge on the go, with maple syrup.'

'Oh, yes, please,' Tess said as she sat down.

Rose flourished a spoon. 'He's put cinnamon in it. Highly recommended.'

'And,' Daz said excitedly, 'guess what?'

'We're staying another day too.' Jamie was delighted.

'It's a perfect day for research.' Robin was already looking at a map. 'Rose and Daz are coming with us.'

'That might be an interesting jaunt,' Rose said.

'It will be,' Daz agreed, his eyes moving to Jamie.

'So what will we do with ourselves, Tess? I suppose we could stay here and read?' Della asked. She looked around a little anxiously. She'd enjoyed cooking and helping out. Now she'd be left alone with her thoughts.

'Murdo's out the back chopping wood. Maybe when he's finished, we can ask him to drive you somewhere...' Roddy said.

'Or,' Tess said, 'what about a girls' day out, a Hens' reunion, like we had in Paris?'

'Can I change my mind about going to look at dinosaur footprints?' Rose asked. 'I think I'll leave the men to their hunter-gatherers and come with you. Where shall we go?'

'Portree,' Tess exclaimed. 'There's shopping and places we can eat and things to do. I'll drive.'

'I'd love that,' Della said.

'Perfect.' Rose ruffled Daz's hair. 'I'll take my walking stick. I'm sure I can toddle around a few shops by myself.' She winked. 'Neither of us need a chaperone today.'

* * *

Rose huddled in her warm coat next to Tess as she drove the Fiat 500 out of Sleat, along the coastal road, passing Armadale, where Sandy lived. The roads were clear now, hardly any evidence that it had snowed except for the white mountain peaks. Della sat in the back, staring through the window at the sparkling sea. She sighed. 'Skye is such a peaceful place.'

'It is,' Rose agreed. 'Too peaceful, perhaps. It needs The Hens to liven it up.'

'It's over an hour to Portree,' Tess said. 'So – what shall we do when we get there?'

'I'm looking things up on my phone.' Della started to read. '"The main town on the Isle of Skye is a bustling port and a thriving cultural centre."'

'The main town. There's only one.' Tess laughed.

'It's got a harbour with fishing boats and pleasure craft,' Della said.

'Pleasure craft?' Tess joked. 'I can imagine a big Scot in a boat in a breeze with a kilt and no boxers.'

Della chose to ignore her and read on. '"Excellent leisure facilities – swimming pool, pony-trekking and shopping opportunities".'

'Ooh, tell me about the shopping opportunities,' Rose said.

Della thumbed her phone. 'Galleries – batik shops – crafts, soap – more galleries – whisky shop.'

'It's hardly Paris.' Rose groaned.

'We could go horse riding... try archery?' Della suggested.

'I'm making progress, Della, but I'm not bloody Robin Hood,' Rose said grimly.

'So what shall we do?' Della asked.

'Leave it to me.' Tess winked in the driver's mirror. 'It's not about the quality of the shops – it's about the calibre of the shoppers. You wait and see...'

* * *

It was almost midday when Tess drove into Portree. It was the prettiest place. The harbour made her catch her breath, a row of brightly coloured houses lining the edge of the water. Behind, a church loomed, majestic.

Rose sighed. 'Oh, the peace. I could live here.'

Tess laughed. 'What would you do for fun? You wouldn't have Monty's club.'

'Monty's is closed until further notice,' Rose said, hugging Della's arm. 'Daz said three customers complained about tummy ache after eating dodgy chicken. There will be all sorts of investigations into food hygiene. The girls are annoyed about losing work.'

'Girls?' Della asked.

'Peaches and Ida have been keeping me in touch with what's going on – it seems Monty's taken off to Brazil in a huff.' Rose gazed around. 'But it's so peaceful here. A good place to heal.' She squeezed Della's arm. 'How are you doing?'

'As expected,' Della said. 'Some days are better than others. But...' She met Tess's eyes. 'I'll always be grateful that you brought me here. I'd be alone at home stuck with my grief...' Her eyes filled.

Rose gave a grim smile as she hobbled towards the centre of town. Little shops and houses crowded around the corner; behind her was the wide blue arc of the sea and snow-iced mountains stretching to the clouds.

'We'll have a great time today. My treat. After all, I seem to have more money than I know what to do with nowadays. The flat in Paris costs me hardly anything as Daz covers it, and my house is sold.'

'Oh...' Tess took in her words.

'You can stay with me,' Della said quickly.

'Jen and Pam said the same.' Tess felt her mood sink. She would be homeless when she got back: it was like being out in the open sea on a raft. In the rain. By herself. Despite the loyalty of her friends, she felt a keen sense that her future was up in the air.

'You can stay with me and Daz in Paris,' Rose offered. 'I do feel responsible. I should have sold you my house.'

'It would still be out of my price range,' Tess said. 'There are some pretty little terraced cottages near Pam's. I might have a look in the new year.'

'What will you do, Rose?' Della asked.

'It all depends on this bloody stroke.' Rose was slowing down, leaning on her stick. 'I need to get my right hand playing piano again, or I can't work. I love being in Paris but it would be intolerable if Daz was performing and I was stuck in a poky flat all day. I'd rather be here.'

Tess agreed. 'It's certainly pretty.' She surveyed a huddle of buildings, pink, white. 'So – what shall we do first?'

'I might buy souvenirs – something for Aston's and Linval's kids,' Della said.

'Oh, look.' Rose pointed. 'A clothes shop.'

'Where?' Tess was staring around, looking for a window full of fashions. There was none to be seen.

Rose pointed her stick. 'There.'

Della and Tess stared at a sign, The Highland Hiker. In the window were wax coats, boots, tartan scarves, an array of woolly hats.

'Come on, girls, we're on Skye – we need to look the part.'

'What part?' Tess asked.

Rose stared at Tess's jeans, old trainers, at Della's cheap walking boots, and she urged everyone forward, her stick banging on the pavement. Excitedly, she hurried into the shop, Tess and Della at her shoulders, blinking in the bright lights, taking in the variety of country wear.

A man approached them, lean, sombre. He drawled, 'How can I help you, madam?'

Rose lifted her stick. 'We are ladies of leisure and we want to be kitted out as such for our Highland holiday. So, if you please, young man...' she indicated Tess and Della, who stood next to her, mouths open '...I want three wax jackets, three scarves, three warm hats, three fleecy gilets and three pairs of sturdy walking boots.'

'Oh.' The man took a step back.

'In whatever colour these ladies want. But for me – the more purple I can get into my wardrobe, the better I like it.'

* * *

Half an hour later, Rose, Della and Tess emerged, three smart country ladies. Rose had insisted they wear their new purchases and carry their old clothes in bags. Della was sombre in a green jacket and matching hat with tan boots, but Tess and Rose had chosen the loudest colours they could find. Tess teamed a yellow Deerhunter hat and jacket with lurid orange boots. Rose had bought herself a purple knitted hat with an outrageously large bobble, a purple padded jacket and red rambling boots. She had insisted on buying three matching tartan scarves, insisting that it was the nearest they'd get in Portree to sharing a tattoo.

The three friends swayed from The Highland Hiker, arms around each other, and Tess said, 'So, what now? I feel dressed for archery.'

Della said, 'I read they do axe throwing... I'm up for that.'

'Axe throwing?' Rose lifted her weak arm. 'With my luck, I'd kill the instructor.'

'So how about a drink?' Tess suggested.

'I'd love a hot chocolate.' Della's eyes lit up.

'Right, I know.' Rose pointed to a majestic building that spanned the corner of the road. In large gold letters, the words 'Grand Highland Hotel' could be seen, and beneath that, the words 'Black Stag Bar' and 'Grill and Tearooms'. 'That's the place,' she declared firmly.

'It looks expensive.' Della hesitated.

'All the better – my treat.' Rose was already hobbling forwards.

'Oh, we can't let you...' Tess began, but Rose gave her a stern look.

'For goodness' sake, Tess, I'm almost eighty, I've had a stroke, I've sold my house. And I'm a working woman with plenty of savings.' She was deadly serious. 'Poor Della's lost her soulmate, you've got rid of a man who was nothing better than a ball and chain. Now, tell me, what are we three ladies of leisure going to do with ourselves on the beautiful Isle of Skye?' She banged her stick impatiently on the ground like a purple Gandalf and grinned. 'Are you going to stand there all day gawping? Come on – this is the grandest hotel in Portree.'

'It's the only hotel in Portree,' Tess said, but there was no telling Rose anything.

* * *

Rose leaned against the bar, flanked by Della and Tess, watching a handsome young man in a crisp white shirt and a tartan bow tie arranging glasses. He approached them, all smiles. His name badge said he was called Jun.

Rose called out amiably. 'Hello, Jun. What do you have for us today? We are three young ladies in search of perfection.'

Jun's smile grew wider. He pushed a hand through thick black hair. 'Do you mean food, drink or the bartender?'

Tess was in her element. 'All three.'

'Don't forget you're driving,' Della whispered nervously.

'So,' Rose said. 'Tell us about this place.'

'The Grand Highland Hotel is the best on Skye,' Jun said proudly. 'We are surrounded here by the majestic Cuillin Mountain range and we offer a warm Highland welcome. We serve breakfast, lunch, high tea, and the restaurant is open in the evening for fine dining. Our wood-burning stoves create a cosy atmosphere. Live music is played on Friday and Saturdays...'

'You've been on the course.' Tess was impressed.

'It's a lovely place.' Della looked around at soft lighting, the burgundy and cream walls, a roaring fire in the hearth, surrounded by armchairs at the end of the bar. Various stags' heads stared down from the walls. A pair of ancient silver swords hung over the door marked 'Toilets'.

Jun waved towards a chalk board with a menu. 'I can offer you lunch. Today our special is Cajun-spiced buttermilk fried chicken, brioche roll, garlic mayo, gem lettuce and tomato.'

'Shall we have that?' Tess said excitedly.

'Definitely,' Della agreed.

'Three of those, please – and do you have mocktails?' Tess asked.

'We do.' Jun nodded. 'I can do virgin mojitos or a delicious alcohol-free passion-fruit martini.'

'Yes to the passion fruit,' Tess and Della chorused.

'For me too,' Rose said. 'But put the alcohol back in mine. I'm recovering from a stroke. I need all the help I can get.' She noticed Tess and Della glaring at her.

Tess said, 'Maybe a mocktail for now, Rose?'

Rose pulled a face. 'All right – I'll have the alcohol-free one.'

'Would you like to sit over there, by the fire?' Jun indicated a table with three wing-backed armchairs.

'Perfect,' Rose said.

'I'll bring everything over.' Jun accepted Rose's card. 'My pleasure.'

'Do you know, I play piano in one of the best drag clubs in Paris?' Rose said with a flourish.

'I didn't know that.' Jun didn't bat an eyelid. 'But it doesn't surprise me at all, madam.'

* * *

The fire crackled and roared, the light reflecting in their glasses, dancing in the pale liquid. Rose snuggled in the high-backed chair, mayonnaise on her lips. She said, 'This is bloody lovely.'

Della smiled fondly. 'It's been special today.'

'The holiday's not over yet,' Tess said. 'We've still got a few more days.'

'A few more days? Rubbish.' Rose snorted. 'Is there somewhere you have to be?'

'Our flight back is at the weekend,' Della said, nibbling brioche.

'Oh, the world won't come to an end if we don't get on a plane or a train.' Rose said. 'I spent too much of my life abiding by rules. I'm not going to do it now.'

Tess agreed. 'I see what you mean.'

'Besides, it's comfy at The Gilded Chicken, or whatever the hotel is called.' Rose glanced around. 'I could do with bringing Roddy here to pick up a few tips. Look at the décor, the warm welcome, the choices. This place has confidence in itself. Roddy's a half-hearted host.'

'Poor Roddy,' Della said. 'It's good that he has Sandy, but he's still quite... I don't know...'

'Nervous?' Tess suggested. 'It's like he's defeated before he starts.'

'I know that feeling. His wife has given his confidence a battering. She rearranged him and made him weak, then she left him and he doesn't know what to do,' Rose said. 'Being married to Bernard was just the same, even though I loved him. It was like I had nothing else than to be a good wife. My self-fulfilment never mattered.'

'That's exactly what Alan wanted, a good little wife,' Tess said. 'No wonder I failed.'

'I was so lucky,' Della whispered.

Rose leaned over and took her hand. 'But we're conquerors,

superstars. We defy the stereotype. We're strong, we're survivors. We're rebels.'

'We are.' Tess smiled. 'I fancy myself as a rebel.'

'But do you fancy Murdo?' Rose asked directly, and Tess felt her cheeks tingle. She didn't know, but it was embarrassing Rose thought she might.

'What on earth makes you think that?' Tess wondered if she was protesting too much.

'He's nice,' Della said. 'You get on well.'

'Murdo gets on with all of us,' Tess said by way of an excuse. 'I think he's grieving.'

'He is.' Della made a sympathetic face. 'We all have our different ways of dealing with it.'

'He lost his wife.' Tess sipped from her glass. 'It's hard sometimes to move forward.' She met Della's eyes. 'You're doing so well.'

'I'm doing what I can.' Della shook her head. 'It's a long road.'

Rose raised her weaker arm. 'The long road to recovery.' She moved her fingers as if playing the piano. 'I'm determined to have the movement back by Christmas.'

'Why Christmas?' Tess asked.

'Why not?' Rose replied enigmatically. She stared around at the high ceiling, the roaring fire, the strategically placed stags on the walls, and licked her lips thoughtfully. There was no one at the bar. She held up her glass and called over.

'Three more mocktails, please, Jun. And could you bring the dessert menu?'

25

Dinner that evening was delicious, although Tess and Della weren't hungry after their long lunch. Sandy had made what he now called the 'Sicín Órga Scottish Menu', consisting of Cullen Skink, beef stew and tatties, and cranachan for dessert. Despite not being hungry, Tess polished off two helpings of whisky-laced creamy oats and raspberries, announcing that she loved Scottish food. Sandy winked and said, 'Tomorrow's pudding's deep-fried Mars bars, then...' Apparently, they were his daughter Maisie's favourite. Rose told him that she was willing to try anything once.

The group sat in the lounge in front of the fire with coffee. Roddy asked Sandy to join them and Murdo announced that he'd give him and his little motorbike a lift back to Armadale. Sandy placed a plate of freshly baked shortbreads on the coffee table and said he'd be happy to stay for a while; Shona would have put Maisie to bed and she'd be watching the soaps. Sandy didn't like soaps – he said there was too much crime.

Rose sat on the sofa, Daz on one side and Jamie on the other, almost as if she was keeping them apart. She asked, 'How were the hunter-gatherers?'

Daz and Jamie exchanged glances. Robin, stretched in a chair, murmured into his cup, 'Wonderful. I had such a good time on An Corran Beach.' He smiled indulgently. 'Of course, it was windy and cold. The boys went to the pub.'

'Did they?' Rose gave Daz a light dig in the ribs.

'But I enjoyed the research,' Robin admitted. 'I'm used to my own company.'

'Too used to it, Dad,' Jamie murmured.

'It was a good day for me too,' Roddy said. 'I've taken more bookings. The website is drawing attention and Isla's stayed away.' He made a hopeful face. 'Perhaps she's given up.'

'Or biding her time,' Murdo said cynically. He turned to Tess, who was sitting in front of the fire on a rug with Della. 'How was Portree?'

'Oh, so pretty. The harbour's lovely, the mountains all around.' Tess's cheeks flushed in the firelight.

'Rose bought some lovely clothes,' Della said.

'And we went for lunch in the best hotel on Skye,' Rose explained. 'I picked up lots of tips, Roddy.'

'The Grand Highland,' Roddy said, closing his eyes dreamily. 'I'd love to be the south Skye version of it.'

'It's simply a matter of keeping a positive outlook,' Rose said firmly. 'If you want something, if you believe it will happen, then you're halfway there.' She wiggled her fingers. 'I managed to play quite a bit of "Gimme! Gimme! Gimme!" with both hands tonight...'

'I heard you.' Daz smiled. 'You're making good progress.' He grunted. 'Although I don't know what's happening at Monty's. I was texting Elton Joan today and it seems there's discontent amongst the artistes, what with Monty clearing off to São Paulo.'

'It will be what it will be,' Rose said. 'So – how about a game of cribbage?'

'What's cribbage?' Sandy asked. 'It sounds dirty.'

'It's a card game.' Tess stifled a laugh.

'What about strip poker instead?' Daz's eyes sparkled.

'I know a good drinking game.' Murdo winked and Tess threw a shortbread biscuit at him. He gobbled it up in one mouthful.

'Can you book Daz and me until the weekend?' Rose stretched her sore arm. 'I'm not ready to go home.' She winked at Daz. 'Stuff the train tickets. We'll get more.'

'I'm up for it,' Daz agreed.

'The room's yours.' Roddy's face broke into a smile. 'I'll crack open a bottle of Scotch.'

'Just a soft drink for me,' Murdo announced, with a peek towards Della and Tess to check they were impressed.

'I know what we'll do.' Rose's eyes gleamed with mischief. 'Let's play Truth or Dare.'

'Truth or Dare?' Robin repeated.

Daz rubbed his hands together. 'Oh yes. It's a blast.'

'What are the rules?' Jamie asked nervously.

'We play it a lot backstage with the girls at Monty's... and by the end of the night there are no holds barred.' Rose pressed her lips together to hide a smile. 'You'll soon pick it up.'

Daz was taking it seriously. 'We have to agree two things up front first.'

'What are they?' Jamie raised an eyebrow.

'In Paris we drink after every question, and no one's allowed to be offended,' Rose explained.

'Alcohol?' Murdo leaned forward eagerly. 'I'll fetch the whisky, shall I?'

'Are you sure?' Tess asked anxiously.

'I'm a new man.' Murdo grinned. 'I'll pace myself.'

'I won't drink – I'll drive you home, Sandy,' Roddy offered.

'I'll go with you,' Della said. 'I won't drink either, but I'll play the game.'

'Is alcohol a good idea with such personal questions?' Tess asked Murdo.

'Depends on the questions,' Murdo grinned.

'Game on,' Tess said.

'We're off home tomorrow, Jamie,' Robin said anxiously.

Jamie deliberately misunderstood him. 'Then it doesn't matter what we say, does it, Dad?'

'How do we play?' Robin asked.

'So, we spin the bottle, and whoever it points to gets to ask the question, truth or dare. They choose who they want to ask,' Daz explained.

'Who spins the bottle?' Della wanted to know.

'We take it in turns.' Rose rubbed her hands together, watching Roddy pour whisky into glasses, cola for himself and Della. 'I'll spin first.'

Sandy was on his phone. 'I've just told Shona I'll be a bit late – kept back for staff training.' He shrugged. 'She won't mind, she's pretty good, Shona. Until she loses her temper...' He mimed a punch on the nose.

The bottle was rotating. It pointed to Rose. Her face was gleeful as she launched in with the first question.

'I get to go. Right, Roddy – I choose you. Truth or dare?'

Roddy was nervous. 'Truth.'

'So, Roddy, tell the truth,' Rose said. 'What made you marry that appalling man-eater Isla?'

'Rose!' Tess exclaimed, shocked. 'That's a bit near the knuckle.'

'The game's hardly started.' Daz raised an eyebrow. 'After we finish a show at Monty's, Rose asks the most evil questions.'

Tess glanced at Robin, whose face was a picture. He'd never played such a game before. Tess hadn't either. Roddy looked mystified. He took a deep breath.

'Isla? Well, she seemed to like me. A lot. I was really flattered. She smiled at me all the time and then she asked me out.'

'Of course she did.' Tess snorted.

'Did she know you owned a big hotel?' Rose asked.

Roddy's eyebrows came together. 'Oh yes – she wanted to come round to see it on our first date. She was so excited by all the bedrooms that – we ended up spending the night in one. A four-poster. And by the end of a month, I'd proposed.' He looked around helplessly. 'She turned my head.'

Sandy helped him out. 'You're best rid of her, boss. It leaves the door open for someone who'll really get you. After all, there are plenty more fish in the loch.'

'There are,' Robin said softly and Tess downed her drink in one.

'My turn to spin.'

She twizzled the bottle. It pointed to Della.

'My question.' Della was thoughtful. 'And I pick you, Rose. Truth or dare?'

'Dare.' Rose met her eyes defiantly.

'Get Rose to show you her knickers,' Daz shouted out.

'I know the rules. I will if asked,' Rose retorted.

Della had decided on her question. 'Right... I dare you to... re-enact your favourite scene from a film.'

Rose thought for a minute, then she muttered, 'Got it!' She began to groan softly, moaning louder. Roddy looked extremely uncomfortable. Daz covered his mouth then fell about laughing. Rose grunted, guffawed, mooed and screamed, a crescendo of pain or ecstasy. Robin was completely confused as Rose threw her head back, growled and howled like a banshee.

Tess said drily, 'I'll have what she's having.'

Robin seemed to have no idea what had just happened. Everyone else in the room was in uproar. More whisky was poured and the bottle was whirled again, again and again.

An hour passed and the whisky bottle was empty. A second one had been found. Robin was asleep. Sandy had just been dared to perform a Highland jig and ended up spinning in a circle and falling on top of Roddy. The bottle was turned again and this time it pointed to Sandy.

He thought for a moment and he said, 'Right. I choose Della. Which is it to be, truth or dare?'

'Truth, always,' Della said confidently.

'So... you seem like a really saintly woman,' Sandy said and everyone laughed. He stared into his empty glass. 'Have you ever done anything that you really, really regret?'

Della thought for a moment, then she said, 'Yes, definitely.' She took a deep breath, all eyes on her. 'I should have used my voice more.'

'In what way?' Roddy asked. 'As a singer?'

'No – to stand up for myself.' Della's eyes flashed. 'As a woman, as an older woman, as a black woman. All the times I've put up with, you know, the looks, the innuendo, the whispered comments, the little incidents that added up, like being pushed back in a queue, being treated like I was invisible, the stares, the nasty smiles, the slurs. I wish I'd used my voice instead of being silent. I wish I'd told more people to – to – to piss off.'

There was a moment's silence then Rose applauded. 'Bravo, Della.' She raised her glass. 'Here's to using what we've learned as we've grown. There are moments in everyone's life when we need to just say it like it is.'

'I was too placid – I'd shrug things off, pretend they didn't matter. But now I'd be very different.' Della's eyes glowed. 'Oh yes, I can be fierce.'

'I'm pleased to hear it. Time to spin again,' Sandy said and the bottle was in motion.

It came to rest at Della, who offered a mischievous expression and said, 'OK, Tess.'

Tess waved her hands excitedly. 'Oh, it's me. Oh, oh, I don't know – I'll do... I'll do truth.'

'Right.' Della took a breath. 'Tess – would you say as you've got older, you've got more comfortable in your own skin?'

'The truth?' Tess refilled her glass. She'd already drunk a lot. 'I suppose – I'd say no. I mean, I wasn't confident as a teenager – you know – I thought my thighs were too big, my stomach wasn't flat but... I was OK about myself before I met Alan. He didn't help. He was never very good with compliments.' She giggled, but that was more to do with the alcohol than the memory.

'A man should make a woman feel like a princess,' Sandy muttered.

'I agree, but it works two ways,' Della said. 'Men need their egos massaged too.'

'Definitely,' Murdo added, looking at his glass. He'd been sipping slowly. 'We aren't perfect and we don't want perfect women – we want that special one. Familiarity, love, the sense of being close to someone else and accepting who they are, totally.'

'Do you know?' Tess gulped her drink again. She was staring at him. 'I remember when I'd just given birth to one of the girls – I think it was Gemma – and the nurse said I should go and have a nice hot bath while the baby was asleep. I got into the water, and I saw myself in the mirror. I don't know why we women expect to have a flat stomach straight after giving birth. But I was horrified – my belly was like an empty carrier bag, floating in the bath water...'

Someone laughed once. Then the room went quiet while Tess finished her whisky and refilled her glass. 'I cried. Not because I was still a bit flabby. But because I was afraid that Alan would see me like that. I knew he'd criticise.'

Robin muttered something in his sleep that might have been, 'Disgusting.'

'He'd won the lottery, having you as a wife, a woman like you in his bed each night,' Murdo said. 'What an idiot that man was.'

'Shona was so gorgeous pregnant,' Sandy said. 'She had a hell of a temper on her though, every day.'

'Sylvester told me I was a goddess,' Della whispered. 'He'd say, you're a real woman, Della, to be held in my arms and loved...'

Tess refilled her glass. 'Alan was just a shit.'

'He was. Good riddance.' Rose spun the bottle. 'Jamie, it's your question.'

Everyone laughed in anticipation as Jamie gazed around the room. His eyes were glazed with too much drink. He checked to see if his father was asleep. Robin's head lolled to one side; he was snuffling in his chair. Jamie said, 'Daz, I choose you. Truth or dare?'

'Dare,' Daz replied coquettishly.

'Right – I dare you to... do a striptease.'

Daz was on his feet. 'Fully naked? You're on.'

'No – just the top half, please,' Roddy spluttered.

Everyone burst into song. 'Dah-dah-dah, dada-dah-dah...' Tess's voice was the loudest.

Rose was waving her arms and Sandy was on his feet clapping. Daz wiggled and posed, pouting as he undid each button of his shirt, wriggling it over his shoulders teasingly until he realised the cuffs were done up and he couldn't remove his hands. Everyone clapped and dissolved into peals of laughter. Daz hauled his shirt back on, sat down again and twisted the bottle. It rotated three times and pointed to...

'Rose again!' Daz said.

Rose's eyes glinted. 'My question. Truth or dare, Murdo?'

Murdo drained his glass. 'Truth's as good as anything – I'm not sure I could get up and do a dare. But I've had enough whisky – pass the cola.' Tess heaved the bottle towards him.

'So... the truth.' Rose glanced around at her audience. Everyone in the room watched her with an open mouth, although it was more drunken stupor than interest. 'Who in this room is your secret crush?'

Murdo shook his head. 'I don't know what that means.'

'Yes, you do,' Rose insisted. 'If you had to pick one person here who you fancy most, who would it be?'

Murdo looked round sheepishly and said, 'I don't know.'

'You have to say truthfully.' Rose leaned forward. Tess put her hand to warm cheeks.

'Mairi was the only one I ever truly loved. I gave her my heart, but...' Murdo took a deep breath. Everyone was waiting. 'I suppose now... there is someone I admire... a lot. I mean, I haven't known her for long but... I like her. She's sweet, kind, good-looking...'

Each person in the room leaned a little bit further forward.

'Och, I've drunk enough to tell the truth,' Murdo swigged from the cola bottle as if to give himself courage. 'So here goes. Rose, my secret is out. I think I'm developing a bit of a crush on...'

'Eeeeewww.' Tess felt her stomach clutch in a spasm and she realised she was feeling sick. Her head was swimming. Her eyes blurred and she couldn't focus. She groaned. 'I feel awful.

Whisky, all that cranachan and… no, I – I have to go…' She staggered from the room. Retching noises could be heard from the hall.

'That doesn't sound good,' Rose said.

'I'll go after her.' Della stood up.

'I'll help.' Murdo followed. There was the crashing of footsteps outside, more retching, then the room was silent.

'What happened?' Robin opened his eyes. 'Is – is it my turn to do truth or dare?'

'It's been a long night,' Daz said, and started to collect glasses.

'I think the party's over, Dad,' Jamie explained.

'I'll take you home, Sandy,' Roddy said.

'We've all had enough.' Rose eased herself from her seat. 'I don't know about the rest of you, but I'm just going to sit at the piano for half an hour and play that darned song again. Not that I'm expecting anyone to gimme a man after midnight. I'm afraid those days have long gone…'

26

It was quiet in the Land Rover as Roddy drove back to Armadale, Sandy and Della next to him in the front. Della had insisted on coming along – it was late, Roddy looked tired and she didn't like the idea of him driving back alone. He clearly wasn't used to Murdo's Land Rover; he kept crunching gears and lurching forward but, as he explained, Sandy would need his motorbike, which was stowed in the back.

Sandy cleared his throat. 'So, how do you think I'm getting on, boss?'

Roddy's eyes were on the road. 'I think you're doing great. So – if you're happy to have Mondays and Tuesdays off each week and work at weekends, the job's yours. What are you cooking tomorrow?'

Sandy tapped his nose. 'I'll do a banquet every night – Mediterranean, Indian, Chinese, English. Then I can just rotate. We can do themed nights if you like, with music or dancing – Tex-Mex, Caribbean, seventies food, whatever.'

'And do you have more bookings coming in, Roddy?' Della asked.

'I do. I was talking to Rose about it. She's really nice, Rose –
so encouraging. She was telling me I could develop the hotel
into a place as big and successful as the one you had lunch in, in
Portree.'

'Do you think you could?' Della asked.

'I'm sure of it,' Sandy butted in. 'I'm confident my cooking
will bring people back. Then we could get a second chef, a
housekeeper.'

'Rose said something like that,' Roddy said. 'She made it
sound so easy. I don't know what we'll do when you've all gone
back to England.'

'We'll be fine.' Sandy sounded confident. 'I reckon we can
really make things happen.'

'You're a talented chef,' Della said.

'That's praise coming from you,' Roddy added.

Della shook her head modestly. 'I'm just a mum, a family
cook. You cook as if you've had experience.'

Sandy shifted in his seat. 'I'm trying to settle down and do
what's right. Maisie's four now and Shona wants her to have
security. She's been on at me about it for a while. Now I've got
this job, I'm going to give it my best shot – for her and the little
one.'

Della understood. 'It was like that with me and Sylvester. We
put everything into raising those boys right. It didn't matter how
many hours he had to work, Sylvester was a good dad.' She
turned to Sandy. 'You're a good dad too.'

'I need to prove it,' Sandy said. 'Shona's had a lot to put up
with.' He laughed, to change the mood. 'She'll be properly vexed
when I get home. Once she smells the whisky on me, I'll get a
right telling-off.'

'Is she from Perth too?' Della asked.

'She was born there. But her father was from Jamaica – St Ann's Bay.'

'So was my Sylvester,' Della said softly. 'Has she ever been there?'

'No, but she's always saying she'd love to go. It's her big wish to show Maisie and me where her dad came from. Of course,' Sandy gave Roddy a hopeful look '…if I keep this job and we can save up a few pennies, maybe all our dreams will come true.'

'She sounds lovely,' Della said.

'Och, she's the best, my Shona,' Sandy admitted. 'Can you stop here, please, Roddy? We're just round this corner…'

Roddy braked gently and the Land Rover slowed down to a halt outside a small terraced house with a tiny front garden. Sandy slipped from the passenger seat with a grin and a wave. Then the front door opened and a young woman came out into the cold, wearing jeans, her arms folded. She yelled, 'Sandy, ye steamin' bampot – you've been drinking and I'm stuck here with wee Maisie and she's been crabbit all night.'

'Shona.' Sandy opened his arms and gave her a hug. 'I want you to meet my employer, Roddy, and the lass I told you about who's been helping me in the kitchen, Della.'

Roddy and Della slid from the car and Della held her hand out. 'Hello, Shona – I've heard so much about you.'

Shona took her hand awkwardly. 'Hello. Sandy's such a fool at times. He said he'd be home late but…'

'I'm sorry,' Roddy muttered. 'We had a drink after work.'

'He said it was staff training.' Shona shot him a look.

'It was – in a way.' Roddy looked guilty.

Della was staring at Shona. With her arms folded and her hair pulled back from her face, she looked vulnerable, tired. She reminded Della so much of herself as a young mum. Once or twice, Sylvester had come home late after drinking rum with friends. She'd forgotten how cross she'd felt at the time, but now her heart was full of warmth and she reached out to hug the exhausted young mum.

'I'm sorry,' Della said. 'Sandy's a brilliant chef, but we should have brought him home earlier.'

'Och well.' Shona seemed surprised at the sudden sympathy. 'I suppose he needs the odd night out with his work pals.' She turned to him, hands on hips. 'As long as you don't make a habit of it.'

'I won't.' Sandy grinned sheepishly, wrapping her in his arms.

'Do you want to come inside for a coffee?' Shona asked.

'Thanks, but – you should get your motorbike from the back, Sandy,' Roddy said, 'and then we should go.'

'We should,' Della agreed. 'There will be some clearing-up to do back at the hotel.'

When they arrived back, Della found Rose still in the dining room, seated at the piano, bashing away determinedly. She had mastered a staccato rendition of the Abba song and was keen to play it to an audience. Della listened while Roddy cleared away empty cups and glasses. He hurried past Della and Rose into the kitchen, a strange look on his face, and muttered, 'Well, I've tidied up all that I can... but there's not much I can do about *them...*'

'About who?' Rose asked.

'Go and see for yourselves.' Roddy looked baffled.

Rose and Della went back to the lounge and peered round the corner. The lights were out; there was a ruddy glow from the dying fire, the low crackling of logs burning down to embers. Daz and Jamie were asleep together on the sofa, their arms around each other.

Rose smiled indulgently. 'Well, I didn't see that coming.'

Della looked surprised until she realised Rose was joking. She suddenly felt sorry for Daz. 'Jamie will be leaving tomorrow for... Where does he come from?'

'Aberdeen, I think,' Rose said sadly. 'It's a long way from Paris. But then again – we're not in Paris, are we?'

'What will you do now the club is closed?' Della asked.

'I'm giving it some thought.' Rose glanced at Daz, who was wrapped in Jamie's embrace as if they belonged together. 'He hasn't had anyone to love for a while now, not since Simon dumped him. And he's such a good person. I don't know what I'd have done without him, especially over these last few weeks. I'd like to give him something back.'

'Such as?' Della asked.

'I'll sleep on it. Let's go up.' Rose took Della's arm. 'It's Thursday tomorrow. We're booked in until the weekend. But we could stay on a bit longer.'

'I don't know...'

They had reached Della's door, room number two. Rose said, 'I'll leave you here. But let's check if Tess is OK first... she sounded terrible.'

'She did.' Della pushed the door and discovered it opened easily. 'It's not locked. Oh...' She stood in the open doorway, staring. Rose joined her, peering at the bed in the half-light, at the mound of two figures lying on Tess's single bed.

'It's Tess... and Murdo.' Rose glanced at Della. 'Well, I hadn't seen that coming either.'

'Are you joking again?' Della was uncertain.

'I've given up trying to understand the ways of the world.' Rose winked. 'But you can't sleep here.'

'So where shall I go?' Della was mystified.

'Daz isn't using his bed,' Rose said. She made a face. 'Well, we've had it all tonight, Truth and Dare and now musical beds. Come on – let's get some beauty sleep...'

* * *

Early next morning, with the birds tweeting outside the window, Tess opened her eyes to look straight into a large bearded face. She jumped in alarm. 'Oh!'

Murdo was fast asleep. She tried hard to remember what had happened. She'd been sick. Murdo had helped her to her room. She'd wrapped her arms around him and burst into tears and told him the world wasn't fair. He'd said something like, 'Aye, lassie, it isn't...' Then they'd kissed.

She couldn't remember much after that. She'd fallen asleep. Clearly, Murdo had done the same thing on her bed. Tess's head was knocking as if someone were banging drums inside it. She was cold – they were lying on top of the duvet. She reached down with tentative hands to check her clothing. It was all there, dishevelled, crumpled, but she was still wearing everything she'd had on last night apart from shoes. She wished she could remember what had happened. She was mortified.

Murdo murmured something, and Tess wriggled out of the bed and scurried to the safety of Della's; it smelled nicer. She wondered where Della had slept. Her head throbbed and she felt decidedly giddy. She snuggled beneath Della's duvet and closed her eyes, shutting out the world, snorting in self-disgust. Here she was, getting drunk, sleeping with men, having a hangover the morning after and she was seventy-seven years old. She'd never learn. It was ridiculous. She squeezed her eyes shut and promptly fell asleep.

Much later, she opened them and felt the dull ache in her head. When she reached out a numb arm and checked her phone, it was half past eleven. There was a glass of water on the cupboard next to her bed. Tess drank it thirstily in four gulps. She wondered who'd left it there.

Murdo was no longer in her bed and she imagined him outside in the cold, chopping wood, or downstairs tucking into a hearty fried breakfast. The thought of food made her feel nauseous all over again. Her body ached; her stomach was cramped. She ought to drink more water. Sitting up precariously, she looked around. The room was dim. Perhaps she'd have a hot shower, then she'd feel better. She eased herself out of bed, imagining the embarrassment of facing Rose and Della, explaining what had happened.

More to the point, what would she say to Murdo when she next saw him? It was her fault he'd drunk whisky after trying so hard not to. She'd encouraged him. She felt suddenly consumed with guilt. They'd kissed, after all: so what else had they done?

Even the details of the kiss were difficult to recall. She'd been in his arms. His beard had prickled her face. Had she pushed her fingers into his hair, snuggled close to him? She might have, but she hoped not. And what had he said in return?

She wished she could remember.

She had no idea where Murdo was now and how she'd react when they next bumped into each other. Should she apologise? How would she find out what had happened? Tess's mind was buzzing with questions. It would be embarrassing to see him. Were they a couple now – or had she disgraced herself and he'd never speak to her again? Neither option sat comfortably.

Feeling confused and truly awful, Tess dragged herself into the shower and turned on the water, stripped off her smelly clothes and stepped beneath the steaming stream. With luck, she'd emerge cleansed of the terrible guilt and feelings of stupidity. She rubbed shampoo into her hair with firm fingers, telling herself she was an adult, a woman of the world. She was human, fallible, allowed to make mistakes. Everyone made them from time to time. In an hour or two, she and her friends and Murdo would laugh about it, chalk it up to a good night and too much whisky.

Then, in her head, Alan's voice muttered, 'Slut.'

27

Tess arrived downstairs to see everyone sitting at the dining table, coffee cups and notepads in front of them. Rose and Roddy had called a meeting. Della was there, Daz, Sandy and a young woman she'd never met before, a child on her knee with cute dark pigtails and freckles. Murdo was nowhere to be seen. Tess breathed a sigh of relief and plastered a wide smile on her face. 'Good morning.'

Della called, 'Tess, good to see you.' She raised the coffee jug in welcome. 'You'll need caffeine.'

Daz dragged a seat between him and Rose. 'Here you are. Take the weight off. You must be shattered – you were the life and soul of the party last night.' He made a sad face. 'Jamie and Robin have just left.'

Tess felt embarrassed. 'I should have said goodbye – they were really lovely people.'

'But we've all been talking over breakfast and—' Rose patted the seat. 'Come and join us.'

'This is Shona, by the way – and my little one, Maisie,' Sandy said proudly. Maisie put a thumb in her mouth and snuggled closer to her mother.

'I haven't seen Murdo.' Roddy was puzzled. 'He must have gone home while I was driving Sandy back.'

'I expect that's what he did,' Rose agreed with a wink to Tess. 'Now, where were we?'

'Making plans,' Roddy said. 'I'm really excited about this...'

'Oh?' Tess plonked herself down, sipped coffee and tried to make her face look normal.

'So,' Roddy put both elbows on the table emphatically. 'Bookings are increasing in number – we're aiming for a full house for Christmas. That's where Rose and Daz come in.'

'I asked Jamie and Robin this morning if they'd come back for Christmas, and they said yes.' Daz beamed.

'We have more guests arriving today.' Rose waved a finger. 'Tess – I'm staying on with Daz until the 26th. Why don't you and Della stay too?'

Della smiled. 'Rose mentioned it last night. It's only two more weeks – and Rose has some interesting ideas up her sleeve.'

'So?' Rose's eyes were keen.

Tess shrugged. 'I suppose so. Yes. Christmas here might be fun.'

'Right. We have a plan,' Daz said.

'We'll fill every room with guests.' Rose clapped her hands excitedly. 'Roddy's agreed to take Shona on as housekeeper. I'm going to project-manage this entire event and we're going to make the whole hotel look really smart. A bit of painting, Christmas decorations...'

'I've been in the attic,' Daz said. 'There's so much space up there. We can improve the dining area though – open it up so that we can find the old stage behind the stud wall and make it grander.'

'The kitchen's perfect as a catering space,' Sandy said. 'Della will help me with some of the cooking ahead of the 25th – we'll be fully stocked and prepped. Christmas will be spectacular.'

'I can help with advertising,' Tess said. 'I used to be an estate agent years ago. Maybe I can do the sales patter.'

'And I'll call Murdo.' Roddy looked really pleased. 'He can help me decorate. And with more guests coming, he can run more island tours.'

'The Northern Lights...' Tess remembered, realising she still hadn't seen them.

'This is so exciting.' Rose clapped her hands.

'So – we have two more guests coming,' Sandy said. 'I thought I might make a buffet dinner this evening, candlelight, canapés, a few substantial dishes, and we could all congregate in here.'

'I'd like to try to play the piano...' Rose's eyes gleamed.

'Can I come, Daddy?' Maisie piped up.

'Och, she'll need to be early to bed,' Shona fretted.

'We can put a makeshift bed in the corner, with cushions and blankets if you like – she can sleep there when she's tired. Lots of the entertainers at Monty's bring their little ones and we let them sleep backstage,' Daz said.

'Then that's decided,' Sandy said. 'We'll have a special night. What do we know about the guests, Rose? Any special dietary requirements?'

Rose was thoughtful. 'We should cater for vegetarians just in case – let's have a good selection. The new guests are travelling a distance, so they'll be glad of a tasty supper.'

'No after-dinner games though.' Tess put a hand to her head. It was still throbbing.

'Right,' Roddy said. 'Meeting over.'

Shona slid little Maisie from her knee. 'Can you help Mummy with the bedrooms?'

Maisie announced, 'I'm a sistant housekeeper, Mummy said...'

Shona smiled proudly. 'That's perfect. We got a lift in this morning with a neighbour who comes this way. It's over an hour to walk it and that's no fun with Maisie...'

'I'm sure Murdo or I could fetch you – it's just minutes by car,' Roddy said.

'Right – we should crack on. You all have plenty to do.' Rose was already easing herself to her feet. 'I'll have half an hour's practice on the piano and then I'm going upstairs for a doze. Last night really took it out of me.' She turned to Tess. 'I advise you to do the same. You've looked perkier.'

Tess decided she'd stay close to Della all day for security. She followed her into the kitchen to plan a menu for the buffet. Della knew instinctively that Tess was feeling awkward, so she said, 'Why don't you make some mini quiches? Maybe then you can cook something sweet.'

'I'll teach you to make cranachan,' Sandy offered. 'It'll look the business in individual glasses, topped with cream.'

Tess nodded emphatically. If she worked, she wouldn't be thinking about Murdo. In truth, she had no idea what she felt beyond being embarrassed by whatever had happened and she was horrified by her behaviour – although she had no idea how she'd behaved. She wished she could remember something that would give her a clue, but there was nothing, except a scratchy kiss and a feeling of emptiness.

She spent several hours in the kitchen, drinking water every ten minutes, busily preparing food, chattering to Sandy and

Della. She was happier listening to the buzz of their conversation.

Sandy was chopping vegetables with a huge knife. 'I'm going to make two stews, one with meat, one without, and serve them up with rice. If I slow-cook them all afternoon, they'll melt in the mouth. I'm going to do cheesecake too.'

'Who doesn't love cheesecake?' Tess said.

'Sylvester used to like an oven-baked one with ginger and rum,' Della remembered.

'I made a dulce de leche cheesecake for my boss's birthday once. He was impressed.' Sandy was chatting as he worked. 'I might do that for tonight.'

'Was this when you were at Queen's?' Della asked.

Sandy hesitated. 'Yes, it was part of our training. We covered everything. But mostly we just cooked simple things when I was doing my NVQ Level 2.' He grinned. 'I was always the one who wanted to try something ambitious.'

'You're a good chef,' Della said kindly. 'They must have been impressed by how you can turn your hand to anything.'

'Och, my boss'd be amazed now if he could see me here,' Sandy said.

'Why?' Tess asked. 'Didn't he expect you to become a chef?'

'I meant – I always wanted to work in a hotel.' Sandy was momentarily flustered. 'As opposed to in a bar. I – I love Rose's ideas for this place. She's so clever. And it's really kind of her to help Roddy out. If we can make Christmas special, then maybe things will look up next year...'

'I hope so,' Della said.

'I might get a few things from out the back,' Sandy said quickly. 'There's some stock in the freezer.'

'I'll go for you,' Tess offered, thinking that she could do with some fresh air. 'What sort do you want?'

'I boiled up some chicken bones the other day with some herbs and veggies. It'd go lovely.'

'I'll get it.' Tess washed her hands.

'It's in a freezer bag,' Sandy called after her. 'With a label that says "chicken stock"...'

'I'm on it.' Tess hurried through the back door towards the outbuilding where the old Aga was. There was one small security light on. Tess hesitated in the doorway and breathed deeply. The air was cold, seeping through her clothes, but in a way she felt revived. It had been too hot in the kitchen. She flicked a switch and a single bulb illuminated in the darkness.

'Hello.' A voice came from behind her.

Tess swung round and felt her heart thump. 'Hello, Murdo.' She took a breath. 'How are you feeling?'

'After falling off the wagon?' Murdo held up a huge axe and laughed once. 'Not proud of myself. It won't happen again.'

'Oh?' Tess wasn't sure if he meant drinking or kissing her. She felt awkward, wondering how to ask the question that hung on her lips. She needed to know what had happened – or hadn't. Instead, she said, 'Chicken stock.'

Murdo frowned. 'Eh?'

'I've come out to get some from the big freezer.'

'Oh.' Murdo stood where he was.

'We're having a buffet tonight. Two new guests are coming.'

'Aye, I'm picking them up from the airport in Inverness later.'

'Right,' Tess said. Silence hung between them and she said again, 'Stock, then.' She smiled to defuse the tension.

Murdo said, 'I came for the big axe... There's more wood to chop, every day.' He brandished the axe again.

'Of course,' Tess said. 'Well.'

'Well.'

Tess said, 'I better get what I came for.'

'Indeed.' Murdo scratched his beard. 'Me too.'

'So...' Tess was about to say chicken stock again but she stopped herself. She hurried into the outbuilding towards the freezer and let out a loud scream.

'What is it?' Murdo charged in behind her, holding up the axe as if expecting to find a rat. Tess was standing in water.

'It's soaking wet in here.'

'Why?' Murdo looked around. 'Oh, I see what's happened. The freezer's off.'

They both lurched towards the large chest freezer. On top, someone had drawn a smiling face in lipstick, and there was scrawled writing beneath. Tess frowned.

'What's this?'

'It's been turned off deliberately.' Murdo pointed to the electric switch on the wall. 'Looking at the amount of water on the floor, it's not been on for some time.'

Tess frowned. 'Is it a mistake?'

'No – look at the scribble.' Murdo pointed to the smiley face scrawled on the top. 'There's a message. That has Isla written all over it.'

'I don't understand.'

'She's sabotaged Roddy's stock of meat.' Murdo scratched his head beneath his cap. 'There will be hundreds and hundreds of pounds' worth in here that Roddy's put away for Christmas. She'll have come in here when we were busy and switched it off.'

Tess felt herself blush for no reason. Her hands went to the freezer where she'd feel cooler. 'I'll just get the stock.'

'Best not to open the lid,' Murdo said. 'Look at the message under the smiley face – the date and time she switched it off. It says, "Tuesday lunchtime. I needed some steak for dinner." That's forty-eight hours ago – the meat will be ruined if it isn't eaten today.'

Tess looked down at her trainers, the soles deep in the water. 'Roddy will be devastated. Will his insurance cover it?'

'I doubt it,' Murdo said quietly. 'There has to be a solution.'

Tess shook her head. 'It's a shame it's not summer – you could have had a big barbecue.'

'Och.' Murdo's eyes gleamed. 'You little beauty, Tess,' he said.

'What?' Tess had no idea what she'd done.

'Give me an hour, then I'll come and find you. Tell everyone what's happened and that it's one of Isla's little tricks. Tell Roddy not to worry, and leave the freezer closed. I'll sort it all out. I have a plan.'

'What plan?' Tess asked.

Murdo placed both hands on her cheeks and kissed her full on the forehead. 'Your plan. Leave it with me. I have people to talk to – things to do.'

And with that he rushed away, the axe over his shoulder, whistling cheerily.

28

Several people stood in the kitchen drinking tea. Sandy was making the biscuity base for cheesecake and Della was taking quiches from the oven. Tess put the finishing touches to a vegetable stew with mushrooms and miso. Shona sipped from a mug of tea as Maisie played with a rag doll with pink hair. Roddy stood with his hands on his hips, looking perplexed. 'Why would she do that?' He shook his head.

'Revenge,' Sandy said. 'Angry women are bad news...' He winked at Shona, who ignored him deliberately.

'She must have crept in while we were all out.' Tess remembered Murdo's words. 'We wouldn't have noticed.'

'She chose her moment,' Della agreed. 'All that food. What a really mean trick.'

'Isla is mean,' Roddy said sadly. 'I have so much stock in there – the freezer is filled to the brim. Chicken, prime beef, deer, pork – all ruined.' He shrugged. 'Isla's won.'

'That's what she wants you to think,' Tess said encouragingly. 'It'll be all right.'

'But how?' Roddy asked.

'It's a wicked trick. What a waste of food,' Shona said.

'What did she do, Mummy?' Maisie's little face puckered and Shona picked her up.

'It's just a lady who's a bully. But we don't let bullies win.'

'What's happened?' Rose swept into the room, leaning on her stick, Daz behind her. 'What's Isla done now?'

'Turned off my big freezer – it's full of meat.' Roddy groaned.

'Can't we save it?' Daz asked. 'Put it somewhere else?'

'Or switch it back on?' Rose said.

'It will need to be eaten today,' Sandy said. 'Forty-eight hours is the safe limit. I should have checked it when I came in this morning.'

'I shouldn't have left the door to the outbuilding open,' Roddy said. 'And she scribbled a message too – just so we'd know it was her.'

'Can you tell the police?' Della suggested.

Roddy shook his head. 'A smiley face? A sarcastic message? They've got more important things to deal with...'

'Can we cook it all and use it for pies or something?' Tess was clutching at straws.

Murdo hurried into the kitchen in boots, leaving muddy prints on the shiny floor. 'It's all sorted.'

'What's sorted?' Roddy asked.

'The meat. I've found a home for it. You remember my friend, Aul Crabbit Harris, whose boat we sailed on Loch Coruisk?' Murdo said.

'*The Nauti Buoy*?' Daz said.

'With the design on the side of a sailor in a cap and a striped shirt, with an oversized pink banana...' Tess stopped there.

'Your friend with more money than sense?' Della said.

'Right. Well, Aul Crabbit has this big house in Sleat, amongst a couple of other places. And he has a garden with an orangery, and he'll be here with a truck in about half an hour to take away a freezer full of meat. He's going to buy it from you.'

'What's he going to do with it all?' Rose asked, horrified.

'Cook it – for the whole village.' Murdo was pleased with himself. 'He wants you to gather all the food you've made so far and take it up to his place – he'll throw a party tonight for everyone in Sleat, Armadale and beyond.'

'That's a mint idea,' Daz said.

'Clever of you,' Rose added.

'Aul Crabbit's happy to fund it all as a Christmas treat, food, drink, everything. So you'll get paid for the meat, Roddy, and you'll be able to buy more stock.' Murdo folded his arms.

Roddy looked shocked, a rabbit in headlights. 'Thanks.'

'Well done, Murdo,' Della said and Murdo beamed with delight.

'I can help with the barbecuing,' Sandy offered.

'Can I come to the Barbie Coo, Mummy?' a little voice asked. Maisie tugged at Shona's sleeve.

'We can all go,' Shona said.

'It sounds like half of Skye will be there,' Roddy said, relieved.

'If life gives you lemons, have a party,' Daz said with a grin.

'I only hope our new guests like a party.' Roddy made an anxious face. 'We were going to provide a buffet here. They'll be tired.'

'Leave that to me,' Rose said with a smile.

'That reminds me – I need to pick them up from Inverness.' Murdo turned to Della and Tess. 'Who's coming?'

'You should go, Tess,' Rose said quickly. 'I need Della for something – I need help to choose what to wear.'

'Oh yes – you'll have to try everything on first.' Della picked up on Rose's hint. 'And I promised Sandy I'd help him with his cheesecake.'

'Oh, I love a party,' Daz said sadly. 'What a shame Jamie has gone back to Aberdeen.'

'This is practice for Christmas... and good publicity for the hotel.' Rose's eyes glinted. 'What this is telling me loud and clear is that this hotel needs to bring the outside in – to make better use of the community.' She smiled with satisfaction. 'Oh, well I never – that's another great idea I've just had.'

'What have you come up with now, our kid?' Daz asked.

'You'll all have to wait and see...' Rose said coyly. 'But I can promise you – it's a Christmas cracker.'

Tess sat in the Land Rover with Murdo. It was cosy inside, with the heater going and New Grass Revival playing too loud through the speaker. Murdo was talking nineteen to the dozen about his love of all things musical from the Appalachian region, although he'd never been there. He was talking too fast, as if he was a little nervous in Tess's presence. He'd clearly wanted Della to come as well. Tess was a little disappointed, but it was at least a chance to find out all she needed to know about the last fateful night.

Murdo was moving his shoulders to the music as he drove across the Skye Bridge. 'Bluegrass music is,' he said as he stared through the windscreen, 'the most uplifting music in the world.'

'I don't really know much about it,' Tess muttered. 'American, isn't it?'

'It gets its name from the band Bill Monroe and the Blue Grass Boys,' he said, still staring ahead. 'It has roots in traditional English, Scottish, and Irish ballads, blues and jazz. Bluegrass features acoustic stringed instruments and emphasizes the offbeat – then one or more instruments each take turns playing the melody and improvising around it, while the others accompany...' He realised he was wittering on and stopped.

'It's nice,' Tess said hopefully.

There was silence, except for a jangling guitar. Tess felt awkward.

'It's about two hours to Inverness, isn't it?'

'Aye.'

'OK.' Tess searched for something else to say. She wished she'd persuaded Della to come. Clearly, Rose thought she was doing her a favour by sending her off solo with Murdo. But the silence was excruciating.

Murdo had stopped bobbing to the music. He was searching for something to say too. 'What music do you like, Tess?'

She took a breath. 'Pop. Abba.' She tried again. 'Wham.'

Murdo made no comment. Then he said, 'Well, are you looking forward to the party?'

'Oh yes.' Tess made her biggest effort. 'I'm so glad you found something to do with all that frozen meat.'

Murdo relaxed a little. 'You'll like Aul Crabbit. He's an eccentric. He made his money in the seventies in property. He has more cash than he knows what to do with.'

'Is he married?' Tess had no idea why she'd asked that. Murdo might think she was looking for a rich husband.

'No, not now.' Murdo chuckled at memories he kept to himself. 'He's had a few ladies: models, an actress who was in one of the soaps – I don't remember her name.'

'Ah,' Tess said and the conversation stopped again.

'No, Aul Crabbit and I are bachelors now – and I suppose bachelors we'll stay for the rest of our days...'

Tess realised she'd have to ask now or there might never be

another opportunity. 'Murdo – what happened to your wife? I mean – is it OK for me to ask?'

'I don't talk of it but – aye, I can tell you, Tess.'

'I know you think about it a lot.' She felt him weakening. 'But it can't have completely been your fault.'

'It feels that way sometimes.' Murdo shuddered a sigh. 'It was this time of year, the run-up to Christmas. I always hit the bottle in December, remembering. That's why you found me drinking on the beach. Christmas will never be the same.' He sighed and was silent for a moment. Then his voice was small. 'We went to a party at some friends' house near Portree...'

'And?'

'We took Mairi's car. She was driving. It was her idea – she was so sweet. She said I could have a couple of glasses of beer and she'd have soft drinks. I always drove us everywhere in this Land Rover. But she wanted us to go in her little Clio. She was short-sighted, bless her. She was used to me doing all the driving.'

'But she insisted?'

'She did. So I agreed and let her drive.'

Tess waited for him to go on. He said nothing, so she repeated, 'So – what happened?'

'The weather was awful. Raining, the icy rain like we often have on the island – that hard, cold, blinding rain so bad that you can't see properly through the windscreen. It was all misty...'

Tess understood. 'Bad visibility.'

'I was singing to her on the way home. It was late. I can remember the song. I'd had a few beers and I was merry and she was laughing.'

'What was the song?'

'It was raining cats and dogs,' Murdo said. 'And I was

singing "You Are the Sunshine of My Life" and Mairi was laughing and telling me I was a numpty, and we were both happy as could be – then a lorry just came out of nowhere and...'

Tess caught her breath. 'Oh...'

'We swerved – the road was wet, we were out of control and we smashed into a tree...'

'I'm sorry.'

'I broke my arm and two ribs. Mairi was killed instantly. If I'd been driving, it would have been the other way round.'

'Oh, Murdo.'

'If we'd taken the Land Rover and she'd been in the passenger seat, maybe she'd be alive now. I wish it had been me. I wish I'd gone in her place.'

Tess struggled to find words. 'That's so hard. But you mustn't blame yourself.'

Tess glanced at him and his face was wet. Murdo took a deep breath. 'You're right. I know that. But I start to move forward and I think I'm getting over her, then something hits me between the eyes and it starts all over again.'

'I can understand that. I know it's the same with Della. She lost Sylvester recently.'

'She's spoken about it,' Murdo said quietly. 'She gets how I feel.' He took a deep breath. 'But I'm doing my best, Tess.'

'I know.' Tess reached out and patted his arm. 'I can see that.'

'It's been better since you came, and Della and Rose. You're good people. You've all had your own problems and I've been too focused on my own. You've helped me to try and see a future for myself.' He turned to her, meeting her eyes for the first time since they'd left the island. 'I'm turning a corner.'

Tess met his smile. 'You are.'

'Thanks, Tess.' Murdo offered a warm smile. 'I'm grateful.'

Tess seized the opportunity. 'I think I owe you an apology for last night.'

Murdo frowned. 'Apology?'

'I was drunk. I was sick.'

'That makes us equal. One all,' Murdo explained. Tess was confused, so he tried again. 'I was sick in your bed when we went to the whisky tasting.'

'Oh, I'd forgotten – yes,' Tess said. There was a moment's awkward silence. 'Murdo?' She wasn't sure how to ask the next question.

'You're going to tell me you've forgotten everything that happened?' Murdo said.

'We kissed?' Tess tried.

'We did.' Murdo grinned. 'It was very nice too.'

'And did we...?'

Murdo glanced at Tess briefly. 'Did we what?'

'You know...'

Murdo shook his head. 'No, of course not.' His eyes met hers and she saw an honesty there. 'You're a nice woman, Tess. I respect you. And I'm not that sort of man. Besides...' he gave a low laugh '...I was steamin' drunk.'

Tess couldn't help but laugh. 'We're a right pair, Murdo.'

'We are.' He thought for a minute. 'I'm glad you're staying until Christmas.'

'Are you?'

'Yes, you and Della and Rose. Rose was telling me about your hen trip to Paris, how one of your friends was getting married and you went to bars and clubs and galleries and casinos. You must have had a right laugh.'

'It was fun,' Tess admitted. 'And Rose stayed in Paris when we all came home.'

'Ah, she's a tough woman, that one,' Murdo said. 'Della's sweet too. I'm so glad we all got to spend time together.'

'Me too,' Tess said. She thought he might take her hand, say something romantic. She recalled last night in the Truth or Dare game he'd been about to admit his feelings. Tess wished he had said it. She could feel something developing between them – trust, affection. Or it might simply be friendship – she didn't know. She wondered what it would become by Christmas.

She told herself to be patient; to allow things to take their natural course. Murdo was still deeply affected by what had happened to his wife. But he'd admitted that their kiss had been very nice and that he respected her. That was a step towards love, wasn't it? Tess wasn't even sure she was looking for love. But a bit of romance might be nice...

The sky was purple now as the sun sank low. Murdo stared into oncoming headlights, driving carefully towards Inverness. Tess's eyelids began to feel heavy. She closed her eyes; she was warm and comfortable. The Land Rover rumbled and rolled and Tess felt her body relax. Very soon she was asleep.

She woke with a jolt as the Land Rover slowed down.

'We're at the airport,' Murdo said gently, lifting her head from his shoulder. 'Have you slept well?'

'Mmm,' Tess said. She felt relaxed, energised, better than she had all day. 'So we're picking up the new guests?'

'We are,' Murdo said happily. 'We'll drop off their stuff at the hotel, give them an hour to unwind and then we'll all get off to Aul Crabbit's place for the big barbecue.'

'So – who are the guests? Where are we meeting them?' Tess asked.

'Here – in the car park,' Murdo said.

She stared out of the window. 'How will we know who they are?'

'Rose said you'd recognise them...'

'Did she?' Tess asked, then she saw two figures tugging cases, emerging from the swing doors of the airport, wrapped in scarves and woollen hats. One of the pair held a small spaniel on a lead.

Tess was out of the Land Rover, running into the cold evening air, squealing and laughing. Then they were in a three-way hug, chattering excitedly. Elvis was barking and Tess was tugging at their arms, pulling them towards the car.

'It's so nice to see you. Rose didn't say it was you. Oh – how typical of her to make it a surprise...' She took a breath. 'How was Iceland? How was Crete? I can't wait to hear all about it. Oh, Pam, Jen, it's just so good to see you both.'

29

Murdo had been absolutely right about Aul Crabbit Harris. He was certainly a strange character. He stood at the iron gates to his mansion, welcoming everyone, dressed in the full Scottish tradition: a tartan kilt, a sporran, a sgian dubh knife, kilt hose, and ghillies. He was an exceptionally tall man in his seventies, clean-shaven except for a tuft of white bristles on his chin, pale red hair tucked beneath a tam-o'-shanter, a loud voice, an even louder laugh. As Rose clambered from the Land Rover, Aul Crabbit bowed to her, took her hand and kissed it before tucking it beneath his own. 'The Lady Rose – I've heard all about you. Erskine Harris, at your service. Anything you wish for, it will be my pleasure to facilitate. May I accompany you to the orangery, where the barbecued meats are currently roasting, melt-in-the-mouth, for your delectation?'

'Thank you.' Rose, dressed warmly in her new country-woman garb, allowed herself to be led towards a huge glass building lit with fairy lights, surrounded by paving stones and grass. Outside, dressed in chef's hats, Sandy, Roddy, Murdo and Daz were barbecuing more meat than she had ever seen. Tess,

Della, Jen and Pam followed behind, their eyes straying to the large mansion in shadows, the long sweeping drive, gardens, orchards. Elvis was leaping up, barking excitedly. They reached the orangery, where there were trestle tables loaded with food, wine and various drinks in punchbowls; a waiter in a red waistcoat, matching tartan bow tie and shorts rushed over with a tray of champagne flutes.

Aul Crabbit said, 'I'm honoured that my friend Murdoch has enabled me to give an early Christmas banquet for my friends and neighbours. I want you to have a wonderful time and enjoy traditional Scottish revelry.'

Rose looked around. There were so many people – certainly over fifty men, women and children – hovering around the red glow of the barbecue, carrying plates stacked with hunks of meat. Aul Crabbit smiled. 'Roddy's wicked, bitter wife has done us all a favour. Let us all eat, drink and be merry.' He smiled at Jen. 'I will dance with each of you twice and kiss you all once before the night is over.'

Pam was unsure. 'Is it all meat here?'

'Oh, no, not at all.' Aul Crabbit held up a hand in protest. 'Just ask, my dear, and it will be given to you. We have catered for all tastes. The orangery is packed with dishes of the most delightful variety – quiches and bean stews, canapés and stuffed vegetables, couscous, rice, salads. And if you can't find anything you like – come to me.' He lowered bushy eyebrows. 'I'll phone the takeaway in Portree and have your favourite dishes brought.'

'Oh.' Pam was surprised by his kindness. 'Thank you.'

'Not at all.' He took Tess's hand. 'Now, you will be the first to dance with me while the others get their fill of food. They'll have their fill of me later on the dance floor. I am a true Scot – I cannot stomach meat without some whisky and dancing first.' He indicated a group of musicians on a stage outside the orangery, all in traditional costume. There was a piper, a harpist, guitarists, an accordion, a violin, various singers. Tess's mouth fell open as Aul Crabbit whisked her into his arms and pulled her around in some sort of frantic waltz. He whispered in her ear, 'You're far too rare a beauty for Murdo to have to himself.'

Tess was secretly pleased. 'Why? What's Murdo been saying?'

Aul Crabbit did the thing with his eyebrows again. 'Ah, the secret talk of men must be kept between themselves. We are wicked creatures, all of us, and our banter is not for the delicate ears of a young woman.' He swirled her round. 'I hear the rather sumptuous Della is recently widowed? It is my intention to offer her a shoulder to cry on and to give her an evening of kindness unrivalled throughout Scotland.'

Tess had no idea what he was talking about, so she said, 'It's very kind of you to help Roddy out.'

'Do you not know Dickens' story, *A Christmas Carol*?' Aul Crabbit said. 'I was once just like Ebenezer Scrooge – hardened, miserable, rich beyond compare, foolish and lonely – now I am the most popular man on Skye. You know, my dear?' Aul Crabbit twirled her so hard, Tess almost fell over. He snatched her in his arms like a possession. 'I should be called Lord Bountiful these days. They call me Aul Crabbit because I used to be so dour and crusty and miserable. But it came to me one night, like St Paul on the road to Damascus in a flash of blinding light... when I was drunk as a lord and wenching.'

'What did?' Tess wasn't sure what to say.

His face was grimly serious, and so was his low voice. 'Ye cannae take it wi' ye...'

'What can't you take?' Tess was confused.

'Money,' Aul Crabbit said. 'It's for spending, sharing, having fun now. What's the point of dying with a big bank balance? Life has bestowed upon me the gift of far too much money, so my intention is to make as many people as happy with it as possible.'

'I see...' Tess began.

'And it makes me happy to see people celebrating. That's the benefit. Murdoch is a good friend of mine, and I rejoice that I can help him out,' Aul Crabbit continued. 'And as for Roddy, I don't like to see a man turned to frozen jelly by the vitriolic acts of a wicked wife. What she did, turning off the freezer, was like turning off his life support machine, and I won't have that. You see, I am the good fairy of Skye... in a Harris kilt.'

'Are you?' Tess was feeling dizzy.

'I am.' Aul Crabbit slowed down, then stopped, supporting her waist in case she fell. 'Well, that was enchanting, my dear. Now trot off and get yourself a drink and a big hunk of roasted deer to gnaw. I'm going to find that rather attractive young woman with the little black dog and see if I can't entice her to a jig.'

'Pam?' Tess asked, feeling very giddy.

'Pam... indeed, the lovely Pam,' Aul Crabbit called, and was off at a pace towards the orangery. A waiter in a Santa Claus outfit approached her and Tess accepted a glass of fizz gratefully, resolving to take it steadily tonight. She didn't want to drink too much and she certainly needed to watch her step around Murdo. He was over by the barbecue, turning steaks with a pronged fork. His eyes gleamed in her direction and she waved feebly, not sure what to do next. It was all too confusing.

* * *

The party continued with ceilidh dancing into the late hours, fires glowing, voices raised in whoops as they changed partners.

Murdo danced with Tess and Della, Sandy with Shona and Maisie, Aul Crabbit was monopolising Pam. Daz and Rose were talking to Roddy, their heads together, discussing the hotel's plans for Christmas. Everyone seemed to be having a wonderful time. Jen stood by herself, with Elvis on a lead sitting obediently at her feet munching the remains of a barbecued sweet potato that Pam had declared was his favourite.

Jen wanted to be alone for a while – she was deep in thought, still preoccupied with memories of her Icelandic cruise. She had met someone who had made a deep impression on her. He was called Gunnar Kristjánsson, a retired naval officer from Húsavík in north-east Iceland. He was a widower, on board for the cruise because his son Jon was chief engineer. He and Jen had met at dinner and had clicked straight away. And now a new message had pinged in from him on her phone.

> I would like to visit you soon in England. Would that be acceptable?

His manners were impeccable, as was his appearance: white hair, ice-blue eyes, an easy smile. And beneath the shirt and smart trousers, in swim shorts, he was toned and muscular. Jen wasn't sure yet but, perhaps, she had met someone who was as romantic as she was. He'd held her hand. He'd kissed her at the door of her cabin. They'd stood on the deck in the moonlight and he'd told her that, for the first time in seven years, since his beloved Sóley had died, he'd learned to smile again. He'd been the perfect host when the ship had docked. He'd introduced her to the culinary delights of Iceland: rotted shark, breast of puffin, sheep's head, ram's testicles, skyr, and she had been pleasantly surprised. They had bathed together in the gorgeously warm Blue Lagoon, seen the loud Gulfoss waterfall, watched Strokkur, the little geyser that leaped in the air every few minutes. Then he'd bought her a beautiful basalt necklace in Reykjavik, on a silver chain. She was wearing it now against her skin. And, before she'd reached Southampton, he had said, 'Ég vil sjá þig aftur.' 'I want to see you again.'

And Jen had said the only words of Icelandic she had learned. 'Já endilega.' 'Yes, please.'

Jen patted Elvis, who was looking up with round eyes as if he knew what she was thinking. Jen was falling for Gunnar. But it was not the convenient relationship she'd had with Eddie, the man she had been briefly engaged to several years ago, when she and Tess, Rose, Pam and Della had taken off to Paris for her hen party. While she'd been there, enjoying herself, she'd changed her mind. Gunnar was nothing like Eddie, who was controlling: Gunnar was wonderful. And now he'd asked if he could visit. Jen was wondering how to phrase the reply. 'Yes' might just be enough.

Pulled from her thoughts, Jen was conscious that someone was standing next to her, a smart woman in a checked coat with a black fur collar, her hair piled high. The woman had a local accent. 'Are you staying in a hotel around here?'

Jen nodded, unsure why she was being asked.

'In the Sicín Órga?'

'Yes.' Jen nodded again. 'Why?'

'You need to be very careful,' the woman said, hardly opening her mouth to speak. 'It's not a good place.'

Jen was filled with immediate loyalty. 'My friends are there – they love it.'

'Just be careful,' the woman said in a low voice. 'It's not what it seems.'

'What makes you say that?'

'It's a shambles – badly organised.' The woman smiled but her eyes glinted. 'I hear this food would have gone rotten and no doubt given you food poisoning if Erskine Harris hadn't barbe-cued it. The hotel is filthy, the driver is a dangerous drunkard, the chef is completely untrustworthy and the owner is useless.'

'How would you know?' Jen frowned. 'It seems lovely...'

'Let's just say that I have inside knowledge.' The woman tapped her nose. 'Don't say you weren't warned.'

She walked away and Elvis yapped once, as if to disagree. Jen went back to watching the dancing. Pam and Aul Crabbit were laughing, whirling round to the music in a bouncing circle with Della, Murdo and Tess.

Jen looked around for the woman in the checked coat, to ask her again what she'd meant by the warning, but she had gone.

30

Jen didn't think about the woman's comment again over the next few days. She was busy texting Gunnar, arranging to meet him in the new year, imagining their wonderful reunion in Exmouth. And in her spare time, she was busy making plans for Christmas with The Hens. Over the weekend, they'd bought paint and brushes and, with Murdo and Roddy's help, they started to decorate the dining room. Sledgehammers and overalls were brought in, and the stud wall that hid the stage area was smashed down to reveal a beautiful ornate arched stage with wings. Rose sat at the piano practising tunes, determined to get them right. She was making progress. Abba and Beethoven, even with occasional mistakes, were the perfect soundtrack to painting.

By Thursday, the dining room was done, the walls freshly white, the floor oiled, the new stage area repainted and bright. Pam had taken it upon herself to have a go at the hall, varnishing the old banister, giving the walls a new lease of life. Roddy had even hung a few pieces of tinsel around the picture of Dougal Fraser, his great-grandfather.

On Friday, a delighted Roddy made an announcement over

breakfast. 'So – we now have the grandest, most beautiful hotel. I can't thank you enough.'

'We're staying for next to nothing... so we don't mind being jills of all trades,' Tess replied.

Roddy was excited. 'Can you believe it? We're booked up for Christmas. And Robin and Jamie are coming back.'

'Oh, that's great,' Tess said, clapping her hands.

Rose looked around the dining hall. 'So – let's think – it's 20 December – what are we missing?'

'We don't have enough Christmas decorations,' Pam said and Roddy's face fell.

'You're right. What can we do?'

'It's easy,' Pam said. 'We go out into the woodlands and find some holly and mistletoe.'

'And I can get some twinkling lights,' Tess added.

'We need to make a big statement in the lounge area and dining room – put in a huge tree, some presents, lights around the fire – make them really Christmassy,' Della said.

Murdo put both elbows on the table. 'So how about we all go into Tormore Forest and see what we can find?'

Sandy was collecting plates. 'There will be lots of berries and stuff you can use for decorating. A centrepiece for each table would be nice.'

'I can make them, and Christmas wreaths,' Pam offered.

'And I'll keep everyone on task,' Rose said.

'I'll be fine here – I have plenty to keep me busy.' Sandy held a huge pile of plates in one hand. 'Shona and Maisie are doing the laundry and I have tonight's meal to prepare. How does a pasta bake and salad sound?'

'Perfect,' Roddy said.

'Then later – maybe we can go through the Christmas menu

one last time and I can do some final prep?' Sandy asked. 'When do the first guests arrive again?'

'Tomorrow – 21st,' Daz said. 'Jamie and Robin will be here in the afternoon for the run-up to Christmas, until Boxing Day.'

'The other guests will follow on 22nd.' Roddy's face was flushed with delight. 'We're so well organised.'

'I'm happy to play piano,' Rose reminded him with a grin. 'For a small fee.'

'What are you going to do for Hogmanay?' Tess pulled a sad face. 'We'll all be gone – there will be just you, Sandy and Shona.'

Roddy was suddenly downcast. 'I hadn't thought that far ahead.'

'You'll be on a roll by then,' Rose said.

'Maybe we can take on more staff?' Sandy said hopefully.

'Let's get coats and boots on,' Murdo suggested. 'I can take five people in the Land Rover.'

'And I'll bring my car – Rose and Daz can come with me,' Roddy said.

The drive to the community forest took ten minutes. With Murdo leading the way, they followed the path, inhaling the sharp scent of damp foliage, into the centre of the woodland where new trees had been planted. Pam and Elvis scurried ahead, Pam carefully cutting branches and berries, placing them gently in a basket. She called, 'Anything you can find, put it in your bag – especially fir cones that I can spray, or spruce. Then later we can make wreath bases out of wire and decorate them.'

'I'm glad you know what you're doing.' Tess paused to watch a squirrel scamper up a tree.

Murdo led them further into the woods and they paused at a river. Della closed her eyes, inhaling the fresh air, thinking how much she'd have enjoyed the walk with Sylvester in such a peaceful place. All the time, her thoughts went back to him. Of course they would. She felt her spirits sink. Rose took her arm.

'Are you all right?'

Della nodded, blinking back tears.

'Do you mind if I hang onto you?' Rose made an excuse to hug her. 'I'm not sure I can manage much more walking – this is exhausting.'

'There are seats in the clearing,' Murdo said. 'You can rest, Rose. I know this place well – it's a community forest. I plant trees here with the volunteers.'

Tess gave him a look of pure admiration. 'That's wonderful.'

Jen paused suddenly, fingers to her throat. 'Oh no – I left my basalt necklace back at the hotel.'

'What's basalt?' Tess asked.

'A hard piece of igneous rock,' Pam explained. 'Jen's Icelandic boyfriend gave it to her. It's beautiful. I'm sure it symbolises something everlasting and enduring.'

'Why haven't I heard about this Icelandic boyfriend, Jen?' Rose wanted to know.

'Oh, I've heard all about him,' Pam teased. 'He's called Gunnar. Jen met him on the Iceland cruise.'

'Tell me more.' Della was interested.

'Maybe he's the one, Jen – maybe we'll have another hen party?' Tess said eagerly.

Elvis barked in agreement. Pam was the only one filling a basket. The others crowded round Jen, fascinated.

'Tell us all the gory details,' Tess insisted. 'Did you share a cabin with him?'

'We swam in the Blue Lagoon,' Jen said. 'It was heavenly – I felt like a film star.'

'Is he nice?' Della asked. 'Didn't we see a photo of him in a tuxedo? What foods did you eat in Iceland?'

'Skyr – that's fresh sour milk cheese. And I even managed to try some hákarl, Icelandic fermented shark.'

'Eww. Not for me.' Della pulled a face.

'Show us all your photos,' Rose insisted. 'If he's not handsome, he's not good enough for you. Only the best for our Jen.'

Jen pulled out her phone and showed a photo to her friends of a man in a smart jacket and bow tie, smiling adoringly into the lens. 'So, he's called Gunnar Kristjánsson, he's a retired naval officer, the same age as me... he's really sweet.'

'Gorgeous eyes,' Tess said. 'Blue like the ocean.'

'More to the point, he looks trustworthy,' Rose said. 'Not like unsteady Eddie, the last one you took up with. I'm sorry, Jen, but I wasn't convinced about him, even before we went on the hen party. But this man looks like a good choice.'

'I hope so,' Jen said with a sigh.

'Let me see too,' Daz insisted. 'Oh, yes, he gets my seal of approval, Jen. Very stylish.'

'We should keep going,' Murdo said. 'There's a nice view from the top of the hill.'

'There's a nice view on Jen's phone,' Daz retorted.

'I mean that you can see the sea,' Murdo said. 'And the mountains in the distance. It's nature in its glory.'

'I'll stop here with Jen and she can tell me all about sexy Gunnar,' Rose decided. 'I need to rest anyway.'

'Well, I'm going to the top,' Pam said, Elvis at her heels. 'I have more foraging to do. Who's coming with me?'

'I am – I need the exercise,' Daz whined, pressing his stomach. 'I've eaten so well since I've been on Skye. I don't want to get porky.'

'I'll come.' Tess glanced at Murdo.

'Me too.' Della smiled. 'It's such a beautiful place.'

'I'm up for the walk – I'm no good at talking about romance.'

Roddy made a face. 'My days of anyone giving me a second glance are over.'

'Don't be silly,' Rose told him sternly. 'Lift your chin, smile. There you are. What a handsome man you are when you put your mind to it.'

'Oh, am I?' Roddy scuttled happily after Murdo, who was already leading Pam, Elvis, Tess and Della up a steep winding path into the dense woodlands.

Two hours later, they had collected all the foliage they needed. Murdo and Roddy drove into Sleat. Murdo stopped outside An Roth, a community café that offered a spectacular view overlooking the landscape towards the sea and the wide expanse of blue winter sky filled with spun clouds. He treated everyone to hot chocolate and was enjoying a moment of blissful relaxation, his eyes closed, when Rose noticed that the café sold groceries. She grabbed Daz's arm. 'Local produce. Come on. This looks like fun.'

'Maybe I can get some things to make Christmas wreaths?' Pam wondered.

'Or some decorations?' Tess added.

'We'll have more back at the hotel, up in the attic,' Roddy said.

'That attic needs a good clear-out,' Rose said firmly. 'Murdo, what are you doing this afternoon?'

'Clearing the attic.' Murdo grinned: Rose was a hard taskmaster.

She was also a demon shopper, especially when her efforts were combined with Daz's. Between them, they bought honey, whisky, gin, three mugs, a ceramic jug, five jars of marmalade and a print of a painting of a sunset over the Cuillin mountains. Della was hunting for presents for her sons and for Aston's and Linval's children. Tess treated herself and Jen to bars of chocolate so that they wouldn't feel left out. Murdo tried to tell them about the café. 'This is a real community place. They sell local produce – and support reinvigorated crofting and create jobs in the area…'

'This place is wonderful,' Pam said excitedly. 'I think we're enjoying being tourists for a bit,' she added before treating herself to some fudge and a pottery mug.

Finally they drove back to the hotel, where Sandy was busy in the kitchen, humming a tune. Shona had finished work and Roddy offered to take her and Maisie back home to Armadale, but the little girl was desperate to stay on, to help with making Christmas decorations. She sat next to Pam, who showed her how to make a three-layered Christmas tree from green cupcake wrappers that Sandy had found in a cupboard.

They worked for an hour, making decorations, chattering away while Rose sat at the piano, doing her best to master all the Christmas songs she knew. She was getting better with every repetition and eventually she became so perfect that Daz started singing along. Everyone was soon joining in with 'White Christmas'. Daz even performed a falsetto version of 'Walking in the Air', causing Roddy to sit upright and marvel at the quality of his voice.

Sandy dashed from the kitchen with a plate of warm mince pies and some squirty cream. He nodded to Pam. 'It's all cruelty free – don't you worry about that,' and hurried back: he had several more batches in the oven that he intended to freeze. Tess took a huge bite of a mince pie, cream on the tip of her nose, as she twisted wire to make another ribboned wreath. Then she said, 'Can we see this basalt necklace, Jen? The one gorgeous Gunnar bought you?'

'Oh, yes.' Jen's fingers flew to her neck. 'I'll pop up to our room and get it.'

Pam said, 'It was on the dressing table this morning – next to your little gold earrings.'

Jen was in the hall, on her way up the stairs, when Murdo said, 'I'll have one more mince pie then I'll be off up to clean out the attic.'

'I'll help you,' Roddy offered with a guilty look towards Rose. She was playing with both hands, oblivious. She and Daz had started to sing 'Have Yourself a Merry Little Christmas'. It was not far from being a faultless performance and Rose beamed. Her right hand was almost back to normal.

Tess pushed scissors and ribbons away. 'Roddy – shall we start on the lounge and put some decorations up?'

'By the way, I've ordered a Christmas tree,' Sandy called from the kitchen.

Roddy was perplexed. 'Have you?'

Sandy's head poked around the door. 'Cut price. A mate of mine in Armadale deals in them. I popped in and bought the last one yesterday.'

'It's coming the day after tomorrow on a lorry,' Shona said. 'It will look perfect in the lounge.'

'Thanks.' Roddy smiled. 'It saves me a job of ordering an expensive one.'

'Can I help decorate the tree?' Maisie asked.

'We only have one of those wee tinsel things at home with glowing lights on it...' Shona muttered. 'It's pink. It sits on the TV and saves space.'

'We can all decorate the tree together,' Della said. 'We can get some sweet treats on there...'

Maisie clapped her hands. 'I'll help with that too?'

Shona ruffled her daughter's hair. 'Of course you will.'

'How much did the tree cost?' Roddy asked.

'Twenty-five pounds – but there's no rush.' Sandy was back in the kitchen.

'No, I'll get it now.' Roddy scampered out to his office, just off the hall, where he kept his petty cash. Tess grabbed another mince pie.

'These are the best mince pies in the world, Sandy.'

'The pastry's so light,' Della said.

Murdo helped himself to another two, one after the other, nodding in agreement. Roddy hurried back into the dining room, his face twisted with confusion. 'It's gone... the petty-cash box has gone.'

Sandy came back in the room. 'It was there first thing.'

'It was,' Murdo agreed. 'You took some money from it, Roddy. I saw you.'

'It's gone now,' Roddy repeated. 'And there was some cash I was going to bank tomorrow – about two hundred pounds. That's gone too...'

'How can it have disappeared?' Tess asked.

Jen stood in the doorway, her face troubled. She was trembling.

'What's happened?' Pam asked.

'My necklace – and my gold earrings,' Jen said, shaking her head. 'They're not in my room.'

'Have they fallen on the floor? Could you have put them somewhere else?' Pam asked.

'No, they've been taken.' Jen's voice was a whisper. 'And my handbag's been tipped out onto my bed – everything thrown around – and my purse has been emptied. Every last penny.' She turned to Roddy. 'I've been robbed...'

31

All eyes were on Roddy. Jen sank down at the table, tearful, and Pam wrapped an arm around her. She stammered, 'My necklace was there this morning. And my things have been rifled through.'

'What about my stuff?' Pam asked.

'I didn't check – but I think your handbag was on your bed.'

Pam met Roddy's anxious gaze. 'You need to call the police.'

'What about the rest of us?' Tess asked. 'Do you think our things are safe? Have we been robbed too?'

'I locked the door to our room before I left,' Daz said.

Della and Tess were on their feet. Daz hurried behind them into the hall, Pam too. Jen was in tears now. 'My necklace was a present.' She sniffed. 'I don't mind so much about the money but...'

'Were your bank cards taken?' Rose asked.

'I didn't check.'

'Daz will check his and mine.' Rose folded her arms.

Roddy turned to Shona. 'You were upstairs this morning – did you see anyone?'

'No.' Shona bit her lip. 'And I locked all the rooms after I'd changed the bedding.'

Murdo gave a low cough. 'And there were no visitors, no tradespeople? Was the front door left open?'

'It's always left unlocked during the day.' Shona looked uncomfortable. 'No one came round. It was just me, Sandy and Maisie.'

Sandy turned abruptly. 'I didn't see anybody.'

Shona could hardly speak. 'Who could have taken it?'

Everyone stared at each other in disbelief, then Pam rushed in. 'You were right, Jen – my handbag's been emptied onto the bed. The money's gone. The cards are still there, thank goodness, but I've lost about seventy pounds. Some jewellery's missing – a charm bracelet.'

Tess hurried in, flustered. 'All my money's disappeared, and the silver bracelet Della gave me for my birthday, which I'm really upset about. Someone even stole my old engagement ring. I don't care about that...'

'My stuff has gone too.' Della stood behind her. 'All my money. And my hoop earrings – the ones Sylvester gave me last Christmas.'

'Oh, no.' Rose clenched her hands. 'Who's done this?' She paused as Daz arrived, panting. 'What's the news?'

'My wallet's empty. No cards taken. Your handbag's been rifled, purse completely empty.' Daz took a deep breath. 'Everything they could get their dirty mitts on...'

'So there's been a robbery?' Rose turned to Roddy. 'You'd better have insurance.'

'Isla dealt with things like that.' Roddy was shaking. 'I can't understand what happened.' His eyes met Shona's. 'Only you and Sandy were here.'

'I don't get it,' Shona said, her face crumpling. 'I locked

everything. The keys were in your office. I didn't see anyone come in...'

'We should call the police,' Pam said.

'Maybe we should wait a bit,' Sandy said, and everyone turned to look at him. He was hunched, awkward, his face darkening. Shona met his eyes and shook her head almost imperceptibly.

Murdo frowned in disbelief. 'We rarely get robberies on Skye. We're on the edge of Sleat, miles from anywhere. We had no visitors, no other guests. There were only two of you here, and the little one.'

'Maisie wouldn't steal,' Shona said quickly.

'No, of course she wouldn't,' Sandy said. He had the cornered look of someone who was trying to hide something.

'Sandy – do you know anything about this?' Roddy asked meaningfully.

'He didn't see anything,' Shona said loyally.

'I didn't... why would I do anything to ruin my chances here?' Sandy took a nervous breath. 'I just got this job. It means the world.'

Roddy was puzzled. 'Someone must have... I wonder if...'

Shona whirled on him. 'Don't you dare blame Sandy. That's just typical, isn't it? He's doing his best to go straight now—'

'Go straight?' Roddy repeated. 'You mean he's had convictions?'

'Once... just the once.' Sandy looked even more embarrassed. 'I learned my lesson – I did the time.'

'What time?' Rose demanded. 'Do you have a prison record?'

'You said you learned to be a chef at the Queen's,' Murdo remembered. 'Was that at the Queen's pleasure?'

'It's all in the past,' Shona blurted. 'He's doing things right now, he's a good dad...'

Sandy took a step forward. 'I swear I didn't steal anything. I swear on my daughter's life.'

'Let's just think things through. No one's accusing you.' Rose put up a hand. 'You'd better explain though, Sandy. When were you in prison?'

Sandy exhaled sharply, running a hand over his face. 'I got three years in Barlinnie, in Riddrie, Glasgow – The Big Hoose. I was in for two and a half years, they let me out for good behaviour.'

'What were you in prison for?' Daz asked.

The silence was unbearable as Sandy looked at Shona, his eyes full of sadness.

'Aggravated burglary. I was young, stupid.' He turned to Roddy. 'Please – don't fire me.'

'I'm not sure I have a choice,' Roddy said miserably. 'Unless we can find...'

'I wouldn't steal from here,' Sandy implored. 'Believe me – I wouldn't. Never again.' He glanced at Shona again. 'You believe me?'

She nodded. 'I know you won't, not now. But the keys were in the office the whole time.' Shona's eyes begged. 'Please don't sack him, Roddy.'

'I'll have to phone the police,' Roddy said helplessly. Maisie began to cry, and Shona swept her into her arms. 'I'm sorry, I can't think what else to do, Sandy,' he groaned.

'That woman at the party told me not to stay here,' Jen said. 'I wonder how she knew.'

'What woman?' Murdo asked quickly.

'Oh no.' Roddy put a hand to his mouth. The penny had dropped.

'Of course,' Murdo said, his voice low. 'We all know who's been here and stolen your things.'

'There was a dark-haired woman at the barbecue on our first night,' Jen said slowly. 'She came up to me when I was by myself. She warned me this would happen.'

'What did she say?' Daz asked. 'Can you remember?'

'I can,' Jen said. 'That... let's see... that the hotel was filthy, the driver was a drunkard, the chef was untrustworthy and the owner was useless.' Her voice trailed off. 'I thought she was being mean.'

'She was,' Murdo said. 'Look, Sandy, we're sorry for thinking it could be you. Roddy – wait there... and don't call the police, at least until I'm back.'

Silence returned like an awkward guest as Sandy inspected his shoes, Roddy peered into the corners of the room and Pam asked, 'What's going on?'

'Roddy has an ex,' Tess said. 'She wants him to sell the hotel. And she's a nasty piece of work.'

'I swear it wasn't me.' Sandy's face was miserable.

'Of course,' Roddy said sadly. 'It's me who should apologise.'

'I'm sure you didn't do anything, Sandy,' Daz said kindly. 'That woman's a mean cow.'

'It must be Isla.' Roddy looked truly sorry. 'I should have thought of her straight away, Sandy.'

'How could Isla have got in, Shona?' Rose asked.

'I've no idea,' Shona said. 'I was out the back doing the laundry most of the time. Sandy was in the kitchen.'

'She still has a set of keys, and the front door was open,' Roddy admitted. 'I feel so stupid I didn't think of her straight away.'

Rose folded her arms. 'The police need to take that woman in for questioning. It's one thing her being a bitter hussy, but it's another being a thief.'

Sandy winced. 'Aye, it is.'

'We believe you,' Tess said.

'I'm so sorry,' Roddy said again. He looked close to tears.

'That mean wife of yours has some explaining to do,' Della flared.

Murdo came back into the dining room, his shoulders hunched. 'Sandy, I wonder if you'd make a tray of tea for all of us for three-thirty, plus two more guests. And enough mince pies to go round.'

'What are you doing?' Roddy was aghast.

'I've invited Isla and her boyfriend round.' Murdo's face was rigid. 'I'm going to explain to her very simply how the land lies. And I'm hoping we'll get back everything she's stolen.'

'You're sure it's her?' Pam asked.

'She didn't admit to it on the phone just now,' Murdo said quietly. 'But I'd bet my left bawbag that she rifled the place... and I'm determined to stop her dirty tricks once and for all.'

* * *

It was almost dark outside as the group assembled in front of the roaring fire. Sandy brought a tray of teas and coffees, a plate of fancy cakes and mince pies, then he retreated to the corner of the room with Shona and Maisie. Murdo offered him a reassuring wink. Isla sat on the sofa, wearing the same checked coat and boots Jen had seen at the party, her arms folded tightly. Beside her sat an uncomfortable-looking man, Isla's partner, Alasdair Barclay, slim with brown hair cut close to his scalp, his eyes small. Roddy stood over by the fire, Murdo beneath the stag's head. Tess and Della sat by the fire, Jen next to them. Daz stood behind Rose, who sat on a chair, and Pam and Elvis placed themselves by the door. No one spoke for a while, then Isla glared at Roddy.

'I can't imagine why I was asked to come, unless it's because you're going to give me the money for my half of the hotel.'

Roddy shifted uncomfortably. 'The thing is, Isla...'

'Let's all have tea – coffee – cake. Let's be civilised,' Rose said, with a glance towards Isla that was anything but.

Alasdair took a cup of coffee, slurped loudly, then reached for a pink iced cake. He crammed it into his mouth in two goes, spattering crumbs as he said, 'Go on, then – let's hear it.'

Isla picked up a mug. 'It had better be good.' She exchanged a complicit look with Alasdair.

'The thing is... some things have been taken,' Roddy said, then he glanced towards Murdo for help.

'Taken?' Isla frowned. 'What on earth do you mean?'

'Taken for granted, on both sides.' Murdo offered a diplomatic smirk that made Tess sit up and take notice. She'd had no idea he could speak so smoothly. 'That's why Roddy called this meeting. So we could straighten things out – discuss the way forward.'

'The way forward is to give us half of the money for this hotel,' Isla snapped. 'So you'd better put it on the market.'

'Unless your bank manager will lend it to you,' Alasdair sneered.

'Well, we'd like to come to a compromise,' Murdo said, smiling like a politician.

Isla was suspicious. 'So why are these people here? What's it got to do with them?' She stared at Rose, then Della. 'It's not their business.'

'It might be,' Rose said sweetly. 'We're long-term guests – almost residents.'

'It was you, wasn't it?' Jen spoke quietly.

'What was me?' Isla asked guiltily.

'You were the person I met at the party who told me that this hotel was a dreadful place.' Jen raised her voice. 'Were you trying to put me off staying here?'

'Why would you do that?' Della asked, leaning forward. 'It was an underhand way to behave – Jen didn't know who you were.'

'I've no idea what she's talking about – I didn't say anything.' Isla turned to her partner. 'I thought we'd been asked here to be given some money.'

'Talking of money,' Roddy took a breath to steady himself. 'Some stuff was taken from the hotel this morning – money, jewellery.'

'So?' Isla bridled. 'Are you accusing me?'

Alasdair snickered. 'You should ask your chef. Everyone on the island knows what he is. A tea leaf. A jailbird. Ask him where your stuff is – I bet he stole it.'

Sandy twisted a tea towel in his hands nervously. Shona muttered an expletive. Roddy muttered, 'Sandy told us all about his time in prison. That's all in the past.'

'I wouldn't believe a word he says – he's a liar,' Isla said cynically. 'And a convicted thief. I bet he went off with the petty cash.'

'Who mentioned the petty cash, Isla?' Murdo raised an eyebrow.

'Well, I assumed...'

'Did you?' Murdo's voice was ice cold. 'Are you sure you didn't come in with your keys, you and Alasdair, and help yourselves?'

'How dare you?' Isla said.

'I hope you're not accusing us while you employ a thief?' Alasdair's face was thunder. 'Ask the delinquent over there.'

Shona snorted quietly. 'I'm not allowing my wee child to listen to this rubbish.' She turned on her heel. 'Sandy, I'll be in the kitchen, making her a sandwich. I'll see you there in a moment.'

'OK, love,' Sandy muttered, watching her stride out.

'The thing is, straight after – someone – turned off the freezer, I had security cameras installed,' Murdo said quietly. 'And there's footage of a woman coming in here, leaving minutes later with several bags under her arms.'

'It wasn't me,' Isla said. 'You've made a mistake.'

'The picture's very clear. I'm happy to show it to the police,' Murdo said.

Isla turned on Roddy. 'I just took an instalment.'

'Really?' Pam spoke from the doorway. 'You've just admitted in front of nine witnesses that you've stolen money and jewellery belonging to the guests of this hotel.'

Isla pointed at Roddy. 'It's money he owes me.'

Rose took over. 'We'd like you to return all our belongings, please. It wasn't just money – you took things of sentimental value.'

'It's his fault. If he'd paid me what he owed, I wouldn't have taken desperate measures.' Isla glared at Roddy.

'I'm sure the police would be interested to know that you broke in,' Della said quietly. 'You stole a pair of earrings from me and I want them back.'

Isla sneered. 'It was all junk. Most of it wasn't worth more than a few pounds.'

'What Isla means,' Alasdair took over, raising a finger to quieten her, 'is that she's entitled to half of this hotel.' He stood up. 'Of course you can have your rubbish back. And the petty cash. We only took it to make a point. That you're sitting on a little gold mine and half of it is ours.'

'Ours?' Roddy raised an eyebrow. 'Yours, Alasdair?'

Alasdair stood up. 'Isla was never happy with you. You're

spineless.' He glanced at Isla and flexed his shoulders. 'It was clear as soon as we met that she could do better for herself. I have a business—'

'A failing decorating business, from what I hear,' Roddy said calmly. 'You overcharge customers, do a shoddy job and you're never asked back. That's why you want to tap into Isla's funds. She's not what really interests you – it's how much she's worth.'

Isla struggled to her feet, clearly horrified. 'You can't say that. Ali loves me. We have plans.' She glanced around, her face bitter. 'We're ambitious – not like you, a pathetic has-been with a load of old guests, a drunkard and an ex-con in the kitchen.'

Murdo was about to reply, but Roddy was quick off the mark. 'When you left me, I was broken-hearted, Isla. I valued myself at the worth you put upon me. A weak, useless man, rejected and broken. But you're wrong.' He glanced at Rose, at Murdo, then at Sandy. 'A person isn't who they used to be. The total sum of their worth isn't the mistakes they've made. I learned that when you left. No, it's about who we are now, how we measure up today. So, Murdo may have drunk too much in the past, Sandy may have broken the law. But now, they are friends, good-hearted people I care about. And what are you now, Isla? I'll tell you...'

Isla opened her mouth but Roddy was quicker. 'Once I loved you, but I'm over it. You're spiteful, shallow, nasty, and you're a thief. I'm glad you left. I'm happier, better off. So – I suggest you get out and take your devious, sly, shifty little grinch with you.'

'Grinch?' Isla took a step forward. For a moment, it looked as if she might slap Roddy. She snarled at him instead and said, 'Right, I'll go. But I haven't finished yet.'

Roddy hadn't finished either. 'Isla, you'll return all the jewellery and the money to the hotel by first thing tomorrow morning, or I'll give the camera footage to the police.'

'You'll get your junk back.' Alasdair's voice was a threat. 'But you'll be hearing from my solicitor.'

'And I'll make you pay every penny you owe me,' Isla said bitterly. 'I'll bleed you dry, and that's a promise.' She threw an angry look at Rose, then Della, and swept towards the door, halting as Pam took her time to move out of the way.

'You've not heard the last of us.' Alasdair nodded towards Roddy. 'We'll see you in court.'

Rose watched Alasdair and Isla leave, then she clapped her hands. 'Well done, Roddy.'

'You were amazing, mate,' Daz said, his eyes filled with admiration.

'Thanks for getting our things back.' Della met Roddy's gaze. 'That was so kind of you.'

'Well said, Roddy. She had that coming.' Murdo slapped his nephew on the back.

'And well done for the security cameras, Uncle Murdo,' Roddy said. 'That was a stroke of genius.'

'What security cameras?' Murdo winked.

Tess laughed. 'Oh, that was a clever move.'

'It was,' Pam agreed.

'We'll get your jewellery back,' Murdo said quietly. 'That's the main thing.'

'I'm sorry I didn't tell you I'd spent time in The Big Hoose,' Sandy stammered awkwardly. 'I'm grateful for the things you said. I mean – I still do have a job?'

'Of course you do.' Roddy smiled. 'I couldn't do without you, Sandy, or Shona. We have Christmas to prepare for.'

'Decorations to put up,' Tess said.

'Fun to have.' Daz's eyes sparkled. 'Jamie will be here tomorrow.'

'I have a pasta bake to prepare... and it'll have a good crispy topping.' Sandy suddenly remembered the oven was on.

'Right,' Roddy said with a flourish. 'So – we'll open a bottle of wine or two, I think.'

'There is one thing,' Murdo muttered. 'We've won the first round of the boxing match. We'll get the stolen goods back. But winning the entire contest is a completely different matter, Roddy. Isla is your wife – in the eyes of the law, she's owed half of the hotel. She'll get a solicitor involved and – then what's our next move?'

'I'll pay her – but I have to make the hotel work,' Roddy insisted. 'It belonged to my great-grandfather...'

'That's not the point,' Pam said gently.

'It's half hers by rights,' Tess agreed.

'It is... and I promised her the money. She wants it now and I don't have it yet.' Roddy's face fell. 'What can I do? I'm running out of time. She said I'd fail. Do you think she's right?' He exhaled. 'Is that it, then? She'll take me to court. After Christmas, I'll have to sell up to pay her off.'

'Then Alasdair will get his mitts on the money,' Murdo murmured.

Roddy looked close to tears. 'So Isla wins. And I lose the Sicín Órga.'

'Hmm...' Rose said quietly, and all eyes were on her.

'What do you mean, *hmm*?' Della asked.

Daz asked affectionately, 'I can sense you're plotting something, our Rose.'

'I am,' Rose said. 'Don't worry, Roddy. Just give me some time to think things through. I might have a plan...'

32

'It's the 22nd, and we haven't finished putting the decorations up.' Tess twisted a piece of tinsel over the stag's antlers high on the wall. 'Better late than never.'

Pam frowned. 'That poor animal. How humiliating.'

Rose was untangling a string of lights. 'I thought we'd put a holly wreath round his neck.'

'No way. It's disgusting,' Pam grumbled. 'Trophy killings displayed on the wall, in this day and age?'

'I agree, Pam,' Rose said. 'It's probably been here since Roddy's great-grandfather shot it in the 1920s.'

'Then it's time Roddy took it down,' Pam retorted.

'Definitely – it brings nothing to the ambience,' Rose said grimly. 'This place has history; it's classy... and it needs glitz.'

Della and Jen were attempting to extend a string of lights over the window. Jen groaned. 'My arms are just too short to reach.'

'Here,' Pam said, stretching up above the curtains. 'Is that better?'

'It is.' Della smiled, touching her gold hoop earrings. 'Do you know, I'm starting to feel a bit Christmassy for the first time today. Now our jewellery's been returned.'

Jen fingered the necklace, safely around her neck. 'It's good to have this back...'

'Daz has gone off around the island with Jamie and Robin... those two boys look so loved up.' Rose waved a piece of mistletoe. 'Now we just need some Christmas romance for someone else.'

Everyone was staring at Tess. She blushed. 'Why are you all looking at me?'

Della mouthed, 'Murdo.'

'You like each other – it's plain to see,' Rose said simply.

'I'm not sure,' Tess said. 'I haven't made up my mind.'

'You spent the night together,' Rose retorted.

'Did you?' Jen was all eyes and ears. 'You slept with him?'

'I never knew that,' Pam said. 'Tell all, Tess. Is something going on between you and the marvellous Murdo?'

'Not really,' Tess said. 'We were drunk. We slept next to each other. There was just one kiss – and that was an accident.'

'If you say so.' Rose snorted.

'He seems fond of you,' Della said.

'I don't know.' Tess remembered a remark he had made. 'He did say he'd started to develop feelings for someone, a while ago.'

'Then he likes you, Tess.' Jen clapped her hands.

'You need to ask him.' Rose waved a finger. 'And while you're at it, ask yourself. Do *you* like *him*?'

Tess made a face. 'I'm not sure.'

'I love Christmas romances... I'm going to text Gunnar today and arrange for him to come over in January,' Jen said. 'It's so nice being here on Skye though.'

'I keep getting texts from that rich man whose party we went to,' Pam groaned, looking at her phone. 'Another one's just come in. I shouldn't have given him my number.'

'Aul Crabbit?' Tess exclaimed.

'I thought Erskine Harris was quite the gentleman,' Rose said.

'He's very rich,' Tess reminded her.

'He keeps asking me out on his boat.' Pam grimaced.

'*The Nauti Buoy*?' Della smiled.

'I'd love to see it,' Jen said excitedly.

Tess remembered the rampant mermaids, the sailor endowed with a banana. 'I'm not sure you would.'

'Daz enjoyed the boat trip,' Rose said. 'And I'd go out on the loch again.'

'Maybe we can persuade Erskine to take us all?' Pam flicked a switch and coloured lights began to flash against the wall. The door opened and Murdo came in, carrying a large Christmas tree as if he were about to toss a caber. 'Look what I found outside...'

'We were just talking about you, Murdo,' Rose said smoothly.

'What a whopper,' Tess said, and was suddenly awkward. 'The tree, I mean...'

'It's gorgeous. I can't wait to dress it up,' Della said. 'And we promised Maisie she could help.'

'There are guests coming this afternoon.' Murdo paused for breath. 'The Christmas countdown has really started. We'll be so busy, I don't suppose any of us will see the light of day until Boxing Day now.'

Della put a hand on his arm. 'You need to relax and enjoy it, Murdo.'

'We'll all have a lovely time,' Jen said.

'You're right,' Murdo agreed. 'I'd like to make it the best Christmas this hotel's seen for a good while.'

'Oh, it will be,' Rose said confidently. 'Trust me.'

'You sound sure of yourself, Rose.' Pam was intrigued. 'What are you planning?'

'I need to have a conversation with Roddy first,' Rose said enigmatically. 'All will be revealed.'

'I can't wait,' Della exclaimed. 'I love surprises.' Just as suddenly, she felt deflated and sad. It happened all the time nowadays – there was a moment's happiness and, like a thump to the heart, the memory of Sylvester would hit her hard. This was her first Christmas as a widow. She felt Rose take her hand and she muttered, 'I'm so glad you're all here with me.'

'So are we,' Pam said encouragingly.

'Good news.' Murdo brushed pine needles from his hands. 'I've had a look at the aurora forecast and it looks like we may be on for a special sky tomorrow.'

'Oh, that's so romantic – Gunnar and I saw the Northern Lights in Reykjavik, and it was heaven...' Jen closed her eyes.

'The best place to see them here is Glendale, over in the west. It's two hours away. I thought we'd go after dinner tomorrow. I can take five people.' Murdo looked around the room hopefully.

'Do you see the lights on Skye much?' Pam asked.

'It varies.' Murdo pulled a face. 'December's not the best time for them, but there are some good places around the island. There's no telling where and when the lights will show face, but they might be visible tomorrow night.'

'It sounds very romantic.' Rose gave a complicit wink. 'Of course, I may be busy tomorrow night.'

Murdo was baffled. 'Well, my Land Rover is ready to go. So – who's coming?'

There was a pause, some meeting of eyes, then Rose, Della, Jen and Pam shouted, 'Tess.'

Tess blinked awkwardly. 'Just me?'

'Elvis and I will be busy,' Pam said, and Elvis leaped up with a cheery woof.

'I'm phoning my boys tomorrow evening,' Della added.

'I've seen the Northern Lights already,' Jen said.

'You've been so keen to see them, ever since we arrived, Tess,' Della reminded her.

'You should go, Tess. You and Murdo,' Rose said enigmatically. 'I'm sure you'll have plenty to talk about.'

'Ah, but...' Tess began.

Murdo seemed oblivious of the plotting. 'That's sorted, then, Tess. Dress warmly. We'll be off tomorrow evening about nine.' He lifted his shoulders in a huge shrug. 'Right, I have firewood to chop. No peace for the wicked.'

He left the room and as soon as the door closed there was a sudden roar of laughter.

'This is your big chance, Tess,' Rose said. 'It's now or never, truth or dare...'

'I suppose so. Oh, I don't know.' Tess frowned. 'I want to see the Northern Lights though.'

'I think the earth might move too,' Rose said and everyone burst out laughing again.

* * *

That evening, the hotel guests sat in the lounge drinking mulled wine, courtesy of Roddy. Rose was in her armchair, Daz and Jamie together on the sofa, their hands touching. Jen, Tess and Pam sat on a rug with Elvis, who was snoring, his black fur rising and falling in the flickering glow of the fire. Della and Robin Craig were sitting on armchairs, leaving the four new guests to sit on the long sofa. Glenda and Elaine Carrick-White were cheerful women in their sixties from Killiecrankie in the Highlands, who'd made a last-minute decision to come to Skye for Christmas based on the attractive website. The other couple, Josh and Meg Hunter, both tall, lean and in their thirties, simply wanted time away from their busy jobs in London. After Sandy's special meal of crab cakes or Mexican stuffed peppers, the guests were happy to relax with a comforting spicy drink.

Rose was not relaxing; she was watching everyone intently, as if she had something on her mind. 'So – Josh and Meg.' She offered them a warm smile. 'What do you do in London?'

'We work for a housing charity,' Meg said brightly.

'We wanted to get away for a proper break this year,' Josh added.

'We'd only have disappointed one set of parents by going to stay with the other.' Meg made a face. 'They both want us to visit and there's no way of keeping everyone happy.'

'But we're glad to have downtime,' Josh said. 'We love walking – so it will be great to get out during the day.'

'And in the evenings, we'll just chill out by the fire.' Meg inspected the twinkling lights. 'They've done such a great job in here – it's so cosy.'

'They have,' Pam agreed with a wink.

'And the food's glorious,' Glenda Carrick-White said. 'Did someone say the chef's from the island?'

'A local treasure,' Tess said. 'Christmas dinner will be wonderful.'

Robin Craig had been almost asleep. He opened one eye. 'The thing I love about Skye is the variety – there's so much to see.' A smile lingered on his lips. 'The company is nice and the island has a rich history.'

'My dad's a writer,' Jamie said, his face full of pride.

It matched Daz's as he said, 'And Jamie's a music journo.'

'What do you do, Daz?' Josh Hunter asked.

'I'm an – entertainer,' Daz began.

'In Paris. We both are.' Rose stretched her fingers. 'Our club's closed down for the time being, so we've taken the opportunity to come away.'

Jamie said, 'And I'm so glad you did.'

'Do you live in Paris, Rose?' Elaine Carrick-White was impressed.

'I do. I have a house in Exmouth that I've just sold. Oh – Tess – I meant to tell you – we're looking to complete at the end of January. Will you be all right?'

'I'm sure I will,' Tess said with a weak smile.

'You can stay with me,' Pam, Jen and Della chorused.

Tess tried to make light of her situation. 'All these choices.'

'It's great to have choices,' Robin said lazily, and closed his eyes again. 'Choices are exciting.'

'Have you found anywhere to live yet?' Jen asked Rose.

'It's early days.' Rose sighed. 'I've looked for apartments in Paris but there's nothing that I'd tolerate for the price...'

'Rose wants a little palace all of her own.' Daz laughed.

'Don't we all?' Meg agreed. 'Our little rented place in Camberwell is tiny and it costs the earth. How Josh and I are ever going to get on the property ladder...'

'It's so hard for young people,' Robin said, his eyes still closed.

'It is,' Pam agreed. 'There aren't enough affordable houses.'

'Thank goodness it's Christmas,' Glenda Carrick-White said. 'I'm a social worker, and, believe me, this break can't come soon enough.'

'I'm a chaplain,' Elaine said. 'The stress level in our jobs is quite high. Glenda and I felt that a break on Skye was just what we needed.'

'You've been staying here a while, then?' Josh addressed Daz. 'You know where to go and what to do for fun days out?'

'We do – we had snow a while ago. It was tremendous,' Daz enthused.

'Snow!' Meg exclaimed. 'Will we get a white Christmas here?'

'I doubt it,' Elaine said with a roll of her eyes. 'The seas often keep the temperatures up. Where we are in Killiecrankie – now it certainly knows how to snow there.'

'I recommend Dunvegan for a visit,' Della said with a smile. 'There's a sandy beach there – it's so beautiful.'

'The community forest in Tormore,' Jen said.

'The Fairy Pools,' Tess suggested. 'Or Loch Coruisk.'

'The Cuillin mountains...' Robin murmured, his eyes closed. 'Skye is full of the most picturesque and romantic settings.'

'Portree's nice too,' Rose added.

'And I'm off to see the Northern Lights tomorrow on the west coast,' Tess said excitedly.

'How are you getting there?' Meg turned to Josh. 'We could go.'

'Murdo – he's the owner's uncle – he does trips in his Land Rover,' Tess said tentatively.

'Can he take us all?' Josh asked.

'That sounds fascinating – what do you think, Elaine?' Glenda asked her sister.

'Oh, I'd love to see the aurora borealis,' Elaine agreed.

'I saw the lights in Iceland recently – it was amazing,' Jen said, wondering why Rose was glaring at her.

'I'd love to see it,' Robin murmured.

Rose took charge. 'Shall I talk to Murdo, who does the tours? I'm sure he'll take everyone out on Christmas Eve. I expect the Northern Lights won't have gone anywhere before then.'

Daz picked up on Rose's tone. 'Oh, Christmas Eve would be even more perfect.'

'It would.' Josh smiled. 'Thanks, Rose – let's all go then.'

'Wonderful.' Rose was pleased with herself. She rewarded her efforts with a sip of mulled wine and closed her eyes. The fire crackled and the warmth from the blaze was relaxing.

Then Robin said, 'I'll go with Tess tomorrow.'

Rose sat up and frowned like an annoyed headmistress. 'Is that wise?'

'Oh, I'd like to,' Robin said.

'But the trip on Christmas Eve might be much more fun – a big group...' Daz tried desperately.

'It would be lots more fun all together on Christmas Eve,' Della added.

'With mince pies and sherry,' Pam said.

'They say it will be perfect conditions on the 24th.' Jen was surprised to hear herself telling a complete lie.

Robin said nothing for a moment, then he said, 'I'd prefer to go tomorrow.' He sat up slowly. 'Would that be all right, Tess? I mean – would you mind? I wouldn't be interrupting anything?'

'Oh, no, no, not at all.' Tess couldn't help the words that came out of her mouth. 'It's fine. I've been on at Murdo to take me to see the lights for ages. No, two's company and so is three... It would be lovely to have you along with us, Robin.'

'Then that's settled.' Robin closed his eyes. 'I'll look forward to it.'

All eyes were on Tess as she looked around for help. None came.

Now Robin was coming along, it would be a completely different evening.

33

Several thoughts buzzed in Tess's head as she stood in the shower, getting ready for the drive with Murdo and Robin. She was dreading the evening. She imagined sitting in the cold Land Rover for hours waiting for the Northern Lights to appear, trying to quiz Murdo about his feelings for her and work out if she had any for him at all while Robin monologued about hunter-gatherers. It would be awkward.

In truth, it had been an odd sort of day. After breakfast, Jamie and Daz had pulled on boots and gone for a long hike; Josh and Meg had set out in their car to Dunvegan; the Carrick-Whites had gone shopping in Portree and Robin had retreated to his room to read. Rose had buttonholed her in the corridor and started to ask strange questions – did she feel awful about having nowhere to live? Would she like to live with Rose? Had she decided to buy in Exmouth or was she prepared to travel? How did she feel about an adventure that would change the direction of her life forever? Tess was worried about the way Rose's eyes glinted. If she hadn't known her better, Tess would have suspected that she was losing her marbles.

If that wasn't weird enough, Jen had knocked at the door asking to borrow shampoo. They didn't even have the same hair type – Tess smelled a rat. Jen had launched into a conversation about Gunnar, how lovely he was, how finding love in her seventies was the best thing that Jen could have done and she didn't regret leaping in with both feet and giving her heart away with both hands. It was the quizzical way Jen had looked at Tess that unnerved her. Tess had the distinct feeling that Jen had not just been talking about herself and Gunnar.

Pam had been strange too. She'd stood outside in her wellies as she was taking Elvis for a walk and told Tess that just because she, Pam, didn't want to date Aul Crabbit, that money meant nothing to her and she'd be happy with her animal companion for the rest of her days, Tess shouldn't feel that she had to be the same. After all, Alan hadn't been good for Tess, the gorgeous Vladimir was back in Russia and Tess would probably never see him again. Murdo might well be her last hurrah.

Even Della had done her best, looking up from the novel she'd been reading with tears in her eyes, saying she had no regrets about her fifty-something years with Sylvester and if Tess could enjoy a tenth of the happiness she'd had with that wonderful man, it might be the making of her.

Tess wondered if she came across a bit needy or if she was just plain desperate.

To cap it all, just before dinner that evening, Roddy had gone into meltdown. He'd received a solicitor's letter that morning courtesy of Isla from a blunt woman called Ivy Quinn, demanding that divorce proceedings be instigated immediately so that her client could receive her due portion as quickly as possible. Roddy had been inconsolable; suddenly, it was very real.

Tess hadn't seen or heard from Murdo all day. He hadn't

been in the dining room for dinner. She wondered if he'd turn up at all. It wouldn't be the first time she'd been left in the lurch.

Then it was nine o'clock and she was standing in the hall, apprehensive, wishing she'd changed her mind. Footsteps padded on the stairs and Robin came down, wearing a wax coat and walking boots, carrying some sort of complex camera with a long lens. He smiled.

'Hi, Tess. I'm really looking forward to this evening.'

'Me too.' Tess crossed her fingers behind her back – she was lying. She wished she'd gone to bed early.

Robin's eyes shone, hazel with flecks of green. 'It's incredible to think that we'll be looking at the same sky that our ancestors did, the same particles interacting with gases in our atmosphere resulting in beautiful displays of light. Did you know it's the oxygen that gives off green and red light?'

'No, I didn't.' Tess couldn't have cared less. She was half hoping Murdo would come soon, and half hoping that he wouldn't come at all.

'I have to admit – I'm really excited,' Robin said with a smile. 'It was Jamie's idea to come back here to the hotel for Christmas – he and Daz have really taken to each other – but I jumped at the idea when he suggested it.'

'Oh?' Tess assumed he was keen to continue his research on Skye.

'It's quite remote where I live. I don't get to meet up socially very often and – well, you and your friends have been such inspiring company.'

'Have we?' Tess was surprised.

'Oh, yes.' Robin beamed. 'There's just me and my books most of the time at home. It can get a bit...'

'Dull?' Tess tried.

'Oh, never dull,' Robin said. 'Just a bit full on. I do need to have more fun. Jamie always tells me that.'

'Don't we all?' Tess wondered if she'd have any fun at all this evening. She told herself she was being unfair – she needed to pull herself together.

'"Happiness, not in another place but this place... not for another hour, but this hour."' Robin smiled. 'Walt Whitman.'

'Walt who?' Tess had no idea who he was – the only Walt she'd ever heard of was Disney.

'A nineteenth-century American poet,' Robin said, placing a hand on his heart. 'He was a brilliant writer. Whitman's the father of free verse.'

'That's good to know.' Tess offered her most encouraging smile. She heard the sound of an engine outside and the toot of a horn. 'That must be Murdo.' She breathed a sigh of relief.

'Great.' Robin clutched his camera. 'Let's get this adventure under way.'

The journey to Glendale took two hours and would have revealed some fantastic scenery if it hadn't been so dark outside. Murdo drove confidently, the Land Rover leaping across bumps in the road, making Tess's teeth rattle as she sat squashed between him and Robin in the front. Murdo had his bluegrass music playing loudly and he and Robin were having a fascinating conversation about how bluegrass lyrics frequently referenced the people who lived in Appalachia on modest financial resources. Tess stared out of the window. This wasn't the evening she'd hoped for.

When they arrived at the prime spot for viewing the Northern Lights, there was nothing to be seen. The three of them sat in the car waiting for something to happen in the sky for an hour. Murdo stared through the windscreen. 'There's no sign of anything changing up there.'

Tess stared at the canopy of stars, the velvet darkness. 'We'll wait.'

'We will,' Robin said patiently. 'It's nice to be in pleasant company.'

Murdo was fascinated by Robin's research. 'So – this book you're writing?'

Robin seemed equally eager to discuss his work. 'It's almost finished. The lives of hunter-gatherers are so important, not just on a factual level, but they inform us about how we should be today.'

'You mean men should be like cavemen? Clubbing their wives?' Tess joked.

'Not at all. They had a very civilised social structure.' Robin turned to Tess with a smile. 'Food sharing and cooperation are central for hunter-gatherers – social rules, friendship and kinship ties. It's how we should all be.'

Tess was surprised. 'I didn't know that.'

'How long did they live for?' Murdo asked. 'It must have been a hard life.'

'Oh it was. 75 per cent of deaths were caused by infection, dehydration and starvation. Life expectancy was thirty-three years.'

Tess met his eyes. 'That tells us how precious our health service is.'

'It certainly does,' Robin said excitedly. 'Theirs was a tight community. The proverb that "it takes a village to raise a child" was certainly true.'

'We should all help each other more,' Tess said.

'But that's what I admire so much about you and your friends.' Robin leaned forward. 'You're such a supportive group.'

Murdo agreed. 'I think all five of you are quite special, the relationship you have.'

'It's like you're a group of goddesses who help each other. Rose is the chief decision-maker, Pam is the voice of wisdom and protection.' Robin examined Tess's face to see if she was offended, but she was fascinated. 'Della feeds you all, looks after you. Jen is the emotional heart of the group and you...'

'Me?' Tess waited.

'I think you're the fun one,' Murdo said. 'The one who's up for a laugh.'

'Oh, Tess is much more than that,' Robin said with so much enthusiasm that she felt the breath leave her. 'Tess is the nurturing one, the thoughtful one – the one who's intuitive and warm and affectionate. She's unafraid of being spontaneous, letting her feelings show.'

Tess stared at him. 'Do you think I'm like that?'

'I do,' Robin said. 'In the hunter-gatherer tribes, such a courageous person held everyone else together in times of hardship.'

'Oh, did she?' Tess suddenly felt flattered.

Murdo glanced at his phone. 'It's past midnight. I think the Northern Lights have let us down.'

'Perhaps we could come back tomorrow?' Robin suggested.

'It might rain,' Murdo grunted. 'We should go.'

'I suppose we should,' Tess was feeling suddenly sad. She'd been enjoying herself. 'It's a shame about the Northern Lights. I'd almost forgotten about them.'

Murdo started the engine. 'We'll head back. There won't be much traffic on the road this time of night. It shouldn't take as long on the return journey.'

'I don't mind.' Robin smiled at Tess. 'I've had a lovely time. It would have been nice to see the lights, but they'll still be there another time.'

The headlights illuminated the road ahead and the Land

Rover was filled with the sound of banjos and violins playing fast, a group of voices blending in harmony. Tess began to feel sleepy, the hum of the engine and the thrum of wheels on tarmac making her eyelids heavy. She found her head leaning to one side, hovering over a place where she wanted to rest and dream. She sat up with a jolt. She had almost placed her head on Robin's shoulder. She turned to him in alarm, to see if he had noticed, and found him smiling.

Tess turned to look at Murdo, his eyes on the road, fully focused on driving. She examined his face. It was a strong face, heavy brows. He was a big-hearted man, but his forehead was etched with deep lines. He was troubled.

She turned back to Robin. His face was calm, gentle, with a neat beard. There was a warm light that glimmered in his eyes. He was fascinating, intelligent, thoughtful. There was so much about him that she'd like to get to know.

Tess shook herself awake. She wasn't sure what was happening. It must be all the talk of hunter-gatherers. The idea that she needed a significant other, a companion, was silly. Tess told herself she was fine as she was; she didn't need anyone at all. She was tired, that was all – she'd feel more sensible after some sleep.

The Land Rover was increasing speed. Murdo was driving up a rising wide road towards the top of a hill, headlights blazing, trees overhanging on either side. Darkness lurked at the side of the road.

Murdo accelerated as he crested the hill, then something leaped from the shadows like a dancing devil, followed by a second hulking shape, and there was a huge thud. Tess heard herself scream. Robin reached for her hand instinctively and covered it with his own. Murdo muttered, 'Shit,' and braked hard.

They stared through the windscreen. Two deer had run into the road. One sprang away, its thigh muscles quivering. The other one had hit the front of the Land Rover. It stood up, staggering, and stared into the vehicle as if perplexed. Then it drew itself to its full height and bounded after the other.

'What happened?' Robin shook his head as if to dispel a dream.

'Deer in the road... usual for these parts at night,' Murdo grunted. 'Just a bump. They're tough creatures.'

'It felt like a big bump,' Tess said. 'We must have hit it hard.'

Murdo reached behind him and held up a torch. 'I'd better check nothing's been damaged.' He slid from the driver's door into shadows.

'Are you OK?' Robin asked gently.

'It was a bit of a shock.' Tess gasped. Her heart was still thudding.

'Murdo did well to stop so quickly,' Robin said.

Murdo grunted, swinging himself back in the vehicle. 'Bad news.'

'Are the deer all right?' Tess asked.

'Oh, they're fine, but we have a problem.' Murdo's voice was low. 'The antlers have dented the front. The radiator's leaking. We won't get home.'

'What do you mean, we won't get home?' Tess asked.

'We're stuck here until someone can get to us,' Murdo said. 'We'll move to the side of the road, then wait until someone can drive here and tow us home.' He raised his eyebrows. 'And no one will want to be picking up stranded people on Skye this time of night.'

34

Murdo was talking into his phone nineteen to the dozen. 'Crabbit – no, man – haud yer wheesht and listen – no, no, I'm not jaked – I havenae had a drop – aye, a big deer, two of 'em, in the middle of the road... Nae danger will the Land Rover get me home – the radiator's leaking all over the road, ye bampot. Aye, we'll be here when ye arrive, pal – we're going nowhere. Make haste or I'll gie ye a skelpit lug...' He laughed.

Tess hadn't understood a word, nor had Robin – she was sure of it as they exchanged confused looks. But Murdo seemed suddenly cheerier.

'Aul Crabbit's a fine lad. He's on his way.' Murdo exhaled. 'He has a Land Rover and a big trailer. He'll be here in two hours.'

'That's good.' Tess took out her own phone and messaged Della – even if she was asleep now, and she probably was, she'd have a message to read when she woke; she'd know what had happened. Tess wasn't sure if she, Robin and Murdo would be back at the hotel by morning – her bed might still be empty. She hoped not – she was shattered.

It was now almost one o'clock as the three of them huddled

in the front of the Land Rover. She felt bone tired. Murdo pulled out a bottle of whisky from somewhere behind him. 'Well, we'll have a dram to keep us warm.'

'Is that a good idea?' Robin asked carefully.

'I'm not driving anywhere for the rest of the night.' Murdo took a swig. 'Besides, it'll calm my nerves.'

'Nerves?' Tess repeated.

'Aye, the bang. Did you not hear it when we hit the deer?' Murdo's eyes were large with fear. 'That banging sound is still with me, after all these years, when Mairi and I hit the tree. It's in my bones.'

Tess gave Robin a warning look that she'd handle the conversation. 'It must be horrible when it all comes back to you in a rush, Murdo.'

He gulped more whisky. 'It's never left me, to tell the truth. That night, Mairi was driving us home, the roads were wet and we swerved to avoid a lorry. We hit a tree with such a crash the noise and the vibrations of it wedged itself in my heart forever.' He drank again. 'She just slumped against the wheel and I was helpless, shaking, looking at her, knowing the worst. There was blood...' He closed his eyes. 'What was I supposed to do?'

Tess prised the bottle from his fingers and held it to her lips, tipping it, pretending to drink. 'It wasn't your fault.'

'If only I'd been driving.' Murdo wiped his face. It was suddenly wet with tears. 'I'd have been gone.'

Tess handed the bottle to Robin, who copied her, feigning a drink. She said, 'It's called survivor guilt. It's a form of PTSD. It's no wonder you feel as you do, Murdo. It's completely natural.'

Robin offered a sympathetic murmur. 'It's not so hard being alone after a failed relationship like mine. But you and Mairi genuinely loved each other.'

'We did,' Murdo said. 'She was my world.'

'It must be so nice to have someone care deeply about you.' Robin gave a low laugh. 'My ex-wife said my beard scratched, I walked like a T-Rex and I snuffled in my sleep.'

'I remember you saying that.' Tess was full of sympathy. 'Alan never approved of anything I did.' She took the whisky from Robin and secretly shoved it between her feet. 'You and Mairi were blessed, Murdo.'

'It took me years to get over the things Susan said.' Robin laughed gently. 'I even watched a video of a T-Rex on YouTube to see if I move like that.'

'And do you?' Tess teased.

'It's in the eye of the beholder,' Robin said with a lopsided grin. 'But I'm over her now. If the chance came along for something real and meaningful, I'd grab it with both hands.'

Tess met his eyes. 'Would you, Robin?'

'I would.' His lips curved; something had popped into his head. 'Do you remember our game of Truth and Dare?'

Tess was mortified; she remembered everything up to being sick, to kissing Murdo in her room, but she hoped Robin hadn't been aware of her awful behaviour. 'You were asleep.'

'I wasn't,' Robin said quietly. 'My eyes were closed – but I was awake.'

'It was totally embarrassing.' Tess groaned. 'I was drunk and ridiculous.'

'Not at all – you were the life and soul – you were so spontaneous, and I was in awe of your energy and sense of fun.' Robin took her hand, then let it go again, as if he'd broken a rule. 'I was hoping someone would ask me a question – like the one they asked you, Murdo. I had my answer ready. Do you remember what it was?'

Murdo nodded. 'I do – Rose asked me who was my secret

crush, and I almost said who it was, then Tess was sick and I didn't get to say.'

'So there is someone?' Tess asked nervously. She hoped it wouldn't be her, not now.

'Oh, there is – most definitely. Someone I have so much respect for. It would be easy to fall for her,' Murdo admitted, looking at his large hands.

Tess had been wanting to ask the question for so long, but now she feared the answer. 'You don't have to say who it is.'

'I'd like to.' Murdo took a breath. 'I may have lost Mairi, but I'm still human. When I'm alone at night and I find myself sometimes thinking – thinking of this woman, how sad she is, how I'd do so much to make her happy.'

'Is it someone we know?' Robin asked levelly.

'It is.' Murdo took a deep breath, preparing himself.

'You don't have to say a name,' Tess said again. She felt the muscles in her neck become rigid. 'If you'd rather not...'

'It's Della,' Murdo said quietly. 'She's such a kind woman, so gentle. But I know she's recently been widowed. There's no way she'd think of me in that way.'

Tess exhaled sharply and closed her eyes. She was relieved Murdo had not said it was her. She had no romantic feelings for him – she knew that now. It had simply been the need to reach out to another person, to feel wanted. But that wasn't enough for Tess. She realised that she needed to be one half of a magnet, equally tugged and tugging.

She felt sudden sympathy for Murdo. 'Della likes you. As a friend. But she's just lost the love of her life.'

Murdo sniffed sadly. 'That's part of the attraction, I suppose – we both know how it is to feel utterly heartbroken.'

Tess glanced at Robin. 'As opposed to someone like me, a

discarded reject who doesn't care any more and has totally got her mojo back?'

'Absolutely – and me too.' Robin smiled warmly. 'We can look forward.'

'Maybe Della will be able to look forward in time,' Murdo said. 'Maybe she'll think of me.'

Tess gazed at him sadly. 'She'll be going home after Christmas. We all will. We have to buy plane tickets – I have to return the hire car to Inverness. They're a bit fed up with me extending it.'

'But it's Christmas in two days' time,' Robin said quietly. 'And Christmas is a time for miracles.' He pointed through the windscreen. 'Look.'

Tess looked. The sky had changed from pitch black to shifting columns of milky white and green, moving like searchlights. She held her breath. Robin was beside her, fitting a lens to his camera, then he wriggled from the passenger seat and Tess followed him. Murdo clambered from the other side and together they stared up into the darkness. Rainbows of light collided and snaked, yellowish-greens, blues and purples, fiery reds and oranges.

Tess gasped. 'I wanted to see the Northern Lights so much.'

'If we hadn't hit the deer, we'd have gone home and not seen this,' Murdo whispered. 'It's beautiful. It makes me feel that out of something bad, there's always hope.'

Robin's voice was hushed. '"A man is a great thing upon the earth and through eternity, but every jot of the greatness of man is unfolded out of woman."'

'That's beautiful.' Tess's eyes were fixed on the palette of colours that filled the sky. 'Walt Whitman?'

Robin nodded and pointed his camera, clicking away. Tess inhaled and let out a long breath slowly.

Life was good. Like the skies, things were always changing. And miracles were always possible.

* * *

Della stood in the hall, clutching her ringing phone. She didn't want to be late for the meeting Rose had called in the kitchen.

'Linval?' She pressed the phone hard against her ear to listen. 'You're at Aston's, with the kids? Well, happy Christmas to you, too, but it's not for another day... No, I'll be fine here – we're all having dinner together tomorrow. Rose has made big plans.' She squeezed her eyes closed, listening. A tear fell. 'Of course it will be tough for us all, Linval. The first Christmas without him. But I'm here with friends – we'll get through just fine. And I'll say a prayer for him, as I do every day. What? Oh, I don't know, I'll buy a ticket today. Maybe Saturday's the best time to fly home.'

Della nodded as Linval's voice crackled in her ear. 'That's sweet of you. I'd like that. Yes, Tuesday would be a good day to come over – we can go through some of his things, if you think that would be all right... Oh, I almost forgot – Tess might be coming to stay in the new year. Just while she's looking for some-where to buy. What?' She listened again. 'Oh, she's been wonderful – all my friends have. Tess is asleep right now – I've no idea what time she came in this morning, but it was late... You can have your presents when I see you next week... OK, and happy Christmas to you too, Linval. Tell Aston I'll ring you all tomorrow. I want to talk to you all. No, just to say happy Christ-mas... yes, you too – so much...'

Della sighed, counting her blessings. She had her boys, the grandchildren. Linval was the image of Sylvester now, just as he'd been in his forties; and he had the same big, kind heart, the same spontaneous humour. It would be wonderful to see him next week, but it would feel strange. Her family had once been a firm square solid block – now one corner had been chipped off. It would never be the same.

Della recalled Tess fast asleep upstairs, a humped shape beneath the duvet, snoring gently. She'd come home from seeing the Northern Lights and gone to bed without waking her. An earlier text message had simply been a heart emoji accompanied by a photo of some creamy colours glowing in the sky. So she'd seen the aurora borealis. Della hoped she'd had a memorable time and wondered if she and Murdo had declared undying love. That would be typical of Tess, to fall in love now they were about to go home. Della was looking forward to being in her own home again, although she was dreading it at the same time. Memories of Sylvester would linger in her house, the furniture he'd sat on, the cup he'd drunk from, the window he'd peered in through when he'd been mowing the little lawn. The smell of him would still be in every room. The familiarity of it would be a comfort and it would break her heart all over again. Della pulled herself together and hurried towards the kitchen.

Rose was already holding court. She winked at Della as she came in and took her place beside Jen and Pam. Sandy and Shona were there, little Maisie in Shona's arms. Daz stood next to Jamie, shoulder to shoulder, exchanging smiles. Robin was oblivious, in a world of his own. Roddy was next to Rose, holding a notepad and pen, writing down details.

'So...' Rose lifted a finger, calling for attention. 'We're all here, apart from Tess and Murdo, who came in during the early hours after spending the whole night in the Land Rover watching the aurora borealis...' She cleared her throat and Daz laughed.

'Dirty stop-outs...' Daz said.

'It was beautiful,' Robin said under his breath.

'Right, well, I'll fill them in with the details of what we're going to do tomorrow later. But I've asked you here because Roddy and I want to put the finishing touches to our Christmas preparations. Now, the guests are out for the day – the Carrick-Whites have gone for a hike in the forest and Meg and Josh have gone to the Fairy Pools. We have two more guests arriving this afternoon, Joan and Brian Cooper from Yorkshire. That's dinner for six tonight, plus us lot.'

'It's all in hand, boss.' Sandy gave a mock salute.

'And – Christmas dinner?' Rose began.

'It's all in hand, boss,' Sandy said again.

Roddy laughed. 'Go on then, Superchef – let's hear the menu again.'

'Turkey, all the trimmings, chestnut wellington, two sorts of gravy, one veggie, roast tatties, six types of veg including sprouts.'

'Ew... sprouts.' Maisie pulled a face.

'It's all prepped, plus a choice of two desserts, one hot and traditional, one cold and decadent.' Sandy looked pleased with himself.

'And you'll eat with us, and Shona and Maisie too?' Roddy asked.

'Oh, we're looking forward to it,' Shona said.

Rose took over. 'What I want to discuss now is – what's happening in the evening?'

'The aurora borealis trip is cancelled due to rain and I believe Land Rover repairs are under way as we speak,' Roddy said.

'We'll sit in the lounge with brandy and a mince pie?' Jen suggested.

'After a vigorous walk?' Pam added.

'No.' Roddy took a breath. 'Rose has been organising something.'

'Roddy and I contacted most of the people from Sleat who were at Erskine Harris's party. We've sold tickets,' Rose said. 'So, after Christmas dinner, Mr Harris and Murdo are going to help Daz set up the dining room for a concert. We're going to use the repainted stage...' she clapped her hands '...for the first time in a hundred years.'

'A concert – oh, that's lovely,' Robin said excitedly.

'Are you playing the piano?' Jen asked.

'Can I come, Mummy?' Maisie wriggled in her mother's arms.

'All will be revealed in good time.' Daz gave his most enigmatic smile. 'But I have to say, Rose and I have been practising...'

'I'm a bit rusty.' Rose feigned bashfulness. 'But a Christmas concert will be so much fun.'

'And the point is—' Roddy said '—it's a sell-out. We'll be packed. We're bringing the community in. The first of many events, perhaps. It will be so good for business. And I've asked Sandy to do refreshments and bowls of punch.'

'It's all organised.' Sandy smiled. 'Canapés, mini pizzas and quiches, salads, rice dishes, pâtés, bread.'

'This hotel's on the way to being the best in the south of the island.' Roddy couldn't help grinning.

'The best on Skye,' Daz said.

'The most famous in Scotland.' Rose laughed. 'And why not? Aim high, I say. So, to that end – Roddy?'

'Of course – I know what to do now. Thanks, Rose – and thanks for the idea and all the organising and—' Roddy began, but Rose tapped him gently on the shoulder.

'Get on with it.'

'Yes, boss,' Roddy teased as he opened the fridge and pulled out two bottles of champagne, an alcohol-free Buck's fizz and apple juice for Maisie. Sandy and Shona were at his side, placing glasses on the counter, while he fussed with the wires and the corks. There was a loud pop and Roddy poured froth into glasses that were quickly handed round. He looked at Rose, and said, 'Over to you?'

'I propose a toast.' Rose lifted her glass. 'To everyone, to a bright future at the Sicín Órga – and to a wonderfully happy Christmas.'

'To Christmas,' came a chorus of happy voices, then the soft sound of slurping bubbles.

The kitchen door opened with a bang and Tess rushed in. She glanced at Robin and caught her breath.

'Oh. Hello everyone. You've got champagne? Is there any for me?'

'Here you are.' Robin's face was filled with undeniable admiration as he passed her a glass.

'Thank you.' Tess blushed. She took a huge glug. 'Cheers. Happy Christmas Eve.'

The door swung open again and Murdo paused abruptly with his hands on his hips and a greasy smear on his face. He glanced at everyone and grinned.

'Sorry I'm late – I've been fixing a leaky radiator,' he said. 'Is there any of the fizzy stuff left for me?'

35

On Christmas afternoon, Della, Tess, Pam and Jen stood outside the hotel, dressed warmly in coats, scarves and boots, staring at the darkening sky.

'What a beautiful day it's been,' Pam said as Elvis sprang at her legs excitedly.

'It rained again,' Della said quietly.

Jen shivered. 'There's a stiff breeze from the sea, but I'm so looking forward to a quick stroll on the beach before all the light goes.'

'Me too,' Tess added. 'I ate too much.'

'Christmas dinner was wonderful,' Della said. 'It was strange being here, not at home, not having to cook, not having to wash up... but I'm so grateful.'

They linked arms and walked across the grass to where the pebbly descent to the beach began. In the distance, the crinkled steel sea rushed in. 'It's been a lovely time,' Tess said sadly. 'I'm not ready to go.'

'So, you can tell us now,' Jen said animatedly. 'How did you get on with Murdo on Monday night? Are you soulmates?'

Pam narrowed her eyes, perceptive as ever. 'I think Tess has changed her mind.'

Tess tried to feign innocence. 'Whatever do you mean?'

'I mean that you and Robin had your heads together throughout dinner last night and again today,' Pam said.

'You did – I saw that,' Della agreed. 'He seems a nice man – and so attentive.'

'I didn't notice,' Jen said.

'You were too busy texting your Viking,' Tess said, enjoying Jen's guilty blush.

'So the question is...' Pam's eyes sparkled. 'Whose hen party will we be planning first – Tess's or Jen's?'

Elvis barked and Jen smiled. 'Well, if and when Gunnar asks me to marry him...'

'If and when?' Tess said jealously. 'Robin and I haven't even kissed yet. He's only held my hand for three seconds.'

'You'd better get a wriggle on – you're running out of time, Tess.' Della winked.

'You certainly do need to get a move on,' Pam agreed. 'Jen and I have been looking at flights home. We can go on Saturday or Monday from Inverness – there are a few seats available.'

'I think we should go on Saturday,' Della said. 'Linval's coming to visit me on Tuesday, so I won't be on my own for too long.'

Tess made an unhappy face. 'I don't want to go. I'll have to pack everything...'

They had reached the pebbles and were walking towards the sea. Pam slipped off Elvis's lead and he was free, running off to the sea, splashing in the waves.

'Oh, I couldn't go in the water,' Jen said. 'It's very bracing here.'

'It'll be more bracing in Iceland,' Tess teased. 'Or will you and Gunnar live in Exmouth?'

'I'd live anywhere he wants.' Jen faked a little swoon. 'That man is a keeper.'

'So – we have a few days left – what will we do with the last of our holiday?' Della asked.

'Do you think Rose will come back to Exmouth with us or will she go to Paris?' Tess asked.

'I suppose it depends on what's happening at Monty's,' Pam replied. 'She's so busy practising with Daz. I hope their concert goes well.'

'She's making a good recovery – I'm proud of her,' Della said. 'She can play the piano as well as ever.'

'Her mobility isn't 100 per cent though,' Tess said anxiously. 'It's a good job she has Daz to look after her.'

'She mightn't have him much longer,' Jen exclaimed. 'He and Jamie are clearly in love.'

'We'll make sure she's all right,' Della said firmly.

'She's a tough cookie,' Pam said fondly.

'But she's not getting any younger – none of us are.' Tess exhaled. She stared at the glittering sea as the iron-grey waves rolled in. 'We have to grab every moment, while we can.' She took a breath and smiled. '"Henceforth, I ask not good-fortune, I myself am good-fortune."'

'I didn't know you were a fan of Walt Whitman.' Pam was astonished.

'Oh, I picked it up from a man I spent the night with, looking at the stars,' Tess said, with a cheeky smile. Then she shivered. 'It's bloody cold out here now. Shall we go back and get a mince pie?'

Pam gave a low whistle and Elvis bounded back, barking, jumping at her legs, shaking wet drops over everyone.

Jen said, 'We ought to help Rose get ready for her big performance. I wonder what songs she's doing tonight.'

They turned, hands in pockets, shoulders hunched, and began the walk over pebbles back to the hotel.

Pam said thoughtfully, 'I hope she plays some Beethoven...'

'A romantic, sentimental ballad...' Della suggested. '"Fly Me to the Moon"... "Somethin' Stupid"...'

'Or Christmas songs...' Jen sighed. '"All I Want for Christmas Is You".'

'Or Abba?' Tess suggested, launching into a song: 'Gimme! Gimme! Gimme! A Man After Midnight.'

Jen laughed. 'Do you ever think of anything but sex, Tess?'

'Is there anything else?' Tess raised an eyebrow.

Della tugged her arm playfully. 'Conversation. Laughter. Good friends...'

'Talking of which,' Pam lifted her phone. 'I've just had an invitation for a boat trip.'

'When? Who?' Jen asked.

'Aul Crabbit?' Tess guessed.

'On *The Nauti Buoy*?' Della said.

'You and him, a romantic meal?' Tess was delighted.

'Yes, Erskine, tomorrow – a Boxing Day voyage around the loch. But it's not a romantic meal. We're all invited,' Pam said. 'An open invitation on *The Nauti Buoy*.'

'It might be fun,' Tess said.

'Before we all leave,' Della murmured. 'What a nice way to end the holiday.'

'Look.' Jen stopped and pointed to the hotel. 'There can't be more guests arriving.'

'There shouldn't be. We're fully booked.' Tess said.

'Then who are they?' Della frowned. 'There's a minibus parked outside... and some people are getting out.'

'Perhaps it's some of Rose's audience arriving early,' Jen said.

'No – look – they're carrying bags and suitcases and trunks. And – is that an amplifier? It looks like they're moving in.' Tess lowered her voice. 'What's Rose up to?'

Pam paused, staring at the people who were staggering into the hotel beneath piles of feather boas, wigs, silk dresses, and she laughed. 'Oh – of course! I know exactly what she's planning,' she said. 'That woman is a genius.'

* * *

The dining hall was packed with some seventy people clad in their smartest clothes, sipping cocktails. The atmosphere was fully French cabaret. Robin and Jamie had helped Murdo, Aul Crabbit and Roddy to set up with little tables and chairs from the village hall, and Daz had rigged a few stage lights Murdo had borrowed from Aul Crabbit's mansion. The place was smokily dim with little candles burning in glasses on tables, a long trestle against a wall laden with food and drink that Sandy had set up earlier. Jamie had organised for scratchy jazz music to be played through speakers. On the stage, to one side, Rose's piano had been covered in tinsel and fairly lights. A pink microphone sat on top, wrapped in more tinsel. A spotlight illuminated centre stage, and the audience stared at it in anticipation.

Sandy sat at a table looking relaxed, a beer in his hand, with Shona and little Maisie. Robin was sitting close to Tess, who was wearing her Paris cocktail dress. Next to them, staring at the empty stage in anticipation, were Jamie, Murdo, Aul Crabbit, Della, Jen and Pam, who were dressed in their most glamorous clothes. Not far away, the Carrick-Whites in their Christmas best sipped from cocktail glasses; Meg and Josh Hunter in Santa hats and newest guests, Joan and Brian Cooper, shared a bottle of wine. The room was filled with low chatter, excited voices. Roddy shambled nervously onto the stage and everyone was suddenly silent.

'It's gone very quiet here,' Roddy said awkwardly. 'Has my wife turned up?'

Murdo guffawed and Aul Crabbit banged the table with his fist several times. The audience cheered. Roddy was inspired with new confidence. 'Thank you all for coming tonight. I suppose it makes a pleasant change from watching the King's Christmas speech on TV followed by *Chitty Chitty Bang Bang...*'

Someone hooted encouragingly and there was more applause. Roddy continued. 'So, tonight marks the first of what I hope will be many concerts at the Sicín Órga. As you know, the hotel was built in Victorian times by my great-grandfather, Dougal Fraser, a man of much importance and dignity in Sleat—'

'Get on with it, man,' Murdo roared.

Aul Crabbit added, 'I need a drink.'

'So – er – without further ado,' Roddy said, and the applause was deafening. 'I haven't finished...' He looked around and smiled good-naturedly, riding the banter. 'My good friend Rose from Paris has brought some artistes from the famous Monty's club here tonight for a Yuletide show...'

Hands thumped on tables, voices cheered, and the rest of Roddy's words were lost. He gave up, scurrying off stage, and a performer in oversized spangled glasses and a glittery jacket rushed on, her arms waving wildly in the air to thunderous applause. She began to bang out familiar chords on the piano: it was 'Crocodile Rock'. She had black lipstick on, her mouth a sullen snarl as she bellowed out the words, shaking the loose locks of her flame-red wig. Then she stood up, wiggling her bottom, athletically placing a muscular fishnet-stockinged leg that ended in a red stiletto on the top of the piano, and launched into 'Rocket Man'. The audience sang along, clapping and cheering when she put her mouth close to the mic and murmured, 'Thank you. Happy Christmas. I'm Elton Joan.'

She rushed off and the stage was in blackout. There was a moment of anticipation, then a spotlight snapped on to reveal a tall, gangly schoolgirl in a very short gymslip and tie, ripped stockings, blonde hair in bendy plaits with scarlet ribbons. Her mouth was a cupid's bow. She pouted and snarled her way through '...Baby One More Time', 'Toxic' and 'I'm a Slave 4 U'.

Jen whispered to Pam, 'I remember her – she's Miss Peaches Beaverhausen... she and I duetted together in Monty's.'

'I remember it well.' Pam took a sip of wine. 'You both sang "Oops! ...I Did It Again".'

'And I might, you know, do it again, have another hen night. If Gunnar asks me or – perhaps I could just ask him.' Jen's fingers touched the basalt necklace.

Pam's hand strayed beneath the table and she felt a warm tongue lick her palm. Elvis was her most faithful companion – she wanted nothing more.

The next performer was Dee Bortsch, an artiste in tight leather with a pink bouffant hairdo, who sang 'Ace of Spades' and 'Born to Raise Hell' by Motörhead. She was followed by a woman who looked like a traditional pantomime dame, wearing a ridiculously low-cut dress with puffed sleeves, heart-shaped beauty spots on her face, arched eyebrows and purple lips. She introduced herself as Fonda Chips and sang ballads in a heart-breakingly beautiful voice. Della had tears in her eyes as she listened to a sweet rendition of 'I Will Always Love You', thinking that her voice was startlingly similar to Whitney Houston's.

A country and western singer with masses of curly blonde

hair and a fringed minidress, Lynne Shmobb, came on next to sing 'Stand by Your Man' and 'Don't Mess with Texas'. Her version of 'Man! I Feel Like a Woman!' brought the house down. Aul Crabbit clambered on his chair and did a little Highland fling. Murdo got down on his hands and knees and would have proposed marriage there and then if Jamie and Sandy hadn't hauled him up.

There was a short interval, during which everyone approached the food and drinks table, bringing back piled plates. Sandy was delighted that his buffet was a success. Then silence returned as the lights dimmed, and Paris Ite and Carmen Gettit took to the stage in glittery evening dresses and high blue wigs and sang a song Pam recognised from a Mozart opera. They performed 'Pa–pa–pa– Papageno' expertly, but the audience clearly thought it was a comedy and roared with laughter throughout. Next they launched into a lip-sync of the 'Duetto buffo di due gatti', often called the Meow song, and the audience fell about in fits of mirth at their grotesque faces as they sang as two competing cats.

Tess spluttered, 'That's the most hilarious thing I've ever seen.'

Pam was unimpressed. 'It's not meant to be funny – well, not funny in that way.'

The singers took their bow and the stage was dark again, the room silent, waiting. Then Rose came on, graceful in her Marie Antoinette costume, a high purple wig, a sumptuous gown. She sat at the piano, her purple lips next to the microphone, her voice soft as crushed silk. 'Good evening...'

The applause hit the roof, cheering and yelling. She waited, then she murmured, 'Some of you may know I had a stroke recently...'

The room was pin-drop silent.

'On the last day of December, New Year's Eve, I will be eighty years old.'

Someone cheered and shouted, 'Go, Rose.'

'So,' Rose offered a secret smile '...don't ever let anyone tell you an older lady is not a force to be reckoned with. Introducing tonight, for your special Christmas enjoyment, Rose-on-Wye and Greta Manchester.'

Rose's hands banged out the same chords that Tess, Della, Jen and Pam had heard her practising for days, the rhythmic left hand, the right hand rippling up and down the notes in the Benny Andersson frill she had tried so hard to master again. Then Daz was on stage in the shortest, clingiest, pinkest dress, long yellow Agnetha tresses, a glittering blue crocheted hat, bursting into 'Gimme! Gimme! Gimme! (A Man After Midnight)' with the most provocative pout he could muster. Everyone in the audience was on their feet. Sandy wrapped Shona and Maisie in his arms, Aul Crabbit was jiving with Murdo. Robin embraced Tess in a smooch, despite the fast music. Jamie rushed to the front of the stage, dancing for all he was worth.

Rose and Daz played their set to a jiving crowd: 'Dancing Queen' became 'Mamma Mia'; 'Knowing Me, Knowing You' became 'Money, Money, Money'. The applause was so loud, hands banging on tables, voices raised calling for more. Rose stood up and the room was quiet again. She moved to Daz; they held hands and bowed, then bowed again.

'Talking of "Money, Money, Money"...' Rose raised a finger. Everyone was listening as she said, 'I have something to say. Roddy?' She lifted a commanding eyebrow and Roddy was on stage with her, three figures together, smiling. She said, 'Shall I make the announcement, Mr Fraser, or will you?'

'You should,' Roddy said. 'You're the boss.'

'Well,' Rose addressed the audience, 'I hope you've enjoyed the show.'

The audience chorused 'Yes-s-s,' applauding and thumping the tables in appreciation.

'Good. This night marks the first concert of its kind on Skye, but we're hoping it won't be the last.'

There was more cheering.

'In fact—' Rose smiled beatifically '—Daz and Roddy and I would like to put the Sicín Órga hotel on the map. We're planning to make this the biggest, grandest place, bring more jobs to the area and really get things moving.'

The applause grew louder. Tess's voice could be heard shouting, 'How are you going to do that?'

Rose drew herself up to her full height and said, 'Roddy and I are going into business together. I'd like to announce to you all tonight that I am now the co-owner of the Sicín Órga.'

36

Della leaned against the rails of *The Nauti Boy*, watching everyone else have fun. She smiled sadly. She was ready to go home, to spend some time in the house with her memories of Sylvester. Today, Boxing Day, was Thursday and they'd agreed this morning at breakfast that she, Tess, Pam and Jen would book tickets tonight for Saturday's flight to Bristol. There were a few seats remaining. Della wanted to be back home in Exmouth now. She'd had special time with her friends, time to think, to heal a little; she was grateful. But she was ready to be alone with her grief now.

Strangely, somehow, the world continued to go round, she told herself with a shrug, even though her own world had stopped for a while. Life went on for everyone else. Not far away, Aul Crabbit was doing his best to endear himself to Pam, offering her the most succulent pieces of venison from his plate. Jen stood nearby, trying hard not to laugh. Della could read Pam's lips as she showed him an unimpressed expression. 'I don't eat venison. I'm vegetarian.' Aul Crabbit took a step back, remembering the barbecue; his face took on a look of desperation as he wrapped an arm around Pam, asked her how she liked his boat, if she'd like him to get her and Jen a drink. He even chucked Elvis under the chin and rubbed his furry ears in a last-ditch attempt to please her. Della knew her friend well; Aul Crabbit had no chance.

Della glanced to where Rose stood chatting to Fonda Chips, supported by Daz on one side and Jamie on the other. Not that Rose needed their help to stroll down the boat now. But they both clearly adored her.

Music boomed from hidden speakers on *The Nauti Buoy*. It was 'You Spin Me Round (Like a Record)' by Dead or Alive. Della felt her mood plummet – it was incredible how something so simple like the name of a group could do that to her in an instant. The other guests were enjoying themselves: Meg and Josh, Elaine and Glenda Carrick-White, the Coopers from Yorkshire. They'd told Roddy at breakfast that it had been their best Christmas ever. Roddy was chatting to Sandy and Shona, his face animated, every bit the successful business-man. Maisie perched on her father's shoulders, waving a mince pie.

Murdo was surrounded by some of the artistes from last night's performance. Della could hear him ask, 'Were you really singing or miming? I mean, ye were all definitely giving it laldy. I haven't enjoyed myself so much in years.'

Elton Joan, now dressed in jeans and a leather jacket, was sharing crisps with Lynne Shmobb and Miss Peaches Beaver-hausen, both drinking hot punch in warm coats and woollen hats. Della sighed. Life still went on.

Tess and Robin were together, staring up at the black moun-tains. Della assumed they were making plans for a future together. She wondered if they'd be satisfied with a long-distance relationship. The thought made her think of Sylvester.

He was a long way away now, but she'd love him for the rest of her days.

She was aware that someone had moved next to her and was patting her shoulder. She turned, her smile ready. 'Jen.'

'How are you?' Jen asked gently. It was a question Della hated. Jen meant nothing bad by it, but Della knew that too much sympathy brought tears; it reminded her that grief clung to her like a heavy coat she couldn't shrug off.

'I'm all right,' Della said. It was the best she could manage.

'We fly home the day after tomorrow,' Jen said. 'Now, tell me what I can do for you when we get there. Do you want me to come round, to stay over?'

'I'll let you know later, if that's all right,' Della said. 'In all honesty, I've no idea how I'll feel.'

'Of course,' Jen agreed. 'Whatever you need.'

'There is one thing,' Della said.

'Name it.'

Della took a deep breath. 'Please don't behave any differently on my account. Be just as you normally would.'

'In what way?'

'Well...' Della forced a smile. 'If you want to talk about the future with Gunnar, just do it. Say what you want. Be positive, optimistic. I want you to be happy. But – please don't clam up and think, oh, I'd better not mention the future because poor Della has lost...' She couldn't finish. Her throat had swollen and tears blinded her.

Jen wrapped both arms around her. 'Like I said – whatever you need.'

Della stifled a sob. 'It's still so raw.'

'You and Sylvester were together for most of your life. Of course it's raw.'

Pam was next to them, wrapping her arms around Della and Jen as Elvis leaped up with a muffled bark. 'I'm here too, lovey.'

'Thanks.' Della snuffled. 'I'm so sorry.'

'Not at all,' Pam whispered. 'We're sorry. He was a beautiful man. We loved him too. And we love you. We're here whenever you need us. You just have to say.'

Della clutched both women tightly, holding on with desperate fingers. Her lower back ached, her heart was heavy and her eyes filled with tears. She had no idea how she would cope. But cope she would. It was the only way. She had her boys. And she had good, good friends.

* * *

Tess and Robin stood together staring at the snow-topped black mountains beyond the shimmering loch. Robin took her hand in his, smoothing her windblown locks with the other. 'It's been good getting to know you, Tess.'

'It's been lovely.' Tess was unsure whether he was about to tell her that a long-distance relationship wouldn't work but, instinctively, she knew that wasn't what he felt. She could tell by the way his eyes lingered on her face.

He took a breath. 'I know it's early days but... can I visit you?'

'I'd like that.'

'And you can come up to the Highlands and visit me.'

'I'd like that too.'

'I'm glad we met,' Robin said simply.

'So am I. We're so different in so many ways but...'

'We're the same.' Robin finished her sentence. He thought for a while. 'I'd like to kiss you.'

Tess smiled, her eyes fixed on his. 'I'd like to kiss you back.'

Their lips came together, cold, warming quickly as they

stayed locked in each other's arms. Tess said, 'It's not scratchy. It's lovely.'

'My beard?' Robin smiled at the memory. 'What if I snort when I'm asleep?'

'I'll snort next to you,' Tess said and kissed him again.

Robin opened his eyes and murmured, '"There we two, content, happy in being together, speaking little, perhaps not a word."'

'Walt again?' Tess said. 'I'm becoming fond of him.'

'The first thing I'll do when I'm back home is send you a book of his poems – with my love.'

Tess turned; Rose was standing next to her, waiting patiently. Tess said, 'Your performance was just so incredible last night, Rose. I'm so proud of what you did.'

Rose's face was a picture of contentment; she looked fragile, snuggled inside her red anorak. She smiled sweetly at Robin. 'Can I steal Tess for a moment, please?'

'Of course,' Robin said. 'I'll get us all a refill.' He picked up Tess's empty glass, his own, and moved over to the drinks table.

Rose arched an eyebrow. 'It's going well, then, the new romance.'

'It is,' Tess agreed. 'He's quoting Walt Whitman. I think he must love me.'

'It'll be your hen party soon, I expect,' Rose quipped. She studied Tess's face. 'You'll miss him when you go back to Exmouth.'

'I will,' Tess said with a sigh.

'Then why are you going?'

Tess shook her head. 'I live there.'

'*I* live there,' Rose said emphatically. 'Well, I used to. I've sold my house now and I'm using the money to buy a share in the hotel. Daz is coming in with me too, so between me, Roddy and

Daz, we'll buy Roddy's whingeing wife out and make the place properly our own. We'll put our stamp on it and make the Golden Hen soar again.'

Tess was impressed. 'You don't stand still.'

'I don't. Daz is in love with Jamie. Monty's is closed. It makes perfect sense for us to put some roots down here. And we had such a fun time performing last night – we could do that every month. Some of the artists have already said they'll come over regularly.'

'Where the hell did they all sleep?' Tess marvelled.

'Up in the attic – Murdo cleared it out. They brought sleeping bags.' Rose grinned.

'You think of everything, Rose.'

'I do. Roddy and I have been making big plans.' Rose gazed out into the dark loch. 'We'll revamp his flat on the ground floor, make it into two flats. We'll rebuild the outbuilding where the freezer is into a small bungalow. Then we'll refurbish the attic, put in another six bedrooms, up the advertising on the website, bring in another chef, a sous chef, more help. Plenty of people on Skye need jobs.'

'Can you afford that?'

'We've looked at numbers and we can make it work. Roddy will pay Isla off. Once we start making money and filling all the rooms, we'll be raking it in. I have a one-year plan, a three-year and a five-year. So what if I'm nearly eighty? I need a project or I'll fade away.'

'A project? Oh goodness – we need to plan your birthday party.' Tess said.

'Oh, that's already in hand. There will be the biggest bash on New Year's Eve. It'll be here, at our hotel. Invites are on the way – it's all arranged. And you have to be here too.'

'But I'll be back in Exmouth.'

Rose met her eyes. 'Tess, I've been thinking. None of us are getting any younger. Maybe one day, if Jen or Della or Pam needed a different lifestyle, we could turn the place into a retirement home near the sea where we friends live together and have fun. It's got to be the way forward for older people. We'd be the silver-haired sisterhood.'

'What a great idea,' Tess said.

'But for now – what's next for you?'

'I don't know.'

'Right. I'll ask you a straight question. What are you going to do with the settlement money from your divorce?'

'I might buy a little terraced cottage near Pam.'

'What then?'

'Who knows? I'd live there and see what happens with me and Robin.'

'What will your life be like?'

'The same as it's always been. My girls would visit from time to time. Gemma's usually busy. Lisa rings me once a week.'

'And is that what you want?'

'No.' Tess looked sad. 'I don't want to go home, not really. I've had such a good time here. I met Robin. I think we may have something special. Skye's beautiful. It makes me feel happy being here.'

'Tess, are you being deliberately thick?' Rose grabbed her sleeve and shook it. 'Use your settlement – buy into the hotel with us. You can have the bungalow we're going to build – it'll be perfect for a couple when it's finished. Move to Skye with me and Daz, help me manage the hotel. Stay. Be here for my birthday bash. Stay forever. You can see Robin all the time. He can move in and enjoy writing and researching book two.' Her face was desperate. 'You can have fun. You can *live*.'

'I see what you mean.' Tess took in her words. 'You're right. I can live – as opposed to exist. Oh, Rose. I could, couldn't I?' Her breath came in gulps. 'I could. Yes. Yes, please. I'd love to.'

'Do you need time to make a decision?' Rose asked firmly. 'It's a big one.'

'It is – but it's also very small,' Tess said. 'It's a wonderful opportunity. It's about having fun, being with friends, falling in love. Why do I need any more time to think?' She burst out laughing. 'Is that all the time a decision takes, a single word, *yes*? Do I – do I part-own a hotel now?'

'You do.' Rose wrapped an arm around her. 'Right. We should tell Roddy – Daz – and Robin. We should tell Jen and Della and Pam.'

'I won't need that plane ticket to Bristol.' Tess's eyes filled with tears of joy.

'You won't. We should celebrate.' Rose glanced around for help. 'Daz – Murdo – Erskine. Would someone kindly open several bottles of champagne, enough for everyone on the boat? Tess and I have something special to announce.'

Daz was the first to spring to action. Murdo and Aul Crabbit followed him to the table, reaching for bottles, popping corks.

'I'm all over it,' Daz called out. 'What are we celebrating this time, our Rose?'

Rose grinned mischievously as she tugged Tess towards Della, Pam and Jen, and they stood in a close circle, hugging, lifting bubbling glasses, the faces shining with happiness as *The Nauti Buoy* cruised along the loch.

'We're celebrating life,' Rose said haughtily. 'Life, every single minute of it. Tell me, girls – is there ever anything better to celebrate than that?'

ACKNOWLEDGEMENTS

Thanks to Kiran Kataria and Sarah Ritherdon, whose professionalism and kindness I value each day.

Thanks to Boldwood Books; to designers, editors, technicians, voice actors. You are magicians.

Thanks to Rachel Gilbey, to so many wonderful bloggers and fellow writers. The support you give goes beyond words.

Thanks to Jan, Rog, Jan M, Helen, Pat, Ken, Trish, Lexy, Rachel, John, Shaz, Gracie, Mya, Frank, Martin, Cath, Avril, Rob, Erika, Rich, Susie, Ian, Chrissie, Kathy N, Julie, Martin, Steve, Rose, Steve's mum, Nik R, Pete O', Chris A, Chris's mum, Dawn, Beau CC, Slawka, Katie H, Tom, Emily, Tom's mum, Fiona J and Jonno.

Thanks to Peter and the Solitary Writers, my writing buddies.

Also, my neighbours and the local community, especially Jenny, Laura, Claire, Paul and Sophie.

Much thanks to Ivor Abiks at Deep Studios. To Darren and Lyndsay at PPL.

Thanks and love go to Ellen, Hugh, Jo, Jan, Lou, Harry, Chris, Norman, Angela, Robin, Edward, Zach, Daniel, Catalina.

So much love to my mum and dad, Irene and Tosh.

Love always to our Tony and Kim, to Liam, Maddie, Kayak, Joey.

And to my soulmate, Big G.

Warmest thanks always to you, my readers, wherever you are. You make this journey special.

ABOUT THE AUTHOR

Judy Leigh is the bestselling author of *Five French Hens*, *A Grand Old Time* and *The Age of Misadventure* and the doyenne of the 'it's never too late' genre of women's fiction. She has lived all over the UK from Liverpool to Cornwall, but currently resides in Somerset.

Sign up to Judy Leigh's mailing list here for news, competitions and updates on future books.

Visit Judy's website: www.judyleigh.com

Follow Judy on social media:

facebook.com/judyleighuk

x.com/judyleighwriter

instagram.com/judyrleigh

bookbub.com/authors/judy-leigh

ALSO BY JUDY LEIGH

Five French Hens

The Old Girls' Network

Heading Over the Hill

Chasing the Sun

Lil's Bus Trip

The Golden Girls' Getaway

A Year of Mr Maybes

The Highland Hens

The Golden Oldies' Book Club

The Silver Ladies Do Lunch

The Vintage Village Bake Off

The Golden Gals' French Adventure

The Silver-Haired Sisterhood

The Morwenna Mutton Mysteries Series

Foul Play at Seal Bay

Bloodshed on the Boards

Boldwood

Boldwood Books is an award-winning fiction publishing company seeking out the best stories from around the world.

Find out more at www.boldwoodbooks.com

Join our reader community for brilliant books, competitions and offers!

Follow us
@BoldwoodBooks
@TheBoldBookClub

Sign up to our weekly deals newsletter

https://bit.ly/BoldwoodBNewsletter

Milton Keynes UK
Ingram Content Group UK Ltd.
UKHW040641221124
2971UKWH00006B/51